BUTTERFLY
ISLAND

ALSO BY CORINA BOMANN

The Moonlit Garden

Storm Rose

BUTTERFLY ISLAND

CORINA BOMANN

TRANSLATED *by* ALISON LAYLAND

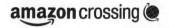

Previously published as *Die Schmetterlingsinsel* by Ullstein Buchverlag GmbH in Germany in 2012. Translated from German by Alison Layland. First published in English by AmazonCrossing in 2017.

Published by AmazonCrossing, Seattle

www.apub.com

Amazon, the Amazon logo, and AmazonCrossing are trademarks of Amazon.com, Inc., or its affiliates.

ISBN-13: 9781477819951
ISBN-10: 1477819959

Cover design by M.S. Corley

Printed in the United States of America

February 15th, 1888

Dearest Grace,
I don't know whether you have forgiven me yet. I can only assume you haven't. But I simply have to write to you nevertheless.

In my mind's eye, you're sitting at the window of your room, looking out over the mist-shrouded park and struggling to come to terms with the way things have turned out. I don't blame you, and I can only say that I'm sorry from the bottom of my heart.

Things have changed here since you've been away. I miss you so much! Papa does, too, even though he'd never admit it. He vanishes for hours on end in his study, refusing to speak to anyone. Mother is afraid he's going to seed. (You know how she can exaggerate!)

As for her, she's immersed herself in a frenzy of activity, organising a party to lift Papa's spirits. In truth, she only wants to know how far-reaching the effects of the scandal are.

Maybe you're smiling bitterly at this, if you're reading this letter at all and haven't consigned it to the flames of the fire. I hope with all my heart that you will give me a chance because I have news for you that may give you hope.

Shortly after you left, he appeared outside my window and told me that he would be coming to find you soon. As a pledge of his intention, he gave me something that I should keep for you, since he no longer has a proper house.

I'm sure he'll come like a fairy-tale hero and whisk you away from the old ruin, and you'll both live happily ever after.

Dear sister, I promise that I will always be there for you and yours, whatever happens. Should you fall on hard times, my door will be open for you—I owe it to you all.

Yours most affectionately,
Victoria

Prologue

Tremayne House, 1945

The young woman arrived at the manor house on a rainy October afternoon. Mist shrouded the park, making the weeping willows, their branches shedding tears of rain, appear more inconsolable than ever. Wind-blown autumn leaves were strewn across the once well-tended paths, littering lawns that had not been mowed for an eternity.

Ignoring the tense, emaciated face of her reflection, the stranger peered through a pane of the front door. She had rung the bell twice, but there was no one to be seen, although the people inside the house could clearly be heard. Their frenzied activity kept them from answering the door.

After pressing the bell a third time in vain, she was about to turn and leave when she heard footsteps, closely followed by the appearance of a woman in a maid's uniform in the doorway. She wore a name badge announcing her as "Linda." With a stern eye she inspected the newcomer, who looked like many women on whom the war had taken its toll. Matted hair, pale cheeks, and blue shadows under her eyes were evidence of hunger and deprivation. Large work shoes, a few sizes too big for her, gaped at the sides.

The slight swell of her belly showed beneath her dirty clothes and tattered trench coat.

"Sorry, we're full," Linda muttered coolly.

On hearing this, the pale figure handed her a worn, dirt-smeared envelope.

"Please will you give this to the lady of the house?" Her words sounded wooden; she was not used to speaking English.

There was a determination in her request that did not befit someone who had come to terms with a life on the streets. Linda looked critically at the stranger, who did not withdraw her request, but instead returned the maid's gaze with a certain defiance until Linda eventually accepted the envelope.

"One moment, please."

One moment stretched to many, but the woman remained standing outside the door as though turned to stone. She did not shuffle from one foot to the other, nor did she sit down, even though the low stone banister gave her the opportunity. She merely stroked her stomach gently, cherishing the valuable treasure it concealed. The child growing inside her was worth every hardship, all the humiliation, she had to suffer.

Instead of the maid, two women appeared, one who seemed to be around fifty with light-brown hair, and another of about the newcomer's own age with strawberry-blonde hair. Although the war had also demanded sacrifices of them, they seemed to be faring relatively well, judging by their healthy complexions and rounded features.

"Are you Beatrice? Beatrice Jungblut?"

The woman nodded. "Yes. Helena's daughter. You're the Stanwicks, I believe?"

"I'm Daphne Stanwick, and this is my daughter, Emily Woodhouse," the older of the two women replied. Her daughter was the spitting image of her.

Beatrice nodded awkwardly, sensing she was unwelcome here. She had no other options. She was not worried about her own life, since she had recently been exposed to danger so many times that death had lost its terror for her. But the child should have the opportunity to see the sun and enjoy the peace that had reigned for a few months now.

The ladies of the house exchanged meaningful glances. Daphne asked, "Where's Helena?"

"She died in an air raid, like my husband," the woman replied.

"What happened to you?" Emily asked. She frowned in consternation at her mother, whose expression remained inscrutable.

"I found a place to hide." She placed her hands on her belly protectively. "My mother told me that if something happened to her I should turn to you."

The two women looked at one another again.

"Do you have papers to prove your identity?" Daphne asked.

Beatrice shook her head. "They were destroyed by fire when we were shot at by low-flying aircraft."

That's it, she thought. *Now they'll send me away. Why on earth should they trust me, after all? It's all meaningless; the letter I've given them is nothing more than an empty promise that's long since been forgotten.*

"Well, you'd better come in for now, and we can talk."

The pregnant woman was met by the smell of carbolic soap and death as she followed the two ladies of the house down a long corridor. There was obviously insufficient medication and disinfectant to deal with festering wounds.

"We've had a makeshift hospital here in the house for a good three years now," Emily explained, clearly attempting to fill the awkward silence. "The rooms are all bursting at the seams. Please don't take offence at Linda for wanting to send you away. We've been overrun with starving people returning from the war."

Beatrice gazed down in embarrassment at her dirty shoes.

"I'm sorry to hear it."

"We're managing," Emily said kindly, and laid a hand on Beatrice's shoulder. "You've come to the right place here."

These words made Beatrice feel dizzy. Was there really a right place for her and her child? The place she had called home was a ruin, sunk in a mire of blood.

Although the kitchen was large, there was an obvious lack of space, as every spare inch of the floor was covered with chests, cupboards, and other furniture.

"Dreadful conditions, but you get used to it." Daphne sighed as she took three teacups from a shelf. "I used to have staff to do this, but the war takes away not only one's freedom, but also all one's privileges. Now we eat at the same table as our servants, who don't actually work for us any more."

Beatrice remembered vaguely that her own family had also once employed a maid. The memory of her house, her room, and the clothes she had once worn had been so thickly overlaid with the suffering she had experienced that she could scarcely recall what her life had been like back then, before the madness took over.

"Who was the woman who came to the door?" Beatrice asked as she sank slowly on to the chair that was offered to her.

"Linda is my maid, but only wears her uniform for form's sake, since she's needed in the hospital. My daughter and I also help out there to the best of our ability."

Daphne lowered her gaze to Beatrice's stomach.

"I could help, too," Beatrice offered, but her aunt shook her head.

"You'd be best off helping in the kitchen, not with the sick. You'd be at risk of losing your baby if you came into contact with any kind of germs."

The unreasonably sharp tone in her voice made Beatrice shrink back from her as her doubts returned. *The fact that she's allowed you to sit with them in a kitchen full of clutter in no way means that you're accepted as part of the family.*

Daphne was about to speak further, but was interrupted as the kettle on the stove emitted a piercing whistle. She got up and made a pot of tea.

The leafy scent had a calming effect on Beatrice. She had always found it soothing, and in the refugee camp where she had found herself after crossing the Oder, the smell of tea reminded her of home. For a moment she felt as though she could wish herself back home, in her grandmother Grace's rose garden and the small greenhouse where she had tried to cultivate exotic flowers. Her grandmother would sometimes sit in there for hours, absently gazing at a frangipani bush with a small piece of paper in her hand that her mother had always claimed was a horoscope.

"This is a wretched Assam, but unfortunately it's all we have." Daphne's voice tore Beatrice from her thoughts. A teacup was placed in front of her. The discoloration from the tea had brought out the fine cracks in the glaze, like veins running down the inside of the cup.

Assam, Darjeeling, Ceylon. In her mind's eye she saw the neat labels on the containers in her grandmother's kitchen. She had lovingly inscribed the letters on squares of paper and decorated them with little vignettes showing stylised tea leaves and flowers. They would now all be reduced to rubble, just like the sea captain's house on the Baltic coast, the garden, and the greenhouse.

The women sat over their tea in silence, each sunk in her own thoughts. Daphne seemed to be staring into space as though she were looking for something, while Emily was lost in contemplation of Beatrice, who pretended not to see her as she was engrossed in her memories of her grandmother.

It's strange that she's the one I'm seeing now, not Mother, Beatrice thought as she traced the lines on the imagined face, allowing her gaze to fall on the fiery-red hair that was her Scottish inheritance, and contemplated the white skin that was inclined to freckles. How envious she had been as a little girl of her bright, radiant grandmother! Her mother, Helena, and she herself were darker in complexion, with black hair and almond-shaped eyes, which Grandmother had said they got from her husband's family. Sadly, Beatrice's grandfather, the sea captain, had died before she was born.

"You can stay here for today, at least," Daphne decided, apparently returning her wandering thoughts to the present. "You can sleep in my daughter's room. Emily will sleep with me tonight."

"But—" Emily began.

"No buts. Our guest will have a room to herself." Daphne's sharp glance put an end to the discussion. "Go upstairs and show Beatrice to the room. Then you can make everything ready for her. I'll go back to the hospital."

Daphne rose and strode swiftly out of the kitchen. The two young women regarded one another shyly.

"I'm sorry about what happened to your mother and your husband," Emily said at last, gently laying a hand on Beatrice's dirt-encrusted fingers. "It's always difficult to lose people you love."

"Did you lose someone in the war, too?" Beatrice asked. Emily looked perfectly healthy and content to her, but her smile froze as the question hung in the air.

"Yes, I did," she replied, staring into her teacup with a strained expression. "My child."

"Did they die in an attack?" Beatrice had heard about the Blitz in London.

Emily shook her head. "A miscarriage in the fifth month. My husband had just been called up to the front. I don't even know if he's still alive. He probably believes that our child can walk by now."

And she's got sympathy to spare for me? Beatrice wondered. *The cross she has to bear is just as heavy.*

"But let's talk about that some other time." Emily got up from the table and forced the memory back with a bitter smile. "Come on, I'll show you to your room. It's lovely, and would have been quite big enough for us both, but if Mother wants me to listen to her snoring . . ."

Emily led her down a labyrinth of corridors, past a former ballroom that was now crammed with rows of beds and mattresses laid out on the floor, then up a staircase. The upper corridors were heaped with chests and furniture that had been cleared from the other rooms. As Beatrice brushed lightly against one of the chests with her arm, she heard a soft clinking of glass or crystal. All these things, packed away and set aside, were waiting, just like the people, for peace to return.

"Here we are." Emily opened a wide double door on to a room that was warm and fairly cheerful. The floral pattern on the wallpaper had faded, but it was still obvious what a beautiful room this had once been. On the floor beneath the high windows were pictures leaning with their backs turned to the room, their frames shimmering gold in the sunlight.

Beatrice was most impressed by the bed. She had never before seen a bed as wide and heavy as this one, which took up most of the room. The clothes Emily wore most often hung from the backs of two chairs, since the wardrobe, its doors gaping slightly open, was stuffed full of other things.

"If you like, I can give you a dress," Emily offered. "The one you're wearing is beyond repair, however much you try to patch it."

"Thank you, I . . ."

"Come over here!" Emily began to open drawers. Inside were various items of clothing, from underwear to blouses and skirts, sweaters and scarves. "Which of these would you like?"

"I . . ."

"Don't be shy!"

"But I don't even know if I'll be allowed to stay. Your mother . . ."

"Oh, Mummy will soon give in, I promise you." Emily fished out a light-pink blouse with a sailor's collar and delicate embroidery. "I think this one will suit you better than it does me. I don't even know why I've kept it—just look at my hair. Red and pink, what a clash."

Before Beatrice could protest, Emily was holding the garment up to her chest. "I knew it! With your dark hair and golden skin, this colour suits you so much better than me."

"But what about my belly?" Beatrice objected. "I won't be able to fit into it in a few weeks."

"I'll have knitted you a sweater by then. In any case, you're so much daintier than I am. I look like an elephant beside you!"

The two women looked at one another, and then broke out into laughter.

Emily wouldn't rest until she had searched out a skirt and a cardigan, as well as underwear and socks. "I'll get hold of some new shoes for you, too. We're about to make a collection for charity; if there's a suitable pair I'll keep them back for you." She went to the door. "I'll let you get some rest now."

Suddenly overcome by all this kindness, Beatrice sank down on the bed. The soft mattress yielded gently beneath her, and a scent of lavender wafted up from the sheets. Beatrice stretched out and for the first time enjoyed a feeling of safety, even though she still wasn't certain how long she would be able to stay.

When Emily returned to check on her, Beatrice's eyes were already closed. She didn't even notice her enter the room.

During the night, Beatrice awoke in terror from a dreadful nightmare. She had once again relived the scene of being separated from her mother and husband, of almost getting trampled in the terrible crush before a stranger's hands pulled her up and dragged her into the undergrowth as the planes roared overhead. She had watched helplessly as bullets rained down on the line of refugees, as her mother and her husband, who had not been called up to the front because of his asthma, had vanished beneath a mountain of corpses.

Imagining that she was still in the American refugee camp, she sat up, but felt the warmth and saw the glow of the fire in the hearth. All was quiet beyond the tall windows. A nearly full moon was trying to penetrate the veil of mist and rain-threatening clouds.

She heard quiet footsteps in the corridor. A door banged. A little later, hushed voices reached her through the wall. Beatrice was unable to make out what they were saying, but a feeling of unease drove her to move a little nearer to the wall and lay her ear against the faded wallpaper, which gave off a strange smell.

"How do we know it's really her? She could have found the letter." It was Daphne, and she sounded angry.

Had she changed her mind? Where could Beatrice go if she had? She knew no one here in England.

"I don't think for a minute that she found the letter." The younger woman rushed to defend her. "There was no money in it—do you think a vagrant would really be interested in it?"

"It did contain a promise of help."

"But anyone would realise it was highly likely that whoever had the letter would be recognised," Emily continued to protest. "Have you seen her hair? And her face?"

"There are plenty of girls with black hair. She could be making the most of that fact."

"Mother!" Emily said, her voice full of reproach. "Haven't you looked at her? It's plain to see. Even though she's the grandchild, it's plain to see."

What's plain to see? Beatrice wondered, ignoring the thirst that stuck her tongue to the roof of her mouth. Her heart began to race as though she were fevered, making the voices all the more inaudible. She sensed that the two women knew something about her that she was unaware of herself. What could it be?

A long pause followed, before Daphne said, "You know our supplies are rationed."

"And you know what Grandma Victoria always said," her daughter countered.

"Yes, that . . ." Something seemed to stick in her throat; something that wanted to come out but didn't dare. "It's all nonsense!"

"Nevertheless, you promised at her deathbed that you'd obey her instructions and help Grace's family if they were in need, just as she had promised her sister," her daughter replied calmly.

"Maybe she shouldn't have made that promise." Daphne fell into an embittered silence; then Beatrice heard footsteps crossing the room. "Very well, she can stay until her baby's born. Then we'll see. We'll be doing our duty if we find her and the baby a safe place to stay. The two of them can't possibly stay any longer in the midst of all this chaos."

"But the chaos will die down sooner or later—"

Daphne seemed to have silenced her daughter somehow.

Could they know I'm listening? Beatrice wondered anxiously. No, that was impossible; she had kept her breathing shallow and leaned against the wall like a statue blown aslant by the wind.

"We'll keep her here until she gives birth, and then we'll see. As you know, all our plans have been destroyed, so we shouldn't be making any more just yet."

They fell silent. The two of them had clearly gone to bed, without saying goodnight or entering into any further disagreement.

As the tension dropped away from her body, Beatrice became aware of a burning sensation in her throat. *Water. I must have a drink.*

Gritting her teeth, she pushed herself away from the wall. Her awkward position had given her a backache, and her ankles, which had been permanently swollen for a month now, tensed up. If it hadn't been for this nagging thirst for water, she would simply have lain down and waited for sleep. But if she were to settle down again she had to have something to drink.

Outside, she felt around for the light switch, but no light came on. Was there a power cut, or was the electricity rationed? Then Beatrice remembered seeing a large fuse box in the kitchen; some fuses had been unscrewed to economise on electricity.

The washed-out patches of moonlight helped her find her way, however. Along the corridor, down the stairs, then through the second door on the right. Down another corridor, following the lingering cooking smells.

Despite her meagre weight, the stairs creaked softly beneath her feet as she crept down as quietly as possible. On the bottom step she had to pause; her thirst had developed into a physical feeling that made her feel faint. Non-existent lights flashed in front of her eyes, and she was unable to drive them away by closing them.

Her heart thumping, she grasped the banister with claw-like fingers. She saw a movement in the corner of her eye. A silhouette stood against the faint light falling from the ballroom.

"Is everything all right, miss?"

Beatrice felt an automatic urge to reply in the affirmative, but she couldn't. The words wouldn't come.

"Miss, I'm Dr. Sayers," the man continued, moving into her field of vision. "I can help you."

Her knees gave way and she sank into darkness.

BOOK ONE

The Secret

1

Berlin, April 2008

Diana Wagenbach woke with the pink morning light on her face. With a sigh, she opened her eyes and tried to get her bearings. The magnificent linden tree in her garden cast a shadow across the tall panes of the conservatory on the side of the living room. Flecks of light were scattered over the dark-red rug that protected the parquet from scratches. A strange smell hung in the air. Had someone spilled alcohol somewhere?

It was a while before Diana recalled how she came to be lying on the white leather sofa. The clothes she had been wearing the previous evening still clung to her body, her black hair was plastered to her brow and cheeks with sweat, and her lips were completely dry.

"Oh my God," she groaned as she sat up. Her arms and legs ached as though she had been dragging removal boxes around all night, and lying in a strange position had given her backache.

As she sank back in the seat, she gazed around in horror. The living room looked like a battlefield—not the aftermath of a wild party, but because she had lost control. Shocked, she rubbed her eyes and face.

Diana was usually a peaceful person, patient almost to excess, or so her acquaintances said. Yesterday she had seen her husband, Philipp, with that woman. True, his job involved business meetings, sometimes after work. But that did not include passionately kissing the business associate while stroking her breasts lustfully.

If only I'd stayed at home, Diana thought as she straightened up and inspected the bruises on her arms.

But no, I just had to go to our regular restaurant because I wanted to treat myself to something special after a hard day's work.

As she stood up from the sofa, trying to rub life into her tired bones, she ran through the previous evening in her mind.

Of course, she didn't have the courage to confront Philipp in the restaurant. She had left without him noticing her and run home, where she had flung open the door in a rage and thrown herself, weeping, on the sofa. How could he do that to her!

After a brief outpouring of tears, she'd begun to pace up and down the house, tormented by innumerable questions. Had there been any clues? Should she have suspected? Was it all simply a mistake and the kiss had been totally innocent?

No, that kiss had been anything but innocent.

And if she was honest, their marriage had been foundering for some time, merely waiting for a gust of wind to dash it on to the rocks.

A thousand curses had shot through her head.

Reproaches, threats, demands.

When Philipp was finally standing before her, keys rattling in his hand, her intention of starting a row with him had come to nothing. Instead, she had simply looked at him, and in a calm voice asked who was the woman he had been embracing so passionately.

"Darling, I . . . She . . ."

She'd refused to believe his protestations that she was just an acquaintance. Lie detection was one of Diana's talents. Even as a child she had always known when someone wasn't telling her the truth. She had even once caught Great-Aunt Emily, normally open and forthcoming, keeping something from her.

"Get out of my sight!" The only words she could bring herself to say. *Get out of my sight.* Then she had turned and gone into the conservatory. Gazing out through her reflection to the moonlit garden, she'd heard the door close behind her.

That would have been the right moment to go to bed and cry all her cares into her pillow. But no, Diana's reaction had been different.

In retrospect, she was shocked by her own actions. A switch had flipped in her, something breaking loose that never had before. It had begun with a vase she flung against the wall with a cry of rage. It was closely followed by chairs from around the dining table. She had hurled them with all her might across the room, shattering the glass coffee table and the display cabinet containing Philipp's trophies.

A bottle of single malt whisky had also fallen victim to the onslaught. The golden-brown contents were now drying to a stain on the carpet.

Maybe I'd have been better off drinking it, Diana thought sarcastically. *It would have made it easier to explain to our insurance company what happened here.*

Shards of glass sparkled at her spitefully and crunched beneath her shoes as she crossed the room. A hot shower would bring some kind of balance back to her spirits and give her the opportunity to put her feelings in order.

After undressing, she regarded herself in the mirror and briefly wondered what the other woman had that she didn't, but gave herself a mental shake/pep talk.

She was thirty-six, but didn't look it. Anyone who didn't know her would have guessed she was in her late twenties. The grey hairs that were supposed to sprout in her mid-thirties had not yet begun to appear. Her fully black hair flowed over her shoulders, which, like her arms, had taken on a golden summer tan—the envy of her female employees and friends. The rest of her untoned but nevertheless slim body was lighter, in need of a beach holiday to bring the skin colour into line with her limbs.

A holiday, she thought with a sigh as she stepped beneath the shower. *Maybe I should get away and forget all about this crappy situation.*

The lukewarm water of the shower revived her senses, but unfortunately also stirred the nervous turmoil in the pit of her stomach. The water might have been washing away the traces of the previous night from her skin and hair, but it couldn't change what had happened.

The shrill tone of the telephone rang out, and Diana tried to ignore it. It was probably Philipp phoning with some stupid apology. Or, worse, asking her how she was. She had switched off her mobile, so the landline was the only way of reaching her.

When the caller persisted and it occurred to her that Eva Manzel, her partner at her law practice, could be trying to reach her, she wrapped herself in a fluffy blue towel, left the bathroom and went downstairs to the hall. *If it's Eva I can just tell her I won't be coming into the office today.* She picked up.

"Wagenbach."

"Mrs. Wagenbach?" a voice asked, mispronouncing her name.

Diana gasped. "Mr. Green?"

Her aunt's butler confirmed it in his halting German, before Diana replied in English.

"It's lovely to hear from you, Mr. Green. Is everything all right?"

How long had it been since she'd spoken to her aunt? Or to the butler, who acted as a kind of go-between and usually held the receiver up for Aunt Emily, whose arm had not functioned properly ever since she had suffered a stroke.

"I'm afraid I don't have good news for you."

The words hit Diana like a fist to her solar plexus. "Please don't keep me on tenterhooks, Mr. Green. Tell me what's wrong."

The butler hesitated a moment longer before venturing into the inevitable. "I'm sorry to tell you that your aunt suffered another stroke two days ago. She's in St. James's Hospital in London, and I'm afraid the doctors don't know how long she has to live."

Diana's hand went to her mouth and she frowned, as though these actions could fend off the bad news. But an image flooded her mind's eye: an elderly lady, her strawberry-blonde hair gradually turning a snowy white and a kindly smile lighting up her wrinkled mouth.

How old was Aunt Emily? Eighty-six or eighty-seven? Diana's grandmother, Emily's second cousin, had died many years ago, though they were a similar age.

"Mrs. Wagenbach?" Mr. Green's voice blew away the wisps of thought like a gust of wind.

"Yes, I'm still here. I'm just . . . shocked. How could it have happened?"

"Your aunt has lived to a ripe old age, Mrs. Wagenbach, and I suspect life hasn't always been good to her. My mother always said that people are like toys; sooner or later they break." He paused briefly as though imagining his mother. "You should come here. Madam has asked me to bring you to see her, while she's still more or less conscious."

"So she's spoken to you?" A small, absurd spark of hope fluttered inside her. Maybe the doctors would pull her through. Wasn't it the third stroke that was supposed to be fatal?

"Yes, but she's very weak. If you want to grant her wish, you should fly out today if possible. If you decide to come, I'll drive to the airport myself and pick you up."

"Yes, I . . . I'll come. I . . . just have to find out the time of the next flight and whether there's a seat available."

"Very well," the butler replied. "Would you be so kind as to email me to let me know when exactly you'll be arriving? I wouldn't like to have you waiting in the rain."

"That's very kind of you, Mr. Green. I'll send you my flight details as soon as I have them."

Another brief pause followed. A crackling in the ether. Had the connection been broken?

"I'm very sorry, Mrs. Wagenbach. I'll do all I can to make sure everything goes as well as possible for you here."

"That's very kind of you, Mr. Green. Many thanks. I'll see you later."

After ending the call, she had to sit down. Preferring to avoid the mess of shattered glass, she made her way to the kitchen. She had always sat in the kitchen at Emily's when she'd visited her every summer with her mother, Johanna.

Her mother had been particularly close to Emily, since it was Emily who had brought her up after her own mother died giving birth to her during the tumultuous aftermath of the war. Diana only knew Beatrice from a faded photograph that had been taken shortly before Johanna's birth. She had never understood why Emily, who had remained childless, hadn't adopted her mother.

The clock in the living room, which Philipp had brought as a souvenir from the Czech Republic and she had always hated but tolerated for his sake, struck the hour. It reminded her that time was passing and aeroplanes didn't wait.

Although she was churning with worry inside and her hands and fingers trembled slightly, she managed to dress in just five minutes. She chose practical clothing: jeans, a short-sleeved blouse, and a lightweight red sweater in case of unpleasant weather. She tied up her black hair in a ponytail, and went without make-up for once. With an ease acquired from innumerable business trips, she was able to pack her things in no time. She wasn't taking much with her; only a blouse to change into, a T-shirt, changes of underwear and a toothbrush, plus her laptop, notebook and charger. There was a small village near Tremayne House that sold everything needed by the cyclists who liked to tour the area.

As long as she had her purse and papers with her, she'd be able to buy anything else she needed.

Pausing at the door, she glanced back at the chaos she was leaving behind. The glass shards glittered in the sunlight like diamonds. *Let Philipp clean it up,* she thought, quietly pleased that she hadn't left a note for once.

Outside, she got into her red Mini, which always served her well in the heavy Berlin traffic, and a little later found herself on the autobahn heading for Berlin Tegel Airport.

Around the same time, Mr. Green was heading for a bookshelf in the study of his former master. His mistress had left him strict instructions about what to do when she died. He should make sure that Diana found it. The secret.

He didn't actually know what it was. During the years he had served at Tremayne House, he had learned to curb his curiosity, although he had to admit that from his very first day there he had sensed that there was something mysterious about the house. The feeling had never left him.

Mrs. Woodhouse had introduced him to the puzzle of the instructions a few years previously. She had believed at that point that the angel of death would be calling at her door before long, but God had granted her more time, enough to leave a trail of clues.

A picture here, a letter concealed in a book there, to be left where the intended person would happen across them by chance. *It will help her to cope in the time after I'm gone,* Madam had said. Although she had not seen Diana for years, Mrs. Woodhouse had never doubted the love and loyalty of the girl who had assumed the role of grandchild in her heart.

Standing before the bookshelf, Mr. Green sought out a specific volume. The books had never been rearranged since the death of old

Mistress Daphne, Emily Woodhouse's mother. Not even during the war, when everything had been turned topsy-turvy, had a single book been out of place.

Ah, there it was! A green binding, faded golden script. A book that looked as if it had been placed there by chance. But once you recognised the cover, it was clear to see. In case his visitor was too sad to be able to think clearly, he drew it out a little, so that it protruded by hardly a finger's width. The sound it emitted was like the sigh of relief of a dying man finally able to turn over on to his other side.

2

The plane from Berlin landed at London Heathrow under a blanket of thick rain clouds that turned day into evening. Light drizzle developed into a storm as fat raindrops pattered down on the airport and against the windows of the bus that shuttled the passengers to the arrivals hall.

After claiming her suitcase from the conveyor, Diana hurried to the concourse, where she hoped she would find Mr. Green. He had replied to her email saying he would be there punctually, but rush-hour traffic could put even the most conscientious butler off his stride.

At first she couldn't see him among the crowds, but she finally caught sight of him by the doors. Their eyes met and his hand shot up in a wave.

Diana hurried towards him.

As she approached, she noticed how little Mr. Green had changed since the last time she'd seen him, five years ago. He was in his late fifties by now, but his perfectly trimmed hair showed only a few traces of silver and his tall frame had not an ounce of excess fat. The greatcoat he wore over his suit was so beautifully tailored that he could easily have been taken for a wealthy businessman.

Aunt Emily had certainly found the perfect butler in Mr. Green, who had been in her service for almost thirty years now.

"Welcome to London! I'm delighted to see you again, Mrs. Wagenbach."

His handshake was as warm and friendly as his smile. Diana couldn't help wondering whether he had another lady in his life. His last had left him a few years ago.

"I'm also delighted to see you, Mr. Green," Diana replied, picking up on a sense of calm in the butler's manner. *She's still alive,* a voice whispered in the back of her mind. *I'm not too late.* "Did you manage to avoid the traffic?"

"An excellent journey, madam," he replied politely, tucking his oversized umbrella under his arm. "I was fortunate enough to find a parking space close to the front of the building, so we should be able to reach the car without getting too wet."

Diana smiled to herself. She knew it was pointless to try to have a meaningful conversation with Mr. Green when she'd just arrived. It was only once she'd been there for a few days that the butler would let his guard down enough to exchange a few personal words.

Outside, they were met by heavy rain. Without flinching, Mr. Green opened the umbrella and held it over Diana.

"Shall we go, madam?"

Diana found it hard to keep up with a man whose legs were a good six inches longer than hers, while avoiding the puddles that had rapidly formed on the asphalt.

They finally came to a black limousine, a 1998 Bentley Brooklands. Although ten years old, the car looked in excellent condition. Emily had probably been driven out in it only occasionally, and Diana doubted that Mr. Green used the car for private journeys—he was far too correct for that.

The butler took her bag with a smile and opened the door. As she got in, he stowed her baggage in the trunk.

"I assume you'll be wanting to go straight to the hospital," he said, sliding elegantly into the driver's seat. A few drops of rain glistened on his shoulders and in his hair as he turned to her.

"Yes, I'd like to," Diana replied. "Do you have any more news?"

"Unfortunately not, since I'm not a relative. However, the emergency doctor mistook me for her son and told me that the stroke has severely weakened her. If I hadn't noticed that she was unable to get up out of her chair, she would probably have died in the night."

"You've always been very attentive towards her," Diana said, unable to think of a better response.

After she had fastened her seat belt, Mr. Green switched on the ignition and the windscreen wipers, and they were soon making their way through the hurly-burly of London traffic.

St. James's Hospital exuded an air of cool sterility that gave visitors a twinge in the pit of their stomachs as soon as they entered the doors. Diana had always wondered why a place where people's lives were begun, saved, or even ended should seem so unpleasant, so unnerving.

Even the friendly nurse at the reception, who asked her to check in at the intensive care ward, could do nothing to mitigate Diana's uneasiness. The building, with its smell of disinfectant, gave the impression of wanting to suck the life from every living soul inside.

She would have been only too pleased to ask Mr. Green to accompany her, but the butler had excused himself for half an hour to go on another errand. He had a guest and a promise to keep, he told Diana. "I'll wait for you downstairs in the reception area when I get back."

Diana had watched him go and now made her way past bustling nursing staff towards the glazed double doors bearing the inscription *Intensive Care*. Before Diana reached them, the doors swung open to allow a patient's bed, pushed by two porters, to come out and along the corridor. The white-haired man was almost invisible between the pillows and sheets; portable breathing apparatus was fixed to the foot of the bed.

Although Diana greeted the porters, they took no notice of her, not deigning to interrupt their conversation about that weekend's football match.

Faced with an open door and an empty corridor, Diana wondered whether she should simply slip in, but something held her back. *She's here, behind one of these doors,* she thought with a thumping heart and tightness in her stomach. Her eyes took in the nurses' station and the tiled walls punctuated at regular intervals by doors. *Will she recognise me?*

"Can I help you?"

Diana jumped and spun around. She had been so busy taking everything in that she had failed to notice a doctor coming up behind her. The medic, who looked to be around forty, was called Dr. Hunter according to his name tag.

"Yes, please. My name is Diana Wagenbach. I'd like to see Emily Woodhouse. I understand she was brought in yesterday."

"Are you related to her?" the doctor asked.

Diana nodded.

"Come with me."

The doctor led her to the nurses' station and instructed one of the nurses to take Diana to room nine.

The nurse nodded, placed her clipboard to one side, and came over to her as the doctor hurried on down the corridor.

"Are you her granddaughter?" she asked. Diana simply nodded again, unsure whether she would actually count as a relation if she told the whole story, and whether the nurse would understand the complicated twists and turns of her family history.

"Good. Come with me, then."

They hurried past doors and were met by the beeping sounds of monitoring equipment. Diana and the nurse continued to the end of the corridor to where the doctor had disappeared. They stopped outside a closed door. The nurse opened a small cupboard next to the shelf for the patient's file. Before Diana had a chance to glance at the notes, the nurse had pressed a light-blue bundle into her hand.

"Please can you put this on. Your grandmother needs to be protected from germs. In addition to her stroke, she's also developed pneumonia."

"So soon?" Diana replied, her head immediately filling with the horror stories she'd heard about hospital bacteria.

"It's probably protracted flu. She was showing the symptoms when she was brought in. If she hadn't had the stroke, the pneumonia would probably never have been noticed." The nurse sounded irritated. *You'd be irritated, too, if someone made a veiled accusation that you weren't doing your job properly,* Diana thought.

"When you've finished putting the gown on, please can you disinfect your hands. If you leave the patient's room, you'll have to repeat the whole procedure when you return."

Diana had no intention of leaving before she had to.

"You can stay for half an hour, but no longer," the nurse continued as Diana tried to fasten the ties of the thin blue gown behind her back, which turned out to be a fiddly job. "Please could you talk quietly and try not to excite her."

Does she think I'm about to burst into a sickroom with a fanfare? Suppressing her irritation, Diana thanked the nurse for the cap she handed her, and assured her that she would obey the rules. Once she had drawn the cap over her hair and a mask across her mouth, she was finally allowed to enter.

Although she had mentally prepared herself, and had experienced seeing someone seriously ill before—her mother had died from cancer nine years ago—she was still shocked by Emily's appearance.

Her strawberry-blonde hair had faded like wool that had been left out for too long in the sun. Her wrinkled face looked shrunken, dark shadows encircling her eyes. Her breathing rattled from her slightly open mouth. Her arms, now completely paralysed, were held in place with straps to prevent them slipping between the bars of the bed frame.

Diana saw with shock how thin Emily had become. The pneumonia had clearly taken its toll.

Fighting tears and a big lump in her throat, she moved softly to the bedside, which was surrounded by at least half a dozen items of equipment quietly beeping in a regular rhythm.

"Aunt Emily?" Diana asked gently, leaning over the sick woman's face. No reaction. Was she able to hear anything? The nurse had left, so she was unable to ask her.

"Aunt Emily?" she repeated a little louder, summoning all her self-control to prevent herself from crying.

"Diana?"

Although Emily spoke with difficulty, Diana listened carefully and managed to understand her. Emily turned her head incredibly slowly in the direction of the voice that had spoken her name, and opened her eyes.

"Yes, I'm here, Aunty." Diana was about to reach for one of her hands, but it occurred to her that she wouldn't feel anything, so she gently stroked her hair and as she did so felt how hot her brow was.

"I'm so glad I've been able to see you again," Emily whispered, gazing intently at Diana. "You've grown even prettier. You look so like your grandma Beatrice. She was also beautiful, once she'd recovered a little from her hardship."

Diana suppressed a sob, but couldn't prevent a tear from trickling down her cheek and dripping on to the sheet. "You're beautiful, too, Aunty."

"I'm tempted to believe you for once," Emily replied, showing a brief glimpse of the sense of humour that had made her so popular. "So why are you crying? Do I really look so bad?"

Diana shook her head. "No, it's just that . . ."

"That I'm nearing my end?" A smiled fluttered across her face. "Oh, child, we all have to go sooner or later. I've had a long life—not always happy, as you know, but a long one, and at least I've been able to assuage some of the guilt that's been hanging over our branch of the family."

Guilt? Diana raised her eyebrows. *What guilt could this kind, loving woman have taken upon herself? Or her family?*

"Maybe once I reach the other side I'll finally be able to meet Grace, the woman who shaped my life in a way, even though I didn't know her in person," Emily continued, as beads of sweat formed on her brow.

Diana would have liked to tell her to rest and conserve her strength, but Emily had never allowed another to silence her. Some things didn't change.

"I'm going to tell her that her love is still bearing fruit, and that I've done all I can to seek forgiveness for Victoria. The dead know the guilt that people have taken upon themselves . . ."

An outbreak of coughing caused the machines to beep. Diana drew back in alarm and was about to call for the nurse when everything settled back to normal.

With a moan, Emily sank back against the pillows. "There's a secret hanging over our family. One that Grace didn't know about." As her eyes opened again, she looked enraptured, as though she could see in the distance those who had died before the war. "My grandmother had a dreadfully bad conscience about it."

Her breath was coming in gasps, as though the words were placing a terrible strain on her.

"I'm sorry I can't tell you exactly what it was about. I always suspected that my mother knew more details, but she never let me in on it. The only thing Mother told me on her deathbed was that Grandma Victoria had a secret that should not be disclosed until only one of us was left. You're the last of our family line, as I wasn't blessed with children of my own. So the time has finally come."

Diana's stomach tightened. It was true; she was the last. The descendants of the Tremaynes were few—and they had all been female, which meant that the old name had long since vanished from the annals.

"In the old study there's a secret compartment behind the bookshelves, towards the middle of the wall. The key has been missing for a long time—not even my mother knew where it was—but it shouldn't be a problem to have another one cut. Take what's in there and do the best you can with it. Draw the threads together to complete the story."

Diana heard footsteps approaching the room. Time had run away from her. Were her thirty minutes up already?

Emily stared at her with wide eyes. A tear ran from the corner of one eye. A tear from the heart, as her mother had always called them. "Promise me that you'll find everything out and put it all together. Grace and Victoria . . ."

"Mrs. Wagenbach?" The nurse was standing in the doorway, her voice ruthless as a prison warder. "Your half hour is over. Please will you say your farewells? Your grandmother needs to rest."

Diana nodded and pondered the strangeness of Emily's revelation as she waited for the nurse to go. Then she leaned back towards Emily and kissed her brow. "I promise I'll put all the pieces together."

Her aunt smiled at her, reassured. "You really are a lovely girl who deserves all the happiness the world has to offer. If you uncover our secret it will bring you peace, too, I'm sure."

Emily sank sleepily back into the pillows.

"I'll come back tomorrow," Diana promised, stroking her hair once again. She did not know whether her aunt heard the words because no sooner had she stood to go than Emily was asleep.

Mr. Green was waiting in the reception area as promised. Diana hurriedly brushed away the tears that had leaked out on the way to meet him. Her glowing cheeks gave her away, but that was better than crying for the world to see.

"Ah, Mrs. Wagenbach!" Mr. Green folded up the newspaper he had been reading to while away the time, and rose. "May I ask how Madam is?"

"She's been speaking to me," Diana said, "but she's very ill. The nurse said she's also picked up pneumonia; she must have been harbouring it for days."

"I'm sorry to hear it. If your aunt was already ill, she certainly didn't show it." Mr. Green looked remorseful. Diana sensed that, as the butler, it was his duty to run the household, but his mistress's personal state of health was not his concern unless she said something to him or he noticed she was unwell.

"That sounds typical of her." Diana's brief laugh sounded more like a sob.

"As you can see, England's showing her best side, as far as the humidity's concerned," Mr. Green remarked drily as he elegantly unfurled his umbrella. The rain had eased somewhat, but there was still no sun to be seen. "Would you like to stop for something to eat on the way, madam?"

"No, thank you, I'd like to go straight home."

Home. It was only as she left the hospital that she'd realised how easily she used the word in relation to Tremayne House, which had been the backdrop to her childhood summers. As though her life in Berlin had never been.

3

The congested city streets gradually gave way to more rural roads lined with hedgerows dotted with trees and wild rose bushes. Lulled by the sonorous humming of the engine, Diana allowed her mind to drift through a series of images.

She saw Emily in her early fifties bending over her bed when Diana was a child and lovingly stroking her hair. A few years later she bustled around as Diana sat drawing at the kitchen table. Diana had spent all her school holidays at Tremayne House because her mother, who had moved to Germany at the age of eighteen, kept returning to the place where she had been born.

The picture shifted to Emily in her sixties, sitting proudly in church for Diana's confirmation, her elegant attire attracting admiring glances from the other guests. She came to Berlin a second time, when she was over seventy, for Diana's university graduation. At that stage she wasn't showing the slightest indication that time was eating away her strength.

The last time Diana visited her was just after she had suffered her first stroke, but she still had not lost any of her courage or determination.

Diana remembered telling her with pride that she was about to open her own legal practice with Eva. After her father was killed in a car accident and her mother died of cancer, grief had threatened to overcome her. But Emily, ready as always with emotional support, had invited her to Tremayne House to give her a whole summer of time for herself.

Philipp had then entered her life, and in the following years he and the practice had meant that she had only been in touch with Emily occasionally, and had no longer visited her, which Diana now deeply regretted.

She was always there for me, she thought. *And I let her down.* Sadness was mixed with resentment towards Philipp. *Maybe if it wasn't for him I'd have come here more often . . .*

But Diana knew only too well that if it hadn't been Philipp, there would have been another man in her life. A better one perhaps, but she would nevertheless have paid more attention to him than to her aunt in England.

"Here we are, madam," Mr. Green announced, as if to make sure she didn't miss her first sight of the house.

From the small rise as they approached, they had a view of practically the whole estate, which consisted of the elegant two-storey manor house, an annex, and a stable block.

Built near the Thames, the property had apparently belonged to a notorious member of the aristocracy who had been involved in a conspiracy against Elizabeth I. The queen's infamous spymaster, Sir Francis Walsingham, was said to have lived nearby. The Tremayne family had acquired the estate in the seventeenth century from Charles II after the restoration of the monarchy. Since then, the family's descendants had managed to keep the house going without having to open it to the public to pay the bills.

On this dismal afternoon, Tremayne House looked like a wet dog lying remorsefully at its master's feet, looking up at him with big, beseeching eyes. Fat drops of water dripped from all the bay windows, the roof, and the gutters, and the run-off down the side of the steps sought in vain to catch the flow.

Mr. Green parked the Bentley on the circular drive with a fountain at its centre and reached for the umbrella he had laid down in the footwell.

"Wait there, madam. I'll see you to the door."

Before she could remark that she could manage the short distance to the front door without dissolving like a sugar cube, Mr. Green was already opening her door, the umbrella up. On his shoulder he was carrying her bag, which she had almost forgotten about.

In the hall she was overcome for a moment by the thought of how it must once have looked in the times of Grace and Victoria. In those days, there must have been an army of servants going about the business of fulfilling their master and mistress's every wish. The butler of the day would have made sure that everything was in order, while below stairs the clattering of pots and pans would have resounded throughout the kitchen.

A little of the bygone activity seemed to have soaked into the walls to be stored there. Why else would it all have come into her mind now?

"I've prepared your room," Mr. Green announced, having stowed the umbrella almost noiselessly in the metal stand by the door. "If you'd like to follow me."

Diana wanted to object that she could carry her bag upstairs herself, but Mr. Green already had his foot on the first step. *Maybe I should simply give in and enjoy being looked after,* she thought as she climbed the marble staircase that although crazed with fine cracks had lost none of its solidity. It would certainly make a change from all the months of neglect by Philipp.

Surrounded by the familiar ornaments, and the paintings of long-dead people and distant landscapes, she was immediately whisked back to her childhood by the creaking of the upstairs floorboards and the smell of old wallpaper—reminders of a time when she had been blissfully unaware of the problems of adulthood. She ran a finger affectionately over the gilded frame of a scene depicting the park that surrounded the house. Beneath the dense weeping willows that surrounded a small lake, two young girls with gorgeous red hair were sitting on a blanket with their mother.

Given the painting's date, 1878, these children must have been Grace and Victoria, the last to have been born with the name of Tremayne. The younger of the two, Emily's grandmother Victoria, sat in front of a small easel, while the elder girl wove a garland of flowers. Their mother sat between them like a queen, in a dress of delicate green adorned with lace and silk flowers.

Diana had always loved the painting, whose realism gave her a window into a time long past. Even now she would have liked to pause and spend a while contemplating the two girls and their mother, but Mr. Green was waiting by her door.

Diana knew immediately that the room had been renovated. The smell of modernity mingled like an uninvited guest with the mustiness of bygone days. Fortunately, the repairs seemed to have been sympathetically done. The faded flowered wallpaper, which was otherwise in excellent condition, had been painted over with a clear varnish that would see it through for a few more years. One of the bedposts had been renewed, although this was not obvious from a difference in colour, but from the texture of the wood—the new bedpost merely lacked the woodworm holes of the others. A welcome change was the soft carpet, with its thick pile that invited her to walk barefoot over it. It harmonised perfectly with the colour of the furniture, but was far too clean to have belonged to past times.

Diana approached the fireplace reverently. The fire blazing in the grate drew the dampness from the air and gave a little warmth to counter the draughts that penetrated the old windows from the rainy day outside. As a child she had loved to sit here, watching the flames dance and trying to count the sparks sent up as a log collapsed.

"If you like, I can bring you some tea in here." The butler's voice slipped unobtrusively between the wisps of memory.

Diana shook her head. After all the day's events, she couldn't imagine sitting on her own in this room, sensing the whispered conversations between the ghosts of the Tremaynes that would begin as soon as the butler left.

"I'll quickly unpack my things and then come down to the kitchen. I assume my aunt no longer employs a cook."

"No, there hasn't been one for several years. I've taken over the role." A smile flickered across the butler's face, almost too brief for her to catch.

Was he embarrassed to admit it, or surprised that a discerning mistress like Emily Woodhouse should be satisfied with his cookery skills?

"I'd be pleased to help you, if you like," Diana offered. "Didn't you say you had a guest today?"

"That's precisely why I can't accept your offer of help," the butler replied politely. "I promised Mrs. Woodhouse that I'd make sure you're as comfortable as possible, and it's a promise I intend to keep."

After unpacking her bag, which only took a few minutes, Diana decided to take a brief tour of the house. First, she glanced at her phone and found emails from Eva and a client she represented. She quickly read the messages, but put off answering them until later. Eva knew from her call that morning what was happening. Diana was strangely disappointed that Philipp had not been in touch, but not surprised. He probably hadn't even noticed that she'd gone.

Suppressing the anger that welled up inside her, she went out on to the landing, which held the same magic for her as it had always done. The creaking of the floorboards beneath her feet, which would have irritated her in a newer house, sounded like the voices of old friends calling out for her to visit them.

Upstairs, as well as her room and a similar guest room, there was a small library where Diana used to hide away on the rainy days of her holidays. Ignoring Emily's warnings that she would ruin her eyes, she would leave the lights switched off and settle down with a candelabra. It was so atmospheric to leaf through an old book, usually lavishly illustrated, by candlelight and to imagine herself living in olden times.

Emily's bedroom had been moved downstairs since illness had confined her to a wheelchair. Mr. Green had written Diana a detailed letter at the time, telling her what had been done to make her aunt's life as comfortable as possible.

At that moment, she heard Emily's voice clear but soft in her mind.

In the old study there's a secret compartment behind the bookshelves, towards the middle of the wall. . .

As though an icy breath had touched the nape of her neck, Diana shivered until she distracted herself with the picture of the red-haired girls and their majestic mother.

The secret. Did it really exist?

Aunt Emily may have been weak and ill, but her understanding had seemed clear enough to Diana. The instruction to sift through their family history and unearth a secret had not come from a confused mind.

Her search in the old study could wait. She went downstairs, following the mouth-watering smell of baking to the kitchen. As she entered, Mr. Green was about to cut a piece of fruit cake, fresh from the oven, with a silver knife.

He's clearly a man of many talents, Diana thought with a smile. *A pity he's twenty years older than me, otherwise I might have tried my luck with him.*

The butler was preoccupied with his activities and didn't notice her standing in the doorway watching him. It was only when he straightened to cover the remaining cake on the plate that he saw her.

"Ah, Mrs. Wagenbach," he said without stopping what he was doing. "I've made the tea."

"Do you remember the days when you used to call me Miss Diana?" she said as she sat down on one of the large kitchen chairs. Although the furniture was relatively new, it nevertheless radiated the charm of the early nineteenth century, the golden age of Tremayne House.

The butler smiled. "Back then you always wanted to know why people didn't just call me 'Green' like the butlers in the old TV series."

"You always kept your first name a big secret."

"I still do. You'll have to ask your aunt if you want to know." With smooth gestures born of many years' experience, he served her tea and a slice of cake.

"Why is that?" Diana asked, revelling in the delicious smell, which helped a little to release the knot that had been cramping her insides ever since her visit to the hospital.

"Everyone has to have a secret, don't they? Mine is my first name, which only Madam and my girlfriend know. And, of course, the registrar who issued my birth certificate."

Diana knew she wouldn't get anywhere asking about his girlfriend—his personal life was also usually kept a secret. "Do you know anything about a secret involving the Tremaynes, Mr. Green?" she asked instead, after trying a sip of the tea and immediately recognising it as Ceylon.

The butler paused for a fraction of a second, which she took to be a good sign.

"This house certainly conceals a number of secrets," he replied evasively. "I'm only the one who looks after the practical side of things. Who knows what lies within these walls?"

"My aunt spoke of a secret when I was visiting her," Diana continued. After all, Emily hadn't asked her not to tell anyone. "She instructed me to look in the old study. To be honest, when I was a little girl I always found that room a bit creepy, as though all the male ancestors of the family were looking down on me, annoyed that a woman had dared set foot in there."

This time Mr. Green kept his poker face intact. "Women have worked in that study since the days of Mistress Victoria. As far as I know, their descendants haven't let a single man who married into the family set foot in the room. Madam kept to that rule."

"But Aunt Emily's husband died in the war." Diana had always wondered why she hadn't remarried, but some people probably did experience the kind of love that lasted beyond the grave and didn't simply vanish like a leaf on the autumn wind.

"Even if a man had entered her life afterwards, he wouldn't have been allowed in that room," Mr. Green replied, clearly rather proud that he was able to go in and out without fuss. "After their time abroad, something must have happened within the family that turned male domination into a matriarchy."

"Maybe the fact that only girls were born into the family?" Diana remarked with a hint of mockery before biting into the cake and releasing a veritable explosion of tastes in her mouth.

"Of course." An enigmatic smile crossed Mr. Green's face as he slipped off his gloves.

I'm on to something, Diana thought as she chewed. *He knows something, but Emily's probably forbidden him to talk to me about it.*

"Come and sit down with me, Mr. Green," she said as the butler moved to return to his work. "It's after five, you've been driving me around, got the house shipshape, and done all you can to make me comfortable. I think you've earned a rest."

A flicker of refusal showed in Mr. Green's eyes, but then he collected himself and sat down in a chair.

After tea, as dusk was beginning to drive away the dismal afternoon, Diana gathered her courage and crossed the chequerboard tiles of the corridor to the large double doors that led visitors to expect a bigger room than the rather modest Tremayne family study actually was.

Although the lamps that lined the walls were all electric now, they had retained the look of old-fashioned gaslights, which gave Diana the feeling of travelling back in time. As a child she had been a little afraid of the place, and so had only ever entered in search of Emily when her aunt was nowhere else to be found. On those occasions, she had usually found her sitting behind the desk, writing.

She paused by the door, laid her hands on the two handles, and traced the cool, ornamented metal with her fingers. She finally pressed down on them—and found herself in the Tremayne House of the late nineteenth century. Behind the heavy mahogany desk was a matching chair, its leather upholstery nailed to the frame with large brass studs. The green shade of the curved lamp was as free from dust as the thick pane of glass, a little scratched around the edges, that protected the ornate marquetry of the desktop from wear and stains.

Expecting to find that the contents of the silver inkwell would long since have dried up, Diana opened the lid. She was surprised to see the shimmering surface of black ink. She smiled. As ever, Mr. Green had thought of everything. His attention to detail had even led him to provide a pad of paper, which looked like another relic from the past. He probably assumed she would have things she wanted to note down.

As she turned to the bookshelves, Diana felt a strange fluttering in her stomach. *The secret,* she thought. *Do I want to know it?*

Even as a little girl it had bothered her that there seemed to be a wall of silence around the death of her grandmother, concealing the more distant past. Of course, she knew the names of her ancestors— letters on yellowing paper, annotated with brief lists of dates—but these revealed nothing about the lives of the people themselves.

Now I have a unique opportunity to find something out about our family. And to make it up to Emily for all the lost years.

Diana carefully pulled one book after another from the shelf and laid them down on the desk, making sure that the volumes were never too close to the inkwell.

Failing to find anything in the first row of shelves she searched, on the second row she found a small door concealed by wallpaper, its existence only given away by a keyhole and a dark-coloured notch.

Thanks to the books, which had shielded it from the light, the colours of the paisley wallpaper were as bright here as on the day it had been hung. She ran her finger over the notch, then tried to open the door using a safety pin, which she always carried pinned to whatever she was wearing.

As Emily had warned her, the compartment was locked. Fine scratches around the edge indicated that someone else had tried to break it open, but this wall safe was very well made and would probably not give up its secret even if the house one day fell prey to the wrecking ball.

Why hasn't anyone tried to have a replacement key cut? she wondered. She supposed the scratches had been made by thieves trying to reach the contents of the safe, presumably in the belief that the family jewels were stashed away here.

As Diana turned away with a sigh, already thinking of how to track down a locksmith, she noticed a book projecting slightly from the others in the row—like a soldier who had forgotten to get into line. It seemed so unlikely to see a misplaced book on these meticulously arranged shelves. Or was it intentional?

Her heart pounding, she drew the volume, with its green binding and faded gold lettering, out from the shelf. Charles Dickens's *David Copperfield*. An edition from 1869. As she opened it, not only were her nostrils filled by a mildewy smell, but she suddenly became aware of something that had been tucked between the pages—clearly recently, otherwise it would not have fallen so freely from the well-preserved book. But the paper that fluttered to the carpet wasn't new.

Diana picked it up. A telegram sent on 15 October 1886. She opened it, and as she read it, the room around her seemed to change, drawing her back in time, a silent witness to the days of her ancestors. It was almost as though she were in the room as the telegram was delivered . . .

With a sigh, Henry Tremayne looked out through the window, his reflection mottled by raindrops. For days it had been raining cats and dogs, with no end to the deluge in sight. The raindrops formed bubbles in the puddles on the path, which according to an old saying meant that even more rain was on its way.

The weather suited his mood perfectly.

A few days ago he had been forced to acknowledge that he would only be able to keep one of his family's properties. The decision shouldn't really have been a difficult one, since he had never really liked the Scottish castle. They had been there two or three times at most since their marriage.

His only connection with the place was the lawyer's letters he received every month reporting on the condition of the estate.

But it was close to his wife's heart, and because he loved her and didn't want to upset her, he was going to find it hard to announce that she would have to sacrifice the castle because of their financial straits. On the other hand, to deprive himself of the family seat, Tremayne House, was unthinkable, and so he faced a dilemma that troubled him more with every day that he delayed making the decision.

A knock at the door tore him from his thoughts. "Come in!" he called as he stretched and turned from the window.

The butler, a gaunt man in his mid-fifties, entered with a small tray in his gloved hand on which lay an envelope. "This telegram has just been delivered for you, sir."

Yet another creditor? *Henry thought irritably as he took the envelope and gestured to the butler to wait in case an immediate reply was needed.*

Suppressing the trembling of his hands, he reached for his silver letter opener and slit the envelope open. The typewritten letters caused Henry to freeze. The message had travelled some distance—Colombo, Ceylon was typed in the top right-hand corner.

"My brother has had an accident," he said in a half-whisper, his voice raw with horror. "They say he fell from Adam's Peak." Although he would not normally permit himself a public display of emotion, he placed his hand in front of his mouth as he read. He couldn't believe it. Richard was dead. Fate had taken him so far away from home.

"Should I send a reply, sir?" the butler asked, his features like a mask. It was his duty not to show his feelings, although he knew Master Richard and was just as shocked by the news.

Henry stormed past him without a word and disappeared along the corridor. Suddenly it was completely unimportant which of the family properties they should sell . . .

A knock drove Henry Tremayne from Diana's mind.

"Yes?" she said as she laid the telegram next to the book on the desk.

"Excuse me for disturbing you, madam. I only wanted to ask when you would like dinner."

"Whenever it's ready," Diana said, a little bewildered. She wasn't used to being asked such a question. "I have no idea. When can you have it ready?"

"Is seven o'clock all right for you?"

"Yes, of course."

A faint smile was on Mr. Green's lips as he left the study.

4

The next morning, Mr. Green insisted on driving Diana back to the hospital, rejecting outright her suggestion that she should take the bus.

"What else would I be doing all morning?" he said. "In any case, I have something else to see to."

Diana sensed this was not true and suspected that Mr. Green simply wanted to look after her once again.

After dropping her off at the main entrance of the hospital, he shot off on his supposed errand, whatever it was. As on the previous day, Diana made her way to the intensive care ward. The flimsy, yellowing paper in her trouser pocket felt like a stone, getting heavier with every step she took towards Emily's room. Diana had spent the night wondering about the possible consequences of the telegram. She had known nothing of Henry Tremayne's brother nor of his tragic death.

Was that part of the secret Aunt Emily was talking about?

When she stopped to enquire at the nurses' station, Diana was overcome by a strange feeling. The doctor who approached was not Dr. Hunter, but a slim, blond man in his late thirties with a shining stethoscope over his surgical gown.

"Are you her granddaughter?"

The nurse, who was also here today, must have told him she would be coming.

"I'm Dr. Blake," he said when she nodded, and shook her hand. "Unfortunately your grandmother isn't doing too well. Her condition has deteriorated to such an extent that we've had to link her up to breathing apparatus. Her circulation is very unstable, but we're doing everything we can."

Diana nodded in shock. She hadn't anticipated an improvement, but had certainly not expected her aunt to deteriorate so quickly.

"Of course, you're still welcome to visit her, but we've sedated her to help her recovery, so she won't be able to hear you. You should be aware of that."

Stunned, Diana thanked him and made her way to Emily's door and into the protective clothing. As she stood before the beeping machines, the situation became even clearer to her.

Emily's face could hardly be seen beneath the breathing and feeding tubes, her eyes were sunk in hollows, and her breast rose and fell mechanically, prompted by the respiration equipment. A dreadful tightness gripped Diana's chest; she had not felt this kind of pain even when she'd discovered Philipp's infidelity.

She sank down on the small stool by the bedside and sat for a few moments silently weeping. No one came to ask her what was the matter or offer help, which was just as well. No one could help her right then.

Her tears began to ebb some fifteen minutes later, and she edged up to the bedside and stroked Emily's hair. An occasional sob still escaped her, but all at once she felt as though her aunt was standing near her with a comforting hand on her arm.

Oh, child, we all have to go sooner or later . . . Once again she saw the hope in Emily's eyes as she'd said that maybe she'd see her forebears on the other side. And she thought of the reports of comatose patients who believed they'd heard the voices of their relatives as they lay there motionless.

"I found the telegram," she said softly, once she had overcome the shyness of talking to an unconscious woman.

"I don't know if it was you who tucked it into the Dickens, but if it was, thank you." Diana was still a little perplexed, but convinced that this piece of paper, which she regretted being unable to show to Emily, was part of the secret. "And I've found the secret door. Locked, as you said it would be. But I'm going to call a locksmith today. I promise you I'll find it."

She heard footsteps and looked up as if caught in some guilty act. A nurse in full scrubs came around the corner. Had she overheard her and now thought her crazy? If she did, she didn't show it.

"You do know you're only allowed half an hour here?" she asked.

Diana nodded. "Yes, I was just leaving."

This time she didn't add that she'd come again tomorrow. She had no desire to tempt fate, nor to be stopped again by a waiting doctor at the nurses' station.

She said goodbye to Emily by kissing her brow through the mask, then left the room and tore the protective clothing from her body.

Before she had reached the reception hall, her phone buzzed. She should have switched it off altogether, but her sense of duty towards her practice kept her from doing so. As she rummaged in her bag for the phone to read the text, she wondered how long she actually intended to stay here. Eva had asked her to stay away for only two or three days, but Emily's condition, the trail of the family secret, and the fact that someone had to be there if the worst came to the worst seemed to be conspiring to keep her from returning to Berlin any time soon.

Would she be able to manage such a long absence? Granted, her team was incredibly reliable and Eva was a very good lawyer, but every now and then clients wanted to speak to her personally.

A harassed glance at the phone revealed a message from Philipp.

*You weren't at home. Please get in touch and tell me where
you are. We need to talk.*

Talk, Diana thought bitterly as she deleted the message without
hesitation. *Talk about what? About your infidelity? Or how you're sorry?
No, my dear, you can stew for a while longer.*

Philipp's message helped her come to a decision. Once she was
back at Tremayne House she'd message Eva saying she shouldn't expect
her back for at least two weeks and she should forward any important
matters to her by email.

As on the previous day, Mr. Green was waiting for her in the hospital
foyer. He was talking to an elderly man, a small package beneath his arm.

Why didn't he leave that in the car? Diana wondered as she gave him
a brief wave and carried on through the glass doors.

"How is Mrs. Woodhouse?" he asked after excusing himself from
the other man.

"Worse. She's on breathing apparatus."

Diana couldn't bring herself to say any more. Mr. Green nodded
in sympathy.

"I'm sorry to hear it. I have something for you here."

Diana looked at him in surprise and swallowed. "You bought something for me?"

"No, I just went to fetch something that your aunt had bought.
For the annual parcel."

All shreds of Diana's self-control vanished—hot tears flowed down
her cheeks. Even though she had been feeling unwell over recent weeks,
Emily had thought about something as inconsequential as the parcel she
sent her once a year for no particular reason. Diana had always jokingly
called it the Care Package, since her mother had always received one
after moving to Germany.

"Now, now, Miss Diana, you have to be brave. Your aunt's a fighter.
She won't give up so easily."

Mr. Green drew a clean handkerchief from his coat pocket and only then did he seem to realise that he'd called her Miss Diana, just like he used to when she was a child. He suddenly blushed bright scarlet.

"Thank you, Mr. Green," Diana replied with a sniff. "And please will you keep calling me Miss Diana? For one thing, I don't think I'm going to be Mrs. Wagenbach for much longer."

The butler looked at her in some confusion before leading her over to the car.

"My husband and I will probably be getting a divorce," she informed him once they were a short way out of London.

At first the butler was rendered speechless, then he cleared his throat and replied, "You should think long and hard about it. These days people often throw relationships away too easily."

In earlier days, maybe the times of Emily or Daphne, he would have been reprimanded for such a statement. But Diana thought he had a point. People simply threw good, long-term relationships to the wind—for a short-term affair, for example.

"He was unfaithful to me," she said, which would also have been unacceptable in the old days.

"Oh, then that's a different matter altogether." Could Diana detect a slight trace of anger in his voice? "I don't understand some men. Why do they throw themselves into affairs and believe that women won't notice? That certainly wasn't the case in the past—women have a sense for it."

"And now they're no longer prepared to hide the fact that it troubles them," Diana added.

"Exactly! But men still assume they'll get away with it. And they bring all that trouble and disgrace upon themselves just to feel another woman's skin for a few moments."

Listening to his wise words, she could have been forgiven for thinking that he'd had the happiest relationship of all times. But Diana knew only too well that wasn't the case. Was he saying it with the benefit of hindsight?

Back at Tremayne House, Diana immediately withdrew with the parcel to the living room, which she had transformed into a kind of headquarters since the previous evening. She had always loved the huge colonial sofa, which had been so lovingly cared for that it showed no sign of wear despite having survived since the turn of the twentieth century.

Her laptop, its cable running to the phone socket, stood on the low, solid table which was more used to holding the fruit bowl. She had brought the pad of paper from the study, but left the inkwell where it was, since she didn't want to risk staining the carpet with a fountain pen.

On the pad was a list of the things she wanted to do that day. For years she had kept a to-do list, which had actually helped her to bring a bit of order into her life. The list, with a call to the locksmith as its first item, now also fulfilled the role of lifesaver for Diana as she sank down on the sofa and took the telegram out from the new envelope she had put it in to protect it.

Yesterday she had tried googling the name of Richard Tremayne, but without success—his ghost had not yet reached the Internet. A visit to the archives here had made its way on to the list.

But for now, Diana reached for the telephone, which seemed to be the most modern piece of equipment in the house. As she had explored the rooms, some of them completely empty, she had seen no sign of a TV.

Diana had tried two other locksmiths before finally reaching a friendly sounding older man on her third attempt. He told her he was planning to retire soon, but since it involved Tremayne House he would come the following afternoon and examine the lock in question.

No sooner had she hung up than she noticed Mr. Green in the doorway. She had no idea how long he'd been standing there, patiently waiting for her to finish her conversation, but there was a delicious smell coming from somewhere.

"Lunch will be ready at about one. Is that all right for you, Miss Diana?" he asked.

"That depends what it is," she replied playfully, despite her sadness inside.

"An English speciality. Wait and see!" His voice echoed down the corridor as he disappeared from view.

Diana was unsure whether she wanted any surprises just now. Her eyes wandered over the neatly tied parcel, which gave no clues as to its contents, or even the place where it had been bought. The brown wrapping paper had no company logo on it, as might be expected, and it was tied up with ordinary string, the kind that could be bought anywhere.

Well, here goes—surprise! she thought, untying the knot.

As she opened it she felt something incredibly soft beneath her fingertips. She gasped in amazement as she saw what it was. An orange silk scarf, printed with a beautiful red-and-gold pattern. It seemed quite old. The edges were very slightly frayed and the design looked Victorian in style. Although Diana was no expert, she thought she had read somewhere that scarves with a genuine Indian paisley pattern were very expensive. That was why people had begun to mechanically reproduce the pattern in a Scottish town called Paisley.

Aunt Emily was famous for the generosity of her Care Packages, but they had never contained anything as beautiful as this before. Was it from her own wardrobe? But if so, why would Mr. Green have had to fetch it from somewhere?

All at once Diana remembered the pattern on the wallpaper that concealed the compartment behind the bookshelf. Was it one of Emily's clues?

There was no way she could confront Mr. Green to ask him whether Emily had taken him into her confidence. He would probably only laugh and give some mysterious reply.

No, I'll get to the bottom of it myself, she told herself as she slid the scarf through her fingers, enjoying its silky feel and losing herself in thought.

5

The English speciality promised by Mr. Green consisted of juicy lamb chops, potatoes, and gravy with a hint of mint. It tasted delicious. Diana was not really hungry, but Mr. Green's cookery skills had enticed her to eat so much that she felt as though she would soon be rolling around the house like a balloon.

During the afternoon, the doorbell rang—a shrill sound that was out of character with the building but which penetrated to every corner.

Mr. Green was out on an errand, so Diana answered the door herself. Leaving her laptop, she got up from the comfortable leather sofa and hurried through the labyrinth of corridors until she finally reached the hall.

The visitor seemed used to waiting. As she approached the glazed door he was still there, a picture of patience with lowered head and a hat in his hand. The art nouveau patterns in the frosted glass hid his face from view, but as Diana opened the door she saw a gentleman of around eighty with thick grey hair and wearing a black trench coat.

"Dr. Sayers?" she burst out.

The man widened his eyes as if he'd seen a ghost, and nodded. After a moment's astonishment it seemed to dawn on him who she was.

"You're Beatrice's granddaughter, aren't you?"

"Yes, that's me, Diana Wagenbach." Diana smiled. How long was it since she'd seen this man? In her childhood he had often called at Tremayne House, since in his role as the family doctor he had formed a bond of friendship with Emily's family. As so much time had gone by since Diana's last visit, she had not seen him for a long while. Aunt Emily had spoken of him every now and then, yet he had gradually receded to a phantom figure. As Diana saw him before her now, his features crystallised from her distant memories.

"My goodness, when was the last time I saw you?" A smile softened his usually severe face. "Would you have been fourteen? It must be more than twenty years ago."

"It could well be. But you haven't changed at all, Doctor."

Sayers gave a dismissive laugh. The ice was broken. He patted her arm.

"Don't go flattering an old man—you don't know what kind of thoughts you might put into his head!"

"I assume you've come about Aunt Emily?"

"Yes. I haven't heard anything for a few days. Is she well? She must be delighted that her niece is here; you were always like a granddaughter to her."

Diana looked down in sadness. He obviously didn't know. "Please come in, Dr. Sayers, and I'll tell you all about it."

In respectful silence, the doctor followed her through the house and into the kitchen, which was flooded by the afternoon sunshine breaking through the clouds. Although Mr. Green was very conscientious about his work, small motes of dust danced in the rays of light. *Old houses collect dust of their own accord,* Diana's mother had always said. Here was the living proof.

"Please sit down and excuse me bringing you here into the kitchen. I'm afraid I've made the living room a bit untidy. Papers lying around, that kind of thing."

The doctor nodded with understanding as he sat on one of the kitchen chairs. "Yes, the authorities never leave us alone. Emily must be pleased you're here to help out."

Diana swallowed the lump in her throat. "Aunt Emily's been taken to hospital—the day before yesterday, so Mr. Green tells me. She's had another stroke."

"Oh, good Lord!" Dr. Sayers raised his hands helplessly. "Where is she now?"

"In St. James's. She also has pneumonia, so she's on breathing apparatus and can't communicate. I went to see her this morning."

Sayers took a moment to grasp the situation. "That's terrible. I'm so sorry, Mrs. Wagenbach."

"Call me Diana. And thank you, that's very kind." Diana took a deep breath, staring awkwardly at her hands. Mr. Green had made sure to leave the tea things out for her before leaving the house, so she got up and made a pot, pouring a cup for herself and Dr. Sayers. This time the smell of the tea was not enough to soothe her anxiety, but she kept herself together in the presence of her guest.

"It's a real pity that I'm no longer practising and so no longer have the right to walk into the hospital and declare myself the family doctor. I would have told the old girl she can't leave us yet. Who am I going to put the world to rights with every Wednesday afternoon?"

A bitter smile crossed his face and Diana couldn't help wondering whether he had ever tried to get closer to her aunt. When she was widowed Emily had still been plenty young enough to have at least allowed herself a lover.

"I remember your grandmother well, Diana," the doctor said. He sipped his tea and closed his eyes as he savoured it. "What wonderful tea! What do you think the chances of Mr. Green revealing his source are?"

"You'll have to ask him yourself."

Sayers harrumphed. "I doubt he'd do that, secretive old devil that he is. It must sound strange for you to hear me calling him that when I must be at least thirty years older than he is."

He laughed and took another drink.

"Oh yes, your grandmother," the doctor resumed. "What a lovely girl Beatrice was! I met her the night she arrived here."

Diana was familiar with a tiny part of her family history. At the end of the nineteenth century her great-great-grandmother, Grace, together with her husband, had built a house on the Baltic in East Prussia, the part that now belonged to Poland. During their flight in 1945, Beatrice's husband and her mother, Helena, Grace's daughter, had been killed. Diana's grandmother had somehow found her way to England, pregnant and half-starved. Emily's mother had taken her in when the house was being used as a military hospital.

"Although she couldn't help much in the hospital because of her condition, she worked hard and helped us in every way she could. Even though Daphne didn't approve."

His eyes seemed to be wandering back to the old days, when he had been a young man and probably many a girl's heart-throb.

"Approve of her doing too much, you mean?" Diana said.

"That was part of it. But Daphne didn't seem to trust her. There was never any proof of her origin. Only a letter."

Diana pricked up her ears. "A letter?"

"Yes, something she brought with her. A letter her mother was said to have given her. I never saw it myself, but I heard Daphne and Emily talking about it. It was the straw that Beatrice clung to—without it, Daphne would have sent her away for certain."

"What about Emily?"

"Oh, she was besotted with Beatrice from the word go, saw her as a kind of big sister."

The male domination was giving way to a matriarchy. Mr. Green's comment slipped into Diana's mind.

"Anyway, Emily and Beatrice were inseparable from the start, coming at first more from Emily—she had her heart set on doing some good for the lost woman. Beatrice was very withdrawn, probably because she was tormented by memories of her flight. It wasn't until a few months had passed that she became a little more approachable. She never confided in anyone about what had happened, but it gave her an inner strength that made her whole being seem even more radiant and beautiful." A rapt gleam shone in the doctor's eyes, soon driven away by a shadow. "Beatrice's death following the birth of her daughter, Johanna, was a great shock to us all. She had been subject to bouts of frailty, but we put that down to the deprivation of her wartime journey and the pregnancy. Although we were relatively well provided for here, it wasn't enough for her to put weight on."

Diana hugged her shoulders. They had never talked about the story of her grandmother's death before. Emily had never told anyone the details. Not even her mother knew more than the very basics. Diana hadn't expected to hear it now.

"During the contractions there was sudden, unexpectedly heavy bleeding. The midwife and I were completely at a loss. We suspected a tear, and hoped to stop the bleeding with an operation. After the baby was born I fought for her life for over an hour, but in vain. She had lost too much blood." Sayers's shoulders, which had tensed up as though he were still in the operating theatre, sagged. "As I was performing the post-mortem on her body, I noticed that she had a piece of shrapnel in her abdomen. I have no idea why she never complained of it. It's possible that it entered her body unnoticed and moved around until it reached an artery."

"In that case her death could have happened at any point," Diana said uneasily. She realised how close her family had come to extinction.

"Yes, that's true. She could have died during her pregnancy. But God, or whoever else, wanted her baby to be born. Given the later events, you could even say that for once, at least, fate showed a little kindness to the descendants of the Tremaynes. Emily remained childless after losing that first baby."

The silence that followed his words was like an echo from earlier days. Images of the past slipped closer, surrounding them like soldiers, leaving Diana and the doctor with no choice but to give in to them.

"Have you seen your grandmother Beatrice's beautiful grave? I wonder if it's fallen into disrepair by now?" Sayers's voice shattered the silence like a hammer on a pane of glass, making Diana doubly attentive. "I haven't been to the churchyard for a long time. Now my own time is approaching, I avoid the place like the plague."

As the past withdrew back into the shadows of the house, Diana shrugged, a little bewildered, ignoring the doctor's joke.

Her grandmother's grave was only a vague shadow from her childhood memories. A shadow with wings, as Emily had set a marble angel to watch over it.

"I still haven't got round to looking. Aunt Emily employs a gardener to take care of it."

"Maybe you should pay your grandmother a visit. Unlike me, you have nothing to fear from death. Beatrice would certainly be interested to see the kind of woman her granddaughter has become. You're the spitting image of her, if I may be so bold as to say."

Diana was suddenly overcome by a guilty conscience. Was it really the case that the dead could see? If so, both her mother and her grandmother would be horrified by what Philipp had done to her—and of course by her reaction to it. She was sure that no woman in the family before her had wrecked parts of her own living room.

"I'll go as soon as I've sorted out the paperwork."

Sayers looked at her as though to check whether she intended to keep her word. Then he nodded and felt in the inside pocket of his jacket. "Here's my card, in case anything happens or for when Emily is well enough to receive visitors. You can call me at any time, whether you want a heart-to-heart or simply need some help around the house."

Diana thanked him and he leaned back, glancing up at the ceiling and smiling as though he had found something he recognised there.

"Yes, this house! It's almost like a second home to me. I can still see the domestic clutter that was all over the place here when I was young. The work in the hospital could be horrific at times, with unbearably cramped conditions and dreadful hunger, but I'd never want to delete that chapter from my biography. Despite all the suffering, there were good times, too."

They talked for a while longer about less serious subjects before Dr. Sayers took his leave, promising to call back in a couple of weeks and make sure everything was all right. Diana knew the real reason behind it—he didn't want to spend his Wednesday afternoons alone—but she enjoyed the doctor's company, even though it had stirred up a lot of suppressed knowledge.

Diana returned to the living room and sank down on the sofa. Her legs had suddenly become incredibly heavy. Dr. Sayers's story had summoned up such clear pictures in her mind that it felt as though her grandmother had died only yesterday. Beautiful Beatrice, whom she only knew from a photo. Her face was somehow overlaid with Emily's—Emily who was now also on the threshold of death.

Maybe I should go to the grave after all and make sure everything's OK, now that Emily no longer can. In any case, a small voice whispered in the back of her mind, *you should think about where Emily is going to be buried if the worst comes to pass.*

Donning a cardigan against the chill, she made the ten-minute walk to the village churchyard. There was something hypnotic about the crunching of gravel beneath her shoes, clearing her head and enabling her to sort out all she had heard.

She had walked about halfway when the sun finally succeeded in breaking through the cloud. All at once the place looked completely different, the wild brambles and grass sparkling with bright raindrops, the birds singing more loudly and a cuckoo somewhere in the distance announcing the onset of summer.

The sun's broken through now, Diana thought. *Could it be a sign?*

Although she didn't believe in that kind of thing, the unexpected sunlight suddenly filled her heart with lightness as she saw the cemetery surrounded by its stone wall. With its chestnut trees and magnificent yews, it always seemed a little more sheltered here than anywhere else. The Tremayne family vault was an imposing sight among the gravestones and crosses. Diana had never paused to wonder why her grandmother had not been buried there, but now the question thrust itself insistently into her mind. Was there no room in the vault? Had Daphne prevented her from being brought here, or had it been her own wish?

It didn't take her long to find the grave of Beatrice Jungblut. The angel holding out a protective wreath over the ivy-covered gravestone greeted her from afar.

The chapel had probably once been at the heart of the graveyard, but time and the gradual expansion of the place meant that the centre point had now moved by some fifty metres. The angel, whose wings made it slightly taller than the chapel, now formed the radiant centrepiece of the cemetery.

It was hard to tell whether it was intended for the shadow of the wreath in the sunlight to create a frame around the dates of birth and death; in any case, the effect was a pretty one and made Diana smile.

"Hello, Grandmother," she said softly, crouching down and tracing the engraved letters and numbers with her finger.

BEATRICE JUNGBLUT
NÉE FELDMANN
1918–1945

Whoever was responsible for tending the grave did their work very well.

She had always thought it silly to speak to the dead, since even as a child she had been convinced that there was no afterlife. But now she felt compelled to tell this woman, whose legacy to Diana consisted of no more than a photo and her genes, what had happened during the years since she had last visited the grave. She began with her studies, how she had met Philipp and established her practice. She ended by telling her about Philipp's infidelity, that Emily lay dying, and that she felt as though her world was about to break apart.

As she looked up at the wreath, which the angel was now holding above her, she noticed something strange about the leaves. She had never seen a wreath with serrated leaves like this! This was not laurel. With a strange fluttering in her stomach, Diana got up and took a closer look. It was the most remarkable piece of sculpture she had ever seen. The leaves were very detailed, as though they had been created following precise instructions. Diana sighed as she ran a hand over the marble, which was so smooth that not a single speck of moss or lichen had adhered to it. *Oh, Emily, if only I could ask you.*

All at once it occurred to her that she had seen leaves like these once before. She couldn't remember exactly where, but they were incredibly familiar. The fluttering in her stomach grew in intensity, and she was overcome by an urge to refresh her memory. It was so strong that she turned on the spot and ran to the gate, where she almost crashed into two elderly ladies on their way to their relatives' graves armed with watering cans and rakes. She barely noticed the disapproving shakes of their heads as she was already racing down the lane.

She had never been particularly athletic, and was reminded of the fact as she dragged herself, puffing and panting, up the Tremayne House steps. Mr. Green had returned and parked the Bentley in the garage, but he left the doors open in case of emergency.

After a brief pause to catch her breath, and ignoring the stitch in her side, she flew into the kitchen, scaring Mr. Green so much that he almost dropped the teapot.

59

"Miss Diana! Has something happened?"

Diana ignored him. She made for the kitchen cupboard, tore open the two small drawers, then opened one of the little doors.

Got it! With a triumphant "Ha!" she picked out a small package. It was only then that she noticed Mr. Green looking at her as though she'd lost her mind.

"I'm sorry, Mr. Green," Diana said in embarrassment, pressing the package to her chest like something of immeasurable value. "I didn't mean to make you jump. I just wanted to be certain."

The butler raised his eyebrows. "Certain? That we haven't run out of tea?"

Diana laughed. "No, Mr. Green. But it looks as though Aunt Emily allowed herself a little indulgence at my grandmother's grave."

"What do you mean?" the butler asked with a frown.

Diana told him about her conversation with Dr. Sayers, which had led her to visit her grandmother's grave.

"It was probably because I haven't been there for so long and could now see the details with fresh eyes," she began. She turned the package she'd fished from the cupboard over in her hands and held it aloft. "The wreath that the angel's holding over the grave, framing my grandmother's dates with its shadow, is made of tea leaves."

A little later, they sat at the kitchen table over tea and cakes. "A wreath of tea leaves," Mr. Green murmured thoughtfully. "Are you sure?"

"Totally sure," Diana insisted after washing down a bite of cake with a mouthful of tea. "The leaves are just like the ones on this pack. Of course they're a little more ornate, but I'm sure the guardian angel's wreath isn't laurel."

Thoughtfully, Mr. Green studied his tea plate, which cutlery had scored with innumerable tiny scratches over the years. "Why would Madam do something like that?"

"Don't ask me," Diana replied. "Whatever the reason, it's very strange."

"Maybe your grandmother was particularly fond of tea? Or could it have been something more mysterious? There must be a good reason why fortune tellers read tea leaves."

Diana shook her head. These explanations didn't satisfy her—Emily wasn't superstitious. If someone had offered to read her tea leaves, she would simply have laughed. It was more credible to think that Diana's grandmother simply had a liking for tea. But would such a liking be enough to have her grave decorated with tea leaves?

"Have you anything against me taking this pack of tea and keeping it as another clue to the family mystery?" she asked.

Mr. Green looked up from his teacup in surprise.

"Of course not. We have plenty. Anyway, you're the lady of the house now—at least until Madam returns."

Diana found it touching that the butler had not given up on his mistress, and she almost felt ashamed of the way her heart told her that Emily's last days were approaching.

After tea she went back to the living room where she added the little pack of tea with its spicy smell to the scarf and the telegram.

I'll have to find a box for them if this goes on much longer.

She worked until the evening, answering emails from her practice and ignoring another—from Philipp. What else could he want but to attempt to justify himself? And what did he want to talk about? Her angry heart had no desire to know.

As she snuggled up wearily against the arm of the sofa, she realised that the search for her family history was like a game she had played with Emily as a child. Emily had been mistress of the scavenger hunt, hiding scraps of paper around the house to be found and pieced together to form a message. It was just a pity she was in hospital and couldn't give her any clues.

6

During the night, beneath the old bed's heavy, slightly musty sheets, Diana dreamed she'd returned to the cemetery. This time it was shrouded in morning mist, through which she thought she could hear voices. She looked down at herself and saw that she was wearing nothing but her nightdress. Her naked feet left slight imprints on the sandy path, and her hair, which was longer than in reality, floated freely like a veil behind her.

Nothing seemed to have changed since her visit, apart from the strange whispering that remained a mystery behind the thick, pinkish cloud of fog. The angel was still holding the wreath over the grave. The sun had been swallowed up by the fog, and there was no shadow to fall around Beatrice's dates, yet the monument was nevertheless an impressive sight.

All at once, something gently brushed Diana's cheek. Recoiling, she saw that a butterfly had appeared out of the mist—a small, exotic-looking creature that flew by her and fluttered around the angel, finally settling on the wreath.

At its touch the leaves awoke and came to life—green and shiny. Then colour began to spread up the arm holding the wreath, too. And so it continued, until Diana was looking not at an angel, but at a woman with flaming-red hair, robed in a white shroud. Tears were running down her face, golden as tea. Suddenly she looked up at her and implored, "Bring him back to me."

These words, full of unspeakable sadness, startled Diana. She looked around in bewilderment and realised a little later that she was back in her room, having kicked off all the sheets.

Sobbing, she sank back down on to the mattress. *It was only a dream,* she told herself, but the thought that her great-grandmother had appeared to her in person to make her appeal sent a shiver down her spine.

Unable to go back to sleep, she lay, agitated, staring at the ceiling and wondering what kind of butterfly it was and how it had come to the cold English shores. On a ship? Carried by a current of air? Stowed away on board an aircraft?

Her eyes finally closed as dawn was approaching, and she slept dreamlessly until her phone alarm woke her. Though she'd had a restless night, Diana rose from her bed. She wanted to visit Emily in the morning so she could be back for the locksmith, who had said something about coming in the afternoon.

After a refreshing shower—the hot water had been somehow reluctant to make its way down the pipes—followed by tea, toast, and marmalade in the kitchen, she went into the living room, where she spent a moment weighing up the possibility of telling Emily about her discovery before remembering it was unlikely she would have been brought out of her artificial coma yet.

Diana had just slung her bag over her shoulder when the phone rang. Both she and Mr. Green, who was waiting in the doorway, froze.

She had no idea why, but all at once she was overcome by a sense of foreboding. Who could be calling them?

"That must be one of Madam's friends," Mr. Green attempted to reassure her, but his voice, too, sounded uncertain.

"I'll get it." Diana reached the phone on the third ring.

"Hello. Woodhouse residence," she said, in case it was one of Emily's friends. Dr. Sayers, maybe, asking after her condition.

"St. James's Hospital, Dr. Hunter." Diana remembered him. "Am I speaking to Mrs. Woodhouse's granddaughter?"

"Yes, this is Diana Wagenbach," she replied, feeling a knot in her stomach.

"I'm very sorry, Mrs. Wagenbach," he continued after a brief pause. "Your grandmother died a few minutes ago. We did all we could."

Diana lowered the receiver. Her arm had suddenly lost all its strength to hold it.

"Hello?" she heard the voice asking down the line.

After staring into space for a brief moment, she hung up, then turned back into the hall in a daze. Mr. Green's expression darkened.

"Everything all right, Miss Diana?"

Diana shook her head as her eyes filled with tears. "She died a few minutes ago."

All Diana knew next was that Mr. Green guided her to the sofa in the living room. He asked if there was anything he could do; she responded with a shake of her head. He nevertheless appeared a little later with a freshly opened pack of tissues and a cup of tea, before withdrawing discreetly back into the kitchen.

After staring for a while into the fireplace, which was surrounded by portraits of people long dead, the paralysing shock of the news lifted and Diana gave herself up to her grief.

In a daze, Mr. Green stood at the kitchen window, where he had a good view of the garden and part of the park, which had never been restored to its former glory since the war.

Although he was not a particularly sentimental man, tears were running down his face. Silent tears, since he would never have allowed himself to cry out loud. After all, this was his place of employment.

But the death of his mistress troubled him, not only because she had been a good mistress, but because the responsibility for revealing the secret to Miss Diana was now his alone. He would no longer be able to consult Mrs. Woodhouse and had to depend on the instructions she had already given him.

He hurried to the bureau near the door and took out the telephone directory that had not been used for a long while. He slipped the envelope inside it into his jacket pocket. Madam had never told him what the letter said, but it was clearly very valuable. Her instructions were for it to find its way to her great-niece surreptitiously—as though she had stumbled across it by chance. Until now, the assumption that Madam would be among them for quite a while longer meant he had not even thought about it. But maybe an idea would occur to him during the journey. Miss Diana would certainly want to go to the hospital after notifying the undertaker.

Grasping the phone directory, he hurried through to the living room.

Diana was very grateful to Mr. Green when he arrived with the phone book already open on the page showing local undertakers.

All at once the memory of her mother's funeral was with her, and the mountain of formalities she had to plough through. Fortunately, this time she had Mr. Green at her side, which did something to mitigate the sense of being overwhelmed.

"Norton and Fenwick have a very good reputation locally—we could certainly rely on them for a tasteful funeral, which is what your aunt would have wanted. Would you like me to call them?"

"No, I'll do it myself in the car. We ought to set off as soon as possible."

"But of course, Miss Diana."

On her way out, Diana's eyes fell briefly on the painting of the scene by the lakeside. For a moment she thought she saw a resemblance to her aunt in the child Victoria's face. Trying to keep control, she got into the Bentley, which then swept off across the gravel.

As the calming murmur of the engine surrounded her like a security blanket, Diana sighed. "To be honest, I don't know whether I'm ready to see her."

"She won't have changed much," Mr. Green replied. "I was also afraid of what death might have done to my mother. But in the end it wasn't too bad. She looked as though she were asleep. Maybe the hospital staff will have taken Mrs. Woodhouse down to the morgue to prepare her for the undertaker."

As if aware of the pragmatism in his own voice, Mr. Green fell silent.

Diana hadn't even noticed. She stared at the landscape passing by the window and said abruptly, "You may think I'm crazy here, but I'd like to see her again, despite my fears. I don't want my last memory of her to be when she was covered in tubes and wires."

"That sounds anything but crazy to me," the butler replied. He accelerated, ignoring the speed limit sign he had just passed.

Fortunately, there was enough activity on the ward that no one had time to look at Diana with pity or sympathy.

The nurses at the station indicated for her to take a seat and wait for a moment in the corridor. As Diana gazed absently at a bed that was being pushed past her, she felt strangely calm. Of course grief raged inside her, but her fears had gone. She no longer needed to worry about Emily. If there was such a thing as a heaven, she would be with her loved ones and be able to tell them what she'd lived through during her years without them.

Dr. Hunter suddenly appeared in front of her, making her jump out of her skin.

"Oh, Doctor, please excuse me!" Diana pressed a hand to her breast. "I was completely lost in thought."

"No one could blame you." The doctor shook her hand. "I'm very sorry."

Diana nodded then rose, assuming the doctor would not want to speak to her there in the corridor.

"We've taken her to the chapel of rest. We knew you'd be coming, so we didn't want to take her straight to the mortuary. I assume you've informed the undertakers?"

"Yes." Diana felt as though the ground had suddenly opened up beneath her feet, as though she were having a panic attack. *You have a doctor on hand,* she told herself quickly. *He'll catch you if you faint.*

"Good. Shall we go? I take it you'd like to see her once again?"

She must have nodded, because Dr. Hunter now led her to a room at the far end of the corridor.

Her heart leapt to her throat, and she felt like telling the doctor she had changed her mind, that the gallery of images of Emily she carried in her heart would be enough.

But then the door opened and Diana saw her.

Beneath the sheet, Emily's body looked as fragile as an old porcelain doll's.

Freed from the tubes and wires, she really did look as though she were asleep. Only the dark shadows beneath her sunken eyes betrayed the suffering she had recently endured.

Her hair, which someone had arranged lovingly on the pillow, looked like a bride's veil interwoven with copper strands.

"She died peacefully," Dr. Hunter said. "She simply went in her sleep. When the alarm sounded, we tried to revive her, but she had made her decision."

Was death really something you could decide on? Could Emily have come back if she'd wanted to? Or had she believed that she would finally be able to leave because she had told her great-niece about the existence of the secret?

Diana pressed her hand to her lips as tears ran from the corners of her eyes. Despite the burning in her breast, she was unable to give in and cry out loud. She couldn't help thinking that Emily had only held out for so long because she wanted to instruct her to uncover the family secret.

These thoughts caused her to miss the doctor's explanation of the cause of death. It was not until he laid a sympathetic hand on her arm that she came to herself.

"I'll leave you alone with her for a moment. Feel free to stay as long as you want. When the undertakers arrive, I'll send them in."

Diana thanked him with a nod and heard the door closing softly behind her.

After standing for a while by the bed, she drew up a chair and sat down.

"I've found the first clue," she whispered as she stroked Emily's hair and felt the coldness of her skin. "But how does it all fit together? I so wish you were here to help me."

Diana fell silent, waiting for an answer she knew would not come. Eventually there was a knock at the door, and two men in black suits entered. Diana greeted them briefly, then withdrew after taking a final look at Emily. *I'll keep my promise,* she thought as she leaned against the corridor wall and cried softly.

As promised, the locksmith appeared in the afternoon. The ringing of the bell tore Diana from sleep. Exhausted when she'd arrived home, she had stretched out on the sofa for a while, but her bones still felt as heavy as lead. She rejected the brief notion of simply not opening the door and hurried to see who it was. *I promised Aunt Emily.*

The locksmith, a white-haired man in blue overalls who looked well into his sixties, stiffened as she opened the door and looked at her in surprise. "Is everything all right, miss? Should I come back later?"

Of course, he could see she'd been crying.

"It's OK," Diana replied, wiping away a tear that had trickled from her left eye. "I received the news today that my aunt has died."

"Oh, I'm sorry to hear it. I knew Mrs. Woodhouse—she sometimes employed me to cut keys for her. She was a lovely lady."

"Thank you, it's very kind of you to say so," Diana replied, blinking in daylight that seemed a little too harsh for eyes.

"Are you sure you don't want me to call back some other time?"

"No, please come in, Mr. Talbott."

As she stepped aside to let the locksmith in, she noticed Mr. Green pass by with a wheelbarrow full of hedge clippings, a dogged expression on his face.

Everyone has their own way of dealing with grief, Diana thought, secretly wishing she also had some physical activity to help her let off steam. *Maybe I should go for a walk, or a bike ride.*

With the indifference of someone who had seen the place plenty of times, Mr. Talbott followed her down the corridors without taking much notice of his surroundings.

"I had no idea that you'd worked for my aunt before," Diana remarked, feeling somehow obliged to make conversation with him. It was like being at the hairdresser's. Even if you had no desire to talk to a complete stranger, you finally gave in and began with the weather if only to put an end to the sullen expression in the mirror.

"Yes, Mrs. Woodhouse wasn't exactly talkative. But a very pleasant woman all the same. As long as everything was done as she wanted it, she let you get on with it. It's just a pity she didn't find another husband. Apparently there were one or two suitors, at least that's what people in the village say."

Was Aunt Emily really the subject of village gossip? Diana wondered. As a child she hadn't been aware of any of it, as she had only left the protected acres of the park occasionally and had hardly had any contact with the village children.

They had reached the study and Diana said no more. The room beyond the double doors seemed to make no impression on the locksmith, either. But the secret compartment behind the shelf caused him to exclaim in surprise.

"What would Tremayne House be without secret compartments and hidden passages! No English manor house was built without one. That's what I always said to Mrs. Woodhouse, although she didn't want to hear any of it."

Were there really any secret passages here? Or perhaps a cellar full of secrets?

Diana stepped aside and watched the man feel his way around the frame of the little door, as though he were expecting magical symbols to appear. After scrutinising the compartment with its little lock, he took a lump of what looked like modelling clay from his bag.

"These days, locksmiths swear by silicone guns," he said as he did so. "But I don't want anything to do with them because they can glue up the lock sometimes. I stand by the old methods."

Diana had nothing to say to that since she knew nothing about the locksmith's trade. She let Mr. Talbott do what he thought right, and nodded in approval as he showed her the imprint of the lock.

"Look at this! I think it will be one of the finest keys I've ever made! Give me a few days and I'll drop it off for you."

Diana thanked him and accompanied him to the door. Instead of retiring to the living room, she went back to the Tremayne study. A strange feeling of calm had descended on her in the presence of the locksmith. She ran her fingertips meditatively over the surface of the desk, then sat down on the chair, which creaked lightly. She glanced at the secret compartment and the books that surrounded it, before turning to the window.

How magnificent the garden must once have been! Mr. Green did all he could to keep it neat and tidy, but it no longer quite fulfilled the traditional image of a luxuriant English garden. And yet there was still a reassuring feel to it. Diana began to realise why her ancestors had chosen this room to work in; this room, which had always given her goosebumps as a child, that had changed now that Emily was dead, she was amazed to realise. It was as though the house had fully accepted her as its mistress now.

Her grief for her great-aunt abated slightly, and Diana soon decided to move her "headquarters" to this room. She fetched her laptop, the phone, the scarf, the pack of tea, and the old telegram from the living room and arranged them in the study.

When she had finished she remembered she had other things to see to first. She needed to notify the vicar, inspect the family vault, and attend to the formalities with the authorities. With a sigh, she stroked the soft silk of the scarf before drawing up a checklist.

7

Over the next couple of days, the funeral preparations took up so much of Diana's time that she had no chance either to think of her law practice or to pursue the secret further.

After selecting a coffin, talking to the vicar, and completing the formalities, she went into town and bought a classically tailored black suit and black silk blouse, black tights, and black court shoes. Now all she had to do was arrange the grave itself.

Mr. Green was a step ahead of her and already had the keys to the vault ready before she even thought to ask.

"What on earth would I do without you?" Diana said. The butler responded with a slight bow.

"It's my duty to help you, Miss Diana, nothing more."

"You're simply too modest, Mr. Green," Diana replied, amused by the old-fashioned gesture. "I should give you a pay rise. And then I hope you'll let me into the secret of your first name."

Mr. Green's only reply was a subtle smile.

This time they drove to the cemetery, attracting curious glances from the people visiting various graves there. Although the days when the village was dominated by its major landowner were long gone, people still tended to stiffen with awe when their eyes fell on a member of the family—especially in a place like the churchyard and following news like that of Emily's death.

With the looks causing the hairs on the back of her neck to stand on end, Diana entered the tomb of the Tremaynes, her distant ancestors, for the first time in her life.

Here, too, the graveyard gardener had done his work well. He clearly had a second key, since when she opened the wooden door, she was faced with neither a huge cloud of dust nor a heap of old leaves.

At first she had wondered how such a small vault could contain so many coffins. Now, standing in the doorway, she looked in vain for sarcophagi and urns.

As ever, Mr. Green was ready with an answer to the puzzle. Armed with a halogen torch, he shone it on a small wrought-iron door, which appeared to lead into complete darkness.

"The actual vault is underground. The narrow silver key opens the door."

Diana found it strange to go down the narrow stairs and enter the little town of the dead. The circular underground room reminded her of an old Egyptian burial chamber that she'd seen in a *National Geographic* feature. Of course, she was well aware that wealthy families had their members buried in vaults such as this, but she had never been inside one. And this one was the tomb of her own ancestors. As a child she had sometimes wondered what it would be like to meet all those who had gone before her, to walk with them or ask them about the times in which they lived.

But now, instead of curiosity she felt only a sense of unease. This room, with its coffins arrayed on shelves and two sarcophagi dominating the space in the middle, showed her only too well what becomes of every person one day.

"The sarcophagi belong to the progenitor of the Tremaynes and his wife, don't they?" Diana asked as she shone the torch over the carved plaques of solid stone.

"Yes, as far as I know," the butler replied, still standing respectfully on the steps, which were bathed in faint daylight. "The other members of the family were laid to rest in their turn on the shelves. In some vaults it's usual to give each of the dead their own compartment in the wall."

Diana began in the front left-hand corner and slowly worked her way clockwise around the circular room. Name after name made its way into her mind, and she used their dates to attempt to form an imaginary family tree with spreading branches.

She finally stopped in front of one of the coffins. The magnificent oak was polished and decorated with beautiful marquetry that showed hardly any signs of age. As Diana rubbed the brass plate free of dust, she read:

HERE LIES VICTORIA PRINCETON, NÉE TREMAYNE, IN GOD'S PEACE. 12 SEPTEMBER 1873–15 AUGUST 1929.

The famous Victoria, Emily's grandmother. Diana's aunt had hardly ever spoken of her, which was hardly surprising since Emily had only been nine when she died.

If she had understood the arrangement of the coffins correctly, Victoria's sister, Grace, would have been laid to rest somewhere near her. But there was no coffin with her name on it, as Diana discovered after shining her light on the others. She found the coffins of Henry Tremayne and his wife Claudia, and that of Daphne and her husband. None of these Tremaynes had lived to a particularly old age. As far as she knew, the same applied to her own family. No one had reached seventy; Emily was the exception.

The absence of Grace might be explained by the fact that her husband had insisted on her being buried with him. He had been a sea captain and was probably buried in East Prussia, where they had settled—Diana had gleaned that much from her mother. But why wasn't Beatrice in here, either? She was a descendant of the Tremaynes.

Why had she been given her own grave—with an angel bearing a wreath of tea leaves?

"Did you ever hear why my grandmother was buried outside the vault, Mr. Green?"

"I'm sorry, I didn't," Mr. Green replied from where he still stood by the door. "That was one of the things that was never discussed. But maybe it was your grandmother's wish."

Diana wondered whether Beatrice, weakened as she was by childbirth, had been in a position to express any kind of wish. When she was on her deathbed she probably hadn't cared where she was to be buried. Or had Daphne, ever mistrustful of her, insisted on it?

As Diana turned to the vacant space beneath Daphne, the beam from the torch fell on something under the coffin.

"What's that?" she murmured in surprise, shining the light further underneath Daphne's coffin. The piece of paper was yellowed and rather crumpled, and lay covered in dust at the foot end of the coffin. At first she thought the gardener must have tried to dispose of his packed lunch wrapper there, but when she drew it out she saw that it was an envelope.

"Mr. Green?"

Her voice echoed unanswered through the vault. The butler had gone back up.

"Excuse me, Miss Diana, did you call me?" he called after a moment, and hurried down the steps. "I just popped up to see whether the gardener is around."

Diana turned, her eyes still on the letter in her hand. "I found this under Daphne's coffin. An envelope." She turned the letter over. It was addressed to Grace Tremayne, but she couldn't see either a sender or a date. Although the envelope was only loosely sealed, Diana decided to open it later. She was finding the vault more unsettling with every moment that passed. She had a strong sense of the eyes of her ancestors upon her.

"Have you looked to see what's inside?" Somehow Mr. Green didn't seem surprised.

"No, I'll look later." Diana shoved the envelope into her pocket. "I think this is the space intended for my aunt. Do you agree? Below her mother."

"I'm sure Mrs. Woodhouse would be satisfied with that."

Diana peered into the darkness beneath the coffin, shuddered, and drew back. *Maybe Grandmother really didn't want to be buried here, but preferred to be up in the open air where she could gaze at the stars. Or up at the tea-leaf wreath.*

She realised the gardener was probably waiting for her outside. After a brief discussion about the arrangements for the funeral, she sent Mr. Green back home. She decided to walk. On the way she met a few people, to whom she gave a friendly greeting, although this only earned her some bemused looks. Once, she reached into her pocket to get the letter out, but then let it be. Instead, she wondered who could have tucked it under the coffin. Emily, maybe? Had someone stolen it and then, struck by a fit of guilt, not known what else to do with it? But who would have been able get into the vault?

Once back at Tremayne House, she went straight to the study and flopped down into the chair behind the desk. A leaden heaviness weighed down her limbs.

She considered going to lie down on the sofa and sleep, but the letter wouldn't leave her in peace. What was in it? Could it have been there waiting for her for all those years since Daphne died? It was dusty enough for that. And since it was cold and dry down there, it was no surprise that it had hardly any patches of mildew. However, there were a lot of dirty fingerprints on the envelope, and its edges were greasy. As Diana turned it over, she even thought she saw a few drops of blood on the front.

She carefully smoothed out the envelope on the desk protector. It had probably been crumpled up at some time and then carefully smoothed, possibly even pressed between the pages of a book. The fine creases had remained, but it looked like a crinkled garment that had been ironed at too low a temperature.

It was addressed in typescript to Grace Tremayne at Tremayne House. Diana's great-great-grandmother. There was no sender's name.

Her hands trembling slightly, Diana pulled out a sheet of paper. It looked no less dirty, but at least there were no traces of blood. The ink had run, indicating that the letter had got wet at some stage. The folds looked fragile, almost as though the fine wood fibres of the paper would fall apart if touched.

The letter was short, but its few lines caused Diana to lean back in her seat in amazement. Emily's grandmother, Victoria, apologised to her sister, referred to a scandal and announced that a man, whom it appeared Grace loved, would be coming to visit. Victoria also promised always to be there for Grace's family.

What had happened? And why hadn't Grace and Victoria been in the same place? Diana turned the letter over but found no reference to where it had been sent from, only the date: 15 February 1888.

That was only a year and a half after Henry had received the telegram informing him of the death of his brother. And now this letter. What did the two things have to do with one another?

Diana looked at the secret compartment regretfully. Did the answer lie in there? It was a pity that the key would take a while longer to be ready. It was now Thursday, and the funeral would soon be upon them.

After reading the letter through again, she suddenly remembered what Dr. Sayers had told her: that Beatrice had been carrying a letter, and used it to ask for help. Was this that letter? That old promise of help?

That was certainly what the wording of the letter implied.

Diana brooded over it for a while longer, but no answer came to her. She finally conceded that she would be better off going to bed. After carefully slipping the letter back into its envelope, she laid it down with the telegram and pack of tea before switching off the light and climbing the stairs.

8

"Sleep well, Aunt Emily," Diana whispered after ensuring her aunt had taken her proper place among her ancestors in the family vault. To her enormous relief, the funeral service had been just as she had envisioned it—and surely how Emily would have wanted it. She thanked the pall-bearers, local men who were hardly younger than Emily herself but who would not have missed the opportunity to pay their last respects to the mistress of Tremayne House.

Meanwhile, the mourners had gathered around the entrance to the church, some of them talking in hushed tones to Reverend Thorpe, whom Diana also wanted to thank.

On the way back to the car, she stopped to look once again at the impassive angel holding the wreath over Beatrice's grave. Remembering her strange dream, she examined the face more closely—but it was not a woman's face she saw. The features were clearly male. Male and somehow . . . exotic.

Diana tilted her head as she tried to work out the possible national-ity of the angel. Did it actually have one? Or had it merely been a per-sonal notion of the sculptor's—someone he knew, perhaps, and wanted to immortalise in this monument?

A hand on her elbow drew her out of her reflections. Mr. Green had appeared beside her without her realising.

"Is everything all right, Miss Diana?" His voice was scarcely above a whisper.

"Yes, I think so. I was just looking at the angel. His face . . ."

Mr. Green raised his head, eyes narrowed.

"It's a man," he observed. "I assume he's one of the archangels."

"Don't you think there's something exotic about him?"

"It never occurred to me before . . ." The butler paused briefly, then nodded. "You're right; his features aren't really European. Maybe it's a personal touch by the artist."

"Could be." A thought flared up in Diana's mind, but she couldn't quite grasp it. "Come on, we shouldn't keep the others waiting."

Almost all the mourners followed them back to Tremayne House. Mr. Green had arranged for some helpers, women from the village who had declared themselves willing to cut the cakes and serve the tea.

After Diana had spoken a few words to the guests and thanked them for coming, a subdued murmur arose, spreading through the old building and ironically giving it life that it had missed for so many years.

Among the many unfamiliar faces, some of whose names she didn't even know, Diana was glad to see Dr. Sayers.

"I'm glad you came," she said as she shook his hand.

The doctor gave her a sad smile. "It was the least I could do for my old friend. It's a real shame she's been called away from the world, but that's the way things go. It's probably my turn next."

Diana didn't know how to reply—who was she to know a person's life span? A change of subject occurred to her. "You must have seen how well-tended my grandmother's grave is."

"Yes, I have. And to be honest, it's a sight that gladdens my heart. I regret that I haven't visited it for so long, but as I've already told you, I'm unnerved by the way death seems to be watching men of my age."

Diana pursued her train of thought. *Should I really ask him?*

"I visited her grave shortly after you came to see me, and a few things struck me as strange."

A knowing look lit up the doctor's face. "You must have wondered why she isn't buried in the vault."

"Among other things."

"Well, that's one of the mysteries Daphne took to the grave with her."

"Could it be that she still suspected my grandma of being an impostor?"

"No, I'm sure that wasn't the case. I believe the reason goes much further back, but no one here knows what it is. All we do know is that something must have happened between Daphne's aunt Grace and her father, which led to him removing Grace from the Tremaynes' inheritance."

Diana raised her eyebrows. That was something she hadn't known.

"Seriously?"

Dr. Sayers nodded. "After the death of old Henry Tremayne, Victoria, the second-born, took over the house and the estate, and later left it to her daughter, Daphne."

"Maybe Grace didn't want Tremayne House. My mother once told me that she married in around 1888. She had her own house on the Baltic."

"As I said, no one knows any details. But Daphne was always cool and reserved with Beatrice, as though she knew about the earlier incident. Beatrice herself knew nothing about any of it. She kept her distance from Daphne, but was really close to Emily from the word go. They were like sisters—and no wonder; they were around the same age. Her death broke Emily's heart and was probably what led to Emily's increasing withdrawal when she was a young woman."

The regret in Sayers's voice was obvious and led Diana to wonder whether the doctor had been in love with Emily—new food for thought. But she felt close to solving the puzzle of the angel, and continued with her questions.

"What about the angel? Does he represent anyone in particular?"

"Not as far as I know. Emily commissioned him after the death of her mother. Before that, Beatrice's resting place was marked only by the gravestone. I have no idea whether the angel was made in the likeness of any real person. It's possible that he represents Beatrice's husband, who was killed when they were fleeing. That would be beautiful, don't you think? The husband is still protecting his wife in death." Tears suddenly glistened at the corners of Sayers's eyes. He brushed them away in embarrassment, his lower lip trembling.

"That's a really lovely thought."

Before the doctor could reply, one of the women appeared with a tray.

"Would you like some cake?"

Diana didn't really feel like eating anything but, like Dr. Sayers, she took a plate with a black-and-white iced cupcake.

"Anyway, it's a lovely memorial to your grandmother, isn't it?" said the doctor, continuing the conversation where they'd left off. "If you find out whether the angel's actually modelled on someone, do tell me. After our conversation I'm dying to know."

"I certainly will," Diana said. She bit into the cake and felt a little of her appetite returning.

When all the guests had gone, Diana stood for a long while by the conservatory windows, watching the grey day gradually fade into black without a single ray of sunshine breaking through the blanket of cloud.

When Mr. Green came to switch on the conservatory light, she stepped back from the windows and turned to him.

"I think I've finished for the day," the butler announced. "I've left you some hot coffee in the kitchen, and there's enough cake left if you're feeling hungry."

"Thank you very much, Mr. Green."

Diana noticed he had his coat over his arm. Was he going somewhere? He was hardly likely to get cold on his way to the east wing, where he had his apartment.

"The funeral went very well, if I may say so. Mrs. Woodhouse would have been proud of you. And I'd be surprised if you haven't made your mark among the villagers. After all, you're the new lady of the house."

Diana smiled bitterly. "I wouldn't be so sure about that."

Mr. Green tilted his head in surprise. "Is there some reason you might refuse the inheritance? As far as I know, Mrs. Woodhouse had no other relatives."

"At the funeral tea, I discovered from Dr. Sayers that my great-great-grandmother was disinherited by her father. Dr. Sayers didn't know the reason, but it's possible that there may still be some legal provision preventing me from inheriting."

"Don't worry yourself about that. Dr. Sayers must also have told you that Mrs. Woodhouse loved your mother more than anything—and you. I can't believe she'd allow herself to be influenced by an ancient dispute. Otherwise she'd hardly have asked you to get to the bottom of the family secret. We'll soon see once the will has been opened."

Although she knew Mr. Green was right, Diana still felt uneasy. Why had there been this rift between father and daughter? Once again she thought of the letter she had found under Daphne's coffin. Why had it been lying there? Had Emily left it for Diana to find after she died?

Mr. Green withdrew and Diana went upstairs, this time glancing only briefly at the painting of Grace and Victoria. In her room she undressed and slipped into a lavender-scented nightshirt from the chest at the foot of the bed. Emily had always left a supply of nightwear for her guests, even though visitors had been an increasingly rare occurrence. Although Diana was exhausted, her mind continued to race as she thought through everything she had found out, finally coming to the conclusion that things would only become clearer once the secret compartment had been opened.

When the locksmith appeared the following morning, Diana had already had a brief crying fit. She had dug out an old photo album in the hope that she might find a picture of her grandfather. Instead, she had found a photo showing herself as a small girl in the park with her mother and Emily. The picture looked so natural that she had felt as though she were back there. She could smell the rose bushes and the grass the former gardener had always kept so neatly mown, and above all Aunt Emily's characteristic violet scent.

All at once she recalled again what Dr. Sayers had said about the angel at the funeral tea, and how lovely it was to think of a man keeping watch over his wife even after death. That had been too much for her shaky emotional balance.

The tears had kept her from looking for a picture of her grandfather. And now, as she went to answer the door, the idea seemed completely absurd to her. Why would Emily have kept a photo showing Beatrice's husband?

"My goodness, it seems like I always come at the wrong moment." Mr. Talbott offered her a clean handkerchief, but Diana shook her head.

"I'm fine, thanks. Have you brought the key?"

"Of course." He held up a small brown-paper bag, fastened by a shiny sticker with the company's logo. "You should try it out first. You never know with old locks like this one."

"I trust your abilities. After all, my aunt always did. Come in, I'll fetch the money."

Diana hurried away and stopped herself just in time from getting out a euro bill from her purse. She noticed her mistake and gave him the payment in pounds. He handed her the bag. "The sticker was made by my grandson. He told me I should improve the way I present my services."

"That was very kind of him."

"Huh, he only wants to show me how he can play around on his computer!" Talbott retorted. "When I was sixteen I was more interested in girls than a machine that spews out images and stickers at the press of a button. But young people are different today, and the old ways are gradually disappearing."

He probably made this speech to his grandson at every opportunity, with the same gestures he was using now to emphasise his words. Diana smiled as she imagined the young man rolling his eyes before disappearing back into his virtual world.

"You see, you're smiling now. At least that means it's not me who's making you feel sad."

"Of course not, Mr. Talbott. And if you keep your business going for a little longer I'll be contacting you again if I need any more keys cutting."

"Or if you lock yourself out. But I think if that happened you could rely on Mr. Green to climb up the drainpipe for you and slip in at one of the attic windows to let you in."

That finally succeeded in making Diana burst out laughing. A laugh that hurt her chest, but at least she was laughing.

After the locksmith had left, Diana opened the bag, taking care not to damage the sticker. She found a small, old-fashioned-looking brass key, with a really pretty bow decorated to match others in Tremayne House, with entwined leaves and a small flower. He had probably spent most of the time on this, as the blade was relatively simple.

Would any other locksmith have gone to the trouble of making such an ornate key? Or had Talbott simply done it because he believed she was a second Emily?

Her heart began to thump in her throat, and her sadness receded a little. The key in her hand seemed to pulsate as if it were magic. Her family's secret. She'd discover what it was today.

She took a deep breath, then turned and started along the corridor that she had not been down for a few days. This time her way was not illuminated by the glow of the lamps, but by light falling through two open doors. Mr. Green had been busy here, probably dusting the scary hunting trophies.

She paused briefly outside the double doors, then took another deep breath and opened it. Nothing had changed. The dust that had settled since she was last here had been conscientiously removed by Mr. Green.

Diana grasped the little key so hard that she could feel every contour.

The metal warming in her hand, she moved to the shelf and pushed the key into the lock. A moment of tension, a moment of holding her breath. Then Diana turned the key. The blade met a slight resistance but pushed it aside, and the lock fell open with a soft click.

Her hand was trembling a little, and she felt a twinge inside as she opened the door. With the smell of old masonry rising to her nostrils, Diana discovered a rectangular object inside.

A casket. About as long as her forearm and a hand's breadth high. It was made of rosewood and decorated with intricately intertwined foliage. At first glance the pattern looked Irish, but Diana strangely knew that this casket had been made in a far-off land.

The compulsion to smell it was suddenly so strong that she raised the box to her nose. She realised with amazement that it didn't smell of mildew or masonry. After all those years, it had a slightly sweet smell that she recognised. Had someone kept cinnamon sticks in it?

Diana took the casket over to the desk, ran her hand thoughtfully over the lid, and then opened it. Inside, nestled on the red velvet lining, were four objects. A pendant with a large blue stone, a long-dried leaf covered in strange marks, a photograph of a mountain, and a little book, which Diana picked up first. She felt a strange tension run through her. This was what it must feel like if you were able to look through a window into the past. If you had the chance to see your own roots.

Diana reverently ran her fingers over the book as she drank in all the details. An old travel guide. It had a blue-green binding with blue print.

The Passenger's Guide to Colombo.

Opening it, she saw that it dated from 1887. There was a pressed flower between the pages. Frangipani, one of India's most beautiful flowers. This one was white and had a blood-red eye.

On the well-thumbed, but not yellowed, pages, a few sections were underlined—presumably places the owner of the book had wanted to visit.

Enraptured, Diana thumbed through the pages, which were illustrated with beautiful vignettes and promised a comprehensive overview of the sights of the city. Had this book once belonged to Henry Tremayne's brother, who had met with his fate on a faraway island? All at once she felt as though someone had come up behind her to quietly whisper the story of this object into her ear.

9

Colombo, 1887

"Look what I've got here!" Victoria handed her elder sister a little book bound in coarse green paper, with *The Passenger's Guide to Colombo* printed on it. Her blue eyes shone like the clear sky above the harbour, across which they had an excellent view from their room in the Grand Oriental Hotel.

"A travel guide?" Grace said, as she turned the book over in her hands.

A frame of stylised flowers edged the otherwise plain cover, which was printed the same on front and back.

"For one rupee!" Victoria announced proudly, taking the travel guide back and hugging it to her as though it were a rare piece of jewellery.

"Papa lets you go into town with Wilkes and there you go buying a travel guide!" Grace shook her head reproachfully and leaned back into the broad window seat of their hotel room.

"We'll be able to make good use of it here!" Victoria said, pouting defensively. "After all, we're in a foreign country. How will you find your way around without help?"

I'd prefer not to at all, Grace almost slipped out, but managed to swallow her words at the last moment.

Although she didn't share her sister's excitement, she didn't want to spoil her fun entirely. It was bad enough that they had been deposited here in the hotel like so much luggage.

While her younger sister immersed herself in her reading, Grace gazed with a sigh out over the deep blue sea, on which modern steamers sailed alongside double-masted dhows and Chinese junks as though they had accidentally found themselves in ancient times.

The quayside was teeming with people at that time of day. Natives scurried among sailors of all nationalities, clothed either in plain white trousers or magnificent yellow and red robes. Many of them wore turbans, and some had a red mark painted on their brows.

Grace's eye fell on two women crossing the street. Their bright-pink and turquoise saris made a delightful contrast with their golden-brown skin and raven-black hair. Naturally they attracted the attention of men of all nationalities.

Grace had to admit that the view of the harbour alone was far more fascinating than anything she could observe back in dreary, grey London. But that foggy city was where her friends were. At that very moment, Grace thought sadly, Eliza and Alyson were probably trying on their dresses for the debutantes' ball. The date, which she had been aware of for months now, had almost arrived—but now, instead of getting herself ready for the ball and the season that followed it, she found herself at the other end of the world, in searing heat and surrounded by the smell of fish. Her presentation to Queen Victoria had been postponed "for as long as it takes for Papa to get the plantation up and running," her mother had said.

Grace knew better. Although an official veil of silence had been drawn down over the situation, it was nevertheless impossible to overlook the fact that they were experiencing difficulties, which could only be overcome by taking over the plantation. The old family estate in

Scotland was draining away a substantial portion of the Tremayne household's coffers, and their family home in London also needed to be maintained.

Her father had not spoken to her late uncle Richard for a long time. Just as silence was maintained over their financial straits, so he maintained his personal silence—even denying that Richard had been the more successful of the two brothers. The plantation was well established and doing nicely, as she had discovered from a letter she had found in her father's study and read in secret. As for the circumstances of her uncle's death . . .

"Oh, look!" Victoria cried, clapping her hands as though she were four rather than thirteen. "There's a map here! And it even marks the location of the lunatic asylum!"

"Lunatic asylum?" Grace repeated, frowning.

"One of the sights listed in the guide. It says the building's new and well worth seeing." Victoria turned the page on the map and carefully leafed through the book until she found the place she was looking for. *The new lunatic asylum, a charitable institution, supported solely by the government, caused the colony a lot of concern in the past. The cost of its establishment, six hundred thousand rupees, seemed unnecessary to many, causing the original building plans to be modified. Four hundred lunatics are housed in this building, which is among the largest of those attributable to the governor, Sir James R. Longden.*"

"You could have gone to see lunatic asylums anywhere in England," Grace remarked laconically. "I don't recall you showing an interest in such charitable institutions a few months ago."

"Because if I'd suggested going to visit one, Mama would no doubt have had a fit," her sister replied, undeterred.

"She would now."

"Which is why I'm telling you and not her!" Victoria retorted.

"You'd be better off visiting some church or temple. Mama would be bound to allow you to go to those."

"Churches are boring, but the temples here are supposed to be really beautiful." Victoria began once again to leaf through the guide. After a while she found what she was looking for.

"Just look here—you must be interested in this, too!"

She held the book under her sister's nose, so close that she could do nothing other than look.

"The Cinnamon Garden," Grace read. "There's a museum close by, so Mother need have no concerns about our intellectual edification."

Grace wanted to reject this suggestion, too, but she had to admit that the Cinnamon Garden had aroused her interest. She loved the spice, which their cook, Mrs. Haynes, had sometimes added to desserts and cakes.

Victoria seemed to sense that her defences were crumbling because she continued, "In the Cinnamon Garden you can see how the cinnamon bark is stripped and then dried. If we go, we may even be able to bring some back with us. You must have missed your cinnamon milk on the voyage here."

"Oh yes, I really did!" Closing her eyes, Grace indulged in the memory of the taste.

Unfortunately, Mrs. Hayes had stayed behind in England, and Grace had had to make do with her uncle's cook here. But maybe she, too, knew how to use cinnamon and could be persuaded to sweeten their exile with her favourite bedtime drink.

As a child she had been veritably obsessed with cinnamon and wanted to know all about the spice. Her father had waved away her questions in a kindly but firm manner, while her mother pretended to know nothing about it. Only the cook, with whom Grace liked to spend many a forbidden hour, let her into some of its secrets. "Cinnamon comes from India and Indonesia," she would reply.

She had long since forgotten these stories by the time she heard they were to move to Ceylon, but now, thanks to her sister's travel guide, the memories had been reawakened, suddenly bringing a little relief to the heat and boredom.

"So, shall we go to the Cinnamon Garden?" Victoria nagged.

"You don't know for how long we'll be staying in Colombo," Grace replied as she handed the guide back to her sister. "Uncle Richard's plantation is near Adam's Peak. That's a long way from here."

"It looks as though we'll be here long enough to put down roots!" Victoria replied, gesturing angrily towards the harbourmaster's building. "Father seems to be well ensconced there. If we just set off in a rickshaw, we can be at the Cinnamon Garden in no time. We'd be back from a visit to the museum before they even knew we were gone."

"Don't be silly," Grace said with a shake of her head. "If we're still here in a few days' time I'll ask Mother myself. I don't believe even she could have anything against the Cinnamon Garden."

"Honestly, how long is all this going to last?"

In the next-door hotel room, Claudia Tremayne was complaining to her butler, Wilkes. She looked reproachfully out of the hotel window at the building her husband had vanished into two hours ago. Since the harbourmaster had to examine their papers in any case, Henry wanted to take the opportunity to meet Mr. Cahill, his brother's lawyer.

"I'm sure he'll be back soon, madam," Martin Wilkes replied. Still a bachelor at fifty, he was just as much a fixture in their household as the trunks they had travelled with.

"So you say, Wilkes! But you know Mr. Tremayne!" Claudia, whose accent always fell back to her native Scottish when she was agitated, looked through the connecting door to her daughters' room. The two of them were poring over a thin book, which Victoria had bought when she accompanied Wilkes to the Harbour Office.

Claudia looked wistfully at her daughter Grace. The girl resembled a younger version of her own mother, whom Claudia could remember well despite her death at a young age. Claudia had always admired Bella Avery for her golden-red hair, pale skin, and green eyes.

She herself had taken after her father—heavy-boned, tough, dark-haired. She sometimes wondered how Henry Tremayne, the handsome son of an influential member of parliament, could ever have noticed her. On the occasion of her debut presentation to Queen Victoria, Henry had been surrounded by so many beautiful young women that she could hardly have stood out among them with her dark hair. And yet, one day, he had appeared at her father's door asking his permission to court her.

Her parents would have preferred the elder son of the Tremayne dynasty, but even then Richard had been showing signs of rebellion against his ancestral family. By the time he had moved out to Ceylon on the adventurous trail of a tea plantation, Claudia's parents had been satisfied, not least because Henry, whom she had married in the meantime, had now become the heir of the Tremaynes and the owner of Tremayne House. A house that had gradually proved to be a curse. Part of the animosity shown towards Richard by Henry was due to the fact that he had assigned the house, with all its obligations, to him. Unlike his parents-in-law, Henry had never harboured aspirations towards inheriting his family estate.

And now, after Richard's death a few months ago in mysterious circumstances, Henry had even been forced to take over his brother's plantation in Ceylon.

With a sigh, Claudia smoothed a few creases from her blue-grey taffeta skirt, which in the tropics felt like a greenhouse concentrating the heat.

Gazing once more out of the window, she thought she glimpsed her husband. Had the meeting finally come to an end?

Clearly not—the figure turned, and she realised that it was not Henry, but probably the man he was to meet.

Hopefully he'll be back soon, she thought, cooling herself with a Chinese paper fan she had found in Victoria's bag.

◆ ◆ ◆

"The plantation extends to three hundred acres of land near Adam's Peak," John Cahill said, lowering the pince-nez, which was gradually beginning to give him a headache. He was with Henry Tremayne, the new owner of the Tremayne plantation, going through the estate's papers now that the formalities relating to their arrival had finally been settled. "This makes you one of the biggest plantation owners, after the Stocktons and the Walburys, and in any case their holdings are on the other side of the mountain."

Henry seemed tense, and no wonder after the strain of the journey and the exhausting meeting in the harbourmaster's office. The room had been stuffy and teeming with smells carried in from the harbour on the wind. They had assured him that when the wind was from the south it would smell of cinnamon here, but right now it stank of fish, seaweed, brine, and an incongruous mixture of the spices and fruits on sale in the nearby market.

If only we could have held the meeting in a nice cool room, Tremayne thought as he suppressed the urge to fan himself with the papers in his hand.

"It produces an excellent yield, as you can see from these figures, and it is expected that the profits will double this year. All the plantation needs to make the problems go away is a strong owner."

Henry looked sullenly at the book Cahill pushed over to him. Despite his attorney's optimistic words, he had no desire to go through the figures. His grief for his brother gave way regularly to heartfelt anger and bouts of hatred. At that moment the former feeling was fast giving way to the latter.

The death of Richard Tremayne, Henry's older brother by five years, had left chaos in its wake. Badly kept books, outstanding payments, and disorder in his personal papers. Although the land was clearly good, it was increasingly obvious that his brother had possessed little idea of how to manage it.

The figures nevertheless lifted Henry's mood a little. If Cahill was correct with his talk of the profits doubling, he wouldn't have to give up the family seat and would even be able to keep the Scottish castle.

"Have they found out yet why my brother fell?" Henry asked as he snapped the book shut. His words made Cahill, who clearly wanted to show him yet more figures, lose his thread.

"No, sir. I'm afraid the enquiries are still continuing. And although there are Englishmen involved in the investigation, it's dragging. But I think we can safely assume it was an accident. Adam's Peak isn't a dangerous mountain, but there are risks there nevertheless. I don't know why your brother felt the need to clamber about the place all the time with that naturalist."

"Was the naturalist there?"

Cahill shook his head. "No, not on the evening in question. It seems he had set off completely alone, strangely enough. The staff say that he was angry about something, and they assume that he went up to the mountain to let off steam."

"Without anyone to accompany him?"

"Yes, as far as we know. But . . ."

Henry looked with embarrassment at the toes of his shoes. "You don't think he might have gone to end his own life?"

"No, that's not possible. I knew your brother. His bookkeeping may have been eccentric, but he wasn't a man who would have left a mess behind him. If he'd been planning to take his life, he would have tried to ensure that things were in some kind of order. Or at least have left a farewell note. But there was nothing of the kind."

"Could it have been murder?"

Cahill paled. "Let's hope that isn't the case. You'd never hear the last of it from the authorities, not for months at least, should grounds be found for such a suspicion."

"Did my brother have any enemies, as far as you knew?"

"No, sir, he got on well with more or less everyone. If any disputes arose, he resolved them amicably. Tea cultivation is a gentleman's business—they're not like Texas cattle barons shooting one another out of the saddle."

Henry fell into contemplation. Could his brother really have been the victim of an accident? Maybe it would be better if he stopped thinking about it or trying to find out more. He certainly didn't want any trouble from the authorities; things were complicated enough as they were.

"When can we move to the plantation, do you think?"

"The workmen are still there at the moment getting the house ship-shape. Over recent months it suffered a little neglect at the hands of your brother. But I'll make sure they get a move on, and I'm confident they'll be finished in a few more days. I'm sure you'll agree that it's worth it. Vannattuppūcci is a very special place—a paradise if you like. You'll soon see!"

Over dinner, in a quiet corner of the hotel dining room, Henry told his family what John Cahill had said—as much information, at least, as was unlikely to overexcite or perplex them. Claudia was unsatisfied all the same.

"My goodness, how long are we going to have to stick it out here?"

She looked around with disapproval at the other guests in the room, who took no notice of her. "You know what workmen are like—they always drag projects out to try to earn more money."

"Mr. Cahill promised he'd hurry them up."

"Even if they do hurry up, I dare say that will mean they make a botch of it."

"Claudia, darling." Henry gave his wife an almost beseeching look. *Did carping make things better?*

As if she could read his mind, Claudia appeared to agree with him. She lowered her head as if in shame. Her husband took her hand.

"Maybe you should have a look around the gemstone markets in the city. I've heard there's some magnificent jewellery to be had at half the price you'd have to pay in England."

"And what opportunities would I have to wear fine jewels in this wilderness?" Claudia asked, still feeling a little ungracious as she saw herself a prisoner between palms and tea plants.

"Mr. Cahill speaks of a lively social life in Nuwara Eliya. Apparently there are hotels there, lots of villas used as holiday homes by some very high-ranking English families and, of course, other plantation owners who are very highly regarded. I'm sure that with your social graces you'll soon find some friends—and you can hold balls that will be the talk of Ceylon."

A smile came to Claudia's lips now. And although Grace knew it would be small consolation for missing the debutantes' ball, she also looked forward to the next opportunity to dance.

10

Berlin, 2008

Diana's return to Berlin felt wrong somehow—as though she no longer belonged there. Even on the plane, she was already missing Tremayne House so much that she was moved to write an email to Mr. Green. *That's bound to surprise him,* Diana thought as she tapped the words on to the keyboard. *But maybe it'll reassure him that this time it's not going to be years before I return.*

In any case, she was now the mistress of Tremayne House. When they had opened Emily's will it had turned out that Diana's aunt had left the house and its grounds to her. If Dr. Burton, the solicitor, was to be believed, there was no one else who could make a claim to the inheritance.

She preferred not to think of the future maintenance of the house. Emily had also left her a substantial sum of money and some stocks and shares, but they were not enough to keep a property like that running.

And there was also the casket from the secret compartment. All through the flight her head had been filled with questions about it. In Victoria's old letter that she'd found under Daphne's coffin, there had been a reference to "something" that the mysterious man had left behind until he could reach Grace. The only truly unusual object in the casket had been the inscribed leaf.

Did this leaf have something to do with the guilty conscience Emily had referred to?

In any case she first had to find out what the marks on the leaf meant. Maybe it was something like a love letter in a secret code. Or maybe it was in an Indian language. She knew someone in Berlin who was familiar with Asian scripts, and intended to get in touch with him.

Unfortunately, there were other matters to concern her. Although she had to uncover the family secret, she first needed to have it out with Philipp. While she was away, she had actually managed to hold back from answering him a single time—although that wouldn't make it any easier when they met face to face.

As she drove up the street, she had a strange feeling that her husband would be waiting for her. His car on the drive confirmed her suspicions. It seemed he didn't have a lunch date with his new girlfriend that day.

She parked her Mini behind his car, steeling herself for his reproaches as she got out. Although with his affair he had forfeited the right to scold her for being unreachable, her heart was nevertheless pounding as if she were a little girl coming home late from playing out, wondering how to justify herself to her father.

As she turned the key in the lock a thought occurred to her that made her pulse race even quicker.

What will you do if you find the two of them in bed together? Maybe he's been making the most of your absence . . .

Listening anxiously for laughter or other telltale sounds, she closed the door as quietly as she could behind her, then slipped down the hallway.

Light shone from the open living room door. The TV was on. No other sound. Diana made no attempt to be quiet as she approached the door. He was sitting there in front of the TV, cool as a cucumber, as though it were a perfectly normal evening. At least his girlfriend wasn't with him.

Diana set her bag down on the floor and he finally turned.

"Diana!" He jumped up from his chair and came over to her. "For God's sake, where have you been?"

"In England," she replied coolly, refusing to meet his eye. His angular face, dimpled cheeks, brown eyes, and short curly hair—the things she had first fallen in love with—almost caused her to regret her behaviour now. But no, she wasn't the one who had anything to feel guilty about.

"At your aunt's?" Philipp planted his hands on his hips. "Why didn't you say anything? You didn't even send me a text!"

"You know full well why." Despite her intention to stay calm, to use Mr. Green's composure as an example, Diana realised she sounded like a sulky child.

"It was only a one-off."

"And? How long has this one-off been going on for?"

"Diana . . ."

"Please could you be honest for once," she snapped.

Philipp pressed his lips together. Not because he was lost for words, but from anger.

"How's your aunt, then?" he asked with a veneer of self-control, as though the previous words had not been spoken.

Diana narrowed her eyes, but couldn't prevent the tears from escaping. *He doesn't need to know,* she tried to persuade herself. *He never took any interest in her before.*

"She's dead," she burst out despite herself.

Philipp looked shocked at the news, and made as if to give her a hug. Diana shoved his arms away. "Don't touch me! You can sympathise all you like, but it won't change what's happened!"

Philipp sniffed, then shook his head. "So where do we go from here?"

"Us?" Diana laughed bitterly. "We should keep out of each other's way. I'll sleep in the guest room."

She picked up her bag and trudged upstairs.

Gasping with suppressed anger, Diana sat down behind her desk. *My suspicions were right,* she thought as she unpacked her laptop. *I should have stayed a while longer at Tremayne House.*

"Next stop, Dahlem-Dorf," came the distorted voice through the hubbub of subway noise. Diana carefully put the travel guide away in her bag and checked again that the envelope containing the strange leaf hadn't got crumpled.

Lost in thought, she stood outside the station with a smile on her face. Not much had changed since she had been a student at the Free University of Berlin. Fashions were a little different, the curriculum would have been revised in line with the times, but Dahlem was still alive with people hungry for knowledge.

Unlike during her student days, she turned her back on the university buildings and headed for the grey glass-and-steel structure that housed the Museum of Asian Art.

She had managed to contact her acquaintance that morning and arrange an appointment the same day—a rare occurrence, so he claimed, as he was usually fully booked.

The excessively loud voices that met her as she entered came from a group of students gathering for a guided tour of the museum, who were attracting disapproving looks from the lady behind the reception counter.

Diana went over to her. "Hello, my name is Diana Wagenbach. I have an appointment with Dr. Fellner."

Looking at her as though she had told her a whopping lie, the assistant picked up a phone and announced Diana's arrival. The person on the other end of the line confirmed the appointment, and the woman's features softened a little.

"Just a moment, please. He's on his way."

Diana thanked her and took a seat on a nearby bench. She didn't have to watch the bored-looking students for long, as five minutes later her acquaintance came towards her. Michael Fellner was tall and still slim, but had lost the lankiness of his student days. He wore a grey jacket over blue jeans, and the collar of his light-blue shirt was open. No one from his younger days as a punk would have believed that he would now be walking around looking like this, least of all Diana.

He held out his hand to her with a smile. "Diana! Lovely to see you! Fancy; we've been working in the same city for years, but our paths have never crossed."

"They have now," Diana replied and hugged him as they always had when their crowds had met.

"You're looking good! You've hardly changed at all."

"I'm the one who's asking you for something, so I thought I'd better try and dress to impress," Diana said with a smile.

Michael stroked his chin pensively. "Well, you've certainly impressed me. It only makes me painfully aware of my growing spare tyre and the grey I see at my temples in the mirror every morning."

Diana shook her head in disapproval. He had no sign of a spare tyre, and he certainly wasn't going grey. His hairline was receding a little, but his features were still those of the boy who used to wear over-sized glasses and sport spiky dyed-blond hair and who had kept trying to lecture her on Asian art. His glasses were a more acceptable size now, his short hair cut to an even length, and she was now eager to share in his knowledge.

"Let's go to my office and you can show me your treasure."

They went upstairs and along a couple of corridors until they reached Michael's inner sanctum. The office, which was full of the clutter of the academic, had a good view of the university grounds, from which buildings rose up like scattered rocks.

"Diana Bornemann," he said as he sat down behind his desk.

How long had it been since she'd heard her maiden name? All at once it seemed as though she'd taken a step back in time. Still unmarried, about to take an exam, full of ideas and ambitious plans. The man before her was once again a budding Asian specialist, whose Japanese and Chinese were still a little shaky, and who was teaching himself Hindi in his spare time.

"You got married," he said, glancing at her ring finger. "At first I wondered who this Diana Wagenbach was, but then I recognised your voice. Do you know that almost everyone in our crowd secretly dreamed of getting you into bed?"

Diana put on a shocked expression. Of course she had been aware of the guys' advances—and all the stupid stunts they pulled to show her who was best. Michael had always been more reserved, but he hadn't held back from giving her meaningful looks.

"And I thought you were only interested in debates on social injustices. But I don't think we need to dwell on the past."

"You're right," Michael agreed, leaning back and studying her. "So what brings you to me? You sounded so mysterious."

Diana took the envelope from her bag and laid the strange leaf on the table.

Michael breathed in sharply. "It can't be!"

Diana kneaded ice-cold hands together. This must be how it felt to take some junk from the attic to an art expert and have him declare it to be a genuine, as yet unknown Da Vinci.

"What can't be?" she asked eagerly as Michael drew the leaf reverently towards him, pulled his glasses down his nose a little, and peered over the frame to see better.

Lost in researcher mode, Michael didn't reply for a while. Then he took a deep breath as though he needed plenty of oxygen for what he was about to announce.

"Tell me, have you heard of the palm-leaf libraries in India or Sri Lanka?"

Diana shook her head. "Forgive me if I seem uneducated to you, but this is the first I've heard of them."

Her friend was trembling slightly, a sure indication that she really had discovered something special.

"In India and Sri Lanka, people have been writing on dried palm leaves for many centuries—no, millennia—and some of them are very intricately decorated."

He typed something into his computer and turned the screen so Diana could see it.

The palm-leaf books Michael was referring to looked at first glance like large boxes. The engravings on the covers consisted of the snail-like letters she had seen on the leaf, framed by ornate patterns. Some of the "book covers" consisted only of the patterns.

"So you think my leaf is a page from one of these books?"

Michael shook his head and pushed his glasses back up his nose. "No, my dear, this is something completely different. Normally you wouldn't be allowed to possess this leaf."

"Why not? Is there a ban on importing them? In my defence I can say that it's probably more than a hundred years old."

Michael came round and sat on the edge of the desk. After shaking his head as though he were unable to believe it all, he said, "I'm convinced that what you've found here is a page from the legendary palm-leaf libraries, an ancient Indian oracle. Most of them are written in Old Tamil, a language that hardly anyone understands these days. One of the legends associated with the palm leaves tells of how Bhrigu, the son of a sage who had the privilege of living among the gods, one day had the insolence to hit Vishnu. Vishnu's wife Lakshmi punished him with the curse of bad luck. Although Bhrigu showed deep remorse and Lakshmi relented, she was unable to lift the curse. However, she granted him sight of the legendary cosmic scroll that enabled him to see the fate of all men, and ordered him to have the fates he had seen written down on palm leaves by Brahmans."

"That sounds interesting," Diana replied, although this information told her painfully little about her family history. "Maybe this leaf was stolen by some colonialist. Unfortunately, I don't know." She kept to herself her suspicion that the palm leaf could be the gift for Grace.

"It's possible," Michael replied. "If so, the colonialist was clearly unaware that taking one of these leaves is supposed to bring very bad luck. Usually palm leaves are not given out, but read and interpreted by mystics known as Nadi readers. People have them read out in order to find out about their past, present, and future destinies. Sometimes there are also insights into earlier incarnations—as you probably know, both Hindus and Buddhists believe in rebirth and Nirvana."

"I know you can only reach Nirvana once you've freed yourself from all sin and done appropriate penance."

"You could put it like that. If you don't manage to have a positive effect on your karma, you go through reincarnation until you have comprehended what you can and can't do. To put it simply."

A shudder ran through Diana. Could Henry Tremayne have brought this curse down on his family? Or maybe the unfortunate Richard—had he suffered his accident because he'd taken a palm leaf from a library?

"Do you think there's any truth in the curse?"

"That's something each of us has to decide for ourselves. There are reports of people who steal sacred Maori objects, for example, being pursued by bad luck or even dying in mysterious circumstances. From a modern scientific viewpoint, I'm only too pleased if something that doesn't belong here is returned to its proper place of origin—of course after plenty of photographs or facsimiles have been made of it. While we're on that subject, would you permit me to have this treasure photographed?"

"Of course," Diana replied a little uncertainly, as her thoughts were still on the curse and what Emily had said on her deathbed.

"It's truly fascinating." Michael's eyes seemed to be boring into her. "I'd be interested to know where you got it from."

"I found it in a secret compartment."

"Where?"

"In an old manor house in England. It's where my aunt lived until recently, when she died. She left me instructions to open a locked compartment. It was in there."

"I'm sorry," Michael said. "About the death of your aunt. But this find is sensational."

Should I tell him about the other things I found? Diana decided against it and asked instead, "Is it possible to find out which library this leaf is from? So that I can give it back, I mean."

"Hmm, that could be difficult. Even if you were to visit one of the libraries, no one would be able to tell you whether the leaf is theirs. As you can see, it hasn't been catalogued."

"But someone, somewhere, must have noticed one missing."

"There are so many leaves that one missing leaf is unlikely to be noticed. The only way would be if someone looking for their destiny was unable to find it. In this case because his leaf has been lying around in a secret compartment for all this time."

"Is there a leaf like this for every person?"

"No, but for very many. Personally, I explain it by the fact that many new souls are coming into the world who have not yet built up their karma. According to the Brahmans, most people who find their fates written on the leaves have experienced many lives and incarnations."

Diana looked at the leaf. Her curiosity was eating into her. What did it say? For whom was the fate prophesied? Grace? Her mysterious lover? Another family member, perhaps? She suddenly felt a longing to speak to Emily again. Why had she never told her anything about her grandmother's time in Sri Lanka, or about the brothers, Henry and Richard? Why had those two, like Henry's daughters, remained mere facts and figures in the family trees, fading faces on gradually yellowing photographs?

Had the thing that gave Victoria such a guilty conscience really been so dreadful?

"What should I do now?" she heard herself asking.

"The best thing to begin with would be to find someone who can read this for you," Michael replied, unable to take his eyes off the leaf. "Maybe it belongs to a family member. If you find the right reader, maybe he can also tell you which library it belongs to. But I'm afraid I can't promise that—there are an incredible number of these leaves."

"So that means I'd have to go to India?"

"It looks that way. I don't think there are any Nadi readers outside India."

"Or Sri Lanka." She thought of the guidebook again. "Is there one of these libraries in Colombo?"

"What makes you think of Colombo?" Michael asked.

"There was also an old guidebook to Colombo in the secret compartment, published in 1887. That's why I assumed the leaf also dated back to the late nineteenth century."

"It's probably much older. If you left it with me for a while I could tell you more precisely when it was made."

"You can examine it over the next few days. I'm going to need a while to find out where I need to go next."

Michael beamed. "If you leave it with me I'll have it photographed and test it to ascertain its age. It's not every day you get your hands on something like this."

"But I want it back!" Diana replied.

"Don't worry, you will. I'll call you as soon as I've got the photos and I've taken samples. It'll only take a few days."

11

Colombo, 1887

The next morning, Victoria did get her mother's permission to go to the Cinnamon Garden. Because of a migraine, which was probably the main reason for her giving her consent, she couldn't go with the girls herself, but she made sure Miss Giles and Mr. Wilkes accompanied them to make sure they didn't get lost.

Victoria didn't seem in the least bit concerned that their escorts would watch them like hawks.

"Maybe the coachman will drive past the lunatic asylum," she whispered conspiratorially to Grace, after they had taken their places in the carriage and were waiting for the others to join them.

"What do you want to see there? A depressing building surrounded by a high fence?"

"That may be what it means to you, but you never know what young women have been falsely committed there because their villainous husbands are after their inheritance."

Grace couldn't conceal her grin. "You've been reading one of your penny dreadfuls again, haven't you?"

"Me?" Victoria feigned a look of innocence—unsuccessfully. "I wouldn't read anything of the sort! You know what Father thinks of that kind of literature."

"That's never kept you from reading them before. Do you hide them in a secret compartment in your suitcase lid?"

A mischievous smile crept over Victoria's lips. "You know about that?"

Grace nodded.

"And you haven't told Papa about it?"

"You're my sister, or have you forgotten that? Sisters don't betray one another."

Victoria grasped her arm and snuggled up to her. "Thank you, darling sister! If you like, I'll lend you a few of them."

"I hardly think I'll be interested in the adventures of Lord Ruthven, but thanks for the offer."

Miss Giles and Mr. Wilkes now climbed aboard the carriage and they set off.

The coachman, a native in the service of the hotel, was skilled at negotiating the crowds of people, rickshaws, and ox-carts. Only once, when confronted with a group of elephants in the road, did they come to a halt.

"What magnificent giants!" Victoria marvelled at the beasts with their colourful blankets and pagoda-like structures perched on their backs.

"Elephants on way to temple," announced the coachman in broken English. "They holy. We must wait."

As the procession of elephants took a while to pass, Miss Giles began to fear for her complexion in the blazing sunlight.

"We're all going to burn dreadfully if we have to stay here much longer. Miss Grace, pull your hat down a little further over your face. And the same applies to you, Miss Victoria."

The two young women obeyed, but Victoria flashed a grimace towards her governess as Miss Giles was looking fearfully out to the side, where a little boy was holding out a carved figurine towards her.

The Cinnamon Gardens were more of a district than an actual garden. A number of houses were dotted among the trees of the plantation and around its edge. In the centre was a large mansion, surrounded by gardens with white sand where the cinnamon trees grew.

"If we're lucky we can go on a tour," Victoria said in delight. "That's what it says in the guidebook, anyway."

Miss Giles looked woefully at the path that wound between the trees, as if she already knew how dreadfully her ankle boots were going to hurt.

"I'm sure it's possible to get a guide to come with us in the coach," said Mr. Wilkes, immediately setting off in search of someone who knew their way around.

Grace noticed that Victoria was staring into space, brooding. She had spent all morning with her nose in the guidebook. Like a character in an old fairy tale, she clearly couldn't get enough of what she wanted.

"You're here. You've got your Cinnamon Garden," Grace said, pointing to the trees that looked so unlike cinnamon. "Why are you pulling such a long face?"

"I'm not pulling a long face!" Victoria objected. "I'm just thinking."

"What about?"

"This and that."

"It's not good for a young lady simply to let her thoughts wander aimlessly," Miss Giles felt obliged to chip in.

Grace had an inkling of why her sister was out of sorts. Contrary to her hopes, the coach had not come past the lunatic asylum—which she herself was quite glad about, as the stories being told around London about such places were completely ghastly.

After a while, Mr. Wilkes succeeded in tracking someone down who was prepared to guide them through the plantation. The small, rather stocky young man, whose skin was the colour of hazelnuts, told them as soon as he got into the coach that they would have to walk some of the way, as the paths between the trees were too narrow to allow the coach to pass.

He also told them, in almost incomprehensible English, the history of the plantation, which had existed since the times of the Dutch settlers and had finally reached its prime under the English. When they finally came to a halt as the paths became too narrow to continue, Miss Giles only got out unwillingly, despite the fact that it was not particularly far to the cinnamon trees and the walk promised to be far more interesting than driving past the rather dull-looking house.

How I'd love to be back in London, Grace thought, a bored expression on her face. She not only mourned the debut that she'd never experience, but also the coming season's balls. She would sorely miss nibbling pastries and confectionery and dancing quadrilles. Instead, here she was, being driven through the searing heat to see how they cultivated cinnamon—which she liked, granted, but was indifferent to how it was produced.

Lost in her own thoughts, she watched the workers peeling the bark from the cinnamon trees, passing it on to be rolled and then tied into bundles to await collection by the side of the path. The bundles were at various stages of drying out. While some looked more like shrivelled wood, others already looked like the cinnamon sticks their cook kept in a sealed glass jar.

"We should take Papa some of these cinnamon cigars," Victoria suggested.

"Do you really think he'll want to smoke them?"

"He smokes those dreadful cigars his friends send him from Sumatra," Victoria countered like a precocious child. "Why not cinnamon cigars? They must smell a lot better."

"Fair enough. We can buy him some as far as I'm concerned," Grace said. "I'll buy a few cinnamon sticks, too, in case there aren't any on Uncle Richard's plantation. I dread to think when we'll next see a shop once we're there."

They went to a small stall where they bought a few packs of cinnamon and some cinnamon cigars, but instead of returning to the carriage with Grace, Victoria walked a few paces to one side before coming to a standstill.

"Victoria!" Grace called after her, but was eventually compelled to follow her.

"Look over there!" Victoria pointed towards the houses beyond the bushes that marked the edge of the plantation. A confusion of voices drifted towards them. A narrow beaten path wound its way through the tangle of frangipani bushes. "How do you fancy an adventure?"

"Are you suggesting we should go over there?" Grace looked over at Mr. Wilkes and Miss Giles, who were still standing by the cinnamon stick stall, talking to the stallholder.

"Why not? I was mistaken when I thought the Cinnamon Garden would be an exciting place. As you can see, it's a crashing bore. But down there," she indicated the roofs from where the tumult arose, "it's vibrating with life. On the way here, in the carriage, I really wanted to get out and mingle with the crowd. Maybe we can find the temple where the elephants were being led."

"But Miss Giles and Mr. Wilkes have been told not to let us go off alone."

"They won't even notice we've gone."

Without another glance at their guardians, Victoria ran towards the little path.

"But . . ." Grace hesitated. All it would take was a cry from her to bring the butler and the governess running, and then Victoria would be dragged back to the coach where she would sulk about the adventure she'd missed out on.

Yet Grace couldn't bring herself to betray her sister. Victoria had already disappeared into the bushes, so she hitched up her skirt and ran after her as fast as she could.

"So you do want to come with me!" Victoria said triumphantly, brushing away twigs and tendrils that blocked their way.

"Only to make sure you don't do anything stupid."

Victoria smiled quietly to herself. Things really would have come to a pass if she couldn't get her elder sister to throw off the shackles of adulthood for a while. In earlier days Grace had always been ready to join in the fun rather than worrying about clothes and parties all the time. They had hidden under rose bushes in the garden or the laurel hedges of the park and told each other stories. But then their mother had begun to prepare Grace to be a young lady. From that moment on, it was a whirl of dances, afternoon teas, and trying on dresses. Victoria shuddered at the thought of all that, which would doubtlessly await her, too, once she reached sixteen. So she wanted to enjoy the last of her childhood to the fullest—and remind Grace how things had once been.

The fact that Grace was now following her through the undergrowth, and risking trouble, too, filled her with hope.

"We're only going to stay a few minutes, though, then make sure we get back safely," Grace hissed in her ear.

A moment later Grace was regretting having given in. The flood of people had closed in behind them and was now sweeping them down the street like a river in full flow. It would be practically impossible to get back quickly.

By the time they finally emerged into a side alley, the cinnamon plantation was far behind them. It was now clear to Grace that they hadn't arrived here by accident. Her sly little sister had planned it all down to the last detail.

"Come on!" Victoria cried, grabbing her hand and pulling her forward. "It must be around here somewhere!"

"You mean the temple?"

"No, something much more exciting!"

"Something you read about in the travel guide?" Grace asked, worried.

"No, on a leaflet lying on the windowsill in the dining room."

"What did it say?"

Grace recalled the tattered pamphlet and now regretted not having looked at it while she had the chance.

"I'll tell you later. For now, don't make me have to drag you along, you stubborn mule."

Grace felt completely out of place among the natives in their saris and sarongs. Sweat ran beneath her corset and down her back, and her skin felt as though it was burning from more than the sun's rays. The looks of astonishment the two English girls attracted at the way they were dressed pricked her like needles.

Suddenly, her sister stopped by a rather dilapidated building. The plaster was flaking off in large chunks, and a shutter hung crooked on its hinges. Instead of curtains, colourful cloths were strung up at the windows, and near the entrance Grace saw a brightly painted statue of a male figure with many arms. Beneath the porch made from woven palm leaves sat a young man in colourful robes with two bright-red stripes on his brow like those she had seen on men around the harbour. He stared at the two young women with a look that was penetrating, bordering on demonic.

"You English?" he asked eventually. "You want know fate?"

"But of course!" Victoria cried out in delight. "Grace, this is a palm-leaf library! Hundreds of these leaves are supposed to be kept here with the destinies of people written on them. That's what the leaflet said!"

So that's why Victoria didn't say anything—she knew I'd say no! Grace caught her hand and pulled her back. "It's nothing but fakery, Victoria! Let's go!"

"If it's only fakery, we don't have anything to fear." Victoria put on her best pleading little girl's face, which she knew her sister could never resist. "Please, Grace, let him predict our futures!"

"But he's bound to try and rob us!" Grace objected, although she knew full well it would have no effect on her adventure-hungry sister.

"There are plenty of other people who could have robbed us if they'd wanted to, aren't there? Even the pushy jewellers around the harbour haven't done us any harm!"

Grace sighed. If she refused to give in, Victoria would be moaning and calling her a scaredy-cat all the way back.

"All right. What does it cost?" Grace asked. The man stared at her so penetratingly with his dark-brown eyes that it seemed he wanted to look into the depths of her soul. *It's probably all part of the trickery,* she told herself, but nevertheless was the first to drop her gaze.

"Five rupees!" He emphasised his words by spreading the fingers of his right hand and holding it up before them.

Victoria nudged Grace in the side with her elbow. "Come on; don't be a scaredy-cat. Two years ago you'd have been the one dragging me into a place like this."

Was that true? Grace was no longer sure whether she had ever been as unruly as her sister. Her lessons in comportment and the duties expected of a lady had driven the pranks of her past into oblivion.

Grace handed the young man the money, which he deftly stowed beneath his robe. Then he rose and led them into a small room, where the blue paint was flaking from the walls. This apparent waiting room was completely empty, although noise could be heard from behind a brightly coloured curtain.

Grace felt the hairs stand up on the back of her neck. What if there was a band of rapists lurking behind there?

"You come." The man pointed to Grace. Her hand flew to her breast in shock.

"Not both of us?"

The man shook his head. "One leaf, one person. You come first, then other miss."

Grace looked at Victoria in panic. Her sister seemed a little disappointed that she wasn't the first to be allowed behind the curtain; despite her avid consumption of florid Gothic novels, she seemed not to share Grace's fears.

"You come!" the man said more forcefully, drawing the curtain aside. Bright daylight reached them down the short corridor behind it.

With a tight feeling in her stomach, Grace followed the man into the back room. She kept half an ear on the front room in the full expectation that she'd hear Victoria screaming as a slave trader took her captive. Back in London such a thing would certainly not be deemed unimaginable in a place like this.

I can't believe I'm doing this, she thought again. *If Mother knew, she'd subject us to a whole week of lectures on proper behaviour from Miss Giles.* On the way here, every glance, every foreign word, had felt like a threat. It would have been better to have stayed in the more respectable areas of Colombo.

Her inner sermon came to an end as she caught sight of a white-haired, brown-skinned man in a white tunic. Despite his considerable age, he was sitting in a strange position on a mat of palm leaves. Next to him was a small bowl from which a spiced aroma emanated.

As her companion spoke to the old man in their native tongue, Grace felt ashamed of her suspicion. The old man could easily have been her grandfather and obviously had no intention of pouncing on a young woman such as herself. On the ground next to him lay a number of long objects that reminded Grace of Chinese boxes, except these were substantially larger and adorned with strange characters.

"I ask you question, you answer," the young man announced as he picked up a pen and a piece of paper.

Grace looked up in surprise and noticed the old man studying her. She gave him a brief nod, then the old man's assistant—the man with the red marks on his forehead could not be anything else—began with the first questions. What her name was, who her parents were, where she came from, when she was born, and so on.

Grace gave her answers extremely unwillingly, since she still expected them to be deceiving her somehow. However, she soon decided against giving false answers, since if this really were an oracle of the future, that might have an evil effect on their prophecies. Not that she believed in it all, but she knew herself well enough to realise that a bad omen for the future would deprive her of sleep for days because she could never be sure if there was anything in it.

After he had noted down all her replies, the assistant vanished into another room, closing the door carefully as though he feared that something might be stolen from behind it. Grace looked around uncertainly. The old man, who had not said a word the whole time, continued to bore into her with his eyes. To avoid his gaze Grace turned towards the curtain behind which Victoria was sitting in the waiting room. Everything was quiet there. Her sister was probably bored already, or wondering where Grace had got to . . .

A rustling caused her to look at the door opposite again. The assistant appeared with a narrow brown leaf that looked like a ruler.

"I find leaf for you," he announced with a smile. "I give it Brahma for reading."

The young man handed his master the leaf with a gracious bow. The old man finally turned his gaze from her and ran his finger down the dried palm leaf. After a while the first strange-sounding words came gushing from his mouth, simultaneously interpreted by the young assistant.

Grace followed the heavily accented words with difficulty.

"Father rich man . . . long journey . . . decision . . . storm change everything . . . wedding . . ."

After a while, Grace gave up trying to follow the words. She allowed the information, which she didn't want anyway, to flow past her like water, until the young man finally said, "Your sixty-third year, you pass to next life. You still three lives till reach Nirvana."

Could he be foretelling her death? She couldn't make anything of the strange word at the end, but it sounded uncannily like the hereafter.

All at once her corset seemed to be stifling her breathing. The heat in the room became unbearable, and her limbs began to tremble. It was only by summoning all her self-control that she managed not to jump up and run from the room.

The old man fell silent, and the assistant finally finished his translation, then picked up a piece of paper on which he had rapidly copied the symbols from the leaf.

As he handed it to her, Grace's throat felt as dry as though she had swallowed a mouthful of sand.

"Take this, miss, to remind and if more questions."

Grace was sure she would never come to this place again. She had already more or less forgotten the assistant's muttered words. And she was sure the things he had prophesied were mere nonsense.

However, she thanked them politely before striding out of the room. Victoria practically flew to her.

"So? What did he foretell for you?"

"That we're going to be in a whole load of trouble, and all for nothing more than a few incoherent mumblings and some symbols that no one can read."

Her eyes shining, Victoria grasped the paper from her hand. "What does this mean? What did he tell you?"

"Nothing of any importance. We should be going."

"But I haven't had my turn!" Victoria protested, grabbing her sister's skirt firmly and holding her back. "Anyway, the five rupees were for us both!"

At that moment the assistant appeared to call the second miss in.

Victoria practically ran in after the man who had come to fetch her. Grace watched her go with a sigh, then sank down on the wooden bench and looked at the paper. Did the writing really mean what they had told her? Had she understood the man correctly? *Maybe I should have the leaf read again by someone else. There must be people on the plantation who could do it.*

But what do I care about it anyway? These prophecies must apply to any English people who come to Ceylon. The old man and his assistant, who could even be his son, were sure to be offering this service to make a living. For all she knew, they had written on these palm leaves themselves and created a great stir about them to surround the whole thing with an aura of mystique. Maybe there wasn't even a library of palm leaves behind that door at all—after all, he'd closed it quickly enough—but a single leaf, which they brought out again and again to people as the old man made up stories.

Who could prove what was really written on the leaf?

I'm going to find out, Grace suddenly decided, *and put an end to this deception.*

After what seemed like an endless wait, Victoria finally returned. She wasn't carrying a piece of paper, and she had a long face. "They don't have one for me," she said, her voice filled with disappointment.

"What?" Grace raised her eyebrows in amazement. Then anger struck. *Of course it's all just a shabby conjuring trick.* She knew it all along! If there were more than one of these ridiculous leaves in existence, they wouldn't have seen fit to disappoint Victoria. They must be afraid of exposure if they made the same prophecy twice. "I'm going to talk to that man!"

"No, leave it . . ." But Victoria was talking to herself, as Grace was already storming through the beaded curtain.

"Can you tell me why you refused to give my sister one of these absurd leaves?"

Grace drew herself up to her full height, her arms folded.

The old man raised his head and looked at her calmly. He smiled, as though he had allowed her a little joke.

"Some people no palm leaf because souls new in world. Still no karma, no former life yet."

He spoke English? As well as that? Why had he been acting as though he understood nothing? Was that part of the deceit?

After a brief stunned silence, Grace began again. "I would like to see your alleged palm-leaf library!"

"You can't," the old man replied without batting an eyelid.

Grace folded her arms aggressively.

"Why not? Could it be because you only have one of these dried-up leaves? I intend to complain to the governor in person that such fraudulent activities are possible in his territory!"

Although the old man was still looking at her strangely with his penetrating eyes, Grace continued to stare at him defiantly.

Finally, the old man turned to his assistant. "Show them to her."

"But they're sacred!" he objected.

"She'll complain to authorities about us. Show them to her."

Giving her a dark look, the young man went to the door and opened it.

"Come, miss."

Grace approached warily. Would the fellow try to hit her? Her heart raced wildly, but her pride prevented her from drawing back. As she peered through the door, the sight took her breath away. In a room about the size of her father's study, an array of crooked shelves held rows of countless box-like books made up of these inscribed palm leaves. Each of the books held about a dozen dried leaves.

Shaken, Grace took a step back. Her outburst suddenly seemed dreadfully embarrassing.

"I sensed your doubt," the old man said behind her. "But fate doesn't care about that. I foretold what will happen to you. If you need my advice about it or want to hear the prophecy again, you can come back at any time."

"Forgive me, I . . ." Shame robbed Grace of her voice.

"You're English. You don't know our ways. Not yet."

To her amazement his voice sounded neither angry nor offended. "Always listen to your heart, and follow what it tells you," he added. "If you don't, you will bring bad luck on yourself and those you love."

Grace looked at him in bewilderment before taking her leave of the old man.

"You don't have a leaf for me, do you?" Victoria asked as she came running out to her.

Grace shook her head. "Come on, Victoria, we have to get back!" After looking around briefly at the man who had followed her into the waiting room, she took her sister by the hand and dragged her outside.

Back at the hotel that evening, after a good dressing-down from their mother and a lecture on good behaviour from Miss Giles, Grace was back on the window seat.

Moonlight glinted silver on the harbour and the sea, while the golden lamplight cast her silhouette as a mirror image on the window-pane. The lights of the ships shone in the darkness, and in the distance the lighthouse sent its beam out into the night.

Try as she might, she could not get the visit to the palm-leaf library out of her mind. *Maybe because I behaved so frightfully?*

The more time that passed since the encounter, the more details that her prejudice had caused her to overlook came into her mind, like a magic spell gradually beginning to take effect.

The way the old man had run the tips of his fingers over the engraved characters and intoned the words in a sing-song drone, to be interpreted by his pupil. The leaf, which must be many centuries old. The scent of incense, patchouli, and other things she couldn't name. And the man's eyes!

Although she told herself that the forecast was nonsense, she picked up the piece of paper and a jotter and pencil. She then tried to remember the assistant's gibberish.

"What are you doing?" Victoria asked, looking up from her beloved city plan.

"I'm writing."

"What?"

"Just jotting down a few thoughts. Nothing special."

"Thoughts about your palm leaf?"

Her sharp eyes had not failed to notice that Grace had placed the piece of paper from the library next to her.

"Thoughts about how I'll probably never again allow myself to be persuaded to follow you to some dubious corner of the city," Grace replied with a vicious tone to her voice that she hoped concealed her embarrassment. After the fuss she had made on the way back, she could hardly admit that she intended to reconstruct what had been said during the consultation.

"It wasn't as bad as that!" Victoria replied, turning over a page of the guidebook. "And we haven't been anywhere near the gemstone merchants yet. I want to go there tomorrow!"

"Only if we go by carriage and avoid the slums! Anyway, I'm sure Mother and Miss Giles will want to come with us—you heard what she said over dinner."

"Yes, yes. 'Promise me you'll never go anywhere near the natives, girls, they'll eat you alive.'"

Grace couldn't help smiling at Victoria's voice.

"You'd better be careful or your face will crack," Victoria added, since she had noticed that it was taking all her sister's self-control not to burst out in unbridled laughter.

"You'd better not let Miss Giles or Mother hear you, or we'll be grounded!"

"Don't worry. I'll be a good little angel tomorrow."

Once Victoria had immersed herself again in her travel guide, Grace went back on the trail of the assistant's words.

What had the man said? That she would find the love of her life before the age of twenty? That she would marry and have a child? It didn't take a clairvoyant to predict that. Her mother was bound to make sure that she would marry and have a family. It was probably the same for every woman. And it was unlikely that she would get away from here. At best she would live in Colombo, by the sea.

One part unsettled her deeply. In the same year in which her baby was born, a great storm would break over her, ending her life as she knew it. Did that mean she'd die in a storm? Or was it the storm of change that awaited her?

The latter was more likely, as among the mutterings that had become increasingly unclear, she had made out that she was destined to have a good end and wouldn't pass over to the next life until she was almost sixty-three. Oh yes, and she would spend the rest of her life by the sea.

Grace noted down all these facts, and after reading them through she shook her head.

It looked as though her family wouldn't be leaving Ceylon any time soon, marriage and children were nothing out of the ordinary, and if she was to live for a total of sixty-two years, it wasn't particularly old, but it was a long way off. Apart from the age of her death—which she found rather macabre—they were things that any fairground fortune teller could have told her.

But then she recalled something else—the advice the old man had given her as she was leaving. *"Always listen to your heart, and follow what it tells you. If you don't, you will bring bad luck on yourself and those you love."*

Something like that. *Listen to my heart,* Grace thought, leaning her head against the windowpane. *What does my heart want? And why should my wishes affect the fate of my family?* The Tremaynes were used to following their intellect, to doing their duty.

Thoughts like these were still preoccupying her as she went to bed and stared, wide awake, at the ceiling.

12

Berlin, 2008

As the underground train rattled towards the city centre, Diana tried to put the information she'd obtained so far about the secret in order. She had found a piece of an oracle, practically an ancient horoscope. She usually laughed over those little predictions in the newspaper, since they were always formulaic enough to apply to anyone. She didn't believe that anyone could know a person's complete future, even if it *were* the case that the hour of death was fixed at birth. But this palm leaf had a strange feel to it. Had Tremayne House breathed a sigh of relief when the leaf was removed from its walls? Did the stones somehow know what they had been concealing? It would be pointless to ask the pragmatic Mr. Green about it . . .

Forty-five minutes later she was back at home. As she entered she was once again struck by the icy atmosphere that had reigned during breakfast and to which she had made her own, not insignificant, contribution.

Damn it, why's he back so early? Diana thought irritably. *He always used to enjoy working late.*

"You're back."

Diana looked up. Philipp was leaning on the banister.

"Are you going to hang around the house every day, waiting for me to get back? You never used to."

"I've got a day off, or did you forget that? This was supposed to have been our holiday together."

"Holiday." Diana sniffed scornfully. "When did you decide that? During the two weeks I was in England? We haven't had a holiday together for years."

"Well, maybe it's time we started to."

Diana shook her head. What had got into him?

"I'm sorry, I've got things to do," she muttered miserably.

"Please can we talk?" he said then. "Believe me, it was only a one-off."

Diana didn't want to talk. Her mind was whirling with all that she had discovered during the day, and she was expecting some important documents by email from Eva.

As she made to pass him on the stairs, his hand shot out and stopped her. Diana looked at him darkly. "What are you doing?"

"I only want to get to the bottom of things."

Only then did she notice the whiff of alcohol on his breath.

Diana realised that anger wouldn't get her very far. She could almost think she was a little afraid of her husband.

"Philipp, let me go," she said with as much self-control as she could muster. Their eyes met and Diana saw that his, which she could never have got enough of in the past, now looked as cold as two dark pits. She knew that any explanation he came out with would be a lie. A lie intended to lull her into a false sense of security and give him the freedom to do it again as soon as the opportunity arose.

"Philipp, please!" She made sure her voice didn't sound pleading, but determined, as though she were threatening him with a thrashing if he didn't obey her. The clamp around her arm suddenly loosened.

"Damn it!" he swore in the next moment, slamming his fist angrily down on the banister. Diana jumped back in shock. She had seen him angry on occasion, but not like this.

"Then don't talk to me!" he snapped. "Creep off into your beloved work. Or maybe back to that derelict English wreck of a house!"

Turning as he spoke the last word, he stormed down the stairs and out of the house. A moment later, his car engine sprang into life. Diana leaned back against the wall.

He's right, she thought. *I should have stayed in England.* And he should have stayed with his girlfriend. Why on earth was he here? Only to pacify his conscience, she was sure.

He's no longer the man I met years ago. Or is it that I'm not the same woman?

As the engine noise faded into the distance, she went upstairs and got out the casket.

"What secrets are you still hiding?" she wondered aloud as she carefully traced the ornate surface with her finger and ran what Michael had told her through her mind. Philipp's anger distracted her momentarily, but she soon managed to get the information in order.

Minutes later she was sitting in front of the computer searching the Internet: eye-witness accounts of Nadi readings, reports on the accuracy or otherwise of the predictions. If people's claims were true—and alarm bells frequently rang in Diana's sceptical mind at the assertions—the palm-leaf oracle was incredibly accurate. Was it possible that what was written on this leaf had actually come to pass?

After thinking about it for a while, Diana picked up the old photograph that had also been in the casket. It nearly fell apart in her hand. She had hardly given it more than a passing glance back in Tremayne House; now, she took the time to look at it more closely. *I must have a copy made of it,* she thought as her eyes took in the yellowing light patches and dark shadows that depicted a mountain landscape against a radiant sky.

Looking more closely, she noticed that the picture showed more than the imposing mountain. In the distance, almost blotted out by a stain, she noticed a white figure. After trying in vain to identify who it was, she rummaged in the drawer for a magnifying glass, which she kept for picking splinters from her fingers. It failed to make the image much clearer, but she could nevertheless make out that it was a woman. A woman in typical Victorian dress. The painting in the corridor of Tremayne House came into her mind. Could this possibly be Grace or Victoria?

Another look through the magnifying glass told her that this person must be an adult. As Victoria would have been around thirteen or fourteen, Grace was the only possibility. Grace—her great-great-grandmother.

Diana sank back in the chair, overcome by a strange feeling. She was already familiar with Grace from the painting, but that would have been influenced by the painter's style and the tastes of the times. The camera didn't lie. It was a pity she couldn't see her face, as she had no way of knowing what Grace was feeling at that moment.

As for the backdrop, she was a little more certain. She had seen a similar landscape to this once in an article about India. Grace was clearly standing in front of a hill cloaked in tea plants. She must have travelled to Ceylon with her family. Because of her uncle's death? Or was there another reason?

Diana suddenly knew where her journey would take her.

She quickly stowed the things back in the casket and tucked it under her arm before rushing downstairs.

Half an hour later, Diana was leaving a travel agency having secured a flight to Colombo and a booking at the Grand Oriental Hotel, the place that was highlighted in the old *Passenger's Guide*. As soon as she had wound up the legal case that Eva had landed while she was away,

Diana intended to fly to Sri Lanka and set out from there on the trail of her ancestors. And, of course, the library from which the palm leaf had been taken.

The travel agent had also given her a leaflet warning of unrest between the Tamil and Sinhalese ethnic groups, and even possible terrorist attacks, but these were far from the areas Diana intended to visit. She felt light with anticipation. The days until her trip would pass quickly if she immersed herself in her work and tried not to think about Philipp. If she handled it well, she would get home when he was out, and leave before he woke in the mornings.

Her head full of these thoughts, she got back into the car and drove towards the office.

Her phone rang on the way. Assuming it was Philipp, she didn't bother to pull over, but continued to follow the tram line until she reached her turn. It was only once she had found a parking space near her office in Charlottenburg that she looked to see who it was.

The caller had left her a voicemail. Although she hadn't yet saved the number, she recognised it and immediately dialled up the voicemail.

"It's me, Michael," the voice said. "I've finished with your palm leaf earlier than I expected to. Please can you get in touch? You have my number."

She immediately pressed the green button and dialled the missed-call number.

Michael sounded breathless when he answered.

"What's up? Are you running a marathon?"

"No, I'm just in the middle of looking for something," he replied. "Thanks for getting back to me so quickly."

"Have I called at an inconvenient moment?"

"No, no, don't worry. I'm glad you've called. So you got my message?"

"Yes, and I thought you sounded in such a hurry that you must have some sensational news for me."

"Not exactly. I photographed everything in detail and took some samples for the age analysis. We won't get the results for a few weeks."

That disappointed Diana a little, but it wasn't as if she needed to hang around doing nothing while they waited. "But I can have it back in the meantime, can't I? I've just booked a trip to Sri Lanka. I'm off next week."

"Well! Are you going on holiday, or do you intend to look for the library?"

"Yes, that's one thing. I also want to find out a bit more about my family. I think Ceylon played an important part in their history."

"Where exactly are you going?" Michael asked. Diana could hear him rummaging through some papers in the background.

"To Colombo. The subject of that old travel guide I found. You remember?"

"Ah! Here it is!"

"Here what is?"

"The business card I was looking for. I'll give it to you when you call. You can come as soon as you like as far as I'm concerned. I'm sure you'll be busy preparing for your trip."

"I don't need a whole week for that! But I do have to show my face in the office. So you have a business card for me? Whose?"

"I've got a friend in Colombo, Jonathan Singh. I was going to suggest you contact him anyway, but if you're going there you absolutely must look him up. Not only will he make sure you don't get into difficulty in Sri Lanka, but you can also make the most of his talents as a guide and source of information."

Diana hesitated. "I don't know. Are you sure he won't mind?"

"We're old friends, and he owes me one. If I ask him, I'm sure he'll make time for you."

"Is he an academic, too? Where's he from? Jonathan doesn't sound like a typical Indian name."

"He's half English and half Tamil. He used to work for the National Museum of Sri Lanka. He went freelance a while ago and now writes books. His works are quite well known in his home country, and I'm in the process of trying to persuade him to help me with a publication for our museum. He's very knowledgeable about the history of Sri Lanka and the country's customs. If anyone can help you, he can."

"But I don't want you to waste the favour he owes on my account."

Even down the telephone, Diana could sense that Michael was smiling.

"No problem. He'd be more likely to be angry with me if I sent a friend to his country without telling him. The Sri Lankans are very helpful, you know, and Jonathan's a really nice guy."

"OK, then. Tell him and let me have his address. Oh yes, and when should I come and fetch the leaf?"

Tremayne House, 2008

After Mr. Green had finished his gardening, gone back into the house, and sat down at his computer, he found an email from Miss Diana.

> *Dear Mr. Green,*
> *I hope everything is OK with you. I just wanted to tell you that I'll be travelling to Sri Lanka in a week's time. Over the past few days I've made a few discoveries that mean I have no choice but to travel there, to the country where my ancestor must have gone with his family. I'm going to be meeting an academic there who has been recommended by a friend of mine, so you don't need to worry. If you need to get in touch with me, you can do so online at any time; I'll have my laptop with me and I'll check my email regularly.*

*I imagine I'll have plenty to tell you when I get
back.
Kind regards,
Diana*

The butler smiled.

He got up, then went over to the cupboard, opened the top drawer, and took out a little package wrapped in brown paper. It had been lying around in there for quite some time. Now, its time had come.

The next clue, Mr. Green thought as he put on his coat and stowed the package in his pocket. He would have to send it by priority mail. He climbed into the Bentley and drove towards town.

13

Colombo/Vannattuppūcci, 1887

After three more days in Colombo, Henry Tremayne received the news that the workmen had finished and the house was ready for the family.

"At last." Claudia sighed in relief, pressing the letter to her lace-bedecked breast. "I thought we'd have to stay in this hotel forever."

"It's not so bad here, darling," Henry said, although his face also revealed his own relief at finally being able to move to the plantation. "Our every need is catered for, and we enjoy wonderful views out to sea."

"Looking at steamers shrouding the harbour in black smoke," Claudia said. "And hordes of traders swarming over anyone in European clothing."

Henry laughed. "Once we're in Vannattuppūcci all you'll see is tea. And palm trees."

"Don't forget the mountain, to remind me of my beloved Scottish Highlands."

Henry came up to her, took her hands, and kissed her. "I know how much you miss your homeland. But I'll do all I can to make sure you soon feel at home here."

"Couldn't you put the plantation in the hands of a manager? This Mr. Cahill seems very capable from all you've told me."

"A place like this needs to be overseen by its owner. Mr. Cahill himself made that clear to me. Since Richard's been gone, the place has gradually sunk into chaos. The tea pickers and other workers need someone in charge of them."

Claudia lowered her head with another sigh. Henry took her in his arms.

"In any case, Vannattuppūcci is our great opportunity. You know how things were in England. If it all goes well, as I hope it will, we'll be able to renovate our country house as well as keep your castle in the Highlands. Maybe one day we will find a suitable foreman who can take over the management of the plantation. But for now, since Richard is dead, someone has to bring order to the chaos."

Grace and Victoria were poring over a rough gemstone which Victoria had bought at Sylvie's in Chatham Street. Although their mother had forbidden them from walking out alone ever since their adventure in the palm-leaf library, she had allowed her daughters to accompany her on shopping trips—on the condition, of course, that they didn't stray more than three paces from her side.

Unlike the traders who lay in wait for foreign visitors at the harbour, the shops were considered to be reputable. Grace hadn't bought anything. In her eyes, these gemstones were a pure waste of money, and maybe even a swindle, but the colourful lights that reminded her of a wildflower meadow and the scent of the incense sticks had caused her to forget her annoyance for a moment.

"I'm sure it's a sapphire," Victoria said as she turned the uncut, deep-blue stone in her hand. "It only needs cutting and polishing, then I'll have a jewel unlike anything that's ever been seen in any English lady's jewellery case."

"A jewel for ten rupees? Don't you think that's a bit cheap?"

Grace took the stone from Victoria's hand and examined it herself. It was the right colour for a sapphire, but she couldn't imagine that even these people would sell such a large, valuable stone for such a low price. Certainly not in this corner of the world. The dealers had seemed very business-minded to her, and ten rupees was probably excessive for the trinket they had palmed off on her sister.

"As if you know anything about gemstones!" Victoria huffed, determined not to let her sister pour cold water on her pleasure at her find. "Anyway, I've read you the description of this place as the land of precious stones. They say they grow on trees here!"

"That's a long way from believing that they're all valuable pieces. I'm sure you've learned from Mr. Norris that there are also such things as semiprecious stones."

It was no secret that Victoria's private tutor, who would also be arriving here in a few days, had a weakness for mineralogy.

"You'll have to show him this lump of rock." Grace laid the stone back in her sister's hands.

"Lump of rock?" Victoria cried. "This could be worth more than everything on Father's plantation put together! This stone, my dearest sister, could make me into one of the best catches in the whole of England!"

"Don't you think that stones like this would be used to adorn the crown of our queen if they were genuine?"

"Who says they export all the biggest stones? The gemstone miners here could well put some aside to sell to visitors from all over the world."

"For ten rupees?"

The argument was stopped by the door to their room opening.

"Miss Giles!" Grace cried in amazement, as Victoria's governess was completely out of breath, pressing her hand to her impossibly tightly laced corset. "What's happened?"

"The time has come at last!" she gasped as though she had just sprinted from bottom to top of the staircase of the Grand Oriental Hotel. In reality, the governess was still overcome by the heat, seemingly unable to adjust to it. "Your mother has just informed me that we'll be departing soon. You should prepare your hand luggage. I'll take care of your clothes."

She bustled over to the chaise longue, where the sisters' dressing gowns and afternoon dresses were draped. As ever when she was in a hurry, she forgot herself, humming a song under her breath to goad herself into action.

"If she keeps lacing herself in so tightly, she'll keel over before long," Victoria took the opportunity to whisper disrespectfully to Grace. The older girl put her hand to her mouth to conceal a broad grin. She always thought the same thing when she looked at Miss Giles. In England she managed fine with the corset, but the climate here was completely different, making breathing more difficult even without tight lacing.

"We all know why she does it," she whispered back. "She wants to look her best for Mr. Norris."

"But if she carries on like that she's likely to die of lung failure before he's set foot on the island."

The two girls snorted with laughter, and Miss Giles turned to them with a disapproving look.

"I don't need to tell you that your mother will be very annoyed if you're not ready in time."

"Yes, Miss Giles," the sisters chorused, and after Victoria nudged Grace with her elbow, they set to work.

An hour later all the cases were stowed in the carriage. The heavy pieces of furniture had already been delivered to Vannattuppūcci. The private tutor and a few servants, whom Mrs. Tremayne felt she couldn't live without, would be following in a few days.

"If you ask me, I'm not too thrilled by the idea of starting my lessons again," Victoria whispered to Grace once they had taken their places in the open carriage, with parasols for their only shade. "Maybe Mr. Norris has been swallowed up by a sea monster during the voyage."

"Just be glad that Father isn't of the opinion that education is damaging for a young lady. Otherwise you wouldn't know half as much about the scandalous painters of the Middle Ages or be able to read your precious adventure stories that Miss Giles is so keen to confiscate."

Grace glanced at the governess, who was hovering in the background as if waiting for instructions from her mistress.

"Anyway our dear governess would be devastated if Mr. Norris didn't arrive. Just look how she keeps craning her neck towards the harbour."

"She's hardly likely to see him from here," Victoria said cheerfully. "But even if he doesn't come, surely there are enough men here. Have you seen those harbour workers with their golden-brown skin? I'm telling you, some of them could even be the talk of the ladies in London."

"You shouldn't be interested in things like that!" Grace replied, feigning indignation.

"Why ever not? In earlier times I'd be of marriageable age already. Some families still marry off their daughters young."

These words brought Grace back to her wistful thoughts of the season in London. *I'll probably end my days as an old maid out here,* she thought. *All the interesting young men in England will be spoken for by the time I set foot there again.*

Victoria seemed to notice her gloomy mood, as she laid a hand gently on her arm. "Don't worry, I certainly won't marry before you. Cheer up—we've got our adventure to look forward to. I can't wait to see the animals in the jungle. Maybe I'll be able to persuade Mr. Norris to forget about his dead old stones for a while and take an interest in living things."

No sooner had she spoken the words than Miss Giles came to join them. She was lost in reverie and looked a little worried.

"Grace, did you know that mail ships usually dock at night?" Victoria had brought out her little guidebook and gave Grace a conspiratorial wink as she spoke.

"No. Where did you get that from?"

"It says so in the travel guide. I'm sure Mr. Norris will be arriving on one of those ships."

Victoria peered at Miss Giles out of the corner of her eye, but she didn't react. Grace, looking more openly, perceived a wistful air about the governess, who usually displayed such outward self-control.

Would I be gazing so longingly out to sea, too, if my beloved was on the other side of the ocean and I didn't know whether he'd arrive safely? she wondered as the carriage began to move.

They reached the plantation the following afternoon, after breaking their journey overnight at a small village inn recommended to them by Mr. Cahill. The mountain against the clear blue sky formed a magnificent setting, blanketed in green and scattered with dark and light patches. The lower slopes were covered with the rich green tea plantations, punctuated by lone palm trees and unidentified shrubs.

The rattling of the carriage and clattering of the horses' hooves seemed foreign in this landscape. Grace looked up at the palm trees moving above their heads and thought she could see a flash of coloured feathers.

"They're parrots," said Victoria. "Maybe I should catch one for Mama's drawing room."

"How do you intend to do that?" Grace asked, craning her neck in the hope that one of the birds would come nearer. She had seen a parrot before in Mrs. Roswell's drawing room in London. But that one had been an ancient, mangy creature with a habit of rubbing its head against the bars of the cage and constantly emitting strange noises which, according to Mrs. Roswell, proved it could talk.

The birds above her communicated in their natural language, which sounded so different from the noises that Polly, Mrs. Roswell's parrot, had made.

"Oh, look!" Victoria suddenly cried out, tugging at Grace's sleeve. She was pointing to a bush, where a little monkey was sitting, closely watching the procession of coaches. It was grasping a branch with one hand, sucking the thumb of the other like a baby.

"Do you think Mama would allow me to have one of those?"

"I thought you were going to catch a parrot."

"I'll do that first, just you wait. I'm sure they must like sugar cubes. I'll leave some on my windowsill, and when they come to get them I'll catch one with my butterfly net."

"You don't have one."

"But I know how to make one!" Victoria argued. "Last year I saw the gardener's son make one from a metal hoop, some netting, and a stick. I'm sure I can get hold of those things. And if not, I'll ask one of the workers. There must be such a thing as a gardener here—just look at the estate!"

Grace had to admit that the garden was really beautiful. As well as the frangipani bushes that were ubiquitous at these latitudes, there were also large numbers of rhododendrons that would have been the envy of any estate in Europe. The lawns were neatly cut like those of an English garden, and although she was no expert in botanical matters, Grace was dying to find out the name of the flaming-red flowers that adorned the beautifully laid out flower beds.

The mansion, in the colonial style, looked like a pearl among all the greenery. It reminded Grace a little of Tremayne House, except that the latter's walls were darker and overgrown with ivy and there was no fountain in the middle of the drive. However, there were a number of outbuildings of various shapes and sizes.

As well as the magnificent gardens, Grace's eye was also caught by the people bustling about the grounds. Women carrying fully loaded baskets of tea on their heads vanished into sheds where they were relieved of their burdens. Their garments were very simple, but glowed with magnificent colours the like of which Grace had never seen before.

The scent of tea and sweet flowers permeated the air—something London could not offer at this time of year except in the stuffy salons whose owners had a weakness for the exotic.

The carriage came to a halt, and the family was reunited. Victoria got distracted by a beautiful tree with orange-red flowers, until Grace led her over to their parents, who were being lectured at by Mr. Cahill.

"Before your brother came, someone had tried to cultivate coffee here." The lawyer gave a self-satisfied smile. "With catastrophic results. The plants were struck by coffee leaf rust, leaving the previous owner with no choice but to sell up. Your brother decided to cultivate tea here, since the soil and climate are ideal for it."

"My brother really seems to have had his finger on the pulse of the times." Henry Tremayne looked around in wonder. If the chaos Cahill described really had reigned, the workers and servants had done marvellous work.

"Oh yes, your brother was admired by everyone here. Believe me, he will be sadly missed. But I'm sure you're the best man to fill the gap he left behind."

When she was sure that Cahill couldn't see her, Grace shook her head. She had never heard such pathetic prattle! Of course the man was talking for his life, or at least his livelihood, since now that her father was the master of Vannattuppūcci, he was free to appoint a new adviser if he chose to do so. But Grace knew her father well enough to be certain that he would keep Cahill in his service, provided he didn't step out of line.

Glancing towards the wonderful flowers of the bush that had caught her sister's attention, Grace saw a tall, handsome man, who was shyly keeping himself apart as if waiting for someone to notice him. Although he was wearing English clothing, he had a foreign air. His dark-brown, almost black hair was a little longer than was usual, and his long, narrow face had a golden shimmer. His thick brows arched gracefully above a pair of amber eyes, and his neatly trimmed beard framed a pair of full lips.

"Oh, there you are, my boy!" Cahill suddenly called out, waving the foreigner over. "May I introduce Mr. R. Vikrama, the plantation foreman?"

"R?" Victoria wondered aloud, earning herself a warning glance from her mother.

Mr. Vikrama smiled softly, but didn't reply. Instead he bowed to Henry.

"I'm pleased to meet you, sir. Even if the circumstances are not happy ones. You have my full sympathy."

"That's very kind of you," Henry replied shortly. He placed a hand on his wife's shoulder and added, "May I introduce my wife, Claudia? And these are my daughters, Grace and Victoria." Mrs. Tremayne bowed her head and the two sisters curtsied.

"I'm pleased to meet you," Vikrama said, nodding briefly to Grace and Victoria before turning to the lady of the house. "If there's anything I can do for you, please don't hesitate to let me know."

"Are you a native?" Henry asked, studying the young man closely. "Your English is truly excellent."

Something about him didn't fit in with the surroundings, Grace found. Was it the colour of his skin, which looked almost European, Italian even? Or his impeccable manners?

Clearly flattered, Vikrama inclined his head. "Thank you very much, sir. My mother was from this area, hence my darker skin."

"And your father?"

"My father is unknown, sir. But my mother always said he was a white man."

"Probably one of your brother's English employees," Cahill added. "It often happens that our boys' heads are turned by the beauty of the Tamil women."

Grace found his accompanying laugh wholly inappropriate.

Even though the affairs between man and wife were not discussed openly, Grace knew by now what awaited women on their wedding night and where babies came from. And she also knew that it was very shabby behaviour for a man to leave his pregnant lover in the lurch.

"So you don't know your father?" Claudia asked, clearly shaken.

"No, madam. He died before I was born."

"You should be aware that the natives weren't always as peaceful as they are now," Cahill felt obliged to add. "Twenty years or more ago it was still possible for a man to be attacked and robbed on the street in broad daylight. Mr. Vikrama's father must have been the victim of such an attack."

The young man's face remained impassive. He clearly hadn't given much thought to his unnamed father.

"What about your mother? You spoke about her in the past tense," Claudia continued. She had clearly got it into her head to find out all she could about their new employee.

Now Vikrama's expression darkened. "She died of cancer two years ago."

Cahill laid his hand patronisingly on the man's shoulder.

"His mother was one of your brother's tea pickers, sir. Mr. Tremayne recognised the boy's talents and sent him to school. You'll find many Tamils in administrative positions here. They even have their own language and script. Forward-looking plantation owners provide for their Tamils to have an education, thus gaining themselves loyal employees who are in a position to take responsibility and keep an eye on the plantation. I don't know what we would have done without him after the tragic accident."

Grace noticed that Vikrama had sunk his head, slightly embarrassed. Was he ashamed of his origin? Or did he find it difficult to accept praise?

Realising that she was staring at him almost impertinently, she blushed and lowered her eyes.

"It sounds as though we've got ourselves a good catch in you, Mr. Vikrama," her father said. "You must put me in the picture of how things are done on the plantation."

"I'll do my best not to disappoint you."

"Very well. Let's meet tomorrow morning to discuss things further and take a tour. The ladies are tired now, and I'm afraid I must confess that the journey has taken its toll on me, too. How about nine o'clock?"

"I'll be there punctually, sir."

"Good! I'm afraid you'll have your work cut out to make me into a tea grower. I never imagined that one day I'd become the master of a plantation like this. But that is God's will, and I look forward to your excellent support."

"I'll do everything I can to support you, sir."

"You can rely on his word." Cahill once again saw fit to add his opinion, unasked for.

Was she mistaken, or did Grace see a sudden flash of resentment in Vikrama's eyes? Before she could confirm her suspicion, his fleeting expression had passed. So that no one would notice her staring at him again, she turned to Victoria with a smile. Her sister's attention had wandered again up into the treetops. There were no monkeys hanging from the branches, but parrots were making their raucous sounds and Grace could see in Victoria's eyes the spark of determination to catch one.

When she turned her attention back to her parents, they were taking their leave of Mr. Vikrama. Cahill murmured something else to the young man, then he turned away. Grace would have liked to see his face again, but he didn't look back.

"Come along, girls! Enough daydreaming," their mother called.

Grace took Victoria by the hand and led her up the steps.

"Did you see those marvellous parrots?" Victoria exclaimed in delight. "I swear I've never seen a completely blue one before. I must have it!"

"Then you should try and entice it with food," Grace replied, a little half-heartedly since, for some reason, she couldn't get the young man out of her mind.

In London, if he had been of noble birth, he would have been the season's sensation. She had never seen a man like him! Those eyes! Was it normal for people to have eyes like amber? She had never seen any like them in England. A tremor ran over her skin, and she had a strange feeling inside.

You have other things to think about, she scolded herself as they stepped through the front door. *He's your father's employee, and he didn't give you a second glance.*

Inside, too, the mansion looked very similar to large houses in England, but as soon as they entered the hall, they could see plenty of evidence of Richard Tremayne's love of the local culture. Whereas in Tremayne House a gold-framed portrait of one of their ancestors gazed down sternly on visitors from the staircase, in a similar position here was a colourful painting like nothing Grace had seen before. Victoria and her parents also seemed surprised by it.

The two men depicted in it appeared to be dancing together. One of them looked out at the observer with a laughing expression, while the other had the head of an elephant wearing a crown. Both wore colourful baggy trousers that hung loose around their legs, with bejewelled golden belts and colourful waistcoats covering their chests. At first glance they looked to Grace like circus artists. But what she found particularly fascinating were the garlands that had been hung around the picture frame and the bowls of flowers placed below the image. They were fresh, and had clearly been set out only that day.

"Is that some kind of idol?" Claudia asked in shock.

"They are the gods Shiva and Ganesha, worshipped by the Hindus," Cahill replied in the tone of a travel guide. "That's the religion of many people in this area. There are also Buddhists here, and some Muslims, though only a few—a reminder of the Arabs who visited the island centuries ago to trade with the natives."

"Why did my brother hang this picture on the wall?"

Henry didn't seem particularly pleased about it, either.

"Maybe he thought it would bring good luck to his plantation? Shiva is the chief deity of the Hindus—wherever he dances, prosperity reigns. Ganesha, whose head was torn off—'

"Mr. Cahill!" Claudia admonished him, indicating her daughters indignantly. "Please don't tell your horror stories in front of the young ladies!"

"I wouldn't dream of it, Mrs. Tremayne," Cahill said, his face turning bright red. "But unfortunately it's one of the myths of this region. Well, however it happened, Ganesha's head was replaced by a goddess with that of an elephant. Since then, elephants have been considered the bringers of good luck in this country."

"Elephants!" Victoria cried out in delight, clapping her hands. Suddenly feeling all eyes on her, she lowered her head in embarrassment. "I'm sorry, but I couldn't help remembering the elephants we saw in Colombo. I'd love to see one in its natural state, without any fancy coverings or jewels."

"If I may say so, young lady, you'll see elephants in the most natural setting possible," Cahill replied, glancing at Claudia, who seemed to be judging his every word. "A new tea field is being established a little further up the mountain. Elephants are being used to remove the palm trees there. It's Sunday today, but maybe you could go and see the beasts tomorrow or the day after."

Victoria's cheeks were glowing with excitement, and she grasped Grace's hand. "Shall we go and have a look?" she asked her.

"If Mama allows us to."

Claudia sighed and said theatrically, "Did I ever forbid anything that wasn't overturned by your father?"

"But I'll only allow you to go if you promise to take care," Henry Tremayne said. "Elephants are no lap dogs; they can crush a person under their feet."

"We'll watch them from a safe distance and run away if they come near!" Victoria promised, stroking her sister's hand restlessly as though to prevent her from voicing any objections.

"Yes, we will," Grace said to keep her sister happy.

"Very well. Then you can go for a walk up the mountainside in the next few days. Maybe our young friend from earlier will act as guide?" He raised his eyebrows at Cahill, who once again inclined his head obsequiously.

"But of course! I'll ask him next time I go to the administration building."

"That's very kind of you, but no hurry," Henry replied, clapping him on the shoulder. "I'm sure the elephants aren't going to run away. As I understand it, the clearance work will last for a while longer yet."

"Of course."

"Good. That means my daughters will have a little more time to get used to the climate." Henry turned back to the picture. "I believe we'll leave this here. What do you think, darling?" He gave his wife a disarming smile. "A little good luck won't go amiss."

As Claudia pulled a sceptical face, Cahill spoke again.

"As you can see from the flowers, this place is a kind of shrine for the workers on this estate. They regularly bring offerings for their gods. It would be most wise to leave the picture where it is."

Henry considered briefly, then nodded. "Very well, it can stay. If you give workers a few freedoms, they work much better. Wouldn't you say so, Mr. Cahill?"

BOOK TWO

The Butterfly Island

1

Berlin, 2008

A week later, Diana was back in an aeroplane heading for London. She would be flying with SriLankan Airlines from Heathrow to Colombo. Although it was not her first long-haul flight, she had butterflies in her stomach.

Diana ran her hand over Emily's silk scarf that she had brought as a good-luck charm. Several things had happened over the past few days, including the arrival of a small treasure from Mr. Green shortly before she left—something he had apparently found in an old chest in the attic when he was up there for his annual spring clean.

Diana was sorry she had not taken the opportunity to look around in the attic. Even though Emily had always claimed that she had given away much of the old junk up there, it seemed that a few mementos remained. But she would never have anticipated anything like this. When she wrote to thank Mr. Green, she had also instructed him to keep his eyes open, although she doubted he would find anything else useful.

After the flight attendant had handed out drinks and her neighbour, a Japanese businessman, had nodded off, she levered herself from her seat as carefully as she could and reached for her hand luggage.

The old travel guide was in the front pocket. Diana smiled as she felt the rough paper beneath her fingers. Back in her seat, she traced the title lovingly with her fingertip and then pulled out the package from Mr. Green.

Inside was an old pack of tea. As well as the name of the trading company that had shipped it, there was also a reference to the grower printed on it. The first time she had read the name *Tremayne Tea Company, Vannattuppūcci*, it had taken her breath away. This had been the first she had heard of it. The fact that the Tremaynes had owned a tea plantation had been another of Emily's well-kept secrets. But why had she kept it from her and her mother? Was the family ashamed of it?

She found that hard to believe, as the wealth of many British families was based on trade from plantations. Diana had researched the subject and discovered that people had first tried to make Ceylon into a coffee island, but the attempt had eventually failed. In the middle of the nineteenth century, the abandoned plantations were made over to tea plantations, which formed the basis of the country's successful tea production. Ceylon soon became a renowned variety of tea which was shipped all over the world.

Her ancestors had made their contribution to ensuring that the tea was enjoyed all over the world, then and now.

That was certainly nothing to be ashamed of. So why had it never been spoken of?

The fact that a pack of tea had survived for all that time in the attic indicated that Emily must have known about the plantation. Had she forgotten about it, perhaps? Or would she have talked about it, if only she'd been asked? Diana regularly caught herself pushing to the back of her mind events in her life that were actually important.

It didn't really matter whether Emily had kept this information back deliberately or unintentionally. With the discovery of the pack of tea, Diana felt as though she had pieced together the edges of a jigsaw puzzle and now all she had to do was complete the inner part.

She now knew why tea leaves had been used to decorate Beatrice Jungblut's grave. And why Richard had been in Ceylon. She now knew what the plants were that grew on the mountainside behind the young woman she presumed to be Grace in the photograph.

And yet the reason for Beatrice being excluded from the vault was still unanswered, as was the question of what linked Beatrice to Sri Lanka. She also knew nothing about the cause of Richard Tremayne's fall, and the biggest puzzle of all was the palm leaf—where it was from, its meaning and how it came to be in the possession of the Tremaynes. She only knew one thing for certain: the family must have moved to Ceylon. And that was where she hoped she'd find the answers.

On the shuttle journey to her hotel in Colombo, Diana looked for the business card Michael had given her the last time she'd seen him. The plain inscription, *Jonathan Singh, Chatham Street 23, Colombo, Sri Lanka*, accompanied by a telephone number, suggested a straightforward, maybe slightly old-fashioned, researcher used to expressing no-nonsense ideas in clear language.

She was nevertheless glad to have a starting point. Maybe this Jonathan Singh would have some interesting information for her.

She set off in one of the minibuses that formed the city's idiosyncratic taxi fleet, getting her first experience of the notorious traffic of Colombo's streets. To the accompaniment of loud Indian music, the driver of the tuk-tuk dodged into the path of larger vehicles at breakneck speed, inciting a concerto of car horns and risking death more than once before they finally arrived at the venerable Grand Oriental Hotel, its façade gleaming in the sun.

Although the backdrop of skyscrapers detracted a little from the effect of the building, which would have been huge in its time, Diana could imagine how imposing it would formerly have been to Western travellers.

Within the old fort area, some of the original buildings and street names had been preserved, which she recognised from the old 1887 travel guide.

The Grand Oriental was one of these remnants from another age.

The hustle and bustle on the street in front of it could have been a scene from a documentary. Among men in dark trousers and light-coloured shirts, which appeared to be the standard dress code for the locals, she saw business people from all over the world, women in both traditional saris and modern clothes, children, and tourists.

Feeling good, she greeted the red-and-gold liveried porter as she passed through the glazed door of the hotel and approached the reception.

The interior of the hotel had also been painstakingly restored. Diana had read in a brochure that in the 1980s it had gone under the name of the Taprobane Hotel, but since then, the owners had decided to restore it to its former glamour as enjoyed by guests of the past, who included the author Somerset Maugham. It now enjoyed the addition of a few modern elements. As well as the book shop, a long-standing fixture, the hotel also had a number of other shops, including a florist with a window filled with wonderful frangipani flowers.

"Welcome to the Grand Oriental Hotel. What can I do for you?" said the receptionist, who was dressed in a smart suit with her hair bound in a tight bun at the back of her neck.

Diana introduced herself and produced her reservation. After filling out a few forms and taking her key, she was shown to her room by a bellhop.

What must the Tremaynes have felt as they climbed these stairs? she wondered as she followed the young man. The lady of the family and her daughters in their luxurious dresses and tight corsets, the husband in his stiff high collar, dragging a train of servants in their wake.

Even in her modern clothing, Diana was sweating. How must the climate have felt to her ancestors?

Although renovated and well maintained, the hotel room whisked her straight back to the nineteenth century. The brown floor tiles, forming an ornate pattern, could easily have dated back to that period, and the four-poster bed that dominated the room appeared to be an exact copy of one that would have given guests in earlier times an excellent night's sleep. The chairs were also new, but harmonised really well with the atmosphere of the room, with its wonderful view of the harbour through the window.

However, Diana looked in vain for a ceiling fan like those she had seen in the movies; it had been replaced by a modern air-conditioning unit.

After tipping the bellhop, she closed the door behind her and drank in her surroundings. She went over to the window and its view of the sea and the harbour. A warm breeze brushed her hair and her face, melting her tensions a little. *I'm on the right track.*

After unpacking, she took the cardboard tube that housed the palm leaf and put it on the desk. Michael had sent her copies of some photos which would help her to locate the library it belonged to.

Maybe it would be better to keep it in the hotel safe, she thought.

Although she was dog-tired, she decided to go out and explore the city a little.

After showering and changing, she let Eva and Mr. Green know that she had landed safely in Colombo. Half an hour later, armed with the old guide and an up-to-date one to help her find her way to Mr. Singh, she tucked the cardboard tube under her arm and left her room.

On the way to the reception lobby, she passed the Lotus Ballroom, where it appeared there was something going on. A shiny sign by the door told her that preparations were underway for a major event. The festive white seat covers with golden bows gave the impression of a wedding party.

All at once she felt a tug inside. Her own wedding celebrations had been very modest. She had wanted a lavish wedding, but she had ultimately given in to Philipp, who was concerned about the costs of accommodating his horde of relatives. Now she felt a pang of regret that they had not had a more extravagant wedding. It wouldn't have changed anything about the way their marriage ended, but she would nevertheless have had a wonderful memory to look back on.

As more employees arrived with armfuls of tablecloths, she withdrew. *You should be concentrating on the present, and the matter in hand, not regretting things that never happened,* she thought. In the hotel lobby she took the old travel guide from her bag. She had marked with sticky notes the pages where places were underlined. Those that seemed particularly interesting to her were the fort, Chatham Street, and the Cinnamon Gardens, a district that now bore the totally unromantic name of Colombo 7. Would the cinnamon gardens still be there?

After depositing the palm leaf in the safe, she left the hotel. *Mr. Singh will be expecting me, if I know Michael. He'll have driven him mad with his instructions. And the sooner I find something out the better.*

Although she had found out a lot about Sri Lanka and read through some illustrated travel books, Diana still did not feel sufficiently prepared for the contrasts that bombarded her as she walked through the city. On one side were skyscrapers and flashing billboards, cars, and phones, on the other, saris, ox-carts, houses from the colonial period, and wooden shacks.

Walking along the street, she had to take care not to be run over by one of the red minibuses that carried passengers through the city at breakneck speed. There was even a man leading his richly adorned elephant through the crowds on York Street. A cacophony of tuk-tuk horns and shrill bicycle bells sounded impatiently behind him.

Chatham Street, too, was thronged with people and bicycles. Many of the old buildings had given way to modern ones. Chinese silk merchants had taken over most of the shops, but there was still plenty of trade in the country's treasures, especially the uncut gemstones sold at fairly reasonable prices.

Diana thought of the large blue stone from the secret compartment, which she had left in her suitcase back at the hotel. *Maybe I should have brought it with me,* she thought, *to have it checked and see if it's genuine—and especially to find out what kind of stone it is.*

She stopped and took out her guidebook to look for the building that had housed the gemstone dealer. She found it after a while, but unfortunately there was no longer a gemstone dealer there. The shop windows were boarded up, with an old advertising poster fluttering from the façade.

Two doors further down she found the display window of a small jeweller, proclaiming the word *Sale* in bold red letters. *It's probably like our carpet shops, who always claim to have a sale on,* Diana thought with a touch of derision.

As her search for the gemstone dealers had proved largely unsuccessful, she continued along the street until she finally found number 23. The colonial-style building looked a little run-down, but had not lost any of its former elegance. The modern bell and intercom system looked completely out of place. Beneath the names written in the characteristic curly script of the country, she saw a sign with a bilingual label. That was him! Maybe he would know whom she could see about the palm leaf.

As her heart began to pound with anticipation, she pressed the button, then took a step back and looked up, in the hope of hearing movement somewhere.

Nothing happened for a while. She was about to ring again when a window opened with a creak and a dark mop of hair appeared above her. The sun was in her eyes, causing her to shade her face with her hand, but even then she could not make out the features.

"Are you wanting me?" he called down.

"Yes, if you're Jonathan Singh," Diana replied.

He paused for a moment, then said, "I'll be right down!"

The head vanished, the window closed. A blood-curdling honking sounded behind her, making her jump with shock. The guidebook fell from her hand and only narrowly missed landing in the rubbish that had collected in the small gully by the downpipe.

As she bent to pick it up, the door opened. Diana straightened hastily and found herself looking into a pair of amber-coloured eyes in a light-brown face. The tall, dark-haired man, wearing light trousers and a white shirt, looked at first glance more like an artist than a fusty academic—the opposite of how she'd imagined Michael's friend to be.

"So you're Mr. Singh."

A smile lit up the man's face.

"Call me Jonathan. You must be Michael's friend. Diana Wagenbach, am I right?"

"Yes, that's right." She nervously offered him her hand, not noticing something fall from the pages of the guidebook. She started in shock as Jonathan bent to retrieve it.

"You've dropped something." With a friendly smile, he handed her a piece of grey paper.

Diana regarded it sceptically at first, then turned hot and cold as she turned it over and realised what she had come so close to losing. The photo of her great-great-grandmother! Or at least the copy she had taken before embarking on her journey. Now she remembered that she had tucked it between the pages of the guidebook while on the plane. She had intended to return it to her bag, but then she had fallen asleep and had simply put the guidebook away when she awoke.

"Oh, thank you so much. I'd hate to have lost it."

The man glanced briefly at the blue-green book in her hand, and his smile broadened.

"Don't you think you should be using something a bit more up to date?"

"Oh, I've got one of those," Diana replied. "I'm only carrying this to compare the past with what's here today."

"Are you a historian?"

"No, a lawyer." Hadn't Michael told him?

"Forgive me, but Michael was really mysterious about the whole thing, as though I might lose interest from the start if he wasn't. It shows what a long time it is since he was here, if he's forgotten how much we like to help people."

On hearing a few voices raised in protest behind them, he drew her a little closer to the wall of the building so they weren't in the way of passers-by.

"I hope he's told you a little more about me, at least," he said.

"Only that you used to be an academic and now write books."

"That's right. As my name suggests, I'm the son of an Indian father and an English mother. Your English is excellent, by the way."

Diana felt the blood rush to her face. No, she really hadn't imagined Jonathan Singh to be like this. Not so charming, not so bewilderingly attractive from the first moment she met him . . .

"My aunt . . . I mean my great-aunt, lived in England. I have English ancestors myself."

"Then we're practically fellow countrymen!" Jonathan replied warmly. "How do you fancy starting by going for a cup of tea? You can tell me more about yourself and your plans. I know a really nice tea room nearby."

"I hope I'm not disturbing your work," Diana said hesitantly.

"No. To be honest, I was waiting for you. My transition from researcher to author has meant that my circle of contacts has shrunk even further. I really appreciate the opportunity to be talking to someone of flesh and blood rather than being stuck with papers."

As they wound their way through the crowds on Baillie Street, he asked, "You're looking for palm leaves, aren't you? That was the only thing that Michael told me."

"Yes, that's right."

"In that case we ought to visit the National Museum. They have a wonderful collection of ola leaves there."

"Ola leaves?"

"That's the correct name for the palm-leaf books here."

Diana couldn't imagine the prophecies being hoarded in a museum. After all, Michael had told her there were special libraries of them, kept by readers, Tamils who were familiar with the ancient dialects of their language. Had he been wrong? Did historical research now include the fates of individuals?

"What's written on these ola leaves?" Diana asked, to make sure they were both talking about the same thing.

"Well, all the knowledge that they considered it worthwhile to write," Jonathan replied. "The Tamils were a very literate people. Most of these writings were destroyed during the colonial era, but a lot of them can still be seen in the museums."

"In that case, I'm afraid they're not the same palm-leaf books I'm looking for."

Jonathan gave her an enquiring look, then his eyes seemed to light up with recognition.

"Oh, forgive me. You want to have your future foretold. That's the kind of ola leaves you're looking for."

"I'm not actually looking to have *my* future told."

Has Michael really not told him anything? she wondered. "Among the things my aunt left me, I found a palm leaf, which I assume was stolen a long time ago. I'd really like to give it back to the library it came from."

Jonathan was speechless for a moment.

"A palm leaf in England?"

"I hope it's not an offence to have brought it here."

"No, of course not," Jonathan replied with a shake of his head. "I was only thinking that the readers are vigilant and won't let a leaf out of their hands."

"That's what Michael thought, too," Diana replied. "But it was in a secret compartment behind a bookshelf at my aunt's. I think it came to England in the nineteenth century. Probably brought back by my ancestors who travelled over here. I've just learned that they owned a plantation here."

Jonathan looked at her, his eyes shining. "That sounds incredibly interesting. I don't understand why Michael didn't tell me all this before."

"It must be because he didn't want to spoil your surprise," Diana said a little uncertainly, immediately reprimanding herself. *You're a grown woman, not a nervous teenager!*

Jonathan stopped suddenly. "Look over there!" He pointed towards a house that looked even older than those on Chatham Street.

Diana frowned as she noticed the inscription over the door.

"That's Dutch, isn't it?"

"Correct. It translates as something like 'Destroyed on a whim, rebuilt by justice.'"

"What does that mean?"

"During the Dutch colonial period there was a governor here called Pieter Vuist. He's said to have been one of the most terrible, cruel rulers of this country. On a whim, some say out of jealousy, he simply had this house demolished. His legal successor, who was a little more modest, had the house rebuilt, and that inscription put in place."

As he told the story, Diana felt a tingle on the back of her neck, as though the cold hand of fate had touched her and was now encouraging her to follow.

With Jonathan Singh she could clearly do that with impunity.

The little tea room on York Street looked as though it had been squeezed in between two buildings, although it was more probable that the other buildings had grown over time to tower over their modest older neighbour, hemming it in.

The interior, painted in a strong russet colour, was narrow and crammed with all kinds of artworks. Indian music tootled from a radio, and a news broadcast could be heard from a TV somewhere. The usual images of Shiva, Ganesha, and other gods were lacking, but in their place Diana saw a wonderful piece of Arabic calligraphy, which looked more than a century old.

"The owner is a Muslim," Jonathan explained as they sat down on one of the cushions. "He's proud to tell anyone who'll listen that his ancestors came from Yemen to spread the word of Mohammed here. They succeeded to some extent, but Hinduism and Buddhism still predominate on the Butterfly Island."

"Butterfly Island?"

"Yes, that's what Sri Lanka is called. Because it's shaped like a butterfly's wing." He emphasised his words with an appropriate hand gesture.

"Something else I've learned today," Diana said, but chose not to tell him about the butterfly that had awoken the angel in her dream about Beatrice's grave.

"Sri Lanka's full of surprises," Jonathan said before ordering two glasses of tea in Tamil from a passing waiter.

"He serves the best in the area," Jonathan said as the waiter hurried off. "I've taken the liberty of ordering a few pastries to go with it. I hope you agree it's still a little early for lunch."

Diana's head was spinning. Was it the jet lag kicking in, or did she simply need a while to take it all in?

"Maybe I should tell you something about myself for a change, rather than interrogating you any more."

Diana nodded. "That would be lovely."

The waiter served them with two steaming glasses of tea and a plate of little pastries, and Jonathan began to speak.

"I grew up in England. My father was an Indian of Tamil origin, which is how I come to have two mother tongues. He came to England as a professor of Indian history, and his interest rubbed off on me, the main difference being that I turned to Sri Lanka for my specialist field. You could say that it's because of him that I come to be taking an interest in a palm leaf carried off to England in the nineteenth century." He paused briefly, chewing his lip as though there was something he wanted to say and he was wondering how to put it. "You don't happen to have your leaf with you?" he asked eventually.

Diana shook her head. "No, I'm afraid not, but . . ." She hesitated. Could she simply invite him back to the hotel? What kind of impression would that give?

The next moment she was shaking her head at herself. *He wants to help you with the palm leaf, not marry you! Just be grateful that Michael gave you this contact.*

"It's back at the hotel. I also have some photos of it, but it's simply too valuable to be carrying around with me all the time."

"I understand." Jonathan swished the tea around in his glass, then said, "I'm dying to see it. Unfortunately, I've got a meeting with my publisher tomorrow. He wants to discuss a new project with me."

Diana raised her eyebrows. "Oh, yes? Can I ask what it's about?"

"It's about the conflict between the Tamils and the Sinhalese—its causes, effects, and history. The tensions between our two peoples have been simmering for decades, with the Tamil Tigers always more uncompromising in their actions. I'd like to think my work can provide a little clarification."

Diana recalled the travel agent's words of warning as she handed her the information leaflet. "It sounds like a very difficult, if not risky, subject."

"It is. But somebody has to tackle it. Silence won't get us anywhere— only by finding a consensus can we one day bring peace to the island."

Diana was impressed.

"But that doesn't mean I don't have time for you. We can meet in the evening if you'd like. That's when the city's at its best. What do you say to that?"

"I'd love to," Diana replied with a strange fluttering in her stomach.

"Which hotel are you staying in?"

"The Grand Oriental."

Jonathan pushed his bottom lip out in admiration. "You seem to be taking your research really seriously. In colonial times the Grand Oriental Hotel, together with the Mount Lavinia Hotel, was one of the best addresses in Sri Lanka for the English. It's the ideal place to begin a trip into the past."

"I found the hotel underlined in my old travel guide. I don't know for sure, but I like to think that it was where my ancestors stayed."

"I'll see you there at eight tomorrow evening," Jonathan said. "It will give me the opportunity to show off the city to you. Wherever you go, hotel restaurants seem to work on the basis that foreign travellers always want to eat the kind of thing they get at home. But you go to faraway lands to be led astray by the local culinary temptations."

With that, he tucked a pastry into his mouth.

2

The next morning, Diana prepared for her meeting with Jonathan Singh by taking a guided tour of the city, including the museum and some very beautiful temples, which she enjoyed photographing. As she had assumed, the palm-leaf manuscripts in the museum were not forecasts, but stories and historical records, as her guide, a Mr. P. Suma, explained. Although he spoke excellent English, Diana's head was soon spinning with all the Tamil terms and names that he used when talking about the history of his country.

In order to distract herself from the brief ride in one of the speeding red minibuses, Diana thought about the forthcoming evening with a thrill of anticipation.

Not only was she hoping for information about the palm leaf, but she also found herself really looking forward to seeing Jonathan Singh again.

Going over their conversation in her head the previous night, she had thought that he was a very engaging man with a great sense of humour. And she recalled his eyes, which she found beautiful. Absurdly, she tried to imagine how those eyes would view a variety of situations.

Back at the hotel, after a shower and a few moments of relaxation, she was standing at a loss in front of her mirror, thoroughly convinced that she had not brought enough clothes. She wanted to make the best possible impression on Mr. Singh—even if he was probably only interested in her palm leaf.

She finally went for a knee-length, flowing white skirt, with floral embroidery around the hem, and a short-sleeved black blouse.

She had found out from Mr. Suma that T-shirts were tolerated, but only really considered appropriate clothing for children. As they were going to be leaving the hotel, she had no intention of attracting the wrong kind of attention with a sloppy choice of clothes.

After dabbing on a subtle perfume and stowing the photos of the leaf and a notebook into her bag, she went down to the lobby, where a group of tourists had just arrived. She craned her neck, but couldn't see Jonathan. Her eyes wandered to the clock above the reception desk. Five to eight. *He probably likes to arrive on the dot.* Or he could be a little late, which would be no surprise given his profession.

Realising she was attracting a few male glances from the tourist party, she went over to the seats, which, like many other features, were in the late-Victorian colonial style. She was no more able to shut out the murmur of voices than to keep her nerves under control.

What was she expecting from this evening?

"Diana?"

Diana looked up in surprise. Jonathan Singh had appeared by her as if he'd suddenly sprung up from the ground.

"Oh, hello!" she replied a little embarrassed, rising and offering her hand for him to shake. "It's lovely to see you."

"The pleasure's all mine. I hope I haven't kept you waiting long."

"Only a few minutes." Diana laughed self-consciously. "You must know all about German punctuality." No sooner were the words out of her mouth than she wanted to slap herself. It was bad enough that the old cliché was still doing the rounds. But Jonathan merely grinned.

"How do you fancy going to Pettah? You'll soon see that the city's fairly quiet at night, but the huge bazaar in Pettah comes to life in the evening."

"That sounds excellent."

They left the hotel and walked through the city.

The traffic on the streets had got a little quieter. There were also fewer pedestrians at large, so she had a better view of the streets, where fruit lay rotting and small dogs snuffled about in search of food. A few of the numerous potholes were so deep that she was amazed they didn't cause major accidents. But everything seemed somehow more friendly than a quiet German street, where houses looked down with empty eyes on the impeccably maintained asphalt.

"How did the meeting with your publisher go?" Diana asked once they had left the hotel.

"Better than I expected. He's very interested, and is hoping for a good response—abroad, too. I think that's probably even more important since, apart from tea, tourism is a major source of income for our country. Many people were concerned after the attack at the airport."

"I can imagine."

"There are no longer warnings against travel, but tourists are still being told to take care. I'm sure that must have been the case with you, too?"

"Yes, but I only skimmed through the leaflets. I'd rather make my own mind up and assess the risks for myself."

"Many people don't think like that. I'd like to help tourists to understand the situation and the risks for themselves."

"I'm sure they'll be grateful to you. As will the whole country."

Jonathan shrugged modestly. "We'll see."

After a while they reached Colombo's seafront promenade, which Jonathan called Galle Face Green. Lemonade stands sprouted like mushrooms after a shower of rain. The view of the sea and sky, separated by a strip of gold, was amazing.

"This isn't a bazaar," Diana said with a smile.

"No, but it's one of the most beautiful views the city has to offer. If you come here in the morning, after it's been raining, you see people appearing out of the mist like fairy-tale characters."

They walked on until they finally turned into a street along which oil lamps flickered in the light autumn breeze. A street grill was filling the air with a heavenly aroma underlain with wood smoke.

After a while they reached a large covered hall that was teeming with life.

"Is this the bazaar?"

"It certainly is, or part of it," Jonathan said. "This is the fabric market. If you want to have a genuine sari cut to length, this is the place to come. It's well worth it."

Diana could believe it, as the stalls were piled high with brightly coloured fabrics. Maybe she would buy something here—after she had solved the mystery of her family.

Jonathan led her past intoxicating spice stalls and jewellers, until they finally found a small restaurant where there wasn't a tourist to be seen.

"This is the ultimate in insider tips," Jonathan said as they waited in front of the small counter to be shown to a table. "For now, at least. The owners of the tea houses and restaurants change all the time, so it's not out of the question that this restaurant might be gone in a couple of years or so."

"I can't imagine that, given the number of customers."

"The restaurants are subject to a unique set of laws. The in place of the moment could go down only a few months later. We should make the most of what we're given here today."

As they waited for service, Diana took the opportunity to look around. Some of the women were dressed in saris, while the men mainly wore dark trousers and plain shirts. The walls were decorated with pictures of the gods and masks; a large framed photo showed a colourfully dressed dancer. Frangipani flowers were piled beneath a small altar dedicated to the god Shiva. Incense sticks sent sweet clouds of smoke into the air.

Over everything drifted a babble of conversation and subtle music. Diana drank in all these impressions so she would later have something to take back with her to Germany, which seemed colourless in comparison.

A table became free, and a young man soon appeared. As a waitress swiftly cleared the table in the background, he had a brief word with Jonathan. A little later they were seated at the table, which had been wiped clean of every crumb and set with fresh palm-leaf place mats.

"So, what's the story with your palm leaf?" Jonathan asked, after the slick waiter had brought them menus printed on thick paper like elephant skin, covered in strange-looking letters and numbers.

"I'm afraid you're going to have to help me here. I don't understand a word on this menu."

Jonathan laughed softly. "Don't worry. Just leave it to me. Have you brought the photos?"

Diana nodded and briefly rummaged in her bag. Trying to maintain the correct sequence, she spread the pictures out on the table. Michael's photos were so pin-sharp that even the finest fibres were clearly shown. The writing on the palm leaf looked as clear as a pattern burned into wood by a pyrographer.

Before Jonathan could begin to look at the photos, the slick waiter appeared again. If he was surprised at the photos lying on the table, he didn't say anything.

Jonathan said something to him in Tamil, and the young man vanished.

"What have you ordered for us?" Diana asked.

"You'll see," he replied with a mysterious smile.

"Aren't you going to give me a clue?"

"It's something you'll like—trust me. Tamil food is delicious, especially if you don't mind hot spices."

"Any time, provided there's a large bucket of water to hand."

"Water only has a momentary effect on hotness. But I've taken care of it anyway."

Smiling again, Jonathan picked up one of the photos and looked at it closely. As she watched him, Diana chewed her bottom lip tensely. Would he be able to read it? He frowned suddenly—not a good sign.

"That's Old Tamil," he said finally. "As I expected."

"So you can't read it?"

"The Tamil script has changed a lot over the centuries. Ola leaves like this one are more than a thousand years old." Jonathan set the photos to one side. "I'm afraid you'll have to find a Nadi reader, someone who still knows this language."

"And I'll only find one of those in the libraries?"

"Or in one of the villages on the outskirts of Colombo. Did you say you want to give this leaf back to the library it came from?"

Diana nodded. "Yes, that's still my plan."

"Then I'd advise you to have it read by an independent source first. That might give you some indication of the library it came from."

"Can that be found out from the text?"

Jonathan shrugged. "Who knows? It would be worth a try, don't you think?"

Diana nodded, and Jonathan looked at her for a while.

"What's the story behind your trip? What's your motivation?" he asked eventually.

Diana took out the photo showing the white-clad woman against the mountain landscape—the photo that Jonathan had saved her from losing. His smile indicated that he remembered it.

"I assume that this is my great-great-grandmother. I can't say for sure, unfortunately, because my grandmother was a refugee during the war and so all her documents, including any other photos, were lost. There's also an old pack of tea, and beneath the name of the producer is the word *Vannattuppūcci*. I'm not sure if that's the name of the plantation or the place where it was located."

"Butterfly," Jonathan said with a smile.

"I'm sorry?"

"Butterfly. *Vannattuppūcci* means 'butterfly' in Tamil. Your ancestors must have had a poetic streak."

Diana had nothing to say to that, but she suddenly remembered her dream. The butterfly that had awakened the angel to life. Had that been a premonition?

"I'd guess it was the name of the plantation. The English usually gave their estates names."

"I can hardly believe that my ancestors would have had the delicacy to give their plantation a name like that. The typical English colonists of that period tended to hide their feelings."

"I'm sure they must have had a reason."

Jonathan looked at the photo again, then sighed.

"You've got a whole lot of work ahead of you."

"I was so fond of my aunt Emily. She was like a grandmother to me. It's a matter of honour for me to fulfil her wishes, especially since . . ."

No, that's going too far, she thought. *I can't tell him the story of my messed-up marriage. He's a helpful stranger, nothing more.*

Faced with her silence, Jonathan looked at her questioningly. Diana searched desperately for words to begin anew.

"In any case, I have to know what lies behind the curtain between my grandmother and previous generations. If you know what I mean."

Jonathan nodded. "Yes, I think I do." His expression became pensive, then he shook his head lightly. "It's very strange. While they're alive our ancestors try and keep any stains on their past hidden. And then they ask us, their descendants, to find them because they want to rid themselves of the burden, but don't themselves have the strength to reveal them."

Diana was amazed at the wisdom of his words. At the same time, she wondered whether her family's secret was such a big stain that Emily was ashamed of it.

"We should see this as doing our duty for those who come after us, shouldn't we?" Jonathan looked at her with a strange expression, as though he had suddenly become aware of some stain on his own past. "Get to the bottom of the past ourselves, to save our children the trouble of having to do so."

"I don't consider it trouble," Diana replied, slightly uneasy. "On the contrary. As a child I always liked to imagine what my ancestors' lives were like. A lot got lost during the Second World War. My grandmother, who could have told me so much, died giving birth to my mother. And Aunt Emily was always so silent on the matter. Maybe she wanted to suppress her own memories . . ."

"I'm sure that's the case," Jonathan said, now looking a little more relaxed. "Otherwise she wouldn't have asked you. Perhaps she believed that you would understand better if you worked out the past for yourself rather than simply hearing a story."

Silence followed. After thinking briefly, Diana could only agree that he was right. Before they could continue their conversation, the waiter appeared with some steaming bowls that gave off a wonderful aroma.

Diana saw some little savoury cakes, a variety of chutneys, and something that looked like the red curry that was also served in Thai restaurants.

The waiter said something in rapid Tamil, then withdrew. Diana gazed at the food in amazement and breathed in the various aromas deeply.

"This is just wonderful! What is it?"

"A cross-section of Tamil cuisine." Jonathan pointed to the dishes one after the other. "Idli and vadai, our name for steamed or fried little cakes of black gram and rice; chutney; rasam, a thin peppered soup; and a red curry. Then there's cool yoghurt for afterwards."

"If I have any room left for afterwards!" Diana replied with a smile, trying to make sure her mouth wasn't watering too much.

"We traditionally eat with our fingers from a banana leaf," Jonathan said, showing her how to hold the stiff green leaf. "You can also eat it with cutlery, but this way is more authentic." As his hand brushed against hers, they looked briefly into one another's eyes. The amber of his looked darker now, almost brown, and Diana suddenly felt as though she could lose herself in them. But no sooner had she felt the sensation than she got a grip of herself, and as she took the first bite her confusion faded before her pleasure in the food, the like of which her tongue had never tasted before.

As she returned to the hotel a little after midnight, Diana felt strange. It was nothing to do with the excellent food, nor with Jonathan, who had come across the whole time as a friendly, helpful travel guide. The fact that she had opened up to him, hinted at the secret to him, made her feel as though she saw a few things more clearly, even though she actually knew no more than before.

Jonathan had promised her that he would make a few enquiries about Nadi readers the following day. Diana could hardly wait to hear what he found out.

After they'd exchanged email addresses, he walked her back to the hotel. They crossed the city in silence, each sunk in their own thoughts. But Diana's gaze kept stealing across to Jonathan. Absurd questions like *Does he go to the gym? What's his shoe size? What does his apartment look like?* kept going through her head, and she had almost felt transported back to her school days, when all the girls dreamed of the older boy who already rode a moped and who won at all the sports.

And now, with the warm water of the shower running over her skin, she couldn't get him out of her head. *When did you last think about a man so much?* It occurred to her that she hadn't given Philipp a second thought since she'd arrived in Colombo. She scolded herself for allowing him in now.

As she slipped between the light sheets and turned her gaze to the lights of the harbour, she was overcome by a deep longing. How long was it since she and Philipp had slept together? In recent months, sex had become something of a duty to be fitted in between business appointments and daily cares. Until the moment she had discovered Philipp's infidelity, it hadn't really bothered her, and after that she had been so distracted by finding him out and Emily's illness that she hadn't been aware of her own body for a single moment.

But here, far from home—surrounded by exotic smells and a quality of air that made her feel as though she could float off, to be borne by the wind far away above the palm groves—her self-awareness returned. She felt the blood pulsing through her limbs, her heart beating regularly beneath her breast, a quiver of excitement in her belly, when she thought of this man, who in reality was no more than a chance acquaintance. That evening alone, which had not involved the slightest commitment on the part of either of them, had given her more than she had ever got from the last few months of her life with Philipp. And she was secretly looking forward to her next meeting with Jonathan Singh, however much she might tell herself that he was just friendly and willing to help and she would probably never see him again after she had finished what she was doing here on the island.

◆ ◆ ◆

She woke at around ten o'clock with bright morning sunshine on her face. The air had warmed up, the deep notes of a tanker's horn sounded across the harbour, and a few dust particles danced like tiny glow-worms in the sunlight that poured in through the window. Diana rose with a smile and immediately felt a pang of anticipation in her stomach. Had he written to her yet?

It took an effort of will not to go straight over to her laptop and check her emails. *He won't have written yet. He's bound to have to work.*

After a refreshing shower and a good breakfast, Diana decided to go for a walk on the promenade.

"Mrs. Wagenbach?"

On her way out, Diana stopped and turned to see the reception-ist giving her a friendly smile. "Excuse me. A letter was handed in for you a short while ago. I called up to your room, but you weren't there."

A letter for me? Diana thought with amazement. *Has Mr. Green written to me?*

As she approached the desk, the receptionist handed her a large envelope inscribed with the hotel's logo and tied with a cord. It con-tained a smaller, cream-coloured envelope stuffed to capacity. There was no airmail sticker.

After thanking the receptionist, she took the letter upstairs and set it down on the desk, her heart thumping. Her name was written on the envelope in neat but elegant handwriting—and nothing else.

She ran her fingertips over the paper before picking up the letter opener.

The envelope almost heaved a sigh of relief as it gave way, revealing the bundle of paper inside. Photocopies, Diana thought. On top was a plain card, with a note in handwriting that had both English and Tamil influences.

Dear Diana,

Thank you for the delightful evening, which inspired me to begin searching for a Nadi reader as soon as I got home. After getting an acquaintance out of bed with a phone call and asking myself if I was crazy, I found out that there's a man who knows Old Tamil living in the small village of Ambalangoda. My acquaintance couldn't tell me his name, but I'm sure there aren't many men like him in the area.

I'd like to suggest that we meet tomorrow morning outside the hotel, provided you don't want to go there on your own. In that case please just let me know by email.

I am enclosing a map on which I've marked the village. If you wish, you could extend the trip to include Nuwara Eliya, where I've located your tea plantation. You'll find the documents enclosed.

I hope you'll allow me to participate further in this adventure, Holmes.

Your obedient servant,

Jonathan "Watson" Singh

It was only once she had read the card three times that she realised Jonathan had actually been crazy enough to slave away for her the whole night long. Although she was outwardly calm, her heart was thumping as though she'd been sprinting, and her hands were suddenly icy cold.

She continued to feel the same way as she leafed through the photocopies and studied the map tucked among them. Her plan to walk along the promenade had evaporated—she knew now that she'd be sitting over the documents all day, drinking in all the information the papers could give her.

But first she had to send Jonathan a reply.

She crossed the room to the desk, opened her laptop, and typed an email.

> *Dear Jonathan,*
> *I didn't realise you had a liking for Conan Doyle. But I can certainly set your mind at rest. After the extremely impressive sample of your detective work, for which I'm very grateful, I can't imagine a better companion for the trip to Ambalangoda than you. I hope you will manage to free yourself from your professional obligations and accompany me, as I fear I would be completely stuck without your knowledge of Tamil.*
>
> *Warm regards,*
> *Diana "Holmes" Wagenbach*

3

Vannattuppŭcci, 1887

Grace and Victoria's room, which they were forced to share until more renovations were completed, was on the ground floor. It had an overall Oriental appearance, reminiscent of an Arab or Turkish house; the pointed arches of the windows were decorated with filigree ornamentation in the style of a seraglio. Bright-orange silk curtains embellished with intricate embroidery billowed in a warm breeze that blew gently through a half-open window. Wind chimes tinkled somewhere in the background. The rest of the room was quite plain and looked as though it were desperate to be brought to life.

On the ochre floor tiles were a desk, an elaborately inlaid wardrobe, and a chest of drawers. Two beds stood against the other wall, with a narrow carpet running along their feet. Heaped in the middle of the room was a pile of suitcases and bags containing the sisters' possessions.

"Perhaps our uncle kept a harem here!" Victoria exclaimed once Miss Giles had gone. The possibility that her scandalous uncle could have indulged in polygamy made her eyes shine like precious stones catching the light.

"I don't think Uncle Richard changed his religion," Grace said. "You have to be a Muslim to keep a harem."

"Who knows, maybe he was converted!" Victoria insisted, eager for sensation. "I've heard Father say that he had himself cremated like the Hindus. We won't find his grave."

"Nevertheless, I don't believe he actually changed his faith. There was probably a practical reason for his last wish—a corpse must deteriorate dreadfully fast in this heat."

Victoria wasn't to be put off. "Who knows what our mysterious uncle was like? Even you didn't know him when he was alive—after he left Tremayne House, he was never seen in England again."

She was right about that. Their uncle Richard was little more to them than a portrait hanging in one of the lonely corridors of Tremayne House. A man with dark hair and attractive grey eyes who looked as if he were being choked by the high collar of his shirt. No one had truly known him, if their father were to be believed, not even he or their grandfather.

Victoria jumped up impulsively, stretched out her arms, and twirled around. "Wouldn't it be exciting to live in a harem?"

"Rather boring, I should think." Despite herself, Grace was similarly overcome by an urge to dance around the room. Victoria's enthusiasm could be contagious. But should she? After all, she was eighteen now and considered an adult. "You lie around on silk cushions all day, listening to the same old stories, without the opportunity to live your own life, your only company fat eunuchs in tiny loincloths forever asking you in squeaky voices what you desire. Your only excitement the intrigues put about by the other women." She was taken aback to realise that her image of life in a harem could have been lifted word for word from one of Victoria's penny dreadfuls.

"But my husband would be a rich sultan, who would heap gifts on me and spoil me in every way because I'd be his favourite wife!" Victoria spun around in another circle. Instead of getting dizzy she seemed to be enjoying her dance more and more.

"How do you know that?" Grace replied, jumping up suddenly.

"I look in my mirror every morning, and it tells me that I'm beautiful enough to be a sheikh's favourite wife."

"Don't you think you're being a bit vain?"

"Of course, but others are, too. Come on, join in, Grace—it's like flying!"

Grace only hesitated a moment. Grown-up or not, in her little sister's company she lost all inhibitions and felt as though she were still only thirteen herself. Now she, too, began to spin on her own axis. Faster and faster, her laughter blending with her sister's. The dizziness in her head felt delightful and after a while really did feel like flying.

"Ladies, please!"

Miss Giles's reproachful voice stopped them in their tracks. Reeling, they managed to fall into each other's arms before collapsing to the floor.

Their governess shook her head in disapproval. "I'm sure you have something more useful to do than indulge in this ridiculous behaviour! Your mother was asking whether you're ready for afternoon tea."

Gasping for breath, and still giggling, the two sisters sat up.

"But of course, Miss Giles," replied Grace, having enjoyed a carefree moment for the first time in a long while. "If you would be so kind as to find us two dresses from our suitcases? You know our mother won't like us to appear for tea in our travelling clothes."

Grace was kept awake all night by the strange noises coming from outside. The heat made it impossible to close the window completely, as the slight cooling effect from the night breeze was essential. She could hear the calls of nocturnal birds, the distant cries of monkeys, and the rustling of leaves and grass. When the tossing and turning finally became too much for her, she lay on her back and stared with wide-open eyes at the curtains, which looked strangely bleached in the moonlight. They were still billowing lightly in the wind like a fairy queen's lost veil. Every now and then there was a slight glitter from one of the embroidered patterns—Grace had noticed earlier that they had gold threads running through them. When she told Victoria about her discovery, her little sister said, "I bet only the queen has curtains like this."

All at once Grace felt a compulsion to get up and look out of the window. Perhaps she'd catch sight of some exotic animals creeping through the garden. Or snakes. There had been no sign of any on the way there, but they had seen one in the city, in a young snake charmer's basket. A shudder ran down Grace's arms as she recalled how the boy had tamed the cobra, which looked at him angrily as he made it dance. Would it be a good idea to carry a flute at all times here, just in case a cobra came into view?

At the window, she drew up a floor cushion and sat down on it. The very low windowsill meant she could sit and enjoy a view over a large part of the garden.

Grace drew her knees up towards her chin and, although no one could see her, demurely pulled her nightdress down over her legs before losing herself in the sight of the moon, which hung above the treetops like a huge glow-worm.

The moon had never looked like this in England. It was usually ringed by a hazy halo indicating more rain to come. But here the moon was as richly yellow as a Dutch cheese, and even in the dead of the night, the sky never seemed to lose its purple undertones.

Suddenly, something dark darted above the trees. At first Grace thought it was a bird, but its movements were far too frantic.

Then it occurred to her—it must have been a bat! They had seen bats back at Tremayne House as evening fell, but those were not half the size of the one she'd just seen. A pleasant tingle, the kind she'd only ever experienced when reading a horror story, ran down her spine. Could these huge bats be some kind of blood-sucking vampires? Or even the flying foxes that hung in large groups in the trees throughout India?

Grace made a mental note to talk to Victoria about them in the morning. She was bound to be excited about them and insist on wanting to catch a flying fox, to their mother's horror.

Her gaze dropped towards the ground, and she thought she caught sight of a white gleam against the dark hedge.

At first she thought she might have been mistaken, but then she saw that it moved. Victoria would now be claiming that she was seeing a ghost, but Grace's rational mind knew it was a person she was looking at, dressed in baggy white trousers.

As the moonlight fell on the figure, Grace's eyes widened. It was a man—a man with a naked torso! She forgot to breathe. She had never seen a man like that. Although the blood shot to her cheeks and Miss Giles's voice of warning echoed through her mind, she couldn't look away.

The man, who seemed to believe he was unobserved, was carrying a long bundle wrapped in fabric beneath his arm. He looked like he was returning from somewhere.

As Grace slowly released her breath, a ray of light fell on his face. His dark moustache and beard stood out against his skin, which was too light for a Tamil and too dark for an Englishman. She could clearly make out that this was the young Mr. Vikrama!

After the brief moment of recognition, the shadows engulfed his features again, but Grace continued to stare transfixed, her cheeks glowing as if from a fever, at the spot where she had seen him.

Where had he been? And why was he wearing clothes like those from an Oriental picture book? Why was he not wearing shoes or a shirt? And what was he carrying?

Sensing that he was about to raise his head, she ducked quickly behind the curtains. Her heart was beating wildly against her ribcage, and her breath seemed incredibly loud. She listened in vain for footsteps. Even if her body had not been reacting so forcefully, she would probably not have been able to hear anything as the grass dampened the sound of his bare feet.

When she trusted herself to peep out around the curtain, Vikrama had vanished.

Grace immediately felt uneasy. The urge to run through the house and see whether he was crossing the courtyard dressed like that became so great that she soon arose and tiptoed out of the room.

The whole house was silent except for a slight murmuring of the wind creeping through the open windows. Grace hurried along the corridor, passed Miss Giles's room with soft snores emanating from it, and finally reached the hall. Concentrating hard, she scanned the courtyard through the window. Was that a glimpse of white?

No, it was only the well gleaming in the moonlight. Behind it loomed the dark stables, with the administration building beyond. Had Vikrama already gone? Had he taken a different route, perhaps?

Grace stood motionless before the windows of the hall. Her heart was still hammering with excitement. Her father had an employee who went about strange business in the night. Should she tell him?

No, better not, she decided. *Not before I know what it's all about.*

As she turned, her attention was caught by the two dancing gods. Only now did she notice that they each held a short sword or knife in one hand, flowers in the other. Their trousers were like those Vikrama had worn, and she recalled what Mr. Cahill had said. Did Vikrama follow this Hinduism, and had he just completed some sacred mission?

Or was it something forbidden that he had done? Why else would he have vanished so suddenly?

She was filled with a longing to find out. *Maybe I should begin by keeping an eye on Vikrama during the day,* she thought. Having resolved to do so, she slipped back to her room, and after a quick glance out of the window that yielded no sign of any further shapes in the night, she lay back down on her bed.

After finally managing to sleep, Grace was awakened at dawn by the screeching of the parrots. Unwilling to stay in bed, she crossed to the washbowl and removed her nightdress. The water had become pleasantly lukewarm overnight. As she dipped her hands in, a butterfly fluttered to the edge of the bowl and settled on it as if there were no better place in the world. Grace froze, afraid that she might accidentally wet it. Mr. Norris always said that this would damage their wings, which was why they always folded them up when it rained.

However, the butterfly seemed not to be afraid of the water. Every now and then it flapped its blue-and-black patterned wings—a magnificent specimen that would have delighted any naturalist—including Victoria. But Grace couldn't bring herself to wake her and therefore condemn the butterfly to an almost certain death. As the water ran over her lower arms, she watched the butterfly until it finally decided to flutter away. Grace watched it go in fascination, touched by a strange magic that she would not have imagined in this place.

After she had finished her morning ablutions, she sat by the window looking at the fog that lay over the tea plantation like an eiderdown. The morning light gave it a gentle blue tinge, a hue that would have been unthinkable back in England. No ball in London, no beautiful dresses, could give her the same feeling as the one that flooded through her at the sight. She felt peace, calmness, and even security—things she had only experienced rarely in her parents' house and which she had never before thought were important.

It was not until the fog gradually lifted to reveal the sunlight and Victoria began to stir that Grace withdrew from the window, determined to stop yearning for the lost glitter of her old world, but to seek new splendour here—starting with the wonderful feeling the early morning had given her.

"After breakfast this morning, why don't we creep across the garden to Father's study window?" Grace suggested to her sleepy-looking sister as she brushed her hair.

"What on earth for?" Victoria replied sullenly, rubbing her eyes. "I'd rather try and catch a parrot."

"But you need a net to do that."

"There must be someone here who can make me one."

"Even if you had a net, you don't know yet where to find the best birds."

"It would be enough for me to get that beautiful blue one."

Grace looked at her closely in the mirror, then raised an eyebrow like Father sometimes did when he doubted something. "Really? But how do you know there aren't some even better ones out there? Purple ones, perhaps?"

"I don't like purple," Victoria grumbled. "If I did I would have bought that amethyst on Chatham Street." She waved a hand at the alleged sapphire that she had placed in front of the small gilt-framed portrait of her dead dog, Oscar.

"But you like red and orange," Grace argued as she completed her sister's braid she was plaiting. "And you never know, you could find a rainbow-coloured one."

"Do you think such a thing exists?" Curiosity sparked in Victoria's eyes.

"But of course! And I'm sure it would look lovely with your blue parrot in the aviary."

"Aviary? But aren't parrots kept in cages?"

"Maybe. But you could keep more of them in an aviary. And they wouldn't slip through the bars." Grace remembered something she'd almost forgotten. "Anyway, I'm sure there are flying foxes here. You've heard of them, haven't you?"

Victoria's eyes shone. "Flying foxes! Oh yes, I've read about them. They're supposed to live in trees and drop down on their unsuspecting prey."

"Do you think so? Remember they sleep during the day."

"Of course they do, but they drop on their prey at night."

The theatrical gesture that Victoria used to emphasise her words almost made Grace burst out laughing. She hadn't the heart to correct her.

"Very well," Victoria said, "let's go for a walk later. We can go by Papa's window, and you can listen in."

"Thank you, darling sister. You won't regret it."

With a satisfied smile, Grace finished the braid at her sister's nape. She could have managed without Victoria to accompany her, but she needed an alibi. If she was noticed, she could claim that she had been walking in the garden with Victoria and happened to have turned up just as her father was setting out on his tour of the plantation with the young man.

She felt a strange fluttering in her stomach as she thought about what she had seen. Since she had woken that morning, she had run through the scene repeatedly in her head, recalling more and more details as she did. The curve of his muscles, his strong calves, his black hair flying wildly around his head . . .

"Why have you gone red?" Victoria said, tearing her from her daydreaming. "Have you been having unseemly thoughts?"

It was uncanny how well her sister knew her and could read her expressions.

"No, of course not!" she said defensively, lowering her eyes in case Victoria could somehow guess there was a man behind them. "Now, keep still. I want to tie off this plait."

In line with the family tradition, breakfast was eaten in the dining room, which the sisters had seen the previous evening. Only if one of them was ill, or had been occupied until very late the previous evening, did the servants take breakfast to their rooms. Henry Tremayne valued his mornings with his family, as he usually came home late from his work and commitments and at best only saw them over supper.

In contrast to the previous day, when the room had still looked quite impersonal, the table was now adorned with flower arrangements in white and orange. The cutlery was polished and shiny.

"It looks like Mama's made a start with the household arrangements," Victoria said cheerfully.

"And she's told Mr. Wilkes to make sure the servants get cracking," Grace added.

As though he had heard his name from afar, the butler suddenly appeared behind them.

"Good morning, Miss Grace, Miss Victoria. You're bright and early this morning. I hope you slept well."

"I had a bit of a disturbed night," Grace replied as she went to her place. Mr. Wilkes stepped behind her and pulled out the high-backed chair for her to sit. "But it's no wonder, with these temperatures, is it?"

"You're completely right," Wilkes agreed, before turning to Victoria to help her into her seat.

"How was your night, Mr. Wilkes?" she asked, apparently innocently although Grace knew there was nothing she enjoyed more than provoking the butler's sense of propriety. The household didn't usually concern themselves with the personal interests of their staff.

"The very best, Miss Victoria," he replied after a brief pause, then turned back to Grace.

"Can I get you anything yet?"

"A cup of cocoa would be nice. What do you think, Victoria?"

Victoria clapped her hands. "Oh yes, cocoa would be good, Mr. Wilkes."

The butler left the dining room, visibly pleased not to be subjected to any more personal enquiries.

That morning, Henry Tremayne looked preoccupied as he came to the breakfast table. Claudia seemed exhausted. As Victoria spooned up her cocoa and Grace sat deep in thought, she complained with a sigh about the heat in her bedroom and the air that seemed thick enough to cut with a knife. If things continued like this, she would probably get a migraine as the day went on.

The breakfast, prepared by the resident cook, was rich in unfamiliar fruits, a kind of cake, and yoghurt.

Grace and Victoria searched the table in vain for porridge. Henry did likewise as he peered up from the newspaper that Wilkes had obtained for him the previous evening.

"Richard allowed some strange customs to take root here. We'll have to inform the cook that she should adapt her breakfasts to the sort we're accustomed to."

"I think the mangoes are quite nice," Victoria remarked. She smacked her lips, earning herself a look of reproach from her mother.

"It may be a suitable meal for the people here, but we'll ruin our digestions with all this foreign food. Who knows what kind of fruits these are."

Grace looked at Victoria, who rolled her eyes, then said, "But Mama, just try some. They're lovely and sweet! I hardly think the servants have a plan to kill their masters and mistresses."

Claudia sniffed as though she were about to object, but she finally succumbed to temptation and tried one of the strange cakes.

After breakfast, Grace and Victoria withdrew before Miss Giles could catch them—she was probably already dreaming of Mr. Norris again. Since her father was not in his study and there was still some time before his tour of the plantation, the sisters disappeared into a corridor of the house they had not yet explored.

"Do you think she'll find us here?" Victoria whispered, constantly looking over her shoulder as though they were spies on the run.

"I'm sure she won't. We haven't looked around this part of the house yet, and you know how timid she is."

"Yes, but I thought that was only playacting so that Mr. Norris could lend her a strong hand."

"Believe me, she won't find us here."

And Mr. Vikrama won't come for Papa for another half hour yet, she thought.

As they moved on, Grace had to admit that she had a slightly creepy feeling. The rooms they had moved into were all freshly renovated and seemed bright enough, but the others were still as they had been on the day her unknown uncle Richard had fallen.

"Maybe we'll meet our uncle's ghost here," Victoria whispered as if reading her mind.

"Don't be silly. There's no such thing as ghosts!" Grace said, but the moaning of the wind here sought to contradict her.

After they had passed two doors without opening them, curiosity won the day.

They carefully pushed open a high double door adorned with dark inlay. The sight that met their astonished eyes was a kind of men's drawing room. The armchair and sofa beneath the window were draped with sheets, as were the two large display cabinets and the desk. There was also a billiard table, a piano, and a large globe, virtually the only object not to be covered, as though its services were still required every now and then.

"Don't you find it strange that there was never a lady of the house here?" Victoria asked, sliding her hand over the piano in a place where the dust sheet had slipped slightly. "You never heard anything about Uncle Richard marrying, did you?"

"Yesterday you had him keeping a harem," Grace replied scornfully.

"That was just a joke. Even if he was the black sheep of the family, I'm sure he wouldn't have sunk so low."

Grace shook her head, gazing at the magnificent globe. It was quite out of date by now, as it showed Ceylon as a Dutch colony. "He probably never found a woman he liked. You've heard Papa's stories. His brother always knew his own mind."

"Or he had a lover who was the wrong class."

Grace drew herself up to her full height. "You're not supposed to know anything about things like that at your age!"

"Why ever not? There are many men who fall in love with women beneath their station."

"But not Uncle Richard. All he ever thought about was work; he didn't even have time for his family."

"But he doesn't seem to have been a stranger to pleasure," Victoria said precociously, pointing at the huge table-like shape that hulked beneath the dust sheet like a sarcophagus. "Why else would he have had a billiard table installed?"

Before Grace could reply, Victoria was already pulling the sheet aside. There was no such item in Tremayne House, since their grandfather had been of the opinion that such pleasures were the province of pubs and bordellos. He deliberately ignored the fact that his gentlemen's club had a billiard table.

With a cry of delight, Victoria ran her hand over the green baize that covered the table. Numerous criss-crossed marks hinted at frequent play, but there was no sign of cues or balls.

"Maybe we should play a game and make ourselves really disreputable," Victoria suggested.

"What do you intend to play with?" Grace said, indicating the empty table.

"The balls must be in one of the cupboards. I'll go and have a look."

"Victoria!" Grace called in warning, but Victoria had already begun to open one cupboard door after the other. As it seemed impossible to stop her sister without putting their walk together at risk, Grace let her carry on and went over to a small chest of drawers near the window. This was certainly not where the billiard balls were kept. It looked as though it had been squeezed in, brought here from another room and simply set down here. There was no sheet over it, which she also found curious.

Grace caught sight of a movement out of the corner of her eye and turned to the windows. She saw Mr. Vikrama's back glide past. A closer inspection of the little chest of drawers would have to wait.

"We ought to go now," she said as heat shot through her veins and a strange impatience made her restless.

"Why?" Victoria asked, stringing out the word like a child who didn't want to be called out of the playroom.

"Because Papa's visitor has arrived. That young man from yesterday, the administrator."

"Is he the reason why you're staring out of the window?"

Grace caught her breath, but fortunately she remembered all the excuses she had thought up during the night.

"Because of him and because of what we can find out from him. Didn't you hear him offering to tell Papa about tea cultivation? I think we should listen, too, since we're obviously going to be here for a while."

Victoria gave her a broad, wordless grin as they left the room and decided to leave by the front door.

"What's the matter?" Grace asked as she felt her sister's smile like pinpricks on her skin.

"Nothing," Victoria replied innocently.

"Have you gone mad? Did you find something strange in that cupboard?"

Victoria giggled quietly then put her hand up to her mouth. "No don't worry, my dear sister, I'm quite clear in the head. I'm just remembering your sour face on the way here and back at the hotel. And now your eyes shine whenever you talk about tea growing. I knew you'd find something to like about your new home."

Grace struggled to keep her composure. "I never said I didn't like this country!" She straightened her back and lifted her chin. "I only regret that I couldn't be there for my debut presentation to the queen."

"Don't worry!" Victoria's eyes had a mischievous spark. "I'm sure Papa will find a suitably rich young man for you here. Or you'll simply marry this Mr. Vikrama, whose first name is a mystery to us all."

"For goodness' sake!" Grace would have liked to retort with something suitably threatening, but then she heard an all too familiar click of heels.

"Miss Giles!" Grace whispered, and the prospect of spending the whole day unpacking their suitcases and having to go through their wardrobes immediately made her Victoria's ally once again.

"Come on, let's vanish into the garden before she sees us."

4

Tremayne House, 2008

Dear Mr. Green,
I'm on the way to Nuwara Eliya and just wanted to let you know that I believe I'm on the right track. Mr. Jonathan Singh, a very nice academic and author, has offered to accompany me to a village where it is said there is an old Nadi reader who may be able to decipher the palm leaf I've found. You can imagine how I'm burning with impatience! We have also discovered that the plantation that belonged to my ancestors is still in existence. Of course it has been in different ownership for a long time now—a state-owned company whose employees were very friendly on the phone and will allow me to look through their archives. Maybe I'll find out more there about Grace and the others. I still have no idea what the big secret is, but my stay

here and all the research work is proving good
for my spirits. I wish Aunt Emily could have seen
it all.
I hope you are well.
All the very best,
Diana

The butler took a deep breath and leaned back in his seat. The secret was still a way from being revealed, but Miss Diana was on the right track. The deciphering of the palm leaf and her stay on the plantation would surely bring the truth to light.

After swiftly reading through the message once again, he went into the kitchen, set the kettle to boil on the stove, and then went to the master's workroom in the basement. There, next to the desk mat, was a brown envelope. The last clue. He would have to plan its release carefully, as it could easily cause more confusion than clarity. He took out the photo carefully and gazed at it as he had so often since Miss Diana had set off on her travels. The picture told him nothing more, but even he had to admit that there was something very remarkable about it.

He was glad that there were modern methods for transmitting information. Green took the photo to the printer and scanner as carefully as he would carry a fully loaded tea tray, lifted the lid, and laid the photo on the glass plate.

The last clue, he thought as the light beam ran along the photo, picking up the pixels ready for display on his computer screen. *Will Miss Diana be able to solve the mystery of the past? And how will it affect her?*

People rarely solved mysteries and remained unchanged . . .

Colombo, 2008

The old, slightly overcautious man drove his minibus purposefully, but slowly, along the red sandy road that made Diana think of roads in Australia. On either side, palms and bamboo canes proliferated, sometimes growing so thickly that they plunged the road into shadow. She looked a little impatiently at Jonathan, who appeared completely unconcerned at the slow pace and the horn-blowing at every vehicle they encountered. He was calmly reading a newspaper, which he had been carrying when they met. Even their near collision with a tuk-tuk that shot like an arrow from a side street was not enough to make him look up from the day's news.

"Maybe we should have hired a different driver," Diana whispered to him once she had got over the shock.

Jonathan lowered his paper and folded it up. There was a smile on his lips, and his eyes sparkled. "Any local would advise you to go with an old driver. The younger ones drive somewhat more . . . speedily."

"Rashly, you mean? Like that guy back there! He could have been on the crazy streets of Colombo."

"Out in the country they usually take more risks when driving because they believe they have the space. The locals typically call it 'Colombo driving.' You can imagine why."

"Oh yes, I've seen enough of it since I've been here." Diana hung on to the nylon strap above her head that prevented passengers from being hurled against the door when rounding bends.

"Anyway, I think Mr. Gilshan will be very helpful."

"But it's going to be dark before we reach the village."

"So?"

Diana frowned. "I thought you had to get back to Colombo."

"Yes, but not today or tomorrow. You want to go on to visit the tea plantation afterwards, don't you?"

"Yes, but . . ."

"I've taken the liberty of giving myself a week off," Jonathan said. "The privilege of being freelance."

Diana was stunned into wide-eyed silence.

"Is that OK with you?" he continued. "I thought you'd need some help in Nuwara Eliya."

"But what about your book? Your publisher . . . After all, I'm a complete stranger to you!"

Jonathan shook his head with a smile. "No, you're no longer a stranger. After all, you've told me your family history. And I promised Michael I'd help you."

"I know."

"As a historian I find it really exciting to be on the trail of this mystery with you. Provided you want me there, that is."

Diana lowered her head in embarrassment. "But I don't know how I'll ever be able to repay you. After all, you're giving up your free time for me, time you could be spending with your wife and children."

"I'm not married," he replied, his voice turned serious. "Not any longer."

"What happened?" Diana burst out before she could tell herself it had nothing to do with her. "I'm sorry, I didn't mean to be rude."

"It's fine," Jonathan replied, but the dark shadow that had crossed his face was still there. "We drifted apart, as people so neatly say. Well, that may sound a bit unusual for a five-year marriage, but that's how it was. She wanted a career with a computer company, but I wanted the opportunity to follow my passion and be a bit closer to the land of my forefathers. The two paths were irreconcilable, so we separated."

"Do you have any children?"

"A daughter. She lives with her mother in Delhi."

"Do you see them much?"

"Yes, I fly to Delhi and visit them. And I take her on holiday. But don't worry yourself about that; I still have plenty of time for Rana." His expression brightened a little. "And when else would I get the opportunity to go on a research trip with a German–English woman? You're one of the most interesting people I've met for months. And that's saying something—at the museum I even meet presidents from time to time."

Diana smiled to herself.

The journey to Ambalangoda finally came to an end without any further near misses, and the driver dropped them off on the edge of a settlement of fishermen's huts and palm trees.

Glad to feel the ground beneath her feet once again, Diana looked around. She could hear music booming out from somewhere, mixed with loud voices.

"There's probably a festival going on," Jonathan explained after listening briefly. "I'm sure most of the village will be there."

"Oh, does that mean we've come at a bad time?"

"On the contrary. The festival will save us a long search, as nearly everyone's bound to be there. Maybe including our Nadi reader. And even if he prefers to remain at home, someone will be able to point us in the right direction."

After walking past a row of apparently empty houses, they finally reached the source of the music and laughter.

Crowds of women in brightly coloured sarongs and saris and men in traditional costume had gathered in front of a richly decorated house. A shining limousine, which looked slightly out of place, was waiting not far from the house.

"Oh, we're in luck!" Jonathan exclaimed. "This is a wedding. The bride and groom will soon be appearing for the Poruwa ceremony."

He moved away from Diana and, uninhibited, approached the guests, who in turn did not seem disturbed in the slightest by his presence. They talked easily to him, every now and then turning to Diana, who stood to one side a little at a loss.

Jonathan finally returned to her with a broad smile. "They've invited us to the party afterwards. I think we should stay here for a while."

"What about the Nadi reader?"

"Ah, we're not so lucky on that score. A. Vijita was taken to hospital a few days ago. It's hardly surprising since he's eighty-five."

His mention of the hospital brought an image of Emily linked up to the life-support machines. "I hope he's not too ill."

"Dasmaya, whom I spoke to, said he'd be back on his feet eventually, but it could take a while."

That upset all their plans. Apart from the fact that, at his age, there was a possibility he might never return.

Jonathan must have seen her disappointment because he said, "People here believe that the gods are in control of everything. We'll have to trust them. The old man is almost a saint to them. If he doesn't have a good line to the gods, who does?"

"And what if he dies?"

"Then we'll find someone else who can help us. But we should think positively; that's the best way we can help Vijita."

Diana's self-consciousness among the wedding guests soon disappeared as the celebrations got into full swing. Almost like a member of the family, she soon found herself near the happy couple, who sat proudly on a wicker sofa that was richly adorned with flowers. A pair of Buddhist monks entered, and a murmur rippled through the crowd. The men, whose orange habits shone against their dark skins, fanned themselves with palm leaves as they approached the bridal couple to bless them. By way of thanks, the couple washed the monks' feet and invited them to eat with them.

During the meal, Diana couldn't take her eyes off them. She had seen Buddhist monks in the movies, but had never been in the same room as one before.

When the monks had finished, they began their ritual singing while the guests listened, enraptured, many of them in the lotus position, which Diana had never managed.

The monks eventually rose and one of them said something that caused the others to kneel before them in turn to have a white band tied round their wrists.

Diana hesitated. Did she have the right to seek a blessing? After all, she wasn't a Buddhist . . .

"Feel free to join in," Jonathan whispered. "You'll be showing respect, and it can't hurt to get a blessing from them."

Encouraged, Diana also knelt and looked at the monk, his face lined by hundreds of wrinkles. With a smile, he moved his hands in the prayer position over her brow, then tied a white band around her wrist.

"That's to bring good luck," Jonathan whispered after he, too, had received his band. "I think you'll need it in your search."

Diana nodded, then gazed at the band, thinking about the unknown Nadi reader and how much hung on his recovery.

5

Vannattuppūcci, 1887

Henry Tremayne felt strange as he entered his brother's study. Part of Richard's soul still seemed to linger there—this room looked as though he had only left it for a brief tour of the plantation. A bitter smile crossed Henry's lips. All those years he had spent hating his brother for throwing his family responsibilities to the wind. But now, recognising his traits clearly in the arrangement of the room, the books, and the writing implements on the mahogany desk, he felt an almost affection-ate pull towards Richard.

He was only too familiar with the cause of his animosity towards his brother.

Henry had dreamed of becoming a scientist—a chemist or a physicist—but since there was no one who could take care of his par-ents' estate, and his father had died shortly before he had finished his schooling at Eton, the responsibility for Tremayne House had fallen to him. While his brother enjoyed his freedom abroad and lived his adventure, such a path would forever be closed to Henry because he was dragged down by the chains that should have bound Richard.

A knock at the door tore Henry from his reflections. He glanced at the clock. It was time for his appointment.

"Enter!" he called out as he took a seat behind the desk.

As he entered, Mr. Vikrama straightened visibly then inclined his head in greeting. "Good morning, sir. I hope you had a pleasant night's sleep."

"I can only repeat what I told my butler this morning: I slept like a rock and couldn't have felt better in my own mother's lap." As Henry offered his hand for the young man to shake, he saw a smile on Vikrama's lips. Henry noticed his gaze was directed towards the window, but as he turned to look, he saw nothing.

"I'm glad to hear it, sir," Vikrama said, his expression turning serious again. "Some Europeans have problems adjusting to this country's climate."

"We had some time in Colombo to acclimatise ourselves. During the first night here I was so tired that I could have slept next to a ship's turbine. Do take a seat."

Henry indicated the chair in front of the desk. His visitor sat with a suppleness that he himself had lost over the years.

"So, you're a kind of foreman over the plantation?"

"You could call it that. Your brother was kind enough to appoint me to the position."

Henry regarded him for a moment. It was hard to believe that this cultured, obviously clever man was the son of a labourer and a Tamil!

"How long have you been in my brother's service?"

"Since I was fourteen," Vikrama replied. "But I've lived on the plantation since I was a child. My mother worked as a tea picker here, and Mr. Tremayne sent me and the other children to school so that we could learn to read and write. He believed that educated employees would be of more use than an illiterate workforce—especially in such a sensitive business as the tea trade. I think it was Mr. Taylor—from whom he acquired the first tea plants—who gave him the idea."

Henry recalled that Richard had referred to James Taylor in one of his first letters, back when he had been trying to get his brother to understand his decision and at least hold on to his affection.

Henry had pretended not to be interested, but the letter, which he had only read once, had remained so well ingrained in his mind that he could still recall how James Taylor had travelled from Calcutta to Ceylon with a trunk of seedlings in order to compete with the coffee plantations that had been the staple trade on the island at the time. Fate had been kind to him, coffee producers became tea producers, and now tea cultivation was becoming increasingly widespread.

Pushing the memory to one side, Henry cleared his throat. "And where did my brother employ these educated young people?"

"Mainly in administration. Unless a pupil turned out to be stupid." A distant memory brought a smile to Vikrama's face. "My mother always urged me to be the best. It was the only way to achieve anything. Of course, everyone else thought she was crazy, but Mr. Tremayne recognised and encouraged my abilities. It was only through him that I became the man I am now, and that's why I regret his dreadful fate so much."

"As do we all." Henry folded his hands on the desk in front of him as though about to pray. He found this unknown side to his brother as bewildering as the young man in front of him, whose abilities clearly exceeded a normal school education. "But I can assure you that my brother's spirit will live on here. The school you refer to—is it still going?"

Vikrama nodded. "Yes, sir, one of my former classmates runs it and teaches the Tamil boys all they need to know."

"What about the Sinhalese?"

A hint of contempt showed in Vikrama's eyes. "They prefer to keep among their own kind. Hardly any of the Sinhalese families are prepared to send their children to school."

"Well, in this world there must always be someone to do the more mundane work, after all." Henry rose. "I'm looking forward to your guided tour very much, and I hope you won't hold back on your knowledge about tea."

"I'll do my best."

He stood up to join Henry, and the two men left the study.

Catching her breath, Grace pressed herself against the wall of the house. Her heart was beating wildly as though she had been caught doing something forbidden.

"You must be mad!" she hissed to her sister. "I bet that Vikrama saw us."

"If so I'm sure he would have told Papa, and he would have come to the window," Victoria replied. "You should be a bit bolder. After all, it was your idea to creep after them."

Grace was about to reply, but the crunching of feet on gravel made the words stick in her throat. "They're coming!"

The two girls quickly slipped behind a white-flowered rhododendron bush from where they could peer through the twigs and watch their father and the foreman. Without a sideways glance, the men headed for the outbuilding that housed the plantation's administrative office. That didn't promise to be too exciting, so Grace decided they should wait where they were for a while until they had calmed down.

"Maybe we should go on ahead to the tea-processing sheds," Victoria suggested impatiently. "That's probably where they'll go next."

"Don't you think people will wonder why we've appeared there with no good reason?"

"They'll also ask questions if we creep around behind Papa. So let's go before the gardener discovers us here."

The dark-skinned gardener was already at work, clipping a hedge not far from their hiding place. The regular snipping of the shears could be heard clearly when the calls of the parrots in the trees dropped enough for it to be audible.

"Very well, then. Come on."

Grace stood up straight, brushed away a leaf that had attached itself to her sleeve, and smoothed her skirt. Holding her sister's hand, she set out along the path as though they were merely taking a walk. A few men passed them, their heads lowered, and a woman with an empty tea basket gave them a friendly smile.

As they approached the tea-processing sheds, they were met by an overpowering scent. The aroma that came from the tea caddies in the kitchen was a pale ghost of the real smell of tea. Tea leaves in various stages of wilting were spread out on grilles and hurdles. Some of the leaves were still fresh, giving off a green scent, while other grilles were covered with light-brown, dark-brown, and even rust-red tea leaves. Some women were sitting at tables near the sheds, rolling up the tea leaves that were at an advanced stage of wilting.

Grace and Victoria had no chance to observe anything more.

"They're coming!" whispered Victoria, whose eagle eyes had been watching the administration building. The two girls vanished behind the tea sheds, where a number of baskets were piled up.

If the women, who were concentrating on their work, had noticed them they didn't show it, nor did they interrupt their work for their new master and his foreman.

"These are the tea sheds, where the tea is still processed by hand, as is the custom in China," Vikrama explained as they looked at the building roofed with banana and palm leaves. "Once the tea has reached the right stage of wilting, it's taken to the drying ovens. Our tea master, Mr. A. Soresh, is an expert at recognising the correct degree of wilting. To date, every harvest that has left our plantation has been excellent."

Henry made no reply, but merely looked around as if some storm had carried him off to a fairy-tale land.

"He seems impressed," Grace whispered as they peered around the corner of the building. "It's not often you see Father rendered speechless."

"This Mr. Vikrama is an impressive man," Victoria replied with a wink. "It's just a pity I'm too young for him."

"You'd wish to marry a native? Mama would have a heart attack!"

"You're forgetting that Mr. Vikrama is half English. I've read that half-castes are held in very high regard here. They even have their own caste."

"Caste?"

But before Victoria could reply, their father and Vikrama set off again. Once they had turned their backs, Grace and Victoria slipped around the tea shed and reached a farther building, ducking beneath a window from which a draught of hot air escaped.

"Your brother had recently begun to introduce mechanical tea processing," Vikrama continued. "Of course, the quality is slightly inferior to that of manual production, but on the other hand we can produce larger quantities at a cheaper price, which is particularly welcomed by customers with tighter budgets."

On they went to the next building, in which a machine could be heard working. The girls didn't dare spy through any of the windows, as their father and Vikrama disappeared into the building for a while. Vikrama's explanations of how the machinery functioned were muffled by the thick mud-brick walls, and the sisters could only catch meaningless snatches of the conversation.

Once they had inspected all the buildings, Henry and Vikrama turned to the bushes, into which led a path reinforced with wooden planks.

After following the two men some way through the greenery, Grace and Victoria saw a kind of village before them—wooden huts with palm-leaf roofs. Some small children were playing with a puppy between the buildings.

"This is where our workers live."

Victoria craned her neck inquisitively. Grace dragged her back down. "They'll see us."

"Don't worry, Vikrama's talking to an old man. Have you noticed how the men wear skirts here?"

"They're called sarongs," Grace told her.

"How do you know that?" Victoria asked, surprised that her elder sister, who until recently had only been interested in balls and afternoon tea, was now a step ahead of her.

"I heard some people in the hotel talking about it. The women's dresses are called saris."

Victoria's eyes sparkled with a desire to shock her sister. "Perhaps we should wear saris, too. As you can see from their naked bellies, they don't wear corsets."

"Vic—!" Grace pressed her hand to her mouth as she watched a smile of satisfaction cross her sister's face. She had won. "You don't mean that seriously, do you? Those dresses are quite unseemly; Mama would—"

"Have a migraine. I know. But don't you think corsets are even more suffocating in this heat?"

Grace didn't reply. She, too, had ventured to lift her head a little above the tall grass. At that moment Vikrama laughed out loud. He threw his head back and laughed so uninhibitedly that even her upright father with all his suppressed emotion couldn't help but be affected. Grace had to smile, too. She would have loved so much to know what had caused his merriment.

But the moment passed and after the men had taken leave of the villagers, they returned by the same path on which they had come.

"Let's get out of here," Grace muttered to her sister. Ducking down, they ran back into the undergrowth. They didn't realise that their father could have seen them until they were sheltering beneath a bush.

Stars swirled behind Grace's eyelids as she tried to suppress her panting. She was no longer accustomed to running. By the time she opened her eyes, Victoria was peering through the branches. "They're going up towards the plantation!"

Grace wondered whether it was time to call a halt to their adventure. Apart from a few moments by the sheds, they had been unable to overhear anything, and she had begun to doubt whether they would actually find out anything about the foreman. But Victoria was aflame with excitement and so, not wanting to lose face, she rose.

"Come on, then, let's go after them!"

The walk was longer than they had anticipated and led up manmade steps reinforced with wooden planks. As her father and Vikrama climbed the steps a substantial distance ahead of them, they were having a lively conversation, and Grace was annoyed that the gentle breeze was not strong enough to carry their words back to her. The only sound was the rustling of the leaves in the trees around them; even the cries of the parrots had faded into the distance.

How far is it up to the plantation? Grace wondered as she looked up at the summit of Adam's Peak rising into the sky like a sugarloaf. A screech above their heads made her jump. The bird that circled above them looked like a bird of prey, but Grace wasn't sure.

She stopped in shock as she saw a group of tea pickers coming towards them. But Victoria drew her on.

"Just act normally, as if we should be here," she advised.

But Grace worried that the women would look at them in surprise after leaving the two men behind and coming across the girls. It almost made her miss the magnificent colours of the women's clothing. Their saris were of simple fabrics, but made up for it with their bright pinks, fiery oranges, and sunny yellows. In contrast, Grace and Victoria in their beige dresses looked like hens next to a parrot.

As they passed them, the women's quiet conversation faded into silence. Concentrating on where they placed their feet, they carried their baskets past the girls. Once they were some way past, their exotic sing-song voices resumed, reminding Grace of the meeting with the remarkable old man.

A strange shudder ran down her spine.

"Always listen to your heart, and follow what it tells you. If you don't, you will bring bad luck on yourself and those you love."

These words, to which she had not attached much importance a few days ago, suddenly paralysed her.

"What's the matter with you?" Victoria tugged at her sleeve.

"Nothing," Grace replied, perplexed. "It's nothing. Let's go after them."

Victoria looked at her uncertainly, but Grace walked on, leaving her no choice but to follow.

The tea pickers among the green tea plants looked like the first rosebuds in spring. Henry Tremayne was overcome by the magnificent greenery that was now his.

"This is the biggest of the three tea fields," Vikrama said with a sweep of his arm. "This is where we grow the tea that's rolled by hand in the sheds. The two other fields and the new one that's being cleared at the moment are intended for mechanical production. The tea in those grows more densely, but due to the higher altitude, the quality of the leaves isn't as good."

Henry looked at the young man, whose eyes lit up whenever he spoke about the tea as though he were talking about his own estate.

"You seem to feel a lot for the plantation."

"It's been my home for as long as I can remember. I can't imagine any more beautiful place in the world. Besides, the plantation provides work and food for my people. It's impossible to dislike such a place."

Henry was moved into silence. *This lad's really good. I'd almost think dangerously good, if the light in his eyes didn't show complete devotion.*

"Tell me about the tea that's grown here," he said eventually, as the silence between them threatened to become uncomfortable.

Vikrama smiled briefly, then began. "These were originally Assam plants, but thanks to Mr. Taylor's help with the grafting, we've been developing our own variety, which has even been given its own name—Ceylon."

"Like the island."

"That's right. And I can assure you that one day we'll outdo all the other varieties."

Holding their breath, Grace and Victoria listened to Vikrama's comments about the tea. Grace would have liked to remark to her sister about how impressive she found his knowledge, but they had gained on the men by too much for them to risk speaking without their father overhearing.

As the two men finally turned to go back, the sisters hid motionless among the tea plants and only stood upright again once they were out of range.

"What now?" Victoria asked, brushing a little dry tea dust from her dress.

"Let's stay here for a while," Grace said. She had no desire to be back between the stuffy walls of the house. "Maybe we could go and have a look at the elephants clearing the forest. What do you think?"

Victoria nodded, her eyes shining. Doubt crept in immediately, however. "But Mama will notice we're missing. The morning's almost over, and Miss Giles is bound to have told her that we're nowhere to be seen."

"We can tell her later where we've been. Anyway she can work it out—we did talk about the elephants yesterday. Perhaps we'll see some more of those beautiful parrots on the way."

That was enough to convince Victoria. Although the only clue they had of the direction was that the freshly cleared field lay higher up the slope, they set out determinedly along the path that led through the tea field. Every so often Grace met the eye of a tea picker, but she would immediately turn back to her work.

After a while they reached an area of forest loud with echoing cries. The slope was steep and difficult to negotiate, but there was a broad, stony path dappled with the huge footprints of elephants. A pile of sawn logs was heaped at the side of the track. They were heading in the right direction.

"Watch where you're treading," Grace warned, her own eyes glued to the ground to make sure she didn't miss any dangerous bumps. "You might roll all the way down the mountainside and end up nothing but a bag of unidentifiable bones at the bottom."

"That would be fun!" Victoria replied cheerfully. "I always wondered how dice felt."

"Dice?" Grace asked, almost getting her feet tangled in a large root that had been washed clear of soil by the rain.

"They're forever being thrown together in cups!" Victoria grinned. "Anyway you're the one who should watch your step. I'm not the one who just tripped up."

They heard voices and stopped. Soon after, three men appeared leading an elephant. It was not magnificently adorned like the temple elephants in Colombo. The chain around its front right foot, held by one of the workers, was cutting into its flesh. Grace swallowed as she noticed other signs of maltreatment on the animal. Was this why Vikrama had not brought her father here? Because he didn't want to shock him with the way the beasts of burden were handled? Victoria, too, seemed visibly shocked at the sight of the animal, its grey bark-like skin covered in streaks of blood.

"We ought to go back," Grace said, taking her sister's hand. Victoria let herself be led away without protest.

Neither of them said a word as they scrambled down the hill. Before reaching the tea field, they decided to take a different path from the one by which they had come.

Perhaps we'll see something on the way to cheer us up, Grace thought anxiously, resolving to have a word with her father about the elephants.

Still in silence, they trotted along the path. Grace noticed how much the sight of the elephant had affected her sister.

"I woke up really early this morning," Grace said finally. "I saw a brilliant-blue butterfly. You'd have loved it."

"Why didn't you wake me up, then?" Victoria asked indifferently, clearly still troubled by the images in her mind's eye. Grace immediately felt stupid. Victoria was no longer a little child who could be distracted from a bad experience by telling a pretty story.

"You were sleeping so peacefully. And it was still really early. But I'm sure it'll be back. Then—"

Suddenly a rider shot out of the bushes. Victoria cried out in shock. Grace hesitated a moment then grabbed her wrist. She managed to pull her sister aside just in time to prevent her from being trampled beneath the horse's hooves. The bay horse reared up in fright as the rider desperately tried to stay in the saddle. It took a while for him to get his mount back under control. "Bloody hell, children! What on earth are you doing here?"

The man, whose eyes were blazing with anger, had dark hair and a beard. His clothes and his accent revealed him to be a member of the English upper class.

Grace straightened her back and smoothed her dress. "I'm sorry, sir. We're newly arrived here and we hadn't expected to see anyone on the path."

The man examined her from head to foot. The anger in his expression faded a little. "You must belong to the new family. You're Tremaynes, I assume."

Grace nodded. The man dismounted and came over to them without taking his eyes from hers.

"My name is Daniel Stockton. I'm pleased to make your acquaintance, Miss . . . ?"

"Tremayne. Grace Tremayne. This is my younger sister, Victoria."

The man took her hand and kissed it lightly before turning to Victoria with a smile. "Please forgive me for almost riding you into the ground. But it's so rare that one meets anyone else up here, and I fear I've adopted the dangerous riding habits of the natives. You should see the way they drive their carts."

Grace didn't reply. Something about the man made her uneasy. His smell? The way he smiled? The strange spark in his eyes?

"May I accompany you home, perhaps?" His smile grew broader as he found what he had clearly been looking for in her expression. "As you've seen, it can be quite dangerous around here. I'd hate to think of anything happening to my neighbour's two delightful daughters."

"That's very kind of you," Grace replied stiffly, "but we wouldn't want to keep you from your business, since you were obviously in such a hurry. We've found our way here; we can find our way back again. Good day, Mr. Stockton."

Grace took her sister by the hand and led her away. She could feel the man's eyes boring into her back until he finally mounted up and rode away. Her fear that he might overtake them was proved unfounded, as he disappeared down a side track.

"Why were you so mean to him?" Victoria asked after they had walked side by side for a while.

"He almost mowed you down!" Grace said, striding purposefully on ahead. "And then he dares to pass the blame on to us!"

"But he apologised. Just think; he knew we'd arrived! Once he found out who we were he was friendly enough."

"Too friendly, if you ask me," Grace said irritably. She had no idea herself what had antagonised her towards him; she wasn't usually so quick to take against a new acquaintance. "If you ask me, it's nothing special that he knew of our family's arrival. Everyone around here probably knows by now. Did you see all the villas on the way here? The people who live there are just waiting for something new to happen. Just you wait, one day we'll be like that and fall on anyone who moves to this mountain."

6

Nuwara Eliya, 2008

The next morning, Diana and Jonathan were driven by a wedding guest to a small railway station, from where they were to take a train to Nuwara Eliya. When the train appeared, wreathed in clouds of smoke, it was already quite crowded, but the people accepted the cramped conditions with good grace, and no one complained whenever Diana or Jonathan accidentally bumped into them.

After a few stations some seats became vacant, so they no longer had to stand.

"Nuwara Eliya is also known as 'Little England,'" Jonathan said as the train passed through a landscape of green hills. "I'm sure you can imagine why."

Diana was captivated by the view. Here and there the greenery was punctuated by white dots, which would not have been here two hundred years ago.

"That villa up there is in the English style," she replied with a smile. "Tremayne House looks similar to that, except the landscape around it isn't as beautiful."

"There are a lot of villas like that here—more than there are tea plantations. There was a time when this country was very popular with the English as it was such a stark contrast to their cool homeland. The monsoon rains may even have reminded them of their own weather, which made them feel at home. And, unlike the coast, in this region it's never sweltering."

"You sound as though you've been here before," Diana said with a smile—with his in-depth knowledge, he could have been a travel guide.

"I've lived here for quite a while, and nothing pleases the local people more than showing off their country to a foreigner."

"But you can hardly be called a foreigner with your ancestry."

"Nevertheless, I only have English and Indian citizenship, not Sri Lankan. I'm just as much a foreigner as you are. With a residence permit, of course." After looking briefly out of the window he added, "You haven't really picked the best time to come; the monsoon will be starting any time now."

"I wasn't intending to stay very long. Just long enough to find out a little about my family."

Jonathan smiled enigmatically, but he said nothing.

The train pulled into a small station at the foot of the mountain. "This is where we get off," Jonathan said. He fished their bags from the overstuffed baggage rack, which had been bulging dangerously the whole time as it swung above their heads.

It proved difficult to make their way between the other passengers, but fortunately the train driver wasn't in a hurry. He waited patiently until all those who were crowding around the exits had left the train and the conductor gave the signal. As the train, with its heavy, loudly chattering cargo, pulled away from the platform, Jonathan and Diana left the station and turned on to a winding sandy track, following a sign that directed them towards the Hill Club Hotel.

"That's one of the oldest hotels here. It's been providing accommodation for travellers since colonial times. I think it will make a good base for your search."

"There wouldn't happen to be a Nadi reader here, would there?"

"No, I'm sure there won't be—all you'll find here are plenty of signs of English visitors from the past. But I'm sure Vijita will get well enough to leave hospital. You've seen all the offerings they placed at the shrine for him. And our medicine is as modern as anywhere, at least in Colombo. And since that's where he is, you don't need to worry—he'll decipher your leaf as soon as he can."

Perhaps I would have been better off going to the library in Colombo, she thought, but then recalled Jonathan's objection. Of course the readers there would not be pleased if she asked them to decipher a leaf that had been stolen.

After they had walked uphill for a quarter of an hour, the hotel came into view between the trees. The sunshine gave its façade the appearance of a pearl on green velvet.

"Turn around!" Jonathan said suddenly. Diana obeyed and was rewarded with a breathtaking view. The green hills nestled together like lovers who never wanted to be separated.

"Our station must be somewhere down there."

Looking to where Jonathan was pointing, all Diana could see were the rails that snaked through the hills like a vein.

"It looks a little like the Scottish Highlands," Diana observed with a smile as she turned back to Jonathan. As she did so, she noticed that he had been watching her the whole time. He looked away as though embarrassed.

"True, except our temperatures are a bit better than Scotland, especially in winter."

"You're right there!"

Entering the hotel grounds reminded Diana of returning to Tremayne House. The building was similarly dilapidated, maybe a little further gone, since there didn't seem to be a wizard like Mr. Green to care for the house and garden. The gardens laid out below the sun terrace must once have been magnificent, but were now overgrown. Yet the terrace itself gave the impression that at any moment a gentleman in a stiff high collar and frock coat would appear around the corner to enjoy a gin and a good Indonesian cigar in the shade.

The holidaymakers enjoying themselves here looked as though they came mainly from Asian countries. Diana saw a few Japanese and a couple who were probably from Thailand. Two Americans made themselves known by talking loudly in their unmistakable accents.

At the reception, which looked the same as it must have done a hundred and fifty years ago, Jonathan and Diana were greeted by a smartly dressed young man whose white shirt was bright against his dark skin.

"What can I do for you?" he asked in strongly accented English.

Jonathan asked in the local language for two rooms, and the young man hurried to an old-fashioned key rack where a few tarnished brass keys were hanging. There was no sign of modern card keys or those strange heavy keyrings, so common in Europe, that made it impossible to keep your room key in your handbag.

"He says he only has rooms available on two separate storeys," Jonathan said. "Would you prefer the higher or lower one?"

"I don't mind at all."

Jonathan smiled. "OK, then you can have the upper room. You'll see more of the wonderful view from there."

When the receptionist returned with the keys, he asked Jonathan to sign the visitors' book. Once that was done he rang a bell to summon a young man to lead Diana to her room.

"Shall we meet down here in an hour's time?" Jonathan asked as he shouldered his bag.

Diana nodded and followed the bellhop up the lightly curving staircase.

The room's furnishings were nowhere near as modern as the ones in the Grand Oriental in Colombo, but Diana was immediately captivated by its charm. It had a ceiling fan like those that circled lazily overhead in the old movies, watching the lives that played out below them.

Jonathan had not exaggerated about the view. The tea plantations and individual villas that dotted the sunlit landscape looked like a photo from a travel brochure.

Did Jonathan come here with his wife? she found herself wondering, but then she reminded herself that he must have divorced before going freelance.

After unpacking her bag, she undressed and took a shower. As the pleasantly warm water trickled over her skin, she let her thoughts wander. *I ought to get in touch with the office,* her conscience whispered, but at that moment she was looking forward so much to what she might find on the tea plantation that she had no desire at all to think of work.

As they had agreed, they met at one o'clock in the lobby. Jonathan had also enjoyed a shower and smelled pleasantly of sandalwood and lemon.

"I took the liberty of reserving us a seat on the terrace. I wouldn't be surprised to find a cup of iced tea waiting for us there already."

The air outside had changed during the last hour. Its smell reminded Diana of a fall of rain after a spell of long hot summer days, when nature was thirsting for a refreshing downpour that seeped away into the ground all too soon.

"I'm afraid we'll have to hurry with our walk to the plantation. If I'm not mistaken, the monsoon will be upon us soon, and then we'll be caught in the rain for a good month."

If Diana were honest, she would have nothing against that. But an attack of common sense drove the thought away as she reminded herself of her responsibilities in the office.

"I have something for you," Jonathan said once they had taken their seats. He reached into his pocket and drew out a brown envelope.

Diana raised her eyebrows in surprise. "What is it?"

"Some information I've found about the tea plantation. I could have given it to you earlier, but I thought it more appropriate to hand it over once we were on the spot."

Diana smiled. "Thank you very much."

"I must admit it's refreshing to have a break from dealing with the subject of terrorism in this country. I've reached that chapter and it's anything but cheerful."

"The attack at the airport was three years ago, wasn't it?" She was momentarily distracted from her eagerness to examine the contents of the envelope by her equally keen interest in the history of the country.

Jonathan nodded. "Yes, and since then we've had to introduce many new security measures. The south and west of the country have largely been protected by the Tigers, but we mustn't be careless."

"You mean the Tamil Tigers?"

Jonathan nodded. "Here they're usually just called the Tigers. It's strange to think that an organisation formed to fight for the rights of the Tamils became a terrorist organisation that doesn't shrink from attacks, murders, and abductions."

Hence the terrorist warnings, Diana thought. When preparing and researching for her trip she had largely ignored the brochure with the safety instructions.

"Does anyone actually know the cause of this conflict?"

"There have been tensions since long before the colonial era. During British rule the Tamils, who had migrated here from southern India, were literate and given preferential treatment. They were appointed to administrative positions, were made foremen of the plantations, and became senior officials in the cities. The Sinhalese, on the other hand, were always terribly exploited as workers. They see the higher-status Tamils as the agents of their oppressors. When the colonial period ended and the British withdrew, the anger of the Sinhalese, who were more numerous, was aimed at the Tamils. In 1983 there was a dreadful pogrom against the Tamils, and in the years that followed there were even attempts to prevent them from using their own language. That was when the Tamil Tigers were born."

Diana had only vague memories of conflicts in southern India and Sri Lanka.

"Nowadays, Tamils and Sinhalese live peacefully together once again in this part of Sri Lanka. But in the north there are strong demands for an independent Tamil state. The government isn't likely to agree to that any day soon. They probably never will."

In the brief pause that followed, Diana wondered how deep the scars ran in both ethnic groups. Would they ever really be able to find peace?

"With your knowledge you'd make a really good journalist," she said.

Jonathan nodded. "Probably. But believe me, once I've finished this project I'm going to return to ancient history. After all, I'm a historian. Have you ever heard of the Kingdom of Kandy?"

"It was somewhere near here, wasn't it?"

Jonathan nodded. "Yes. That's going to be my next project. I'm going to follow the trail of the old kings and do some research at the famous Temple of the Tooth. It's said that a molar of Buddha himself is kept there as a relic." He smiled dreamily as though he couldn't wait to begin his work, before adding, "Every now and then you need some light relief."

"I doubt that researching into an ancient kingdom will necessarily be easy."

"You have to know where to search. If you do, you'll find what you're looking for. And I believe the Vannattuppūcci Tea Company will be a treasury of information."

He took a pile of papers from the envelope he'd brought her and selected a leaflet that had a small paragraph on the history of the plantation.

Jonathan tapped his finger in a certain place and grinned at her.

"That can't be true!" Diana cried out in amazement.

"It seems it is. I'd bet the whole of the fee from my book on the fact that you'll find what you're looking for."

In the evening, Diana and Jonathan got their things together for the climb to the tea plantation. There was no public transport out there, but Jonathan had found a man in the hotel who would drive them up to a certain point.

Diana was excited by the prospect of finally seeing the place where her great-great-grandmother had once lived.

What would she find there? Had any of the files survived the passage of time? Or would she find nothing at all?

A knock at the door tore her from her thoughts.

"Come in," she said, assuming it was a maid come to stock up the minibar.

"Ah, you're almost packed."

Jonathan leaned against the door with a smile. Diana straightened up and brushed a lock of hair from her face.

"Yes, I've got the essentials together. I wonder if we'll find anything at the plantation."

"Even if we don't, at least you'll have seen the place where your ancestors lived. It's very important to find your roots."

Diana smiled. "I could do with a generous helping of your optimism."

Jonathan spread his arms. "I think I've got enough for us both."

She would have loved to sink into his embrace, even though she knew it was not an invitation to a hug, but a mere gesture to emphasise his words. She scolded herself. *You're still a married woman. Your marriage may be over, but even so, you shouldn't simply throw yourself at him.*

In any case Jonathan didn't seem to have been expecting her to respond to his gesture.

"Anyway, I'm not here to oversee your packing," he said. "I've discovered something you should take a look at. It could move your research a step forward."

"What's that?"

"You'll see. Come down into the club."

Diana raised her eyebrows in surprise. "Am I allowed to just go in there?" She meant the question in jest, since anyone knew that most of the private clubs now also accepted women, or at least tolerated them on the premises.

"Of course, especially since you'll be in the company of a man! An evening dress would be appropriate, though, if you're going to put in an appearance down there."

"An evening dress?" Diana said. "Do you mean that, or is it one of your little jokes?"

"I think the club requires a certain degree of elegance among its members. At least, they offered to lend me a tie before I could enter the club room. Curiosity about this historic place got the better of me and I let myself be talked into wearing it."

Diana looked at his open shirt collar. "So where's the tie now?"

"Sadly, I had to give it back. But the doorman of the club will probably offer the same one to me again. Or a similarly absurd one."

"Fine, I'll be right with you!"

As Diana closed the door and hurried over to the wardrobe, which was now relieved of her hiking gear, she wondered what on earth Jonathan could have discovered here. Or was this simply one of his ruses to convince her to spend an enjoyable evening with him?

After picking out the same outfit she had worn at the Grand Oriental Hotel, she went to the door again.

Jonathan was leaning on the wall opposite. He looked her up and down, reminding her of Philipp on their early dates, back when she had hardly been able to believe her luck—a feeling that had completely vanished by now.

"I know this isn't an evening dress," she said, a little embarrassed even though she could tell from his expression that he was far from unsatisfied with her appearance. "But you don't think they'll refuse me entry because of it, do you?"

"I'm sure it'll be fine if you agree to wear a tie with it."

Diana laughed out loud; she loved his British humour.

She had been expecting some kind of doorman outside the club, but obviously not the burly kind of bouncer who guarded the entrances to German clubs and discos. The doorman indicated Jonathan's lack of tie politely, but firmly, without any indication that he'd seen him before only a short while ago.

The ties in the small cupboard were indeed the most dreadful Diana had ever seen. They probably dated from the seventies and eighties, with clumsy patterns and garish colours. Nevertheless, as far as she could tell they were clean and neat, so they could be worn without worrying about the previous wearer's sweat.

It must have been Jonathan's sense of humour that caused him to pick out the most repulsive one—yellow and turquoise stripes with a pink diamond pattern in the yellow sections.

"If a bomb exploded in the club it wouldn't be louder than your tie," Diana murmured to Jonathan as soon as they were past the doorman. She found it hard to stop herself from bursting out laughing again.

"I knew you'd appreciate my refinement and good taste."

With a grin he led her between the club members, some of whom stared at them with undisguised amazement. She wasn't sure if they were more concerned about her lack of evening dress or Jonathan's tie, which didn't match the rest of his clothing at all.

But no one said a word, and if they had Diana wouldn't have responded as her eyes were glued to a wall hung with old photographs showing the members of the Hill Club in the hotel's heyday. Her hunch was confirmed by Jonathan just a few moments later.

"Look at the names beneath these pictures," he said, pointing at an old photo protected behind glass, in a condition similar to her photo of Grace. In this one, however, the people were shown clearly enough to be able to make out their features.

Most of the men, dressed in elegant suits, looked a little strained, partly because it wasn't usual at the time to smile for the camera, and partly because a long exposure was needed to take a photograph.

Her heart beating hard, Diana scanned the names. Emmerson Walbury, Trent Jennings, Daniel Stockton, Henry Tremayne . . .

She counted until she found the fourth man from the left. Henry Tremayne was tall and light-haired.

"It can't be true!" she exclaimed.

"It seems like it is," Jonathan replied. "Your ancestor seems to have been a member of the club. I hope you realise that only the most well-respected members of society were accepted here."

"I can imagine. It was the same in England. And still is, to some extent."

Jonathan allowed her a little time to look at the photo.

"How do you feel?" he asked then.

Diana had to admit that it sent shivers down her spine. "As though I were looking through a window on to the past," she replied. "Do you think it would be possible to have a copy? As far as I know this is the only picture in existence of my great-great-great-grandfather. Somehow it failed to reach the family gallery at Tremayne House."

"It probably will. I'll ask the doorman later. He owes me a favour for inflicting this tie on me."

"But you picked the tie out yourself!" Diana replied with a grin.

"Did you see what there was to choose from? Each one was more horrific than the last!" Jonathan smiled broadly. "Wait a moment; I'll just go and ask him. With a little encouragement he should grant you your wish."

Before Diana could object that if he was going to bribe the doorman, he ought to use her money, he had gone.

Not ten minutes later Diana was holding a copy of the photo in her hands. For a price of twenty dollars the doorman had readily agreed to take the photo down himself and leave his post to take a copy. It was incredibly good.

"That was way too much!" Diana said reproachfully.

"You think so? I think it was a more than reasonable price to pay for another clue. Or at least to know what your ancestor looked like."

She studied the photo. This was what the high society of tea barons and colonial merchants looked like. She could see clearly that the club had hardly been altered, only renovated. Overall, it was just as it had been.

If only I knew what happened between you and Grace, she said silently to Henry Tremayne as she traced his features with her finger. *What led to you break off relations with your daughter and disinherit her?*

She spent the rest of the evening with Jonathan in the club over iced tea and a light meal consisting mainly of local fruits. The topic of the plantation and what could have happened in her ancestors' days seemed inexhaustible, and it was only when they were discreetly told that the club was about to close that they thought about going to bed.

Although it wasn't strictly necessary, Jonathan walked her back to her room. "You never know what unscrupulous ruffians might be lying in wait for a lady at this time of night."

Laughing, she reminded him that they weren't living in the times of Henry Tremayne—although she had to admit that the hotel gave the impression that time had stood still.

When Diana finally lay down on her bed, she heard rain pattering against the windowpane. The monotonous noise soon lulled her into a deep sleep.

7

Vannattuppŭcci, 1887

Grace's hopes that she wouldn't see the insolent Mr. Stockton again were dashed the very next morning. Over breakfast, between the porridge with honey and brown sugar that Mr. Wilkes had sent for from Nuwara Eliya and the wonderful little cakes to which even her mother had become accustomed, her father suddenly announced, "Yesterday I had a very pleasant meeting with one of our neighbours. He's called Daniel Stockton, and he owns the plantation to the west of ours. He went out of his way to speak to me. Isn't that nice?"

"Oh, very nice," Claudia said. "Did you have an interesting conversation?"

"Very friendly. I think he must have adopted the local tradition of hospitality because without further ado he offered to send one of his workers over to help with the forest clearance."

Had that been before or after Grace and Victoria encountered him? Grace turned bright red and looked at Victoria, who raised her eyebrows in surprise.

"He also told me that he had already had the pleasure of meeting my daughters," their father added. "You didn't mention it. Or that you refused his offer to accompany you home."

Grace cleared her throat. "I didn't consider it important. He came within a whisker of riding Victoria down."

"Didn't he apologise?" their mother asked.

As if that were the most important thing, Grace thought grimly. *What about Victoria? Shouldn't you be asking whether she was hurt?*

"Of course he apologised, and we accepted his apology," Grace replied before turning back to her plate.

"He didn't say anything about a collision. Are you all right, Victoria?"

"Of course, Papa. Grace pulled me out of the way just in time. And she was angry with him then because he could have trampled me dead."

With a rush of relief, Grace looked at her sister, who gave her a brief wink.

"Oh, it seems we have a heroine in the family."

"It wasn't a heroic act, Papa," Grace demurred. "I was only doing my duty and taking care of my sister."

"What were you doing up there anyway?" Claudia asked, her eyes moving between her daughters with a searching look.

"We wanted to see the elephants at work clearing the forest," Victoria said, beating her sister to an answer. "You promised we could, Papa."

"And we found that one of the elephants is in quite a bad state," Grace burst out. She had somehow forgotten to raise the subject the evening before. "I think the workers are mistreating their animals. You really should do something about it."

Her father looked at her rather curiously.

Grace realised she was coming across as snappish—which was definitely not her intention. If she wanted to help the elephants she should go about it with more subtlety and not risk her father closing his ears to her entreaties.

But the mere thought of Stockton staring at her again with those eyes unsettled her deeply.

"I'll take care of the elephants," Henry said coolly, giving his daughters a penetrating look. "Is there any other cause for your resentment?"

Yes, Stockton, Grace thought angrily. "I'm not sleeping very well. It must be the air here."

"You'll have to get used to it. And to everything else."

"Well, I think it would have been polite if you had accepted Mr. Stockton's offer of help," Claudia said in an attempt to get back to the previous topic of conversation, as she feared a row at the breakfast table.

Help? Grace thought scornfully. *He kissed my hand in a completely improper manner.* The way he had looked at her still seemed to cling to her skin. He was at least twenty years older than she was! "I considered it better to refuse. In any case, when we're out I'm the one who's responsible for Victoria."

Grace couldn't fail to notice the look her mother and father exchanged. But instead of scolding her for her tone, Henry set his teacup down and said, "It doesn't sound as though you warmed to Mr. Stockton. But hopefully things will change. I've invited him to tea with us this afternoon. Would that be all right for you, darling?"

Claudia's eyes shone at the prospect of having a visitor at last. "But of course it's all right! We ought to take the opportunity to invite his family on another occasion as well. He *is* married, isn't he?"

"Yes, he is, and he has a son. He's a little older than Grace, and sees to the administration of their plantation."

"I'll send out an invitation today. If you have nothing against it."

"It can't do any harm to get to know our neighbours a little."

Henry turned back to his breakfast. Grace sat motionless as if rooted to the spot, before reminding herself that a lady kept her emotions under control and hid her feelings.

If I raise any objection, I'll only make matters worse. It's almost as if this afternoon tea is a punishment for my behaviour.

Her parents seemed satisfied by her silence.

Only Victoria recognised that she was still angry, and when they were walking around the garden after breakfast, she asked, "Is it so bad that he's coming here? He didn't really do anything; he was only trying to be nice. First impressions can be deceiving sometimes. Anyway it's Mama who'll be the centre of attention over tea. He'll hardly remember you, and it'll be over before you know it."

"You're right." Grace lowered her head in embarrassment. "I don't know what got into me. Sometimes I . . . I mean, sometimes I think I can sense when someone's being dishonest. He was a little over-friendly for a first meeting, don't you think? And then the way he kissed my hand! The moment before he'd been looking at us as though he wanted to thrash us with his riding crop."

"You're right there. But Papa wouldn't have reacted any differently if someone had run out in front of his horse. You know what dreadful accidents can happen. Just think of Uncle Richard."

"He fell from Adam's Peak, not from a horse."

"A fall is a fall!" Victoria insisted. Something distracted her. "Oh, look, here comes Mr. Vikrama! Do you think I should ask him if he'll catch me a parrot?"

"You'd be better off concentrating on catching butterflies."

"But a parrot would look wonderful in Mama's drawing room!"

"Then you should try and catch a red one. Miss Giles said yesterday that they've ordered red silk from India."

As though he had noticed them looking across at him, Vikrama turned, briefly raised his hand in greeting and smiled.

"So, what does your intuition tell you about him?"

Grace looked away quickly. "What do you mean?"

"What do you think of Mr. Vikrama?"

"I've never spoken a word to him, so I can't say."

"But we watched him with Father. He seemed very nice to me."

"I don't think your ability to judge is mature enough to say." Grace knew full well that a minor argument was a good way of changing the subject.

"My ability to judge?" Victoria rose to the bait. "You're one to talk! Your experience of the world is as limited as mine!"

"But I've been around for five years longer than you."

"Four!" Victoria corrected her. "And Mr. Norris always says that intuition and insight into human nature have nothing to do with age. Even very young people can tell which way the wind's blowing."

"I'm sure he didn't say that."

"No, but he implied it. And I feel fully mature." Victoria raised her chin defiantly, but Grace had no desire to continue the argument. Her gaze was still on Vikrama. Two women were talking to him, gesticulating wildly. What was that about?

It was impossible to tell from that distance, and she didn't want to go any nearer. But she suddenly wondered whether Vikrama had a wife, or at least a fiancée. He was the right age, and he was handsome enough for her to imagine him with a wife. The tea pickers were probably all crazy about him, as his position on the plantation also made him a good catch.

"Grace, are you daydreaming?" Victoria asked, pinching her arm.

Grace looked at her in surprise, only noticing the pain a moment later.

"What's that about?"

Victoria smiled mischievously. "I asked you whether you think he'll ever arrive."

"Who?"

"Mr. Norris. If not, we'll have to pair poor Miss Giles off with one of the local people. Maybe even with Mr. Vikrama."

Grace tried to hide the pang of jealousy she felt.

"I don't think she'd want him. He's not an Englishman, after all."

Her gaze wandered back to Vikrama, who had taken his leave of the women with a smile and was now heading for the administration building. "No, he really isn't the man for her."

That afternoon, Grace was sitting with her mother and Victoria in the drawing room, as they all waited for the arrival of her father and Mr. Stockton. Back home, Grace had always loved it when visitors came to Tremayne House. Every now and then they included writers and artists, usually introduced by acquaintances. Now all she could think about was how the collar of her pink afternoon dress irritated her skin and how much the time dragged, as if someone had laid a curse on them as they waited.

What would Stockton have to say? The question didn't inspire Grace especially. He would probably rattle on at boring length about tea cultivation and then ask inquisitive questions, such as whether she had been presented at her debut. And she would be struck by the desire to strangle him with his ascot.

Hoofbeats were heard outside, and all three Tremayne ladies took a deep breath. The visitor had arrived. Tea would soon be served. Grace glanced surreptitiously at the clock. One hour. Maybe two. Then he would leave and she would have time to write to her friend Eliza Thornton, who was at this moment probably sweating her way through a dancing lesson, eager to embark on the ball season.

As the butler's voice echoed down the hall, Grace looked across at her sister. They had agreed in advance that they would both keep an eye on Stockton and compare notes about their impressions afterwards.

Stockton entered alone. Where was their father? Bewildered, the sisters looked at one another.

"Ah, Mr. Stockton!" Claudia cried out and rose to greet her guest. "I'm delighted to meet you. My husband has already told us so much about you."

"I hope it's all good," he replied gallantly, without paying the slightest attention to Grace and Victoria. "It would be a shame if I didn't prove worthy of your hospitality."

"You have nothing to fear if my first impression is anything to go by," Claudia replied coquettishly. She turned to her daughters. "May I introduce Grace and Victoria."

"I've already had the pleasure," Stockton replied with a small bow. "I hope you've both now recovered from your fright."

"Of course we have, Mr. Stockton," Victoria replied, looking at her sister. Grace forced a smile. *Maybe I've judged him unfairly,* she thought. *I mustn't cause trouble for Mother.*

"We're well aware there was no bad intention on your part," she said, offering him her hand. Stockton smiled as he took it.

"I'm glad to hear it. I would be inconsolable if I'd upset you in any way."

"You most certainly haven't," Claudia broke in. "My daughter is simply a little impulsive and naturally protective of her younger sister."

"All good characteristics in a future wife," Stockton said, still smiling and giving a light-hearted bow.

Fortunately, this concluded the pleasantries, and Claudia led their guest to the tea table.

"Please excuse the fact that the cakes are a little different from what you will be used to. My brother-in-law neglected to instruct the cook on how to bake proper scones."

"I don't think your brother-in-law is to blame for that," Stockton replied. "My cook is also somewhat unconventional, but she's very hardworking, and that's what counts in my opinion."

As they sat to the table, Grace felt a strange tension. Stockton had not yet done anything to cause her displeasure, but there was something in the air, like an approaching storm building up before finally discharging itself with sudden force. Was it because of his remark about a future wife? She didn't actually have anything against marriage, and after all, the fortune teller had predicted a wedding for her . . .

"I'm very sorry about what happened to your brother-in-law," Stockton said. "It was a shock for us all, and I can assure you personally that I don't give any credence to the malicious rumours that have been flaring up every now and then."

Malicious rumours? Grace looked from Victoria to her mother. But as ever, Claudia was a picture of self-control. If the remark had affected her in any way, she didn't show it, and her manners prevented her from asking about the rumours.

She rang the bell, and one of the Tamil maids whom Claudia had appointed to serve the meals appeared. She didn't have the efficiency of English maids, but under her mistress's stern gaze she made every possible effort.

Stealing a furtive glance at Mr. Stockton, Grace noticed his eyes following the maid in her bright-blue sari.

"You allow your servants to wear traditional clothing. That's very progressive of you."

A faint blush tinged Claudia's pale face.

"Unfortunately we've discovered that there isn't a single maid's uniform in the house. My brother-in-law clearly allowed the staff to work in traditional clothes. But proper uniforms should be arriving on the next ship to reach Colombo."

"It wasn't meant as a criticism," Stockton replied, as he stirred his tea and breathed in the aroma. "I find the women's clothing delightful. They're almost as colourful as the parrots in the trees. With all the green that surrounds us, a few splashes of colour are very welcome, wouldn't you say?"

As he drank, Grace looked at her mother. *Does she still think he's nice now?* Back in England, remarking on the clothing of the servants quite definitely implied a criticism of the hostess.

"Your tea is truly excellent," Stockton said after trying it. "Yes, I can say with a touch of envy that this harvest even surpasses my own. First flush, isn't it?"

Claudia looked baffled. "Forgive me if I'm unable to reply. I haven't yet familiarised myself with tea cultivation."

"Oh, I'm sorry if I've caused you embarrassment. I've been familiar with tea growing since my youth, and I frequently let slip jargon without thinking that others might not understand me."

"What is the first flush, Mr. Stockton?" Victoria asked inquisitively.

"It's one of the four picking seasons." Stockton's gaze was fixed on Grace as though he would have expected this question from her. She lowered her eyelashes nervously, but could still see that the man was smiling. "It's mainly used for Darjeeling, but it's also common to differentiate the picking seasons for Assam. The variety of tea grown here is mainly Assam, even though we now call it Ceylon."

She recalled the explanations Vikrama had given to her father, which made her smile. Needless to say, Stockton noticed.

"Your daughter is truly charming, Mrs. Tremayne. Has she had her debut yet?"

Grace hadn't expected the question to come so soon. Fortunately, he had not asked her, but her mother.

Claudia looked nonplussed. "No, unfortunately we didn't have time for it. My brother-in-law's death was a frightful surprise for us all. But we're planning to catch up next year, once the situation here has stabilised somewhat."

"Well, if that's the case, I can tell you now that the young lady should find a good dressmaker. The Nuwara Eliya society is small, but very particular. With a beautiful dress, your daughter would without doubt be in a position to catch the eye of any young man here."

"You're too kind, Mr. Stockton," Claudia replied, clearly flattered. "Perhaps your wife can advise me on the choice of dressmaker."

"It will be her pleasure."

Grace finally felt his eyes moving away from her. But that didn't mean that Stockton stopped focusing on her as a topic of conversation.

"What do you think about your daughters meeting my children?" he began after trying a piece of cake. "George is twenty and Clara fourteen. I believe they'd get on well."

Grace knew what his stares meant. *He's measuring me up like a brood mare.*

She felt like jumping up and leaving the room, but held on to her self-control. Nevertheless, her silent wish for the afternoon tea to come to an end became all the more urgent.

"We would find that a great pleasure, Mr. Stockton," she heard her mother reply. "I'm planning a small house-warming reception. But before I do, I need to introduce myself to the other ladies."

"I think it will be enough for you to send them invitations. I can assure you that my wife is bursting with curiosity about you. News spreads fast in Nuwara Eliya, and the ladies are all eager to meet you."

The way he stared at her convinced Grace that he was keen to pair her off with his son. But before he could go on, they heard steps approaching the drawing room. A moment later her father came through the door.

"Daniel, what a pleasure to see you here!" Henry greeted his guest warmly, and Grace only just managed to suppress a sigh of relief at the thought that Stockton's attention would now turn to their father and the tea plantation. But she was mistaken.

"Please forgive me for being late," her father said as he took a seat. "I had to go out to the new field to set matters straight. My daughter had drawn my attention to an irregularity."

"An irregularity?"

As though he knew from whom the information came, Stockton looked at Grace again.

"One of the elephants was injured, and the girls were afraid that the workers might have mistreated him. However, the animal sustained the injury in a fight with another bull elephant. My workers have decided to use him in another location to prevent any further conflicts."

Henry looked at his daughter, causing her to blush.

The afternoon tea went on almost into the evening. Grace had to use the pretext of a slight dizzy spell to extricate herself from Stockton's company. At least there was no more talk of marriage or debuts, but she nevertheless felt incredibly relieved when she couldn't feel Stockton's eyes on her any more.

She stepped outside, intending to go for a walk and let the wind blow Stockton out of her head, and immediately bumped into Mr. Vikrama, who was on his way into the house.

"Excuse me, miss," he said once he had collected himself. "I didn't intend—"

"I'm the one who should apologise, Mr. Vikrama," Grace said quickly. "I should have looked where I was going. I almost knocked you over."

They were silent for a moment, then she said, "Did you want to see my father? He's with Mr. Stockton in the drawing room."

"Oh," he said and took a step back. "Then I'd better come back another time."

"Why should you?" Grace said. "If it's important, my father won't mind being disturbed."

"It isn't," Vikrama replied, looking at her as though he had already said too much. "I'll discuss it with him later. There's no hurry."

He turned to go, but Grace held him back. "Mr. Vikrama!"

"Yes?" he asked, his gaze sending a rush of warmth through her veins, making her forget what she had been going to say. *Or had she actually been going to say anything?* At a loss, she struggled to find the right words, finally coming up with something that wouldn't make him think she'd lost her mind.

"My sister has fallen in love with the parrots. Do you think you could show her how to catch one?"

His expression mixing incredulity and surprise, he replied, "Of course I can. But I must tell you that the birds are anything but happy in cages and aviaries. They love flying with their flock, and even the most beautiful ones are all the more delightful if you catch sight of them by chance in the palm trees."

Grace felt a lump in her throat. She had a mental image of her acquaintance's deranged bird. It was probably truly crazy—crazy with longing.

"But if your sister would like to see a parrot up close, I can arrange that."

His warm smile drove away her concerns that she had offended him.

"That would be really kind," she said. "If I'm honest, I'd also like to see more of a parrot than its underside. I promise you we'll release it once we've had a good look."

Vikrama nodded with a smile and was about to turn away again when something else occurred to Grace.

"Please could you explain to me about the tea picking seasons? Mr. Stockton said something about a first flush."

Vikrama's face lit up with the same smile she had noticed when he was talking to her father. Was it really possible for a man to have so many different kinds of smile? Grace was bewildered, so much so that she almost missed what he was saying.

"Have you got a few moments spare?" he asked. "We shouldn't really be talking like this on the steps."

"Of course!"

Grace followed him down the steps into the gardens, towards the rhododendrons where she and Victoria had hidden to listen.

"So you want to learn something about growing tea?" he asked.

Grace nodded, completely off her guard. She'd expected him to launch straight into his explanation. "I'll be living here from now on, won't I? So I ought to know something about the tea. Since I don't have a brother, not yet at least, I could even be mistress of Vannattuppūcci one day."

Another thought suddenly flashed through her mind. "What does *Vannattuppūcci* actually mean?" she asked before Vikrama could respond to her previous words. "It's your native language, isn't it?"

Vikrama nodded. "It means *butterfly*. Your uncle noticed that we have a great many beautiful specimens here on the plantation. He named the estate accordingly."

"I saw a lovely butterfly a few days ago—a gorgeous blue one. Sadly, it had gone as quickly as it came."

"Some people believe that butterflies are the souls of the dead. The Hindus believe that in the next life a person can be reincarnated as an animal, not necessarily a human. Maybe the one you saw was your uncle wanting to see who had moved on to the plantation."

Grace liked this idea, even though she didn't feel any kind of bond with Uncle Richard. But a hint of real sadness flashed in Vikrama's eyes. He had clearly been really fond of her uncle.

But he only let his feelings show for a brief moment.

"Well, I think he'd be delighted by his niece's interest in his life's work. You wanted to know about the picking seasons, didn't you?"

Grace nodded, and Vikrama explained that there were four harvest seasons. The first flush referred to the first leaves picked after the winter, and the second flush was the summer harvest, which was under way at the moment. The rain flush was during the monsoon season, and the growing year ended with the autumn flush—the last leaves picked before production ceased for the winter.

"If you like, I can tell you about the differences in the quality of tea in each season. Every flush gives a different quality. The first flush is light and bitter, the second flush a little milder, but darker in colour. You just have to pay attention when drinking the tea."

Grace was going to comment, but her words dried up in her throat. Looking towards the house, she saw that her father was just outside the front door with his guest and they were now walking across the courtyard. Stockton was looking around as if searching for something. He finally turned towards her. Grace froze and looked to the ground in embarrassment.

"What's the matter?" Vikrama asked.

"I think my father will be able to see you now," she said with some disappointment. "He's just saying goodbye to his visitor."

Vikrama raised his eyebrows in surprise, but Grace didn't feel she could stay with him any longer.

"I have to go now. Many thanks for your explanations, Mr. Vikrama."

She hitched up her skirts and hurried along the sandy path to the house.

A smile played on Daniel Stockton's lips as he left the plantation behind. Young Grace was a promising prospect—he had realised that as soon as he saw her pulling her sister out of the way of his horse. She had character and courage; she was fiery and apparently in good health—all characteristics he would like to see in a daughter-in-law.

All the things his wife was not. Delicate Alice had almost died giving birth to their second baby, and the children she had borne were frail. George, his son, was absorbed from dawn to dusk in stuffing birds instead of showing an interest in tea growing. His daughter, Clara, was sickly and spent most of the time, whatever the season, closeted away in her room.

It hadn't bothered him too much to begin with, but now he was getting on in years he had to start thinking about what would become of his plantation in the future.

Grace was from faraway England, but he sensed she would take to tea production. And even in these early days she seemed to have developed a good relationship with the workers—why else would she have been talking to her father's foreman?

The alternative explanation made his mouth go dry.

Did the fellow have designs on the young woman?

The mental image of her naked in a passionate embrace with a man excited Daniel Stockton so much that he had to halt his horse. Here and now, away from the watchful eyes of society and his pale wife, he could give himself over to his fantasies undisturbed, and that meant a vision of the young woman's face flushed with desire, golden-red locks falling over her naked shoulders and breasts as they moved back and forth in passionate thrusting. All at once he became the stranger who lay between her thighs and . . .

Gasping, he tore open his collar. He had to collect himself. He was on his way home to supper with his family, not an occasion to be faced with eyes blazing with lust. Even though his marriage bed had long been cold, his wife nevertheless had a sixth sense, as did all women, that made her fear losing her man. She would see that he had been thinking about another.

As he urged his horse onward again, he tried to steer his mind on to other subjects. But even as he passed through the gates of his plantation, he couldn't get the gentle lips and blue eyes of Grace Tremayne out of his head.

I'll make sure George marries her, he told himself. *Whatever the cost.*

The next morning, Grace and Victoria were setting out on a little walk with Miss Giles when Vikrama approached them, carrying a cage made of pipework in which a fiery-red parrot with green and blue tail feathers was screeching loudly.

"Good morning, ladies!" he said with a small bow. "I heard that Miss Victoria wanted to see a parrot up close. This morning I happened across one that declared itself willing. But only under the condition that it regains its freedom afterwards."

While Miss Giles peered at it as though she expected to see a flea circus dancing all over the bird, Victoria's eyes shone with delight.

"Oh, thank you, Mr. Vikrama! I promise I'll be as quick as I can with my drawing."

"But, Miss Victoria!" Miss Giles cried out, appalled. "Surely you can't want to get too close to this louse-ridden bird!"

"This bird is perfectly healthy and won't harm your charge in the slightest," Vikrama said, giving Grace a conspiratorial glance. "But I do advise you not to touch it. If you approach a parrot in the wrong way its bite can be very painful."

"Have you ever been bitten by a parrot?" Victoria asked animatedly as she took the cage from him.

"Yes, when I was a child, often. When you catch one you have to take care to hold it carefully from behind, so it can't reach your fingers with its beak. If you don't hurt it, there's a good chance you won't be hurt back, but you never know when something you do will hurt an animal."

"Nevertheless, I'm really not sure—"

"Miss Giles," Grace interrupted her. "I asked Mr. Vikrama to look out for a parrot. It was very kind of him and we're very grateful. How is my sister supposed to learn about the natural world if not through looking closely at specimens? Unfortunately, Mr. Norris isn't here to instruct her."

The mention of their private tutor brought a flush to Miss Giles's cheeks. Grace noticed with satisfaction that she had succeeded in distracting the governess's attention. As she turned with a smile to Vikrama, something lit up in his eyes that made her heart beat faster.

"Come on, Victoria, let's draw the parrot quickly," she said, laying her hand on her sister's shoulder. Before turning away she gave Vikrama another smile, and observed the effect it had on his expression.

8

Hill Club Hotel, May 2008

The rain made a mess of Diana's plans. For the next two days it poured down in bucketfuls. It made it impossible to go up to the plantation—in those conditions, she would have found the hazardous local driving style even more dangerous than usual, and hiking would also have been extremely difficult.

"Do you think the monsoon's begun earlier than anticipated?" she asked Jonathan over breakfast. "I did hear people saying on the train that it would be starting soon."

"It's possible. But I don't think this is monsoon rain yet. Maybe we'll get an opportunity in the next few days to hike up to the plantation."

Diana nodded, a little despondent. She had been hoping so much to gain some clarity soon, but all she had to date were fragments, and the palm leaf still hadn't been deciphered. All kinds of wild notions ran through her mind as she stared out of the window at the green landscape and low-lying clouds, but she suppressed them. No, she wouldn't prejudge her ancestors. She would allow the facts to speak for themselves, and only once she ran out of discoveries would she allow her imagination to fill the gaps.

Shortly before meeting Jonathan for dinner, she switched on her laptop again to look through her emails. The hotel Internet was sluggish, and it took ages for all her messages to download.

You should be grateful that there's a connection here at all, she told herself.

Looking down the list, she sighed.

Messages from Eva keeping her up to date with work were the pleasant side. But Philipp had also written to her three times, each email without a subject line, as if he hoped that would make her more likely to read them.

Diana suppressed the impulse simply to delete them. *I'll look at them later. Maybe he's even announcing his intention to seek a divorce.*

The email from Mr. Green promised to be much pleasanter. He gave a brief report on life at Tremayne House and said that he'd had to call in a handyman because part of the guttering on the main part of the house had come down. This was followed by a request for her to open the attachment and look at the contents closely. It was a picture, entitled simply "IMG7635489." Had Mr. Green taken a photo of the new gutter?

Diana groaned when she saw the size of the file. How could she pick up five megabytes with this poor connection? *Perhaps I should save the message until we're back in Colombo,* she thought. *Why would he go to all this trouble for a photo of a gutter?* But her curiosity got the better of her. *The file can load while I have dinner with Jonathan. It should be here by the time we've finished.*

She clicked on the button, got up, and went downstairs.

Over dinner they talked about colonial rule in Sri Lanka and about the Tamils.

"If we have time, we really should visit one of the mountain temples," Jonathan suggested. "The Hindus built magnificent temples, even if they themselves didn't have much to live on. Their gods are very important to them."

Diana had seen one of these temples in a book on the region. To stand in front of one, to be able to touch its colourful paintwork and breathe in the scent of the floral offerings, hugely appealed to her.

"That would be lovely. Do you know of any temples in the area?"

"There's one really close to Vannattuppūcci. And two more in the surrounding area. As soon as the rain stops we should be able to reach them easily. But"—he reached for his glass of tea which had cooled enough to drink—"your family history takes priority."

"Perhaps my family history is more closely linked to Hinduism than I realise." Diana sighed. "Oh, if only I knew a little more. All I have to date are suppositions and general information that doesn't have anything to do with the secret."

"I think that's the nature of secrets," Jonathan murmured thought-fully, as if to himself, as the same shadow settled in his eyes that had struck him when he referred to his ex-wife. Did he also have a secret?

As Diana watched him, she suddenly felt a need to know more about him. The story of his failed marriage and his child were per-haps enough for a stranger, but by now she had found out so many of his little characteristics that she wanted to know how he had acquired them. And every time she had the opportunity to look longer into his eyes, she was overcome by a longing to be embraced and kissed—and to experience in bed what she and Philipp had long since lost.

They sat for the rest of the evening in front of a sketchy mind map they had scribbled down on a napkin. They drew together all they knew, padded out with general information. At last Diana had some idea of what her ancestors' lives would have been like. Once on location, she might even get to the bottom of the secret itself, around which all the events had played out.

On the way back to her room, Diana took the leaflet about the plantation from her bag and folded it so that the telephone number was showing. Tomorrow was Monday, so the employees would be there and she could maybe make an appointment—provided the rain stopped.

When she entered her hotel room, she had forgotten the photo she was downloading. It was only the screensaver switching to a new picture that reminded her.

The computer showed that the file was fully downloaded. When Diana clicked on it, at first she saw nothing but a grey-and-white area that looked similar to the photo of Grace in front of the plantation. Then the pixels sharpened to show a landscape that had nothing to do with Sri Lanka. The photograph must have been taken in Europe, she supposed in around the 1960s, as indicated by the border around the photo and the lack of mildew spots. To her great amazement it was a picture of a cemetery. At its heart was a gravestone marked with a cross that towered above all the others, its inscription frustratingly unclear.

The next day, Jonathan's guess that the downpour did not herald the start of the monsoon seemed to be proved correct. The clouds thinned a little, finally allowing a few rays of sun to break through. The sight of the glittering drops on the leaves reminded Diana of the fairy story of a princess who wanted a crown of dewdrops because the water glittered like precious stones. Emily had told her the story, and after Mr. Green had watered the lawn, she had sometimes imagined that she was walking through a garden full of roses made from gemstones.

Oh, Emily, she thought, glancing at the desk. *Why didn't you leave me some clearer clues . . . ?*

When Jonathan knocked she was in the middle of gathering up her clues and stowing them in a plastic bag to protect them if it rained again. She had a feeling that it would be good to have them with her. Maybe she would be able to link them to what she found at the plantation.

"Come in!" she called. Jonathan appeared in the doorway. He was dressed in hiking gear, his small travel bag slung over his shoulder. "What do you think. Should we risk it?"

"Of course!" Diana replied. "If we wait any longer we'll have missed our chance. My flight home is in five days, so we don't have much time left. Anyway, I called the plantation this morning. The secretary said the next few days would be a good time, as the manager is there and will be able to show me around."

Jonathan had succeeded in finding a driver with a jeep that would save them from trekking through the jungle.

"Were you joking when you said we had to walk?" she asked sceptically after they had climbed in.

"It's usually a beautiful route," he said. "A walk through the jungle can be wonderful. But with the weather like it is, it's better to have someone drive us. Besides, we don't want to run into any sloth bears, do we? Those fellows can be very dangerous, especially if they're scared."

Before Diana could reply, the driver had started up the jeep and they set off on the bumpy ride. The loud roar of the engine made it virtually impossible to hold a conversation, and the additional fear of rolling or getting stuck weighed heavily on her. In the event of an accident, how long would it take for them to be rescued?

Glancing at Jonathan, she saw only a calm, thoughtful expression, but she suspected he was putting on a poker face so as not to unnerve her any more than she already was.

Finally, her imagination having run through every possible manner of getting killed in the jungle, she gave herself up to the rocking motion and allowed her thoughts to return to the strange photo that Mr. Green had sent her. A cemetery in some godforsaken place.

She hadn't yet asked what he intended by it and where he had found it, but she would do as soon as they were back from the plantation.

9

Vannattuppūcci, 1887

Inspired by her close encounter with the parrot, Victoria now went out frequently with her drawing pad to catch the impressions of the world around her. As though the animals somehow knew she was no longer intent on catching them, they seemed to show themselves more frequently, and she soon had a fine collection of sketches of parrots, butterflies, and other insects. But the flying foxes were still proving elusive.

"Could you ask Mr. Vikrama if he can find me a flying fox?" Victoria asked after another fruitless search for the animals.

Grace started and realised how the mere mention of his name caused blood to shoot to her cheeks. She didn't know why, but whenever she saw the foreman she was overcome by an unprecedented attack of nerves that she couldn't explain. He was always friendly and helpful towards her, without the oily manner of Daniel Stockton. Yet whenever she met him she couldn't help feeling that she was completely inappropriately dressed, had the wrong hairstyle, and appeared childish. What was wrong with her?

Mr. Norris's eventual arrival had heralded an end to their morning walks. From now on, Victoria had regular lessons, while Grace was condemned to spending the time with Miss Giles, concerning themselves with their dresses—as they had unpacked their clothes, the need for repairs had become woefully obvious.

When the sewing and patching became too much for her, she would slip into Victoria's teaching room, where Mr. Norris was informing her about the native species—not a subject he was particularly knowledgeable about. Her father had probably demanded that his second daughter was familiarised with the flora and fauna of her surroundings.

Grace was a little envious of Victoria for the fact that she could still receive schooling and didn't have to devote herself entirely to household duties, particularly one morning when the Tremaynes' tutor was talking about the native flowers.

"The bush you see outside the house is called frangipani here, or *Plumeria* in Latin. There are various varieties and colours, with yellow and red predominating. This shrub, which belongs to the dogbane family, is found throughout the Indian subcontinent."

"Is there also a blue frangipani?" Victoria asked after she had finished taking notes.

"To be honest, I'm afraid I can't answer that one, but one never knows what range of colours God has appointed for this plant." Mr. Norris removed his metal-rimmed glasses from his eyes and laid them down gently on the desktop. "Perhaps you and your sister will find a few blue specimens on one of your walks."

Victoria whirled around, and Grace, caught out, stood up. Disbelief was written all over the younger girl's face—disbelief that her sister would voluntarily come to a lesson when she was free to do other things.

"I just wanted to listen for a while," Grace said, embarrassed. Although she had not had lessons for three years, she suddenly felt like the pupil she had once been, full of respect for her teacher. "I'm sorry for interrupting."

The tutor grinned. "That's what I find strange about my pupils," he said, as though talking to himself. "When I'm teaching them, they all seem to want to escape from my classes. And once they've left the halls of learning forever, they're constantly drawn back."

"It's simply that you never used to tell me about exotic plants and animals," Grace replied.

"You're right. And I must confess that, although rocks are my primary interest, I find myself fascinated by the flora and fauna of this region." He placed his spectacles back on his nose. "If you like, and if your household duties allow it, you're welcome to listen in on my classes again. Without any troublesome requirement to note down what I say, of course."

Victoria pouted. "But I'm not released from taking notes, Mr. Norris?"

"Of course not," Norris replied sternly. "Miss Grace has already completed her schooling, and I'm sure she won't be able to attend these classes all the time. She's bound to marry one day and set up her own household. And to make sure you'll be able to do the same when you're older, Miss Victoria, I think we should continue the lesson now. Next week I'll be asking you to write an essay."

With a sigh, Victoria turned back to her notebook.

As Mr. Norris pronounced on the uses of the coconut palm, Grace looked out of the window and tensed. Mr. Vikrama was passing at that very moment, probably after visiting the drying sheds to make sure things were running smoothly. Once again Grace found herself pondering on what he had said about the tea picking seasons. Did Mr. Norris know about that?

Unlike the previous night, when she had watched him again, Vikrama was now wearing normal British clothing, his brown trousers tucked into high boots and a beige patterned waistcoat over his three-quarter sleeved shirt. The box under his arm looked important.

Where's he going all the time? she wondered. She felt like jumping up to ask him, but she fought down the impulse and gazed out at the distant palms while the tutor's voice drummed down around her like summer rain.

The monsoon season brought with it dull days, constant rain, and a little cool relief, if it could be called that with the temperatures only dropping by a few degrees and remaining hotter than those of an English summer.

For Grace and Victoria it meant long days indoors, which Victoria in particular found trying. She no longer considered her lessons to be a waste of time, but she sorely missed the compensation of her afternoon walks.

During their free time, the two sisters frequently retired to the conservatory, where they set up their easels. Within a few moments the fresh smell of the rain would be permeated by those of oil paints and turpentine.

"Do you remember that time by the lake?" Victoria said, as her brush loaded with blue paint conjured up a parrot's wing.

"You mean when we had our portrait painted?" Grace asked as she began to apply the first pale-pink hues of a frangipani branch laden with blooms.

"Yes, that's right. Wasn't it a wonderful day? Do you recall how we kept upsetting the poor artist as he tried to commit our likenesses to canvas?"

"I'm surprised you remember it at all," Grace said in amazement. Even she had only a faded memory of the afternoon by the lake. She had been nine and had had her fill of having to sit still for the artist. Despite her mother's warnings, she had finally got up and walked around, her legs grown numb from sitting for so long on the lakeside, the air swarming with midges.

"I was five then," Victoria protested. "I even remember some things I did when I was four."

"Like what?" Grace asked, ducking behind her easel to conceal her smile. Teasing Victoria was still great fun despite the fact she was now eighteen.

"When Papa lifted me up to the top of the Christmas tree so I could fix the angel in place. And how we went for a walk in the woods in winter and almost froze because you lost the way."

Her sister's reproachful tone made Grace explode with laughter. "We were rescued. How long are you going to hold that story against me?"

"For as long as you keep doubting that I can remember my early childhood." Her eyes widened suddenly, and she laid her brush down on her palette of blue paint.

"What's the matter?" Grace asked, already preparing her defence against another of Victoria's jests.

"Mr. Vikrama seems remarkably interested in art."

As Grace whirled around, he realised he'd been spotted and took a step back. It looked like he'd been watching them for a while. Victoria waved to him cheerfully, and he responded casually, before nodding at Grace in greeting and withdrawing. Grace was rooted to the spot. Why could she not simply turn back to her painting? Why did she feel a compulsion to stare at the space where his boot prints were gradually fading into the grass?

Vikrama didn't appear that night. It seemed as though whatever he was doing was impossible in the torrential downpour that drummed on the house and nearby foliage like ghostly fingers. Grace regretted it a little, having become accustomed to him slipping past in the night, her curiosity growing each time she saw him disappearing into the bushes and reappearing later.

When the rain lessened slightly after a week or so and the courtyard dried out enough for them to venture outside without sinking to their knees in mud, she ran over to the shed in which the tea leaves were dried. Although the drying racks were empty, she found Vikrama there, checking the condition of the building. After the rainy season it would not be long until the next harvest. Everything had to be repaired and shipshape by then.

"Miss Grace!" he cried out in surprise when he noticed her. "You could have sent one of the maids if you required my services."

"I'm here because I wanted to ask you something. In any case I'm fed up of being cooped up in the house. Back home in England I'd never have dreamed that one day I'd get so much pleasure from being outside."

Vikrama smiled, but didn't interrupt his work. "I've heard your homeland is damp and cool. We have plenty of humidity here, but the temperature is much pleasanter. You ought to get up a little earlier in the next few days to see the beautiful mist over the mountain and the tea fields. It's a wonderful sight at dawn."

"I've already seen it," Grace replied, then fell silent. Should she dare to say it? When would she get another opportunity to ask him?

"I recently happened to catch sight of you in the night," she said with a wildly beating heart. "At least, I think it was you."

Vikrama stiffened. Every muscle in his body seemed tense, and his features hardened.

"Where are you going at that time in those strange clothes?"

"I don't know what you mean, Miss Grace."

All at once Grace felt as though she would have been better saying nothing. What business was it of hers, what Vikrama did during the night? He was an employee and a Hindu. *Maybe his night-time activities have some religious purpose. I really should find out more about the beliefs in this country.*

She cleared her throat and took a step back. She didn't want to makes things any worse than they were. "I think I ought to go."

"Miss Grace, I . . ."

But she was already hurrying off in the direction of the house.

Despite her own explanation, which seemed plausible enough, Grace tossed and turned in bed that night. As soon as she closed her eyes, she could see the young man's face in front of her. He had looked angry, but a little scared—as though he feared being found out. As the daughter of the landowner she could of course have forced him to reveal his secret, if necessary even threatening to tell her father. But she hadn't, and in retrospect was glad about that.

But the burning question of what his religious pursuit could be preoccupied her until well into the night. As quietly as she could, taking care not to wake Victoria, she rose and went to the curtain at the window.

Maybe she should follow him.

As she considered a hundred possible ways of how to follow Vikrama without him seeing her, she stared spellbound at the patch of grass by the bushes beyond which the nocturnal secret must lie. But Vikrama didn't appear. Only the shadow of a parrot passed over the moonlit surface.

After a while Grace gave up staring out. She slipped back into bed and pushed the sheet, which felt as heavy as an eiderdown, aside.

Her heart felt incredibly heavy. *Now I've spoken to him about it, he must have found another way of getting to his secret meeting . . .*

10

Vannattuppūcci Tea Company, 2008

Contrary to their expectations, they survived the journey to the plantation, although the jeep had considerable trouble crossing the sodden
ground. Several times, Diana feared they might fall off the edge and
tumble down a steep slope. But every time, the driver managed to
regain control of the vehicle—sometimes in silence, sometimes cursing,
as though the vehicle could do something about his style of driving.

"I'm just glad that it isn't the true monsoon season, or we'd have
needed a helicopter," Jonathan said with a wink.

Because they needed the driver for the return trip, Jonathan gave
him some money and a packet of cigarettes and asked him to wait.

After announcing their arrival at the gate via the intercom, Diana
tried to catch a glimpse of the main house that lay hidden behind
palm trees and overhanging rhododendrons. The builder had probably
designed it to prevent inquisitive glances at the residence from the gate.

The wrought-iron fence to either side of the gate must have stood
for over a hundred years, as its design was clearly Victorian with its
spear-like tips.

The gardens also looked very English. Diana tried to imagine Grace and Victoria walking along these well-maintained paths in their white dresses, protected from the sun by delicate lace parasols.

A man dressed in khaki trousers and a beige bush shirt finally appeared. Diana guessed he was in his mid-fifties. His bearing suggested a man who was used to giving orders and being obeyed. He pressed a button with a casual gesture and the high wrought-iron gate swung open.

"You must be the lady from Germany." The man, who had surprisingly European features, shook her hand. "I'm Jason Manderley, managing director of the Vannattuppūcci Tea Company."

Diana briefly introduced herself and Jonathan. "I'm grateful to you for finding the time to see me."

Manderley smiled broadly. "The pleasure's all mine. My employee tells me you're a descendant of the former owner."

The only descendant now, Diana thought, but merely nodded. "One of my ancestors was Henry Tremayne. I'm descended from his daughter Grace."

The name appeared to mean something to the man.

"If that's the case then I'm sure you'll find plenty to interest you in our archive. Come in; I'll show you."

Manderley led them along the well-maintained driveway, past a collection of ancient-looking buildings that looked empty, but not completely abandoned.

"These are the former wilting and drying buildings. Until 1950 the frames to hold the drying leaves were in here." He pointed to a freshly painted building in the middle. "That was where the women used to sit and roll the tea by hand. In the early days, Vannattuppūcci was famed for selling one of the best handmade teas. Unfortunately, in later times the owners had to move over to mechanical production because trade in handmade teas was no longer profitable. But we're going back to manual production on a small scale now, because connoisseurs are happy to pay more for the quality."

As Manderley spoke, the whispering of the palms and heveas echoed in Diana's ears like the voices of the women who used to live and work here. The strange inner peace that she had felt at Tremayne House came over her now and had a calming effect on her nerves. It was as though she had come home. Was there so much of Grace passed down in her genes?

"I don't know how familiar you are with the history of tea in Sri Lanka," the managing director continued as they crunched across the gravel drive to the house.

"Not too much, I'm afraid," Diana replied. "My search so far has been concentrated on specific people and items. I wanted to find out as much as possible about my great-great-grandmother and some things I found in my aunt's house."

"Interesting. What did you find there?"

Diana stopped briefly and drew the photo from her wallet.

"My goodness!" Manderley exclaimed. "That really is our tea plantation. I can even see where this must have been taken. Come with me; I'll take you there!"

They turned off the driveway and followed a path that led directly to the tea fields.

When they finally came to a stop, Diana saw they were near a relatively young-looking forest. A quick look at the photo showed it was the same mountain, but she could see neither the tea field nor the open space on which Grace had been standing.

"A few years ago we began to reforest this part of the plantation. For some unknown reason the yields from this part weren't so great as the other fields. The tea pickers say there's a curse on this area."

Diana shuddered. "A curse?"

"Yes. Stories like that are still passed round. But I consider them to be pure folklore. If you were to show one of the women your photo, I'm sure she'd say your ancestor was a ghost. Maybe even the ghost who took the fertility from this patch of land. But I simply think we overstepped a limit with this field. The higher the altitude at which tea is planted, the lower the yields. Like everywhere in the world, it's a question of achieving the right balance, and here the scales reach a tipping point at which the climate is more damaging to the tea. As you'll have noticed, the air here is substantially cooler than down at the foot of the mountain."

Diana was sure her shudder hadn't been caused by the cold air. Perhaps the tea pickers were right.

"If you like, you can go and have a closer look at the place," Manderley offered. "Or take the files out with you. The archive is a rather prosaic place, where only lifeless things are kept. I can let you have a table, and maybe even a tent, if you like."

"That's very kind of you—thank you!"

"Well, first let's have a look what treasures are to be found in the archive."

As he turned to go, Diana remained where she was for a moment, and murmured to Jonathan, "Maybe there really is a curse."

"In that case we really should take a closer look at the place. Maybe there's something there."

"What did you say?" Manderley turned.

"Oh, nothing. I was just pointing something out to Mr. Singh."

The managing director nodded and walked on ahead of them.

As they followed him, Diana saw a strange tree near the house, which seemed somehow familiar to her.

"Is this an apple tree?" she asked Manderley, since this tree seemed completely out of place.

"The English had a habit of adapting their new environment to the old in many respects. They introduced foxes for hunting and planted fruit trees. According to the stories, this gnarled old tree goes back to Richard Tremayne's day. But he must have soon realised that the native fruits are also delicious, because this tree is the only one he brought from home."

A symbol of the strangeness of the British in these latitudes, Diana thought. She resolved to share her thought with Jonathan for his book—if he hadn't already come to the same conclusion himself.

A little later they reached the old mansion, which was now used as the administrative building. Two storeys pointed up to the sky, whitewashed and punctuated by slender windows. Alongside the typically British elements, Diana also recognised subtle but clear European classical and native influences.

"Isn't it wonderful?" Manderley said effusively. "In the 1970s, the former owner toyed with the idea of using the building as a hotel. Holidays among the tea fields, sampling local culinary delights. The idea never came to pass, as the man soon ran out of money. You could say that was fortunate, as hordes of tourists would have both damaged the fabric of the building and interrupted the smooth running of the plantation. But we are pleased to offer accommodation to individual guests who have business here."

"We're staying in a really nice hotel nearby," Jonathan said.

"Oh, you must check out at once! I could let you have rooms here, and they wouldn't cost you a single rupee."

The prospect of living in the house that had once belonged to her ancestor filled Diana with delight. What would Emily say to that?

"I think we should accept Mr. Manderley's offer," she said, turning to Jonathan. "Provided we're not disturbing anyone here."

"Not at all. The guest rooms have a separate entrance. And I'll take care of your food and drink personally. My wife is an excellent cook, and she'd be delighted to meet you."

"All that without taking any money from us?" Jonathan said in wonder.

"Why not?" the managing director said with a disarming smile. "Consider yourselves my guests—after you've fetched your luggage from the hotel."

As they entered the hall, which looked as well-tended as a museum, they were met by two young women who worked in the administration of the plantation. Over their tight black and khaki skirts they wore tops that were modern, but with a traditional influence. After giving Manderley a brief nod in greeting, they disappeared in the direction of one of the other buildings.

"They probably want to make sure things are OK in the dispatch centre," the man said as they crossed the magnificent hall that was a clear indication of the plantation's success.

Diana noticed a light patch on the wall, beneath which a few bouquets of flowers had been placed.

"Why are those flowers there, Mr. Manderley?"

A sad smile crossed the man's face.

"It's said that a wonderful picture used to hang there. Shiva and Ganesha dancing, or something like that. The picture was . . . destroyed."

"The workers treated the picture as a kind of altar, did they?" Jonathan said, indicating the flowers.

"Yes, and as you can see, they still do to this day. The place where the picture was hung is sacred for some reason."

"So why wasn't it replaced?" Diana asked.

The managing director shrugged as though he knew a story he didn't want to tell.

"You'll have to ask the owner. I only run the business side of things here. In any case, the picture's been gone for a long while. I think it was lost as long ago as the Tremaynes' time. You might find something about it in the files."

He gestured to Diana and Jonathan to follow him to the basement, thus cutting off any further questions about the picture. Diana resolved to get to the bottom of how the picture came to be destroyed.

"As was usually the case in British mansions, the staff worked downstairs here, too, while the family lived upstairs."

His words reminded Diana of a TV series she had watched as a child, and which had constantly led her to question her aunt and Mr. Green about all aspects of servants' lives.

"Since we don't need servants here any more, we've set up the archive down here." With a grand gesture he opened the door to reveal long rows of shelves and cupboards. At first glance all Diana could see were books containing commercial records. The real treasures must be concealed in the cupboards.

"This is really impressive!"

"Don't be afraid of exploring. It's more a private library than a place where you need be nervous about documents threatened with destruction. The air here is ideal for preserving old papers. Not too dry and not too humid. The archives in Europe would be envious of these conditions."

It was as though they had stepped through the door to a mysterious fairy-tale land, Diana felt as she approached the old-fashioned desk that was similar to the one at Tremayne House. To one side of the worn leather desk protector stood a Tiffany lamp with a rather battered shade whose notches around the edge had not been restored. Was it somehow significant?

"You can do as much research as you want here, provided you make room for my employees if they need to see specific files."

"We'll do that," Diana said. For the first time, she had the feeling she was in exactly the right place. "I don't want to get in your way."

"You won't. I'm really glad that someone's finally looking into the history. In principle, you won't mind me using what you find in the publicity for this place, will you?"

"Provided I don't find anything too dreadful," Diana replied hesitantly.

"Don't worry, I won't be asking for private details. But you may very well find out some more general information about the plantation. That would be excellent for our information brochure. It's still rather slim."

Diana nodded. "OK, under those circumstances I'll be happy to let you have anything relevant we find."

◆　◆　◆

While Jonathan agreed to go and fetch their luggage from the Hill Club Hotel and clear up the formalities, Diana set herself up in the archive. Her laptop was still at the hotel, but she had a notepad to jot down anything important she found. And of course there was her guidebook of Colombo, which didn't directly have anything to do with the plantation, but was where she had tucked the photo of Grace and the photocopy from the Hill Club.

Jonathan returned two hours later.

"I hope I haven't forgotten anything," he said as he handed Diana her bag. She noticed he hadn't just stuffed her things inside, but had packed them away neatly.

The evening sky was by now spreading swathes of purple silk over the plantation. The setting sun made black patterns of the trees and palms, which now looked like silhouettes from an animated film. The calls in the trees—birds announcing either that they were settling down for the night or just waking up—now seemed much louder.

"Surely the weight of this bag means I've got everything I need in it," Diana groaned in reply. "I see you've brought my laptop, anyway. That's the most important thing. I can manage without underwear and clothes if need be."

Jonathan's right eyebrow shot up. "Really?"

Only then did Diana realise what she'd said. "Of course not! But I'm perfectly used to managing with minimum luggage. Clothes can be washed."

He grinned and she realised with dismay that she was blushing.

"I think I got everything," he said. "You hadn't even fully unpacked. Were you secretly wishing we'd be staying here, perhaps?"

He winked, then shouldered his own bag and accompanied her into the house.

"Mr. Manderley came to see me earlier and gave me the keys to our rooms," Diana said as they crossed the hall, the keys clinking softly in her bag. "He thinks they were the two Tremayne sisters' rooms. Sadly, there's nothing left of the original furnishings, but my room has a fire-place and a window that looks as if it could easily have been there back then."

"Maybe you'll find a secret diary stuffed up the chimney," Jonathan replied with a smile.

"If I'm honest, I hope I do. But I don't believe in coincidences like that—it would be like hoping for a lottery win and then not getting it."

"Never say never." Jonathan looked down the corridor. "Who knows what's been left behind within these walls? Perhaps you'll even meet a ghost you can ask. The people of Sri Lanka firmly believe in spirits who watch over the living."

"I thought most Tamils were Hindus."

"They are, but they still believe in ghosts. Some souls resist the divine scheme of things and don't pass to a reincarnation, but are left behind as shadows." He suddenly fell silent, and Diana was struck by the strange atmosphere of the house.

At the first door she handed him a key.

"You weren't here when he was allocating us our rooms, so of course I chose the best one," she joked. "Mine has a nicer view of the garden."

Jonathan unlocked the door and smiled as he opened it.

"Well, I can't complain about my own view, and I seriously doubt you'd be so selfish as to take the best room for yourself."

Diana grinned. "Actually, I think our rooms were once one. Look at the wall."

Even a layman could tell that it was positioned too close to the window.

"You're right. The room probably used to be too big. A ballroom, perhaps?"

Diana shook her head. "No, the former ballroom is now an open-plan office. If this was the Tremayne sisters' room, they must have had an incredible amount of space."

"Well, if that's the case I'll definitely check my chimney for documents."

Diana pointed to the small tiled stove on the right-hand wall. "I don't think you'll find anything in there. At most they'd have burned a few old papers in it."

"In that case, let's hope they don't include any important papers concerning your ancestors."

Diana wanted to object that it most definitely wouldn't be the case, but she recalled Emily's reluctance to betray secrets. It would hardly be surprising if the Tremaynes had attempted to make anything that wasn't intended for the eyes of the public disappear.

"Anyway, I'm happy with my room." Jonathan's words brushed aside the awkward silence. "I'll tell you if I find anything important."

After stowing their bags in their rooms, Diana and Jonathan went back to the archive. She proudly presented him with what she had uncovered so far.

"I've only got as far as the first cupboard. The files are all over the place."

"I'm not surprised," Jonathan said, his eyes shining with an eagerness to explore and his fingers running down the leather spines of the commercial records. "After all, this isn't a museum, but a private archive. The main focus is on tea production and not research into old files. In this age of productivity, the past takes second place."

"But it still affects what happens today, I'm afraid," Diana replied, unable to take her eyes from his face. She noticed for the first time a slight twitch at his temple and the fine hairs at the edges of his eyebrows.

"Well, let's get down to it," he said. Their eyes met. "But not without something in our stomachs. I'm starving!"

Mr. Manderley had kindly given them the run of the kitchen, and Jonathan offered to cook a Tamil-style rice dish.

"With coconut milk," he said as he positioned himself at the stove. "This is a traditional birthday meal in the rural parts here."

Diana looked at him dreamily. *What would Michael say if he could see us here now? When I get back I'll have to give him a blow-by-blow account. He deserves it, since he's been such a great help.*

Half an hour later, they sat down to eat. To accompany the rice, Jonathan had cut up a few mangoes that he had bought from the jeep driver. The man had brought a whole box of them for his family, whom he was going to see after dropping Jonathan off.

"Like it or not, we're stuck here for a while," Jonathan said as he took a slice of mango. "The driver's not coming back for four days."

"Four days?" Diana said, shocked. "But my flight . . ."

"Isn't there any way you can postpone it?"

Diana wanted to say no, but it was suddenly as if a small voice whispered in her ear: *Why not?*

"Of course it would be possible . . ."

Jonathan beamed at her. "Excellent! In any case, I doubt we'll find anything here in a hurry. Those cupboards need to be thoroughly investigated. We don't want to miss anything, do we?"

11

Vannattuppūcci, 1887

As he had promised, Mr. Stockton took Henry to the famous Hill Club and introduced him to numerous plantation owners and other influential men. They didn't hesitate long before accepting him into their midst and making him a full member of the club. After all, Henry Tremayne was from a good family, and there was sympathy for his brother's accident from all quarters.

Out of gratitude for obtaining him this apparently all-important membership and contacts that would certainly be useful in future, Henry invited Stockton, together with his family and some other men from the club, to their house-warming reception, which Claudia had been planning for quite a while.

In the days leading up to the reception, Mr. Wilkes drove the maids to work ever harder, and successfully asked for the appointment of a houseboy, a young Tamil who had only recently left the school that Henry had generously allowed to continue. Mr. Wilkes also gave the cook the benefit of his experience. He showed her how to make scones and how to adapt the recipe for tea loaf to suit the local ingredients.

When the delivery man arrived punctually with the vegetables and fish he had ordered, the butler seemed to be floating in seventh heaven. Claudia, too; even if she did not feel that Mr. Stockton was particularly likeable, she was determined to show the Stocktons that it was not the maids' dress that mattered—the uniforms still had not arrived—but the manner in which a good hostess entertained her guests.

The reception also meant that her two daughters were to wear new, or at least new-looking, dresses. As the developments in fashion over recent years could not be fully adopted due to their straitened financial circumstances, Miss Giles had had to alter their existing dresses with the help of a magazine that Wilkes had obtained for her in Colombo.

To help her in her task, she engaged two young Tamil girls, who in addition to their picking work on the plantation also mended the clothes of the other workers. The girls frequently broke out in giggles as they worked, and Grace was sure that this was over the clothes and undergarments that seemed so strange in their eyes. Victoria was right in that the local women did not wear bodices or corsets; their hard work kept them slim, and their dark skin seemed to defy ageing more effectively than the skin of white women.

Whenever Miss Giles tugged at her lacing, making it even harder to breathe, she envied them.

Growing weary of being constantly present during the alterations, Grace left the room under the pretext of fetching herself something to drink. Miss Giles was about to ring for a maid, but Grace stopped her, saying that they already had too much to do, and immediately vanished from the room.

She made her way downstairs towards the kitchens. Back in Tremayne House her mother had frowned upon the sisters being seen in the kitchen because it would upset the servants, who were not used to having members of the family among them.

She was still some way off when the sound of a commotion drifted towards her. The cook was giving her assistants orders in strident Tamil, which Grace could not understand, but she nevertheless sensed that the cook was anything but satisfied with the girls. Grace peered cautiously around the corner. For the first time she saw the cook, who was around her early forties and herself a Tamil.

The girls were all about her own age and cringed fearfully at the cook's commands. Mr. Wilkes remained aloof, limiting his involvement to polishing the silver.

After she'd observed the activity for a short while unseen by the servants, Grace's eye was caught by a girl under the table. The child clearly did not belong here. She must have slipped in unnoticed, and now she was trapped in her dark hiding place.

She didn't seem unduly concerned, as she had swiped a few pieces of fruit from the table. But when the girl saw Grace looking, she froze and turned pale. She dropped the fruit from her fingers. Mr. Wilkes would probably have boxed her ears if he had seen the theft, but Grace smiled at her. Miss Giles would have argued that it was not helpful to the child's moral well-being to ignore an act of stealing, but the girl looked at her with such dark eyes and soft cheeks, smeared with traces of fruit, that Grace did not have the heart to betray her.

After a while, the girl's features began to relax and she glanced towards the back door, which was ajar.

At once Grace realised what she could do to help. She moved away from the doorway and entered the kitchen.

"Good morning, Mr. Wilkes!"

For a moment they all turned to look at her. The servants' eyes widened, the cook wound a strand of hair around her finger, and Mr. Wilkes hastily put the cutlery down.

"Good morning, Miss Grace!" The butler straightened up and indicated to the maids and the cook that they should do likewise. "Forgive me. I hadn't noticed you arrive."

At the very moment when everyone except Grace had their backs to her, the little thief made a dash for it. Concealing a smile, Grace said, "I've only come to see how things are coming along in the kitchen."

"I presume your mother has sent you."

Grace didn't contradict him. The fact that her interest in proceedings below stairs was hers alone would only have thrown him off balance.

"The preparations are in full swing, and I can assure you that everything will be to the full satisfaction of Madam Tremayne. We're well aware of the great responsibility that lies with us, and we will all"—his gaze wandered to the kitchen assistants, who had only moments before been on the receiving end of the cook's scolding tongue—"every one of us do our very best to meet the expectations of the Tremayne family."

"I'm sure my mother will be delighted to hear it, Mr. Wilkes. Please continue with your work and . . . please could you be so kind as to pour me a cup of iced tea?"

With the house-warming imminent, Vannattuppūcci radiated all the magic that had transformed the old Tremayne House on special occasions. The ballroom, which had probably not been used for years, was prepared by an army of servants. Since there were not enough staff, Claudia had brought in a few tea pickers from the village. Even though her doubts about this place had by no means vanished, she put them aside in her determination to celebrate a major triumph.

On the evening of the reception ball, Grace was sitting nervously by the window. Fully aware that Daniel Stockton and his family would soon be appearing, she would have liked to flee to the garden and disappear.

"What do you think? Will one of the gentlemen ask me to dance?" Victoria raised her right arm and performed a pirouette.

Grace turned. At least her sister seemed to be enjoying herself.

"You can think of this ball as your debut," Victoria said in an attempt to cheer her sister up a little. "After all, you're being presented to the society of Nuwara Eliya."

"And I've no doubt that Mr. Stockton will lose no time in hanging me on the arm of his son."

"Maybe his son's handsome. Even if you can't bear him, you can't deny that his father's good-looking."

"As if you had any idea about it," Grace muttered. As her eyes wandered back to the window, she wondered what Mr. Vikrama was doing that evening. He certainly wouldn't have been invited, as he was one of the staff. Matters were different with the Cahills—Mr. Cahill had asked her father if he would mind him bringing his wife and daughters. As a matter of courtesy, and because he felt obliged towards the lawyer, Henry had consented. Grace preferred the idea of spending time with those two wallflowers, whom she had met on one of her walks, than with Stockton and his son.

Before Victoria could object that she had eyes in her head and knew perfectly well whether a man was good-looking or not, Miss Giles appeared. As governess she did not have the means to compete with the elegant ladies, but she had made the best of the clothing she had available.

She and Mr. Norris were employees, but since they were responsible for overseeing the girls' upbringing, they had been given leave to appear at the ball.

"You look stunning, Miss Giles!" Victoria said as she skipped around her governess. "I doubt Mr. Norris will let you off the dance floor all evening!"

Miss Giles had probably been about to give them yet another lecture on proper behaviour at the ball, but Victoria's flattery distracted her so much that she blushed. By the time she had composed herself she had lost valuable moments, finally conceding that her lecture would cause them to be late.

As Grace rose from the window seat, she felt an unpleasant tension inside. *The evening won't last forever,* she told herself. *I'll behave as a society lady ought and try not to let my family down.*

When she reached the hall, she saw her parents waiting for her. Claudia was wearing a blue taffeta dress picked out with white lace. Henry looked splendid in his grey frock coat with a black waistcoat and dark-red cravat held with a pearl pin.

They both inspected their daughters critically before Claudia stepped forward and yet again straightened the bows on Grace's light-blue striped dress.

"I do believe you'll make a wonderful impression on the people here. Although that should be small wonder among Englishmen and women who haven't seen their home shores for a long time."

"Darling, please don't prejudge the people here. The men whom I've met at the club were all very friendly and cultured. I hardly expect their families will have gone to seed."

Henry bent towards Claudia and gave her a kiss. They heard the clattering of a horse-drawn carriage outside the house.

"I do believe the first guests are here. Let's put our best foot forward!" Henry Tremayne brushed a non-existent speck of dust from the lapel of his frock coat and struck an appropriate pose while Wilkes moved to open the door.

Within the next few moments a large part of the society of Nuwara Eliya flowed through the door of Vannattuppūcci. Coaches drew to a halt on the drive, and elegantly dressed people made their way up the steps.

"Ah, here come the Stocktons!"

Her father's exclamation pierced Grace like the lash of a whip, and she lost control of her features.

"Don't look so gloomy," her mother warned. "You'll scare the boy off."

This, of course, was exactly what she wanted to do! Pale and red-haired, George Stockton resembled his mother much more than his father. Despite this, she could see nothing about him that made her want to get to know him. She couldn't even begin to imagine him as her husband.

Dressed in a blue-green brocade frock coat, Stockton walked ahead of his family like a puffed-up cockerel. His eyes took in her parents first before falling on Grace. Satisfaction spread across his face as Henry greeted him.

"I'm delighted to welcome you here, Mr. Stockton!"

"The pleasure's all mine," Stockton replied, before introducing his family. George, who wore a light, reddish beard on his cheeks, was accompanied by his sister, who had inherited her father's dark hair, but who also seemed to be quite frail with translucent skin and delicate limbs.

Grace gave them all a friendly smile, noticing as she did so that the boy was eyeing her keenly, as though his father had already told him a good deal about her.

Her suspicion was confirmed—Stockton wanted to pair her off with his son. And from the look he exchanged with his father, he, too, would be pleased at the prospect.

"Your ladies look delightful, Mr. Tremayne," Stockton said after kissing Claudia's hand with perfect elegance.

"May I return the compliment," Henry replied politely. "And I should add that you have a most impressive son and heir. I congratulate you. I'm sure this young man gives you much to be proud of."

"He does." Stockton laid a hand on his son's shoulder. "And he's been dying to meet your daughter. After all, one day they'll both be in charge of the plantations, won't they?"

Grace didn't miss the implication of his words. As a woman, she wouldn't be able to run the plantation on her own, but only with a husband by her side.

Only a few weeks ago she wouldn't have cared. She would have submitted to what was expected of her, giving herself up to the duties of a wife. But now she felt a growing resistance, which surprised and shocked her in equal measure. With a man other than George Stockton she would be prepared to bow to the conventions of society, but not with this lad, whom anyone could see was none too impressive.

Fortunately, the guests continued arriving. Henry and Claudia had to take their leave of the Stocktons for the moment. The mere fact of her release from the appraising eyes of Mr. Stockton and George made the greetings and compliments of the new arrivals much easier for Grace to bear. She noticed that some of them meant their remarks sincerely, and she even found she took a liking to some of them, especially the ones who weren't eyeing her critically like a prize heifer at the cattle market.

Once all the guests had arrived, her father gave a short speech, saying how delighted he was to greet the refined society of Nuwara Eliya and to have the opportunity to put down roots in this beautiful country. He made only brief mention of his brother's memory—which he handled delicately so as to avoid putting a damper on the atmosphere. He quickly turned his talk back to the occasion and indicated to the musicians, whom he'd had brought from Colombo with Wilkes's help, that they should begin.

Halfway through the evening, her head swirling from the many conversations and pleasantries, and from keeping a smile fixed on her face, Grace left the house for a short walk. She had to admit that the guests were not so different from the society in London. Although they had been in Ceylon for a long time, it seemed to have altered nothing about the way they behaved.

The garden welcomed her with soothing calm and darkness that got deeper the further away she moved from the house. In former days she wouldn't have dreamed of going outside in her beautiful ball gown, but the past few weeks had changed her. She didn't know what it was. Her aversion towards this place had completely reversed, her interest in tea cultivation had awoken, and she was gradually coming to feel like Victoria, for whom their stay here was one big adventure.

"Miss Grace," said a quiet voice.

She turned to see Vikrama nearby. He was wearing neither his work clothes nor his mysterious night-time apparel, and Grace could do nothing other than stare. He wore a black shirt, the collar open and the sleeves rolled up a little, wide black trousers and bare feet. He looked strikingly like an Oriental knight from one of the stories she used to read many years ago. Unlike the fictional knights, however, he did not cover his face. In the moonlight he looked a little pale beneath his black locks, dark eyebrows, and neatly trimmed beard. He looked even more handsome than she remembered from the previous days' encounters.

"Mr. Vikrama, I . . ."

He raised his hand with a smile. "I must apologise. My reaction before was inappropriate, and I fear I gave the impression that I was engaged in illegal activities. But that's not the case."

Grace smiled at him in relief. *He's obviously not angry with me.*

"I never believed you were," she replied. "I'm just very inquisitive, a characteristic my mother has always disapproved of. In recent years I've managed to curb it, but here everything's so new and different that I'm afraid it's been reawoken."

"It's not always a bad thing to be inquisitive," Vikrama replied. "Sometimes it helps open your mind to other cultures."

"Is that something by one of the poets?" Grace raised her eyebrows in surprise.

"No. My words. From my own experience. And that of my people. We're also very inquisitive, particularly about new people. That's why you'll always find people here who are willing to help you. Because in doing so, they get to know you."

Silence fell between them. In the distance a strange cry rang out, probably a bird.

"Nevertheless, I had no right to ask you about it," Grace said contritely. "You may be my father's employee, but you have your own life."

Vikrama looked at her strangely. Something seemed to be on the tip of his tongue, but he dismissed it with an almost imperceptible shake of his head. Then he spoke. "Kalarippayatu."

Grace looked at him in amazement. "I beg your pardon?"

Vikrama smiled. "That's what I'm doing. Kalarippayatu."

"What's that?"

"A martial art. I practise it every evening with a few friends. The doctor in the pickers' village is the gurukal, the master. I'm one of his pupils."

"What do you do in this martial art?" Grace asked breathlessly. Whatever she may have thought lay behind this friendly, polite foreman, she had certainly never envisaged him as a fighter.

"We fight with swords and shields, and also with hands and feet. It's more like a dance than pure combat. When we practise, we fight with our opponent, not against him."

Grace tried to imagine what that looked like. Did all the men who practised it dress like Vikrama? What sounds did the swords make? How were they wielded?

"There's an interesting history behind our martial art," Vikrama added as he moved a little closer, his hands clasped behind his back. His movements were as silky-smooth as a big cat's. Or was Grace only imagining that now she was armed with this new information about him?

"Tell me about it."

"In earlier times the Indian rulers were so wise that they wanted to avoid unnecessary bloodshed in battle. So the two opposing parties would each send forward a kalarippayatu fighter from among their bodyguards to duel to the death. The prince of the fighter who died had to concede defeat."

Grace was impressed. "That sounds very wise."

Until then she had only heard of the Indian Sikh warriors, who were renowned for their daring and cruelty.

"It was. Unfortunately, the tradition has fallen somewhat into oblivion over time because there were fewer wars between the Indian princes and the armies had to face invaders who were not familiar with the custom. But the kalarippayatu fighters still form the elite guard of a maharaja."

Grace remained silent, completely carried away by his account.

"We fight in the southern style of the kalarippayatu, although we're no longer allowed to practise the art in broad daylight as the custom would have us do."

In her enthusiasm, Grace didn't notice that Vikrama had fallen silent as though he'd already said too much.

"What does a fight look like?" Her eyes were shining. "Could I come and watch, perhaps?"

Vikrama frowned. "That won't be too easy, I'm afraid. Our practice fights are only attended by men. Women stay away. They're not forbidden from watching, but people don't like to see them there, because they represent a distraction or tempt the fighters to be reckless because they want to impress them."

"Just like at home." Grace smiled. "Young Englishmen also get up to all kinds of mischief in an attempt to impress the ladies."

"Maybe we can find a way of letting you watch in secret," Vikrama relented. "But before you do, you should be able to find your way around the grounds much better. I might be able to take you there, but I couldn't bring you back very early."

Grace's cheeks glowed as if she'd been looking into an oven for too long. How exciting it all was! There wasn't anything like this in good old England.

She noticed Vikrama's expression suddenly become serious.

"What's the matter?" she asked. He stopped moving and gently laid his hands on her arms. "It's very important that you don't tell your father any of this. Please, keep what I've told you to yourself."

Grace was surprised. "But . . ."

"I'm not sure yet what kind of man your father is. During the conquest of India, kalarippayatu fighters fought hard against the English. I know of some plantations where fighters were severely punished when it was discovered that they practised their art. Our way of fighting is forbidden."

Gasping, Grace managed to say, "But surely you don't want—"

"No, we don't want to attack the English. We don't have sufficient numbers, and anyway, for men like me it's merely a matter of keeping up the tradition. That's why I creep across the courtyard at night and meet the others in the forest. And that's why I didn't want to tell you about it."

So her comparison with a knight had not been so absurd. Grace needed a while to digest what she had heard. This friendly young man practised a forbidden martial art under the noses of the colonials, something for which he could be severely punished. And he had taken her, his master's daughter, into his confidence.

"Why have you told me all this?" she said breathlessly. "I could go straight to my father and tell him everything."

"You could." Vikrama smiled again. "But I know you won't. I knew it from the moment you refrained from betraying that little girl who'd stolen fruit from your cook. Maybe you don't know, but among the masters here, theft—even if it's to put food in your belly—is considered a serious crime and is punished by flogging."

"Surely not for children."

Vikrama nodded sadly. "Yes, for children, too. The sex or the age of the thief has no bearing on the punishment."

Grace shook her head in bewilderment. "How do you know about me and the little girl?"

"She told me earlier. She's the daughter of friends of mine. That's how our paths crossed just now—I was on my way home."

Vikrama smiled again and let go of her arms. Although he hadn't been gripping her tightly, Grace could still feel his hands, and a strange shiver of excitement ran through her.

"I promise he won't find anything out from me," she said, and before Vikrama could reply, quickly added, "but please promise me you'll be careful. I'm sure the punishment, should anyone discover you, would be even worse than for thieves."

"Don't worry, Miss Grace. Provided no one discovers what I'm doing, no one will punish me. But now I ought to accompany you back to the house. I imagine they'll already be missing you at the ball."

As they made their way back in silence, Grace wondered if people had begun to miss her. Her father and mother were probably so involved with the Stocktons that they wouldn't have noticed her absence. And Victoria was bound to have made friends with some other young guests, and at worst would be trying to annoy the maids or get hold of a glass of wine.

"Ah, Mr. Vikrama, you've found my daughter!"

Grace started as she saw her father approaching. Although they had done nothing wrong, she was overcome by worry that he could be thinking the wrong things.

"I was feeling a little unwell," she said quickly. "I needed a moment's fresh air.

"And Mr. Vikrama has made sure you're safe."

"I was on the way home, sir," he said calmly and dutifully. "I had been visiting some friends in the pickers' huts. Your daughter looked a little lost, so I offered to accompany her."

"That was very kind of you. Come, Grace, there are some people I'd like to introduce you to."

Grace turned to Vikrama, who bowed slightly and withdrew after giving her a penetrating look.

She saw that Stockton had appeared behind her father and over-heard the conversation. His smile looked partly grim, partly scorn-ful, and Grace could imagine the reason. That time when he had nearly ridden Victoria down, she had refused his offer to accompany them, and now she was accepting the company of a Tamil. Grace pretended not to notice, but Stockton's eyes bored into her like an arrow.

Back in the ballroom, Grace felt out of place. She smiled when it was expected of her, made a few remarks, but whenever her attention was not required, her gaze wandered to the windows with the darkness pressing up to them like a great beast.

Is he practising now? she wondered. How she would have loved to be out there watching him!

After what seemed like countless hours, the reception came to an end. The Stocktons said their farewells, but not without Daniel once again complimenting her father on his "beautiful ladies" and promising to visit again soon. The other guests also left—some of the ladies tipsy and laughing and the occasional man weaving like a sailor.

"Stockton's daughter is utterly boring," Victoria announced as they strolled back to their room. "Did you see how pale she is? That's because of the endless illnesses she has. The doctor is a permanent visitor to their house."

Grace hadn't been listening properly. "Hm."

"I'm sure you're wondering how I know. One of her characteristics is to brag about the various complaints that keep driving her back to her bed. She said that she's currently suffering from dizzy spells and palpitations. Apparently she didn't want to come at all, but her mother insisted."

The words washed over Grace, even once they had reached their room and begun to undress.

"Mary Cahill's much more interesting. Did you see Mr. Cahill's daughter?"

Grace shook her head mechanically, as the words penetrated her mind.

"I tell you, she won't have a problem netting herself the right husband. I'm just glad we're not boys, or she'd be bound to have made eyes at one of us." Noticing that her sister wasn't really listening, Victoria fell silent and turned to her. "Is something wrong? You're so quiet."

"No, nothing. I'm just dog-tired. Father and Mother presented me to literally every guest. I couldn't begin to tell you which son or which daughter belongs to which family."

"Well, when it comes to sons, I imagine your chances of not having to marry into the Stockton clan have been increased substantially by this ball." Victoria laughed briefly, but when she saw that her joke hadn't registered with Grace she sat down next to her big sister on the edge of the bed. "Where were you when Father went outside to look for you?"

"I went for a walk," Grace replied. As she undid the buttons of her dress, she wished only that she could be in bed or alone by the window with time to think.

"For a walk? Alone in the darkness?" Victoria's eyes widened as though she had seen something dreadful. "You could have been whisked away by a monster."

"Not here. The only ones remotely approaching monsters were in the ballroom. It was all quiet in the tea sheds, and I doubt that there are such things as tea ghosts."

"You don't know that!" Victoria raised her index finger in warning. "Every place has its ghosts; there must be some here, too. Maybe Uncle Richard wanders through the tea fields by night, watching over his estate."

The sinister tone her sister used so masterfully when imitating the content of her horror novels sent an involuntary shudder down Grace's back.

"Nonsense," she said eventually and rose to step out of her dress. "Uncle Richard isn't haunting this place. Otherwise he'd have shown himself to us. Ghosts want an audience, don't forget."

Grace kissed her sister's brow, then extricated herself from her remaining skirts before slipping between the sheets dressed only in her shift and drawers. Her sister heaved a resigned sigh and also went to bed.

That night, Grace did not go to sit at the window. Her eyes wide open, she stared at the plain whitewashed ceiling, chasing the questions that swirled around in her head.

She would have liked to have asked the most important ones to Vikrama in person as she walked through the park with him. Did he have a wife? Or a fiancée?

Bewildered, she realised that she felt something akin to jealousy, even though she didn't know what his answers would be.

To prevent these imaginary women from confusing her any further, she tried to picture what this strange martial art looked like. Did they fight like knights? Or did they set about one another like those wrestlers in the backstreets of London? Of course she had never seen anything of the kind, but Victoria's lurid novels had been enough to fuel her imagination. Gripped by a strange excitement, she closed her eyes and slipped into an uneasy sleep full of dreams of strange men in even stranger white costumes.

During the weeks that followed, Grace constantly sought opportunities to find out about the lives of the tea pickers, to explore her surroundings and maybe meet Vikrama by chance as she did so. She had the feeling that, beneath the veneer of his sense of duty, his character and feelings were gradually becoming more apparent.

He continued to disappear between the bushes every night, reappearing several hours later. Sometimes he looked up, smiling if he caught sight of her at the window. But sometimes he was so deep in thought that he didn't raise his head, causing Grace to rack her brains about what he might be thinking.

As the wakeful hours took their toll, Grace slept in a little later.

"You never come to the lessons any more," Victoria said one morning as Grace rose lethargically from her bed. "Mr. Norris is missing you. And Father's wondering why you've been having your breakfast sent up to your room for the last two weeks."

"I'm observing life on the plantation," Grace replied evasively, hoping that her sister hadn't realised the real reason for her solitary walks.

"What are you doing at night after we've all gone to sleep?"

Feeling trapped, Grace remained silent.

"I've recently noticed you sitting at the window, staring at the moon. You're not a sleepwalker, are you?"

"I . . . I can't sleep properly in bright moonlight," Grace replied, hoping that would satisfy Victoria. She knew her sister couldn't see from her bed what was happening outside.

"I've also seen you smiling to yourself, as though you were thinking something nice," Victoria added, close to rejoicing in the fact that she had uncovered one of her big sister's secrets. "You're not like one of those poets who write odes to the moon, or that German artist who paints nothing but moonlit landscapes, are you?"

"You mean Caspar David Friedrich? No, I don't think I'd ever master his skills." On hearing her sister's innocent musings, Grace now felt a little safer. "Believe me, since we arrived here, I keep waking from a bad dream at about the same time every night, and it's not until way past midnight that I can get back to sleep again."

"That doesn't sound right," Victoria said. "You should tell a doctor."

"We don't have a doctor, silly," Grace replied, stroking her hair. "Anyway, I feel perfectly healthy. It must be the fact that the time is different here than in England. I read in one of Father's journals that the sun rises many hours earlier than back home. I'm probably having difficulty adjusting to it. In any case, evening falls earlier than it does there."

The more she talked, the more she liked this explanation. Not even Mr. Norris could object.

As it turned out, her father talked to her about the situation that evening. When she confidently trotted out the explanation, Henry looked at her mother reproachfully. "Our daughter must become accustomed to the circumstances here. Can't Miss Giles do anything?"

"What could she possibly do for insomnia?" Claudia asked in astonishment. "Sing her lullabies, maybe?"

She bent towards Grace with a smile. "Darling, I think we can manage without you at breakfast for now. But you really should work on getting your body's proper rhythms back."

"I will," Grace promised earnestly, although her thoughts had already drifted back to her window and Vikrama slipping between the bushes in his strange garb.

The topics discussed by Mr. Stockton with her father at the reception included recruiting English employees for the plantation. They were to be used for arranging transport and overseeing the tea pickers' work. Henry appointed a second foreman, a big-boned, blond man called Jeff Petersen, who had formerly worked on a New Zealand sheep farm. His most striking feature, in addition to a large nose, was a braided leather whip that he carried at all times. Although he had a quiet voice, his words were tinged with a threatening force. He was not a man who tolerated failure. Once he had won the confidence of his employer, he would rule with an iron fist.

Vikrama was displeased. Sheep were not tea, and the workers didn't need a slave-driver. They had always given their best because they valued their life on the plantation and because they still valued Richard Tremayne, even after his death. And because their caste, their position in life as predetermined by the gods, would condemn them to a life of misery if it weren't for the plantation.

"Forgive me, sir, but are you not satisfied with my work?" Vikrama asked Henry when they met for their daily talk. The new foreman had not yet arrived, but that was soon to change.

"On the contrary, my good man, I'm very pleased with you. So pleased that I've decided to make you my estate manager."

Vikrama stared at him in surprise. "But Mr. Cahill . . ."

"Mr. Cahill is my lawyer, and I believe he performs that function admirably. But I consider your talents to be completely wasted in the position of foreman. I will put you in charge of Mr. Petersen; should he do anything that your experience tells you is wrong, I authorise you to instruct him accordingly."

Vikrama was nevertheless not satisfied. He knew the pickers and how to motivate them without using a whip. One look at Petersen had told him that things were going to change as soon as he was out in the fields.

"You look as though you're not pleased with my decision."

"You're in charge, sir. You will always do what's best for the plantation."

Henry looked at him searchingly, then nodded. "Please have a cup of tea, Mr. Vikrama. You're right, our plantation really does produce the highest quality."

Vikrama drank in silence, then said, "Have you ever noticed that the women sing in the tea fields?"

Henry frowned. What had made him think of that? "When we toured the plantation, all was quiet."

"That's true. The women had seen us coming. But if you approach the tea fields without being seen, you can hear them singing."

"That's all well and good, but what does it have to do with our conversation?"

"Nothing. I just wanted to tell you. The songs are beautiful; they show how happy the pickers are. As long as those songs are heard among the tea plants, Vannattuppūcci will continue to produce tea of the same excellent quality, and you'll enjoy an excellent name worldwide."

Henry found what he said odd, but said nothing. What did he mean by that? A clever man like Vikrama didn't say something for no good reason . . .

All at once he felt a stab of mistrust. Did the lad intend to stir up his workforce against him if he didn't do what he wanted?

He looked into the eyes of Vikrama, who seemed unmoved, although Henry couldn't shake off the impression that something was simmering beneath the surface. *I'll have to keep a good eye on him,* he thought.

When Henry's new employees took up their posts, a few things changed on the plantation. Productivity increased—and a silence fell over the tea fields. The women worked faster than before, but no longer sang. In Mr. Petersen's opinion, singing would distract them from their work.

Henry Tremayne didn't notice the change. He had forgotten Vikrama's words, and his estate manager had not brought it up again.

But Vikrama had changed, too. He had become quieter, more inward-looking. He knew that Petersen and his people would not take any notice of a half-caste. And that, should a dispute arise, Mr. Tremayne would take their side.

He put it all down to the fact that he had been seen in the company of Tremayne's daughter on the evening of the ball. Stockton must have made it clear to him that this was not seemly. Stockton, with whom Master Richard had fought bitterly, and whom Vikrama secretly held responsible for his death. But could he claim that Mr. Tremayne was similar?

He ultimately deemed it better to say nothing—after all, the British stuck together, he knew that—and to keep out of the way of Tremayne's daughters as much as possible, although he would find it hard to forgo Grace's company. Grace, with her milk-white skin, who was so different from other women. He had never felt so much for a woman within such a short space of time.

But for the good of his people he forced himself to avoid her. Not that Tremayne would get the wrong impression . . .

If her father was completely oblivious of the change in Vikrama, Grace certainly noticed it. When they met, he no longer chatted uninhibitedly with her. He was reserved, sometimes really stiff, so that after a few moments Grace would withdraw, completely unnerved, and chide herself for her thoughts in which he frequently played a leading role. But once her disappointment had faded, she would wonder what could have led to it. Were there problems on the plantation? Problems with her father? She hadn't failed to notice the arrival of the men whom Stockton had recommended. Or that Vikrama was more frequently confined to the office instead of walking around the estate as before. Did that also have something to do with Stockton? Although she didn't have any proof of it, it nevertheless increased her anger at their neighbour even more.

One beautiful warm morning, while Victoria was sweating in the classroom over a dictation with Mr. Norris, Grace decided that it was time to write to her friends in London. She had intended to ever since they arrived in Colombo, but had never got around to it; there had been too much to see, too much happening.

A shrill cry caused Grace's pen to slip, causing a hideous line to spread like a gash across what she had written.

Assuming that something bad must have happened, she hurried to the window. She could see nothing from there, so she ran from the room.

She was surprised to find that no one else in the house seemed to have noticed the commotion. Peering out of the tall windows of the hall, she saw a crowd of people gathered by the tea sheds. The cries were still echoing across the courtyard.

At first she thought she should tell her father, but he had left the plantation early that morning. Her mother was in bed with a migraine again.

As no one else appeared to be about to do anything, Grace hitched up her skirts and ran outside.

The sharp hissing sound she heard between the screams turned her blood to ice. She had heard it once before, in Plymouth, where they had boarded the ship for Ceylon.

The women drew back as Grace forced her way between them.

A woman was tied to a palm tree and Petersen was thrashing her with a riding whip.

Grace froze as she saw the blood on the woman's clothes.

"Stop it!" she cried out, but the man brought the whip whistling down again on the woman's back.

Grace jumped, then ran on. Some of the men shrank back in shock; one called out something she didn't understand to Petersen.

All at once she realised there was only one thing to be done to stop the foreman. She stepped in front of the woman, and his arm stopped.

Petersen muttered angrily, but then seemed to realise who she was.

"Get out of my way, Miss Tremayne!"

Impertinent swine, Grace thought angrily. *Who does he think he is, giving me orders?*

"Raise your hand again if you like, but it's me you'll hit!" she said to Petersen, whose arm was still raised. "And I can tell you that if you do, you'll have to explain to my father why his daughter has a bloody gash across her face!"

Time stood still around them. The murmuring that had flared up among the tea pickers fell silent. Petersen chewed his lower lip as though he was weighing up whether to strike. He finally lowered his arm.

"I have the right to punish this woman!" he snarled. "She was stealing."

"What did she steal, Mr. Petersen? Tea?"

"She was picking fruit from the apple tree."

Grace gasped and shook her head. "You're whipping her because she took a few apples? From that tree?" She pointed to the tree that looked as though it didn't belong in this place. "Have you ever tasted one of those apples?"

"I'd never dare, ma'am," Petersen replied, puffing out his chest proudly.

"Then you should," Grace snapped. "Those apples are completely worthless for cooking or eating. That's why they're still there. If anyone on the plantation wants to eat one, there's no reason why they shouldn't!"

"But I'm sure your father wouldn't . . ."

"My father doesn't care about the apple tree! And even if he did, he wouldn't agree to a woman being whipped. Punishments like this, Mr. Petersen, belong in the Middle Ages, not in a cultured society. You will let the woman go and ensure that she's given medical attention!"

The foreman ground his teeth. But since Grace was not in the least bit intimidated by it, he rolled up the whip. "I'll tell your father about this incident!"

"Please do, but don't forget to tell him about your own behaviour because I most certainly will, Mr. Petersen!"

Their eyes met briefly, and Grace saw that the foreman intended to pay her back for it somehow. *But I'm the daughter of the house,* she told herself. *And one day I'll run this plantation, with or without a husband.*

When her father returned, it was only a few minutes before he heard about the incident and summoned Grace. When she entered she saw that Vikrama, who was standing by her father, was as white as a sheet.

Henry looked enraged. "Sit down, Grace," he said.

As she sat down on the chair in front of the desk, her father got up and paced a few steps around the room. Grace looked at Vikrama, but the fear on his face was so great that she didn't dare catch his eye. Her father would probably punish her severely for her intervention.

"Mr. Petersen has just told me what happened out on the yard."

"He was whipping a woman, Father!" Grace burst out. "If he's told you anything else, it's a lie."

"Grace!" The rage in his voice silenced her.

"I'm sorry." Grace lowered her head, only keeping her anger under control with difficulty. Was she now to be punished for the fact that the foreman had behaved like a medieval torturer?

"I don't have to tell you that your actions were completely inexcusable for a young lady. You could have been injured!"

"So you've given Mr. Petersen consent to whip the tea pickers? Because of apples from a tree that we don't even touch?"

"It's a matter of principle. Theft is theft!"

"She was only taking something to eat! In England theft is no longer punished by whipping."

"No, but the thief is dismissed and sent away without references."

"You should at least compensate that woman for the injuries she's suffered." Grace's eyes were gleaming. What had happened to the father she knew? Had Stockton replaced him with an evil marionette? "Since when have we acted like barbarians?"

Henry pressed his lips together. His cheeks flushed. All signs of an attack of rage. A knot gripped Grace's stomach. Not from fear, but from the realisation that her father was not on her side.

"You will never again interfere in the affairs of my employees," he said, quietly emphatic, his voice filled with the threat of anger. "For your disrespect I'm placing you under house arrest for the rest of the day. I don't want to see you outside under any circumstances, do you hear?"

Grace looked at her father in stunned silence. The last time he had placed her under house arrest was eight years ago, when she had been caught at a garden party climbing trees in a white lace dress to enjoy the view over the park. The dress had been ruined, and she had been confined to a day's boredom in her room on her own since little Victoria had to stay with her mother.

You don't mean that, she wanted to say, but the words stuck in her throat. She looked at Vikrama, unable to read his expression, then got up from her seat.

Her father's eyes blazed with rage. "I expect an appropriate apology from you tomorrow. You may go."

Grace's heart felt tight. Tears rose up inside her, tears of anger and disappointment, but she suppressed them as she turned slowly and left the room. She continued to control herself as she crossed the hall. Her mother was on the stairs, talking to Miss Giles about the picture of the Indian gods and the flowers that were still regularly laid before it by unknown hands. Even after a month here, no one had seen the faithful, who seemed prepared to wait for the optimum moments.

Grace managed to slip silently past them into the corridor. Here, protected by the half-light, she gave free rein to her tears. She wept quietly about the injustice she had suffered, and about her father's disinterest in the well-being of his employees. She wept about the fact that Vikrama had been witness to her father's reprimand of her. That weighed heaviest on her.

On reaching the end of the corridor, she stopped. She could clearly hear Victoria sighing to herself. She was probably at her easel again, painting.

No doubt she would ask Grace why she had a tear-stained face. Although she knew Victoria would be on her side, Grace didn't want to tell her anything, to show her how much her father had hurt her.

After brief consideration, Grace thought of the billiard room. As far as she knew, her father had not yet taken it over. With a lump in her throat, she turned and ran to the door she and her sister had opened a few weeks ago.

She could still hear her mother's and Miss Giles's voices drifting through from the hall. Fearing they might hear her, Grace turned the doorknob carefully.

She had hardly stepped over the threshold when she seemed to be gripped by a strange magic—as though Uncle Richard were waiting in person to comfort her. Her tears dried up; her mind became clearer. The injustice she had suffered was forgotten as other thoughts took its place.

Who was Richard Tremayne?

Grace suddenly regretted that she knew so little about him.

Would he also have punished her because she had tried to help a woman on his estate? How had he dealt with his people? The few words Vikrama had spoken about him had been full of admiration.

Grace dismissed any hope that Richard might have left behind some kind of record. It wasn't the way of the Tremayne men to keep diaries. If Richard had resembled his brother in the slightest, he had to have been a purposeful man who lived in the here and now, without clinging on to memories and deliberations.

The fact that she, the heir of the Tremaynes, did so must have come from her mother's side. Her mother, too, tended to think too much, a habit to which her doctor ascribed her migraines, but which she persisted with nevertheless.

Closing the door behind her, all that remained of her furious crying was the occasional slight sob, as though she were a little child who had soon forgotten the reason for her tears. She crossed the room cautiously, running her hands over the dust sheets and feeling the contours of the furniture beneath. She opened the lid of the piano and pressed one of the white keys. The tone that rang out at the gesture sounded out of tune, indicating that the instrument had not been played since long before her uncle's death. Why had he bought it? Had he wanted to learn to play?

She considered that improbable, too. It was more likely because he wanted to impress his friends and fellow club members.

Driven by a sudden impulse, she went over to the little Empire chest of drawers that stood beneath a landscape painting showing a lake and a country house. On closer inspection, it was obvious that Grace's initial assumption that this was Tremayne House had been wrong. This painting was clearly not here for nostalgic reasons; her uncle must have hung it there merely to decorate the room.

She opened the top drawer, her heart beating loudly with expectation. Would she find anything here to help her form a picture of Uncle Richard?

The dry scraping of wood on wood was followed by a glimpse of dusty red velvet. Indents in the fabric indicated that something must have been kept here, something that had long since been removed. Grace ran her finger over the velvet lining. Finding nothing there, she closed the drawer and moved to the one beneath it. In this one were a few pieces of paper, yellowed bills inscribed with Tamil writing, an empty tobacco tin with a missing hinge, and a link of a brass chain. Junk that had been left behind when the important items were removed from the drawer.

At first glance, the last drawer, which was particularly difficult to open, seemed to yield nothing of importance, either, but as she drew it out she heard a muffled knocking along with the scraping. Intrigued, Grace pulled the drawer out further—and was finally rewarded by something that glittered.

She had no idea whether the object had deliberately been shoved so far back or whether it had rolled there as she pulled, but that didn't matter. She drew it out reverently. The locket was very old, its silver tarnished and blotchy, the chain almost black. Her hands trembling, Grace tried to open it, but was unable to at first. Were the contents somehow resisting revealing themselves to her gaze?

She froze as she heard voices outside the door. Had Miss Giles and her mother come to find her? She resisted the impulse to run out of the room and act as though she had just come from her talk with her father. Instead she pressed herself up against the wall near the painting, the locket clasped tightly in her hand as if it were a magical talisman that could make her invisible. The voices passed on, faded away. A door opened and closed somewhere. *Our room,* Grace thought with a start. *Victoria will tell Mother I'm not there. That Father summoned me.*

Would she come and look here? But why was she afraid? Wasn't this room part of the house?

Breathing quietly and feeling the locket gradually warming in her hand, she heard the door again. Footsteps approached, this time unaccompanied by voices. The two people—her mother and Miss Giles—passed by the door to the billiard room, finally returning to the hall.

Grace released her breath, then looked at the locket in her hand. She wouldn't be able to open it without a letter opener or a needle. She hung the tarnished chain around her neck and hid the locket beneath her dress. Then she closed the drawer, replaced the dust sheet, and, glancing once again at the painting, left the room.

As she had suspected, she found Victoria sitting at her easel. She was painting an arrangement of frangipani flowers standing before her in a silver vase.

"Oh, it's you! I thought it was Miss Giles again. How did your talk with Father go?"

"Not particularly well."

"I've heard what you did. People are talking about nothing else. One of the workers told Mr. Norris when he thought I was absorbed in my work. It was incredibly brave of you."

"You think so?" Grace sank down on the bed with a sigh. "If nothing else, it's earned me house arrest for the rest of the day. And the worst thing was that he told me off in front of Mr. Vikrama as if I were a little child."

Victoria raised her eyebrows. "House arrest? But you're eighteen! How can he put you under house arrest?"

Grace shrugged defiantly. "It's what happens when you don't behave like an adult. I don't know what's wrong with me, either. Until a few weeks ago I was capable of doing what others demanded of me."

"You're not in England any more. Back home we don't have such barbarities as whipping among the cultured classes. You can rest assured that Father will do something against the foreman. He's the master of Vannattuppūcci, not you!"

"But who else would have helped the woman? No one else was there to stop him." But Grace couldn't help wondering what Vikrama would have done if he'd been there.

Instead of touching the supper brought to her by a maid, Grace sat by the open window. Her father couldn't forbid her from doing that. The green bushes were blurred by a veil of tears as she yielded to self-pity. After Victoria had left to go to the dining room, Grace had been overcome again.

Why hadn't he been fair with her? Why did he have to punish her in front of Vikrama? That and the fact that Petersen would now be laughing at her expense bored into her like a red-hot blade.

Her father had betrayed her.

"That was very stupid of you!"

Grace started. Looking out of the window, she saw Vikrama in his black clothes. His face was pale, his eyes flashing. What was he doing here by the house? If anyone saw him . . .

But Grace didn't have the strength to send him away.

"It was the only thing I could have done," she replied, brushing the tears from her face in an agitated gesture. "I couldn't watch that woman being whipped. She'd done nothing more than take a few sour apples."

"Apples that belong to your father," Vikrama said.

Was he, too, taking her father's side now? All at once a great longing to be back in London overcame her, with the thought that she had allowed this beautiful landscape to deceive her. It seemed that people were overcome by the beast within when they were far from their homeland.

"Those apples belong just as much to me! I could just as easily have picked them and given them to her," she said defiantly.

"That would have been different. This was theft, and I will tell the woman not to do it in future. We have a new master now, who isn't aware of his predecessor's ways."

Grace was shocked by the contempt in his voice.

"Do you mean to say that my uncle allowed people to pick the apples?"

A melancholy smile crossed Vikrama's face. "Yes, he did."

"Why didn't you tell my father that? He can't have known . . ." Grace hesitated as she saw the sadness in his eyes.

"Things have changed since he brought in those new people," he said quietly. "He's turned me into a lapdog, a man who hardly has anything to do with the people out there. I have to accompany him to meetings and give instructions to his foreman. But I know that the others are gradually getting to call the shots. One day I'll be superfluous, and he'll urge me to go. It simply isn't proper for a Tamil half-caste to hold an important position on the plantation."

Damned Stockton, Grace thought angrily. *He's the only one who could have put such an idea into Father's head.*

"I don't think my father would do something like that. He values your skills and keeps you close by him because he's still very unsure of himself when it comes to tea production."

"Maybe," Vikrama replied, looking at his fingers in a vain attempt to hide his inner turmoil. "I'm probably wrong. But I'm very worried about the fact that I hardly have anything to do with the pickers and other workers any more. They trust me, and under my command they gladly worked for their master. Now Petersen's people patrol the plantation, carrying weapons though there's no need for it, and Petersen whips a woman for the alleged theft of a few apples."

He shuddered, clearly longing to haul Petersen and his men over the coals. He looked at Grace and his gaze sent a wave of heat through her veins. "Thank you for standing up for my people. For protecting Naala."

"That's her name—Naala?"

Vikrama nodded.

"I'll remember that."

"She'll carry the scars of the whip all her life. She'll never forget what was done to her, and why. But she'll never forget, either, that it was the master's daughter who saved her from worse. None of my people will forget that."

Their faces were suddenly so close that he could have kissed her at any moment. But then he looked down to the ground and stepped back.

"Mr. Vikrama!" she called before he could turn.

"Yes, Miss Grace?"

"Would it be possible . . . ?" She stopped, afraid of asking too much.

"What is it?" Vikrama was smiling again.

Encouraged, Grace said, "Would it be possible for you to teach me some Tamil?"

"But most people here speak English."

"I know, but I . . . during the incident I would have liked to be able to talk to the woman . . . to Naala, in her own language. And I would have liked to be able to understand what the other women were saying. I think it would only be . . . courteous to understand their language, don't you?"

Her throat was tight and there was a knot in her stomach. She suddenly seemed silly to herself. Vikrama was right; they all spoke English here. And after that afternoon's incident the people certainly wouldn't want the masters to understand their language. That was the only way in which they could complain without fear of punishment by the foreman.

"Tamil isn't an easy language to learn," Vikrama said after regarding her for a few moments. "But I'll do my best to teach you."

He turned and vanished into the bushes.

Grace watched him go with a smile, before remembering the locket. She drew it out from her bodice, looked at it, and was about to get a hairpin when Victoria stormed in at the door.

She quickly slipped the locket back beneath her dress.

"Aren't you eating?" her sister asked in surprise as she saw the untouched tray.

"I was about to."

"You should. The poultry is excellent! Anyway, sulking will do you no good. Father's seen sense and told us that he's taken Petersen to task for the whipping. He probably only held it against you that you interfered."

No, he held it against me that I wasn't the good little girl he's become used to over the years, Grace thought, but nodded. "I'm going to go to him and apologise first thing tomorrow morning," she announced. She already knew what she would do when her freedom was restored.

The next morning, after apologising to her father and he had lifted her house arrest, Grace made her way to the tea pickers' accommodation. Naala was among those who lived on the edge of the tea plantation with their children. It seemed she did not have a husband, although she had two children. Her son was old enough to help with the work, but her daughter was only three or four. The girl stared at Grace wide-eyed as she approached the hut, then whirled around and ran inside.

As if turned to stone, Grace looked at the dwelling, which couldn't be called a house, hut, or shed. The walls were formed from boards full of holes, and the palm-leaf roof looked anything but watertight. It almost made Grace feel ashamed for the luxury in which she lived.

A little later, the girl appeared again and waved Grace inside. It was dark, the air full of the smell of dried blood and bitter herbs.

Next to the bed, on which Naala was lying on her stomach, an old woman was standing, her skin as brown as walnut shells. Life had traced a furrowed map on her face. She looked Grace up and down, then a spark of recognition flared in her dark eyes. "You are young miss."

Grace took a moment to understand the heavily accented words, then she nodded. "I am."

"You help Naala."

"Yes, and I came to find out how she is."

"She is bad," the woman said and pulled the sheet down a little from Naala's back. The wounds were covered with a paste that did nothing to hide their severity, but on the contrary made them stand out. The skin gaped apart like bloody lips.

Grace's hand shot to her mouth in horror.

"That should be looked at by a doctor."

The old woman shook her head. "No doctor. I am here. I care for her. My medicine heal wounds, but take time."

A firm emphasis in her voice stopped Grace from insisting on calling a doctor. But she doubted whether traditional medicine would be enough. What if the woman got gangrene? She had read in a newspaper article about the painful death that could cause.

"May I come back and see how she's getting on?"

"Mistress can go where she want," the old woman replied simply, then pulled the sheet back up.

Grace felt completely useless. She really wished she could have helped the woman. But how?

The silence between them eventually became so uncomfortable that Grace took her leave, promising to call again during the next few days.

She went back through the tea fields, which looked like a soft green blanket, followed by the surprised glances of the pickers, who turned straight back to their work when they saw her looking. She made her way along the narrow path, raising her eyes regularly to the clouds that formed dramatic shapes against the deep-blue sky.

"Miss Grace!" someone called from one side.

She shaded her eyes and made out Vikrama. Today he was wearing a waistcoat over his shirt, and his shirtsleeves were rolled up. His dark pants and high boots were streaked with dust. He was clearly on his way back from a tour of inspection.

"Yes, Mr. Vikrama?" Grace said with a smile.

"Are you still interested in learning our language?"

"But of course!" she replied. "Only a moment ago I was wishing I could speak it. I've just been to visit Naala. The woman who was with her is a healer, isn't she?"

Vikrama nodded. "She came straight from the village yesterday to tend the wounds. She'll make sure that Naala's able to work again soon."

Grace detected the hint of reproach. *When will he stop seeing me as merely the master's daughter?*

"My main concern is that she survives the whipping and doesn't get gangrene. I've read about the practices on old sailing ships. It wasn't unusual for men who were whipped to die from their injuries."

"You're very different from all the other English women I know, Miss Grace."

"I take that as a compliment," she replied with a smile. "For a long time I didn't know anything different, but this place has worked some kind of magic on me."

"Yes, it can change people if they let it." He smiled to himself, lost in thought for a moment, then folded his arms. "How about meeting tomorrow for our first language lesson? I have the afternoon free."

"And you really want to spend it giving me a language lesson?"

"I don't have anything else to do. And it's for a good cause. Maybe your father will take an interest in Tamil at some stage. You could teach him yourself then."

Grace almost laughed out loud. Her father allowing himself to be taught anything by her? The man who still punished her like a child for making her own decisions?

"I will if he expresses an interest," she replied simply, not wanting to appear like a sulky child in front of Vikrama. "Thank you very much. I'll see you tomorrow!"

Back at the house, Grace began to have her doubts. Should she tell her father? She recalled the look in the foreman's eyes. A look that promised retaliation for her intervention. If he saw her with Vikrama, he might tell her father a pack of lies that could get them both in hot water. She decided to lay her cards on the table.

As she broached the subject nervously, almost fearfully, over supper, she was met with astonishment.

"But what do you want with that uncultured language, when almost everyone here speaks English?" her mother asked. She must have known about her daughter's punishment, but clearly considered it a closed chapter.

"I want to know what the people are really thinking," Grace explained. She looked at her father, who gave the impression he wasn't inclined to grant her wish.

No sooner had she said it than it occurred to her that she could be misunderstood. But it was too late.

"You mean they might be conspiring against us?" Her father's expression was serious.

"No, it's just that . . ." Grace hesitated. There was no way she wanted to give the impression that the people here were hatching anything, or it would not be long before Petersen found another woman to whip. "I just want to be able to talk to them. I find it difficult to understand their accent, and it would be polite to be able to speak their language."

"Polite? With these people?" Henry sniffed scornfully before picking up his glass and drinking two rapid gulps. "These people know nothing but orders and duty. They wouldn't know what to do if their masters were friendly towards them."

Grace pressed her lips together. Did that mean *no*?

"But I grant that it would be an advantage to know the language. At least you'd find out if they're plotting to rebel. You could be doing me a valuable service if you kept your ears open among them. I too would like to know what they're really thinking."

Grace felt as though she'd swallowed a stone. The smell of the roast meat suddenly seemed stale. Her father wanted her to spy for him. Now she was sorry she'd asked—he was so busy that he probably wouldn't even have noticed if she'd gone ahead in secret without mentioning it to him.

"Then I want to learn the language, too!" Victoria exclaimed.

"You will concern yourself with your own lessons and the work Mr. Norris sets you," her father snapped back. "He showed me your last dictation a few hours ago. I can't believe that a young lady has such dreadful handwriting!"

Victoria pouted as Grace scarcely managed to suppress a sigh of relief. She loved her sister more than anything in the world, but for a reason she did not really understand, she didn't want her there when she was practising with Vikrama.

"Very well, Grace, you can have lessons with Mr. Vikrama. But only under the condition that you don't keep him from his real duties."

"He's agreed to teach me outside his working hours."

"And you will take Miss Giles with you to the lessons as a chaperone."

"Chaperone?" Grace exclaimed. "What do you think is going to happen?"

"Hopefully nothing. That's why she'll accompany you. If you don't agree, I'm afraid you'll have to go without the lessons."

Grace sniffed, but she knew that she couldn't push her luck. The fact that her father was allowing her to have language lessons was a blessing in itself, and she didn't want to jeopardise that.

"Very well, Father. I'll take Miss Giles with me," she said sweetly. "I hope the poor woman won't be bored to death."

"She must have some needlework or something that she can take to while the time away," Claudia said, clearly pleased that she wouldn't have to find something to occupy the governess herself. "I agree that it would be better if you weren't alone with this man. He may be a good employee, but we know nothing about his private life." She glanced at her husband, as though hoping he might enlighten her. "It was very bold of you to ask him. He could have misunderstood you."

Grace pressed her lips together. What on earth did they think he was like? Some rake who'd pounce on her given the opportunity?

"If you say so, Mother," she replied. Although she had lost her appetite, she shovelled a little more meat into her mouth and chewed slowly as a defence against answering any more questions.

"What gave you the idea of wanting to learn Tamil?" Victoria asked after they had returned to their room. "I thought you couldn't bear this country. At least, that's how it seemed three weeks ago."

Grace smiled to herself as she examined her embroidery. A few days ago she had begun to embroider a small frangipani flower on a silk handkerchief. "It's because of that woman yesterday. The one who was whipped."

Victoria looked at her in incomprehension. "What's she got to do with it?"

"The other women were all agitated and whispering. I'd like to have understood them."

"So you *do* want to spy for Papa?"

"Of course not!" Grace replied indignantly. "I don't think those people would say anything bad against us."

"Perhaps that's changed since the foreman whipped that woman."

"Let's hope that isn't the case. Anyway, I don't intend to listen in on them and give them even more grounds for suspicion. I just want to be able to talk to them."

Grace turned back to her embroidery. She had just finished the edge of another flower when Victoria suddenly said, "You like Mr. Vikrama, don't you?"

Grace narrowly avoided pricking her finger with the needle. "What put that nonsense into your head?"

"Don't deny it! I'm your sister. I can see the way your eyes light up when his name's mentioned. And when you talk about him. No wonder Father's sending Miss Giles along with you."

Grace was horrified. *Are my feelings really so obvious?* she wondered. Her cheeks turned deep red.

"He's very nice," she admitted. "And he's handsome, don't you think?"

"He looks like a London dandy who's been sitting for too long in the sun." Victoria's eyes shone with glee.

"What do you know about dandies?" Grace said with studied indignation.

"Have you forgotten the guests at our farewell party?"

Victoria moved to sit across from her sister on the window seat. "Mr. Hutchinson looked as though he were out to catch a wife. Yet he's already got one who's rich—and good-natured to boot, if the other women are to be believed."

The memory of the man, who really was a dandy, drove away Grace's indignation and made her laugh.

"Oh, that ridiculously patterned jacket!" she said. "Like a scarecrow!"

"And at his age! The young women were all making fun of him."

The two girls burst out laughing.

"You know," Victoria said once they'd got their breath back, "I haven't been totally honest. I do miss London and its parties a little."

In a gesture that was almost clumsy, Victoria grasped her sister's hand. "You would have been the most beautiful of them all at the debutantes' ball. I mean it."

"Honestly?" As her sister spoke, Grace realised that she no longer regretted not having danced in front of the queen. Something had filled the gap left by the missed opportunity. Something she couldn't put a name to—not yet, at least—but which was much more fulfilling than the glitter of a ballroom.

"I wonder if I'll have a debut?" Victoria swung her legs, kicking her heels against the panelling beneath the window seat. "Do you think we'll go back to England?"

"If you pester Papa about it for long enough . . ."

Grace was sure that would have no effect at all, but she didn't want to deprive Victoria of all hope.

"Anyway, I've heard that there's an annual debutantes' ball in Nuwara Eliya, too," Victoria said.

"They hold it at one of the hotels in the area. It's financed by the men from the Hill Club. I bet that's an attempt to make sure their bored wives have something to do."

Grace winked conspiratorially in response to Victoria's smirk. "I don't suppose they have the queen's double there, do they?"

"No, but I think they hang a copy of her official portrait on the wall," Victoria said. "So we will get to dance in front of the queen."

The two girls laughed.

12

Vannattuppūcci Tea Company, 2008

When Diana woke around seven, the early-morning mist was covering the plantation, bathing everything in a mysterious blue light. As though in response to the effect, the parrots' early calls were timid and sporadic. Stillness reigned over the rest of the plantation. Only the distant rustling of the wind moving over the leaves of the tea plants reached her ears like elfin whispers.

Diana rose and went barefoot to the window. The cold tiles beneath her feet drove away most of her tiredness; the rest was dispelled by the view she now saw. The light was completely different from that in Europe—there was nothing depressing about this morning mist; rather, it looked like the veil of a bride eagerly anticipating the moment she would show her face to her beloved.

Diana sat on the window seat, looking at the silhouette of her own reflection in the glass. Did anything of Grace really linger in this room? And where should she begin to look?

As the morning light grew stronger and the mist gradually dissipated under the sun, she noticed a small notch in the window frame.

It was easy to overlook, but once Diana had seen it, its presence in the wood was obvious.

A butterfly, Diana thought, her heart beginning to pound as though she had just found Grace Tremayne's diary. Standing up from the window seat, she leaned over the frame, and found it was actually quite a complex, artistic carving. Was it by Grace? Or Victoria?

Emily's grandmother had been known to produce wonderful drawings and etchings. Unfortunately, almost all of her works had been lost over time. All that remained were two charcoal drawings in the Tremayne House drawing room, which had faded in Diana's memory. What she would have given to be able to compare them now with this butterfly.

She rejected the idea of asking Mr. Green for a photo or a scan. Instead she reached for her camera, which until now she had only used to capture a few impressions of her guided tour.

None of the pictures she took truly captured the effect the butterfly had on the viewer, but they would be enough for a comparison.

Looking at the images on her camera, she noticed that the gap between the windowsill and the frame was a little wider by the butterfly. Wide enough for something to be hidden there!

Obeying a sudden impulse, she opened the window and inspected the gap. At first she couldn't see anything. *I need some light,* she thought, then went over to the bedside table and fetched her mobile. In the weak glow from the display lighting, she saw what she was looking for.

There was something tucked into the gap! A note? Or just a remnant of wallpaper? There was no way she could pull it out with her fingers, but maybe tweezers would do the trick.

Putting the phone down, she took her make-up bag from the bedside table. She always carried a pair of tweezers in case of emergencies. She used them to reach the greying tip of the paper, which was no easy undertaking. The difficulty in reaching it presumably explained why no one had found the piece of paper before. As she managed to grip it and carefully pull it out, she noticed that this was not a mere piece of paper or scrap of wallpaper.

It was a letter! A letter in a brown envelope that had been hidden behind the wall panelling!

"This can't be true!" she murmured in amazement, her heart beating wildly.

It bore the inscription *By Way of Farewell, 1907.* It was secured with a small seal depicting a butterfly.

Who was its author? Victoria, perhaps? The handwriting was similar to that of the letter from the crypt, but looked more mature and a little agitated, as though the writer had been in turmoil. In any case, there was proof that Victoria had returned to England by then.

Diana weighed the rough brown envelope in her hand for a moment. It felt like there was more than one page. What could it say? Was it a message someone had left behind for a person they loved? Would this reveal the reason for Victoria's uneasy conscience?

Although her curiosity was killing her, Diana decided not to open the letter until later. Twenty-one years lay between the death of Richard Tremayne and this letter. Much could have happened in that time. Although it was possible that part of the story was recorded here, she decided she would look for other clues first.

After gazing out over the early-morning scene for a while, lost in thought, she rose and tucked the letter into her bag to avoid the temptation of opening it too soon. She then took the cardboard tube containing the palm leaf that Jonathan had carefully stowed beneath her clothes. It slipped out into her hand with a light rustle.

"Did you predict a girl's fate?" Diana murmured, gently tracing the characters with her finger. "Or are you nothing to do with any of this?" Silence followed her words; a silence that contained no answers.

As the sounds of activity grew in the courtyard and the first employees of the Tea Company arrived to begin their workday, Diana stowed the palm leaf back in its tube and held herself back from taking another look at the letter from 1907. *All in its own good time,* she thought as she made her way to the small bathroom she shared with Jonathan.

He seemed not to be up yet, as the shower cubicle was dry and it was a while before the lukewarm water ran hot.

When she was ready and about to set out along the corridor, the neighbouring door opened. Seeing Jonathan in a T-shirt and pyjama bottoms was a completely new experience for Diana.

"Good morning!" she called out to him with a grin, as she could see he was not yet fully awake. His reply was more of a mutter than a cheerful greeting, but a shower would probably put that right.

"I hope you slept well." Mr. Manderley greeted her as she entered the kitchen. She had been intending to repay Jonathan for yesterday's dinner, but now she saw that the breakfast things were already out.

"I took it upon myself to put together a little breakfast," Manderley said with a smile. "I went to the archive earlier to get some of last year's books for a market analysis, and I saw that you've already made a good start."

"Yes, the old cupboards in there provided us with plenty to go on. And now I've got someone to help me."

"Your fiancé's an academic, isn't he?"

Diana paused. "My fiancé?"

Manderley looked at her in confusion. "Oh, you're not . . . I'm sorry—the perils of the English language! I really thought you two were . . ."

"No. Jonathan—I mean, Mr. Singh—was recommended to me by a friend and has kindly agreed to help me with my research."

"Ah, then . . ." To hide his embarrassment, Manderley turned and set the kettle to boil on the stove.

"I made a discovery," Diana said to fill the uncomfortable silence. "There's a butterfly carved into the old window frame in my room."

"I know," Manderley replied. He turned and his unease had vanished. "We assume that it was one of the Tremayne daughters who carved the butterfly. Or a secret lover."

"Did the girls have any particular admirers? All I know is that Grace married a sea captain."

Manderley looked at her strangely. "A sea captain?"

"Yes, a German captain. That's one of the few things I know for certain about her. Maybe that was the scandal that caused the rift between her and the rest of the family."

"Well, I'm afraid I can't shed much light on that. However, I do suggest you might spread your search to the Stocktons. They're on the neighbouring plantation, which unfortunately went bankrupt last year. However, the process brought to light some interesting documents. As far as I know, the Tremayne family are referred to."

Diana's eyes widened. Stockton was the man who had been standing next to Henry Tremayne in the club photo!

"Thank you for that information," she replied. "If I can, I'll go there and take a look at the documents."

Manderley nodded kindly, then suddenly looked towards the door.

"Good morning, Mr. Singh. Miss Wagenbach and I were just talking about your research."

"Mr. Manderley has kindly told me about some documents at the neighbouring plantation. He thinks the Stockton family may also have some information about mine. Isn't that great?"

"Stockton? Isn't that the man in the Hill Club photo?"

"The very same!"

"I think you're on your way to getting some results," Manderley said. He glanced at his watch and looked a little harassed. "Please excuse me, I have to go on a tour of the plantation soon. Don't forget the tea!"

Before Diana could thank him for the breakfast, he had vanished. The water in the kettle had come to the boil. Manderley had thoughtfully set out a tea caddy and two cups, which suggested he had never intended to have breakfast with them.

As the tea gave off its heady, herby scent, Diana took care of the toast, while Jonathan set the table.

"So, how was your night in the divided room?" Diana asked when they had finally sat down together and were busy spreading butter and orange marmalade on the toast. Without knowing why, she kept quiet about her find from the window frame. It was as though she wanted to keep that card up her sleeve for the time when all other avenues had come to an end.

"Not particularly good. But you could see that when we met in the corridor."

Diana gave him a searching look. He still looked a little worse for wear.

"Did you see a ghost, perhaps? You didn't have any problems sleeping back at the hotel."

"No, and I don't usually suffer from insomnia, either. I just had a few things going round my head. Usually I can put them out of mind, but there's something about this place that breathes new life into thoughts—good ones and bad ones."

What could he mean?

"Maybe I shouldn't have taken you away from your work," Diana began guiltily. "Here I am dragging you around the countryside and back home your publisher's going crazy."

"It's not that," he blurted out. "It's about my ex-wife."

"I see." Embarrassed, Diana bit into her toast, washing it down with the best Ceylon tea she had ever tasted. Manderley had clearly given them a pack of the hand-produced tea.

"She sent me a message yesterday telling me that she'd met someone else," Jonathan continued unexpectedly. "A computer specialist from Melbourne. She's even considering moving out to Australia and taking Rana with her."

"I'm sorry to hear it."

"There's no need to be. I've been suspecting something of the kind for a while now. Or maybe I should say that Rana's suggested it in her letters. Of course she can't write well enough yet to explain what she feels in great detail, but I've been sensing that something's bothering her."

"What if you seek to get custody? After all, you're an Indian citizen."

"But that would mean I'd have to move to Delhi. I'd have to leave Sri Lanka and with it all the plans I had."

Diana remembered the Kingdom of Kandy that he'd told her about.

"It sounds horribly selfish, doesn't it?" He smiled self-deprecatingly and took a drink of tea.

"What if you were to bring your daughter to Sri Lanka?"

"Then the argument about her change of school would no longer hold water because she'd have to go to a different school here. Anyway, she's too attached to her mother." He set his cup down with a sigh. "I'm afraid my book's going to have to be a real bestseller before I can afford to visit her in Australia."

"Is it out of the question for your ex-wife to pay for your daughter to fly here?"

Jonathan shook his head. "Rana's eight. I don't think any mother in the world would place her daughter alone on a plane at that age if there wasn't a serious reason for it. For better or for worse, I'll just have to get used to the idea of not seeing my daughter for long stretches at a time."

Diana felt keenly how much this was affecting him, and without thinking reached for his hand. "I'm sure you'll find a solution. And if necessary I'll pester all the publishers in Europe to buy the rights to your book."

Jonathan smiled to himself, then changed the subject with a light shake of his head. "We ought to talk about the archives and what you intend to do. You definitely want to visit the neighbouring plantation, don't you?"

Diana nodded. "Yes, provided we can get there. Our driver isn't coming back for three days."

As she spoke she remembered she had to rearrange her flight.

"I'm sure Mr. Manderley will lend us a vehicle. Even though this has nothing to do with him, he seems to be really keen on our project."

The way he stressed the word *our* made Diana feel warm inside, but she concealed her smile behind her teacup.

Half an hour later, they were on their way to the archive and the plantation came to life. Out in the courtyard, workers were calling to one another, women were adjusting their saris and shouldering their baskets. A phone was ringing somewhere in the house, and someone was bashing away on a computer keyboard behind a door.

Downstairs, in the former servants' quarters, everything was quiet. The only sound in the corridor was the humming of the fluorescent lights. In the archive room, dust motes were floating in the rays of sun that fell on to the desk. Overnight, another table had been brought in and was now waiting to be filled with commercial records and books.

Jonathan rubbed his hands together before opening the doors to a cupboard. He looked at the mess inside with a kind of reverence, then smiled. "You know, in a way I've missed this kind of chaotic filing. Earlier, in the museum, we were constantly making finds like this, which had to be worked through and catalogued. Sometimes it seemed like a real burden, but now I realise how much I actually miss it."

"Well, you've got plenty of opportunity here to get it out of your system," Diana replied as she went over to the desk. "I've found a few books here that date back to the relevant time. As soon as I know what's in them I'll get the next ones out."

Nodding eagerly, Jonathan turned and immersed himself in the old cupboard.

"If I understand correctly, Henry Tremayne must have taken over the plantation in 1887," Jonathan said, looking up from his pile of books. He had spent two whole hours sorting through the files from the cupboard and putting them in order. "All the books until then were made out by Richard Tremayne."

"Henry must have come out here a few months after receiving the news of Richard's death," Diana replied. "He received a telegram dated October 1886 saying that his brother fell from Adam's Peak."

"Was he a mountaineer?"

Diana shrugged. "No idea. Maybe he liked hiking. There must be a temple up there. Do you know?"

"There's a pilgrim track, certainly," Jonathan confirmed. "It's really steep in places. If someone was careless it would be easy to fall. The ascent must have been even more dangerous a hundred plus years ago."

"If we have enough time I'd like to see the path," Diana said, running her hand thoughtfully over the pages of the book in front of her.

"Is there any indication of the place where Richard Tremayne fell?"

Diana shook her head. "I don't think so. Maybe there's something in the old police records, but I'm sure they won't be kept here. If at all."

"The English were pretty meticulous about things like that. There must be hundreds of old files languishing in some cupboard or cellar. But you'd need even more time to sift through those, and I don't know if your clients could do without you for that long."

He was right. Her old life was waiting for her back home, and at some stage she would have to bring this adventure to an end. But she didn't want to think about it right then. She had managed not to look at her emails at all yesterday, and maybe her work could live without her doing so for the next two days.

As afternoon came to Vannattuppūcci, Diana leaned back with a sigh and pressed her fingers to the corners of her eyes. How many books had she gone through? Dry columns of figures, composed in beautiful handwriting, but telling her nothing. The enticing thought of simply reading the letter she had found kept resurfacing. But she had held out, recalling the words of her former professor who had warned his law students to choose the right moment to examine any piece of evidence.

Jonathan got to his feet. "I think we should take a little break. How do you fancy a walk around the plantation?"

"Good idea." Diana pushed the documents back across the desk.

A pleasant warmth greeted them on the steps outside the house. After hours of artificial light, it took some time for Diana's eyes to become accustomed to the sunlight. But she drank in the bright colours eagerly and tried to imagine how Grace Tremayne must have felt when she left the house for a walk.

"Maybe we should head for the garden first," Jonathan suggested. "I saw some wonderful old rhododendrons from my window."

He was forgetting that Diana had the same view, but she held back from reminding him.

Their feet crunching on the gravel, they rounded the house and came to the garden, which had a kind of communications aerial in the middle. It was probably there to ensure that the people here had a phone signal—a home comfort that seemed indispensable here, too.

Jonathan was right—the old rhododendrons were wonderful. The magnificent colours of their flowers ranged from snowy white to deep crimson.

Some of my gardening neighbours back in Berlin would kill for specimens like these, Diana thought with a smile. As well as the rhododendrons, they passed some bushes that must be the frangipani she'd read about in the guidebooks. They looked no younger than the rhododendrons, and had probably been here before the plantation was established.

Their magnificent flowers made Diana think of the white flower with a red eye that had been pressed between the pages of the old guidebook. It must have come from here. She was so fascinated by the idea that she felt compelled to go up to the nearest bush and touch the fleshy flowers. Had Grace and Victoria also done that? What a lovely, sweet smell! Diana hadn't been conscious of it before, but now, standing in front of the source, she was reminded of the sweetness on the air that morning.

"Frangipani. Isn't it beautiful?" Jonathan said as he came up behind her. "These bushes grow practically everywhere throughout India and Sri Lanka."

"In Germany, magnificent plants like these would only flourish in a botanical garden or a good greenhouse."

Diana stood for a while admiring the plants, playing out little scenes involving the girls from the painting in Tremayne House—except they were no longer little girls, but young women. She was suddenly overcome by a strange longing, and wished more than anything for a window in time through which she could observe her ancestors. But at best she had only fragments of such a window, its panes blurred by a dark film with only small tears in a few places to shed light on the scene.

Long moments passed before she could finally tear her eyes from the vision of the frangipani. As she turned, she saw the rear façade of the mansion in all its glory and noticed the typically English design of the gardens. They were similar to the grounds of Tremayne House, although those were a little better cared for.

When they reached the wing that housed their rooms, Jonathan stopped suddenly.

"Look there!" He pointed to a small gap in the hedge and a bald strip across the lawn that led to it, looking just like a beaten path. "Shall we have a look what's through there?"

Diana looked up at the house. Would Mr. Manderley have anything against them slipping through it? Seeing no one at the window, she nodded and followed him through the hedge.

"What's the likelihood of coming across a snake here?" she asked sceptically.

"It's not very likely," Jonathan replied. "I'm no biologist, but I think snakes are more afraid of us than we are of them. We should be more concerned about big cats. But they're shy, too. Though you must have noticed there are plenty of monkeys around here. And parrots."

After beating their way through the bushes for a while, feeling they were getting nowhere fast, they suddenly saw a palm-leaf roof rising up out of the undergrowth.

"Is that a hut? Here?"

"Let's have a look!" Jonathan pushed the branches aside eagerly. The path had faded away in places, overcome by encroaching greenery, but they finally managed to reach the building. The hut, built of timber poles and boards, reminded Diana of the stilt houses she had seen on the coast, except that here the design was not to protect it from flooding.

The roof had been practically destroyed, and the hut itself was crooked from years of wind-battering. Its windows looked out like sad eyes from a dense tangle of heveas and palms, as though remembering better days.

"What sort of a building is this?" Diana asked as she looked around the cleared space in front of it that was lined with timber planks. Although the grass had pushed through the cracks, the original shape could still be made out.

"I'm not sure. It could have been the house of a guru, a religious leader. Or a meeting place for the inhabitants of the nearby village."

"But why would it be out here?" Diana wondered.

"You'd have to ask the people of the village. I'm going to take a look inside."

Jonathan climbed the steps and entered the room to look around. He emerged with a broad smile and a long staff in his hand.

"I think I know what used to go on here."

Diana raised her eyebrows. "You know that from the stick in your hand?"

"It's not any old stick; it's a practice stick. I can't be completely sure, but I'd say this building is a former martial arts school."

Diana approached, climbed the ladder up to the veranda, and looked into the room. A number of objects and old rattan furniture lay all over the floor, covered by a thick layer of dust.

"A martial arts school? Do they have something like karate here?"

"Something much better!" Jonathan whirled the stick through the air and cried out, "Kalarippayatu!"

"I'm sorry?"

"That's the name of the martial art. Kalarippayatu."

He briefly explained to her what it was all about. Impressed, Diana said, "A very wise way of measuring strength. Just think how many of the overwhelming losses in the two world wars could have been avoided by it . . ."

"But there are risks involved," Jonathan said. "Imagine if the wrong side had the better fighter and would then be entitled to subjugate an entire population on the basis of that victory."

"You're right. Of course that would be unfair."

Diana watched Jonathan looking around the building reverently. "Do you practise this martial art?"

Jonathan shook his head. "I'm an academic, not a sportsman. Kalarippayatu is very demanding. Fighters usually start training at a very young age, like in judo or karate. The fighters literally spring at one another, and undertake a complicated series of moves with swords or their bare hands. You can only recognise the patterns if you watch incredibly closely and have practised a little yourself. It's a fascinating spectacle."

Diana pushed her lower lip forward in wonder, as she imagined the young pupils sitting on the broad veranda, trying to learn from watching the fighters on the wooden platform. "A martial arts school near my ancestors' plantation! I wouldn't have expected that."

"It was probably already closed by Henry Tremayne's time and fell into disuse. But it's also possible that men from the village met here to practise. If so, you have to marvel at their courage—if they'd been caught by the plantation owners, things would have gone very badly for them."

Since they hadn't expected to make any such discovery, Diana didn't have her camera with her to record it.

As if reading her mind, Jonathan said, "I'm going to come back and take photos of it all. A testimony to the past like this would make a great addition to my book."

"Really?" Diana asked with a smile. "It's only a martial arts school."

"But also a symbol of the Tamil tradition in colonial times. As I'm examining the causes of the present-day conflict, it's entirely relevant."

They fought their way back through the undergrowth, and this time Diana thought she saw a monkey above their heads. She caught only a brief glimpse of the brown pelt, which in retrospect could have been the plumage of an exotic bird, but she wanted to believe it was a monkey.

They had barely left the hedge behind when they saw Manderley coming towards them, a few tea leaves clinging to his khaki pants.

"Well, where did you two pop up from?" he said.

"We've made a fascinating discovery," Diana replied. "Did you know there's a former martial arts school behind the plantation?"

"A martial arts school?"

Jonathan pointed to the gap in the hedge. "Haven't you ever noticed this narrow path?"

Manderley shook his head. "I haven't. But my mind's usually on things other than the lawn."

"Well, perhaps you should have a look at the building. It's looking a bit the worse for wear, but it's a piece of history," Jonathan said. "If you had it restored, you could either use it as guest accommodation or market it as a local attraction. There aren't many clandestine martial arts schools from the colonial period left. The English kept a stern watch against it, and not all the fighters who practised despite them had buildings like this to use."

Manderley's eyes widened. Diana knew that look. It was the same one her clients would show when she explained the potential that lay in a particular defence strategy.

"I'll think about it. Thank you very much for the information."

He excused himself and hurried on.

"We ought to get back to work, too," Jonathan said to Diana.

"True." She turned again to look at the gap in the hedge, then looked across to the Turkish-style windows behind which her room lay.

She suddenly had a thought. Would Grace or Victoria have been able to see the fighters slipping by here? Had either of the girls ventured to the school?

Diana shook her head. Probably not. After all, they were well-bred young ladies. But she really liked the idea that Grace might have been able to watch the men fighting.

13

Vannattuppūcci, 1887

Miss Giles looked a picture of displeasure when Grace fetched her to go to the language lesson. The role of chaperone did not suit her routine, and it robbed her of the opportunity of more frequent chance encounters with Mr. Norris. But, for better or for worse, she had to obey her master's instructions.

Grace's satchel contained a wad of paper from her father's study, along with a freshly sealed inkpot, a fountain pen, a little box of spare nibs, and a pencil.

She felt a little as though she were back in her childhood, when she obliged to take her school things with her on Mr. Norris's natural history walks. Her heart was beating nervously as she saw Vikrama standing by the door. She had nurtured a small hope that he would be wearing Tamil traditional dress, but he was in the same clothes as he had been wearing about the plantation earlier in the day. He smelled of soap, was wearing a new white shirt with subtle red stripes, and had trimmed his beard—she could almost see where Victoria had got her "dandy" notion from.

They found a suitable place for the lesson in an open space near the new tea field with a wonderful view of Adam's Peak. Grace felt a shiver of pleasure at the thought that one day she would climb the mountain from where, as the sailors claimed, she would be able to survey the whole island.

Miss Giles, on the other hand, had little time for the wonders of nature. She kept making comments about the condition of the ground, and when she wasn't complaining, she was flapping her hands at various insects.

"And where do you think you're going to sit around here?" she finally said to Grace and Vikrama.

"Over there, Miss Giles!" he said, pointing to a number of rocks that had rolled down the slope a very long time ago and settled here.

"We're supposed to sit on rocks?"

"For the time being, Miss Giles," Vikrama replied, to Grace's amazement remaining calm and friendly despite the carping.

"I'm going to ask Mr. Tremayne to provide a table and chairs for the purpose. Miss Grace's decision to learn Tamil was rather sudden, and I don't know whether she'll actually take to it."

He gave Grace a look of inquiry and she nodded. Oh, she'd take to it, all right! If only for the fact that he was the teacher!

Once they had all found somewhere to sit, Miss Giles withdrew to the shade and Vikrama began with some simple words and phrases. He spoke sounds that seemed impossible to her with enviable ease. He listened patiently to her clumsy attempts, managing to pass over Miss Giles's bored interjections with a friendly smile.

At the end of the lesson, Grace felt exhausted, but filled with a satisfaction she had rarely experienced before. She finally had the feeling of doing something meaningful!

Her parents' hopes that her enthusiasm would be short-lived were dashed over supper, as she chattered effusively about the words she had learned and their meanings.

"It's amazing how rich this language is! And the script—it's like a secret code!"

It may not have been her intention to incite her father's suspicion of his employees, but she quickly corrected herself after the remark about a secret code by saying she hoped he would allow her to continue with the lessons. She could only reassure him by telling him what she knew: that the people here were far from plotting against him.

"I wish I could learn Tamil, too," Victoria complained as Grace sat that evening copying the characters into a small notebook that she had obtained from Mr. Norris.

"It's more complicated than you realise," Grace replied without looking up from her work. "Learn French first. There'll be plenty of time after that to learn the local language."

"But French is no use at all to me here."

"Of course it is, for when you receive invitations from the society ladies. You heard how enchanted they all were with you."

"But I'm not interested in spending my time with their boring daughters. They're not interested at all in walking in the countryside."

Victoria fell silent and Grace sensed something else hidden behind her words.

She set her pen down on the desk and went over to her sister. Victoria refused to meet her eye.

"What's the matter?"

"Do you like Mr. Vikrama?" Her eyes blazed.

Grace was caught unawares. "Of course I like him. He's very kind."

Victoria gave her a searching look. "You will tell me when you fall in love with a man, won't you?"

Grace was speechless now. Could she tell her? She knew what her father and mother would think of it. They would never tolerate a union with a native man!

But what was she thinking? She liked Vikrama, nothing more. And even if she'd never admit it, the prophecy on the palm leaf kept niggling at her. She certainly didn't want to bring misfortune on her family!

Grace drew Victoria into her arms. "Of course I'll tell you. But there's nothing to tell. Vikrama is very nice and a patient teacher, that's all."

The two sisters remained in their embrace for a while, then Grace picked up the exercise book to show her sister that it contained nothing other than Tamil characters, and nowhere near enough of those to constitute a secret diary.

Grace gradually learned her first few phrases and expressions, and took great delight in using the foreign words when she visited Naala to ask how she was. Her wounds had begun to heal, but Vikrama was right when he said the scars would never disappear. She would not forget who was responsible for them. At first the villagers regarded Grace a little suspiciously, but the healer made sure they knew who she was.

As it was time for a pause in the picking season, the colourful saris had vanished from the tea fields, giving the plants a chance to grow some more. The pickers were now mainly employed in packing the tea. This didn't mean they were free from Mr. Petersen's constant harrying—his gaze roved over their heads like that of a bird of prey. None of them had time for "sloppiness," as Petersen called it. As soon as he caught a woman packing slower than the others, he went up to her and stroked her back menacingly with the rolled-up whip. He might be obeying the ban on whipping the workers, but the women couldn't be sure of it. Whenever they got chance, they complained of it to Vikrama, but there was little he could do. As long as Petersen held back from beating one of the women again, Tremayne left him to his own devices.

As far as she could, Grace kept out of the overseers' way. When she did encounter Petersen she tried to suppress the anger his grin kindled in her. If it had been up to Grace, she would have allowed things to carry on like that, hardly having any contact with him, but one day her father turned to her over supper.

"I'm afraid you're going to have to do without your lessons for a while. I need Mr. Vikrama with me throughout the day. The books need to be brought up to date and new trading deals negotiated."

Grace looked at him in shock, but realised it was not her place to protest. The estate work was more important than her lessons—the plantation was what supported them financially.

As she no longer had anything to do in the afternoons, Grace would either go on walks or sit in front of her easel in the garden capturing the magnificent flowers of the frangipani and rhododendrons. Once, a photographer came to take portraits of the family members in turn outside their house. Unfortunately, it began to rain, so Grace was the only one photographed.

One night, when Grace was waiting as usual for Vikrama to appear, Victoria began to moan in her sleep. At first Grace thought it was a wild animal, one of the monkeys Victoria was so fond of. But when it recurred and her little sister tossed and turned on the bed, her teeth chattering, Grace left the window and hurried over to her.

"Vicky, darling, what's wrong?"

Victoria didn't reply. Grace felt her brow and shrank back in alarm. Her sister was glowing with fever!

She stepped back from the bed, horrified, and stood for a moment kneading her nightdress, before whirling around and running from the room. Someone had to call a doctor. There must be one in Nuwara Eliya.

Although it was not seemly to simply storm into her parents' room, she tore open the door nevertheless. A moment later she was roughly shaking her father's shoulder.

"Papa, can you hear me?"

Henry Tremayne grunted indignantly, then asked, "What are you doing here, Grace?"

"Victoria's sick. She's burning with a fever. We need a doctor."

Claudia sat up before her husband stirred.

"Henry, send Wilkes to fetch Dr. Desmond, the one you met in the club."

Without a word Tremayne got out of bed and threw on his dressing gown.

Grace followed him out to go back to Victoria. She had hardly gone out into the corridor when she heard her mother's imperious voice ordering a maid, who had appeared on hearing the commotion, to heat up some water.

Grace had no idea where her father had gone; probably to wake Mr. Wilkes. Victoria was writhing on her bed in the grip of the fever. As Grace approached her she tossed her head back and forth.

"Victoria, darling," Grace said, but neither her voice nor her touch were enough to bring her sister out of her nightmare. What was wrong with her?

"Come away from her, Grace," her mother called from the door.

Grace, who had been about to crouch down at her sister's bedside, looked at her inquiringly. "But, Mother, she . . ."

"A fever this serious could be contagious. We should wait for the doctor."

"But we have no idea when he'll come!"

"There's nothing we can do until he does. Come away from the bed, Grace. I don't want two daughters struck down with this illness."

Crushed, her heart brimming with worry, Grace turned back to her own bed, refusing to go as far as to leave the room. Her mother seemed to be so afraid of the strange fever that had overcome Victoria that she didn't even enter the room. If Grace wasn't allowed to go near, then it should be her mother's place to try and wake Victoria. Or at least to calm her. But nothing of the sort happened. Like a hesitant angel of death, she remained at the threshold and stared at the bed.

◆ ◆ ◆

An eternity passed before the doctor arrived. As it turned out, Henry Tremayne had ridden out himself to fetch him.

Dr. Desmond, a kindly, red-bearded man, whose hastily thrown-on clothes attested to the nocturnal crisis, greeted Claudia and Grace briefly before turning to Victoria.

As if the presence of the doctor had enfolded her in a protective aura, Claudia also found the courage to enter the room. Behind her, in the hall, Henry was barking out orders.

A little later, two maids appeared carrying bowls of warm and cold water. Claudia indicated to them to set them down on two chairs, then the girls slipped away.

Dr. Desmond's examination was brief. After listening to Victoria's lungs with his stethoscope, feeling her pulse, and feeling her brow, he put a thermometer under her tongue and looked at his watch.

"It's as I thought," he said as he stowed the stethoscope back in his bag and went to one of the bowls to wash his hands. "I fear the girl has contracted malaria."

Grace looked anxiously at her mother, who had turned pale and looked at least ten years older.

"What are you going to do, Doctor?" Claudia asked huskily, hugging her own shoulders.

"I'll give you a prescription for quinine, which you'll be able to get in Colombo. Give it to her in the stated dose. You must also take care to ensure that her temperature doesn't rise to a dangerous level. Your daughter looks strong to me, but she's still a child and she could easily . . ."

Grace pressed a hand to her mouth with a sob, and the doctor fell silent.

"Of course, we don't want to assume the worst. Just see to it that the girl's kept sufficiently cool, if necessary bathing her whole body. And you should mix quinine with your drinking water as a preventive measure."

He went over to Grace's desk and made out a prescription. "Here, give this to your servant and have him set off immediately. Until he gets back it's up to you to keep the fever in check."

Grace took the prescription and ran from the room. She met her father in the corridor. "Dr. Desmond says this must be fetched from the city immediately."

"What's wrong with her?" A glance at the paper in Grace's hand told him faster than she was capable of doing. "Malaria. In our house!"

"We're supposed to take the medicine, too," Grace added.

Henry nodded, then whirled around and hurried back into the hall. A few moments later a rider galloped from the courtyard.

After the doctor had taken his leave, Claudia called the maids back. "I think it's better if we don't tell them what the matter is," she murmured to Grace. "We don't want the servants to spread panic throughout the plantation."

All through the night, she tried to get Victoria's temperature down a little, but as fast as she could cool the cloths, they warmed up again. Victoria began to moan in her fever, periods of calm alternating with violent shivering.

As morning began to break, Grace felt like a marionette, her movements determined only by a puppeteer pulling the strings. The cool water in the bowl shimmered dully, and the cloths looked like shrivelled creatures.

Her mother had sat down, intending to snatch a few minutes' rest, but she had been asleep for three hours now. Grace didn't want to wake her. When the day had fully dawned she would lie down herself for a while, but she was determined to hold out until then.

Tears sprang into her eyes as she looked at Victoria. The early daylight showed even more clearly the effects of the disease. Dark rings around her sister's eyes gave her the appearance of a skull, but her crimson cheeks clearly showed that there was still life in her body. Life that hovered in unbearable danger.

At last her mother awoke and stretched with a painful sigh.

"I'm long past the age where I can sleep anywhere."

She stood up, reeled a little, then approached the bed.

"How is she?" she asked, as though Grace were a doctor.

"No change, I'd say," Grace replied. "As you can see, her skin's still glowing and the water's no longer cold."

"I'll have them bring some fresh." With an unexpectedly gentle gesture, she stroked Grace's hair then carefully ran her fingers over Victoria's brow, before turning to go.

Scarcely had Claudia left the room when Vikrama appeared at the window. Grace left her vigil at Victoria's bedside where she had been changing the cold cloths and hurried over to him. She was a little ashamed, still dressed as she was in her night attire and her hair dishevelled, but how was someone who had been looking after a sick patient supposed to look?

"I heard your sister is ill."

Grace nodded, then cast a worried glace at Victoria, whose face still glowed red. "Last night a doctor came from Nuwara Eliya. Our houseboy's been sent for quinine, but he'll be gone for a while yet. Mother's gone to fetch some fresh cold water, but the fever keeps rising. At least she's not shivering any more, but that could change at any moment."

"It's malaria, isn't it?" Vikrama asked gravely.

"How . . . ?"

"Quinine. That's the remedy the English use for it. They all put it in the water as a preventive measure. And if someone has a fever here, it's often malaria." He reached for her hand. "Please be careful."

Grace shook her head anxiously. "Don't worry, I won't fall ill."

"Let's hope not. I'll ride to the village immediately and ask the healer there if I can do anything to help."

"Do you think she'll have any quinine?"

"No, only the cinchona bark itself. I'll hurry."

He vanished. Grace watched him go, then turned to Victoria's bed, where a sour smell hung in the air. Moaning, her sister was rolling her head back and forth, her lips moving as though she was trying to speak. But no sound came.

Her heart contracting and a sob rising in her breast, Grace removed the cloth yet again from Victoria's brow and immersed it in the luke-warm water. *Please, dear God,* she begged silently, *don't take my sister away. If You think I've sinned, punish me, not her.*

During the morning the fever rose so much that Victoria began to talk deliriously, rambling in confusion about parrots and monkeys. Grace and her mother finally felt they had no other choice but to have a bathtub brought and to lay Victoria in cold water.

The girl's teeth chattered as the cold water surrounded her skin, but after a while she grew calm and the deep crimson of her cheeks paled a little. When they lifted Victoria out, her skin felt cooler, but that changed back within minutes.

"That bloody houseboy!" Claudia muttered angrily after instructing the maids to bring fresh cold water. "He's probably taken to his heels with the money and the prescription."

"He'll be here soon," Grace said, trying to pacify her mother. "You've seen what the terrain's like here. I'm sure many of the tracks have become boggy after the rain we've had."

Claudia was not listening. "This damned country," she muttered. "Why didn't he sell the plantation?"

"The plantation isn't to blame, Mother." Grace stroked her mother's arm. "Anyway, Mr. Cahill should have told us to add quinine to the water like everyone does here."

It was only then that Grace realised her mother could question how she knew that. But Claudia was so wrapped up in her anxiety and anger that she didn't notice.

The maids struggled in with more water, and the whole process began again. It looked as though Victoria would awaken, but then they realised that, although her eyes were open, she was unseeing.

Around midday the tension became too much for Claudia. "I want someone to ride to Colombo and look for that bloody houseboy!"

Before Grace could stop her, she had left the room. The next moment, she heard a knock at the window.

Her heart thumping, Grace turned. Vikrama!

She quickly laid the partially cooled cloth on her sister's brow, then ran to the window.

Vikrama produced a small fabric pouch from beneath his clothing. As she opened the window, he handed it to her. "This is from Kisah. She says you should mix it with water."

"Is this the cinchona bark?"

"Yes, but it also contains other herbs against fever. She says her condition may worsen slightly at first, but she'll improve quickly after that."

"Could the medicine be dangerous for her?"

Vikrama shook his head. "In our village people use it as a preventive measure against malaria. I should have told your father, but I'd assumed that you put quinine in your water like all the English here."

"Don't worry. You couldn't have known. Even we didn't know."

Vikrama gave her a worried look. "Maybe you should take some yourself. Not that you . . ."

"I still feel perfectly healthy," Grace replied, realising as she spoke that she was pleased by his concern. "But thank you. I will take some."

Their eyes met briefly, then Vikrama hurried away.

"Thank you very much!" she called after him. He turned and waved.

Once he was gone, she opened the little pouch. The blend of herbs looked a little like manure, but the smell was much more pleasant. How could she mix it with water without her mother noticing? What would she say if Grace gave her sister medicine the natives used? She would be shocked and immediately throw the medicine away.

Doubt began to creep in. Would this medicine really be any use? *Listen to your heart,* an inner voice whispered.

Then she recalled how the healer had got Naala back on her feet. Slowly, yes, but the tea picker was now working again.

Since Claudia was probably still hounding her father about sending someone after the messenger, Grace went to the sideboard, poured out two glasses of water and quickly added some of the herb mixture. She gulped down the content of one glass, then went over to Victoria with the other.

Would she drink it? If it were poisonous, Grace would have felt the effects herself. But she could feel no ill effects, so she was hopeful. At worst it would do nothing, but at least it wouldn't kill her sister.

"Victoria, darling," she said softly as she raised her sister's fever-hot body a little. "I have some medicine here. You've got to drink it."

Victoria replied with an absent moan, and Grace shook her gently. "Come on, darling, open your eyes. Just drink a little, that's all."

Nothing but a moan. Grace looked in panic towards the door and listened. She couldn't hear footsteps, but her mother wouldn't be gone for long. And the maids could appear at any time with more water.

"Victoria, please."

The girl's sticky eyes opened a little. Grace doubted that Victoria knew what was going on around her, but this small movement encouraged her to hold the glass up to her lips.

Despite her fears that Victoria could choke, Grace managed to make her sister drink the brownish solution. The bitter taste woke her a little, and as Grace spoke soothingly to her, Victoria finally drank half a glass before falling back into a deep sleep.

After laying her back down on the bed, Grace went over to the window and poured the rest away. She tucked the pouch inside her dress, silently praying that it would work.

◆ ◆ ◆

The healer's warning proved true—after drinking the concoction, Victoria's condition got worse. The shivering gave way to delirium, before the girl fell back motionless, as if dead. Grace's stomach clenched. What if she had killed her sister?

She looked at her mother, who was pacing the room, nervously wringing her hands. Grace kept hoping that the herbs would soon take effect. Her father appeared briefly and asked about Victoria's condition, but didn't venture close to his daughter's sickbed.

Late in the afternoon, without anyone having had to ride out after him, the houseboy appeared. Grace, who had just gone to the dining room to fetch some fruit, spotted him first and saw as he came to a halt that the horse was at the end of its strength. Unthinking, she put the fruit bowl down without noticing it was right by the sacred picture, where fewer floral offerings had been left recently.

The messenger, a young tea worker, was exhausted and had to drag himself up the front steps. Similarly, the horse swayed a little behind him.

Grace opened the door.

Sweating profusely, the boy said he had returned from the pharmacy and handed her a box wrapped in brown paper.

"*Nanri,*" Grace thanked him in Tamil, then sent him to the kitchen, while she ran with the package back to her room.

As Grace rushed through the door, Claudia jumped up.

"He's brought it!" Grace cried out in excitement before she could ask. "He's just arrived. He almost rode the horse into the ground. But we've got it!"

Claudia breathed a sigh of relief. Her hands were shaking so much that she left the preparation of the medicine to Grace. When at last she crouched down beside Victoria to give her the quinine water, she noticed that the sweat on her brow had dried a little.

She lifted her gently and once again spoke to her softly. Victoria opened her eyes, and this time she seemed to look at her. Her eyes were still glazed, and it took a while for her to open her mouth, but this time she was better able to swallow.

Maybe she was deceiving herself, maybe she was imagining things, but she had a feeling that Victoria was a little more aware.

After giving her the quinine water, she laid her back down on the sweat-soaked pillow and arranged her hair around her face.

During the hours that followed, Grace did not let her out of her sight. Her stomach rebelled, but although she was hungry she couldn't bring herself to eat anything. Together with her mother she replaced the cold compresses, and although the cloths still warmed up quickly, Victoria remained a little calmer and her delirium passed into proper sleep.

"I must say this quinine seems very good," Claudia said as the day came to an end. Exhaustion had drawn dark shadows beneath her eyes, mercilessly revealing her thirty-eight years, which she usually concealed with make-up and powder. "Her temperature is bound to rage for a while, but I have the impression it won't get any worse now."

She was right, but as Grace lay down to rest, exhausted, she was sure that the real cure was down to the herbs from the Tamil village.

During the days that followed, Victoria's high temperature persisted and she was regularly plagued by bouts of shivering, but the symptoms finally began to recede. As her temperature sank, Victoria got visibly better. Thin and weak, she sat propped up by pillows in bed, ate light fruit soups skilfully prepared by the cook, and after a little more time was even asking for paper and a sanguine pencil.

Although the recent days had also taken their toll on Grace, she felt freer and more relieved than ever before. As the angel of death was no longer hovering over her sister's bed, she once again had room in her head for other thoughts. The first revolved around Vikrama, whom she wanted to thank for his rapid help.

He had looked in at the window whenever it was safe to do so, and had often asked Grace how Victoria was. One cloudy afternoon, after Dr. Desmond had given Victoria a further examination and reassured them that she was out of danger, Grace went out to look for Vikrama.

She found him in the tea shed, checking the quality of the tea.

"Mr. Vikrama, please could I have a brief word with you?"

He turned and nodded, then spoke to the women in Tamil and left the shed.

"What is it? I hope nothing's happened to your sister. The girls told me she fought very bravely against the illness."

Grace smiled for the first time in days.

"Don't worry, it's nothing bad. Victoria's much better. Dr. Desmond has said she's out of danger. She'll be a little weak for a while yet, but that will pass, too."

Vikrama sighed with relief. "I'm glad to hear it. Kisah was asking me last time I saw her how the girl was."

"You can tell her from me that her medicine had the best possible effect and we're all very grateful to her."

"You didn't tell your mother about it, did you?" Vikrama frowned.

"No, she . . ." Grace lowered her head in shame. "She would certainly have claimed it was poisonous. I gave it to Victoria when Mother was out of the room."

"So you trusted me."

Grace looked at him. "Yes, I trust you."

A hint of a smile crossed Vikrama's face, as fleeting as a breath of wind.

"Perhaps your sister recovered because you made an offering to Shiva and Ganesha," he said.

"I did what?"

"It was you who placed the bowl of fruit beneath the picture, wasn't it?"

Grace puzzled for a moment before remembering.

"One of the maids told all and sundry that you'd left an offering to the gods. Everyone believes now that Shiva and Ganesha brought your sister back to health."

Vikrama grinned at Grace, then without warning reached out his hand and brushed a lock of hair from her cheek. The touch of his finger sent a shiver through her like a flash of lightning. Bewildered by the tenderness of the gesture, she took a step back.

"I'm sorry, I didn't mean to . . ." Vikrama blushed as he lowered his hand.

"No, it's . . . it's fine." Grace nervously raised her own hand to brush her hair from her face. Her heart was in her mouth and her cheeks were glowing. Everything in her longed to feel his touch again, but she was sure she had ruined the chance of that by flinching away.

"In any case, I'm very grateful to you. We all are."

"It was my pleasure to help you." Vikrama gave a small bow, his eyes locked on hers. He'd never looked at her in such a dark, mysterious way. And never before had she felt such a strange, secret tug of longing inside as the one that took her over now and remained with her as she turned and walked back to the house.

"We've been invited to the Stocktons'," Claudia announced over supper. "Now that Victoria is recovering and has regained some of her strength, we're in a position to accept."

"I agree," Henry said, dabbing his mouth with a napkin. "What do you think, Victoria?"

The girl's eyes, still shadowed by her illness, lit up.

"Oh, that would be wonderful! I'll finally be able to tell their daughter about my illness and even outdo her, since she's never had malaria!"

"It would be better for you not to mention your illness to the Stocktons," her mother said. "We don't want them thinking you might be infectious—their daughter has a weak constitution, and we don't want her mother worrying."

"But Dr. Desmond said malaria isn't passed on through personal contact."

"I wouldn't be so certain of that if I were you, young lady," her father replied. "Scientific knowledge is constantly on the move. Who knows how findings will change from one week to the next? Maybe they'll discover that malaria actually is contagious, and then we'd be putting our nice neighbours at risk."

Henry laughed briefly and then swept his napkin over his lips. Claudia patted him on the arm. Victoria stuck out her lower lip sulkily.

Grace remained silent the whole time. The mere idea of spending a whole afternoon in the company of the boring George made her shudder. And the looks his father gave her! Her parents must be blind if they hadn't noticed it.

She secretly wished it was she who had contracted malaria. A few of the employees had also come down with it, but thanks to the Tamil healer, no one had come to any serious harm.

"What's the matter, darling?" Henry turned to Grace. "You're so quiet. Wouldn't you look forward to a little trip out?"

"Of course I would."

"But you look as if you've been forced to eat a whole crate of lemons."

"I'm not feeling well."

It was the best excuse she could think of, and one she knew her father wouldn't pursue.

"Oh. Then let's hope you'll be feeling better again in a few days. It would be a real shame if you couldn't come with us."

It would not have been a shame at all for Grace, but she knew she would have no choice. She nodded with a smile. "When are we intending to go?"

"This coming Sunday, immediately after our morning service. If you like, we could even go to church in Nuwara Eliya."

Not a bad idea, Grace thought, hoping her expression didn't betray her scorn. *If we did, I could pray that George Stockton has no interest in me at all.*

The week flew by. Together with Grace and Victoria, Miss Giles made improvements to the dresses the girls were to wear for the visit.

"I'm beginning to feel like a lady's maid," she muttered whenever she felt no one was paying any attention to her. If her complaint had reached the ears of Claudia Tremayne she would have reprimanded her, but neither Victoria nor Grace had any interest in telling on her. While Victoria worked at catching up on the schoolwork she had missed during her illness, Grace distracted herself with walks or daydreamed about being able to resume her lessons with Vikrama as she listlessly sewed braid and lace. He had still not been able to make time for teaching her, and she feared she might forget all her carefully learned lettering and vocabulary.

On the Sunday afternoon, after a visit to the recently built church in Nuwara Eliya and a brief luncheon, they set off to the Stocktons'. The track through the jungle was bumpy and rutted from the passage of numerous wagons. Every now and then there was a buffalo in the road, chewing the cud and staring at them as though it couldn't imagine what people and horses could possibly be doing here. Above their heads, parrots and small monkeys sported in the treetops. Every so often one of the comical little creatures would appear near the carriage, like a scout sent to report back to the clan on who had come to disturb the peace of the forest.

All these scenes passed Grace by as she tried to convince herself that it wouldn't be as bad as she imagined. After all, she had survived various unpleasant visits back in England to her father's creditors. And Stockton wouldn't bite her—at least not if she stayed close by her family.

After about an hour's journey they saw the Stockton plantation before them. The three-storey mansion stood resplendent like a pearl on green velvet. The estate was substantially larger than Vannattuppūcci, and there were more commercial buildings around the place. The house was ringed by a tall, decorative fence, which caused Henry to exclaim, "That's the finest example of wrought ironwork I've ever seen!"

"Our fence is just as beautiful," Grace couldn't help remarking. The house may have been magnificent, but in her opinion it was far too ostentatious for a man with no claim to nobility. The Tremaynes, no more aristocratic themselves, preferred a more modest two-storey house.

As the carriage rolled up on the circular driveway before the sweeping stairs to the front door, Claudia took the opportunity for a final warning. "You will behave respectably, both of you. I don't want to hear any peculiar comments. Victoria, you will not regale the daughter of the house with tales of your malaria, and Grace, you will put on a more affable expression than your present one and behave properly towards the Stocktons."

When did I ever not behave properly? Grace thought, but kept the comment to herself.

While they were both nodding dutifully, the driver brought the carriage to a standstill.

A supercilious butler conducted them into the hall where the Stocktons waited to greet them. Their sickly daughter was there, as was their pale son, who, despite his slim build and scrawny neck, looked as though his silver ascot tie were strangling him.

"My dear friends!" Alice Stockton trilled, approaching them with outspread arms. As her husband shook Henry's hand enthusiastically, he allowed his eyes to wander, as if accidentally, in Grace's direction. She felt his gaze like an unpleasant touch to her cheek.

After the welcome, during which Grace couldn't escape having her hand kissed by Daniel Stockton, they were led to the drawing room, a magnificent circular room entered through a leaded sliding door. Claudia was not the only one to stare in wonder at the beautiful rattan furniture, luxurious carpets, and paintings depicting fascinating landscapes.

Tea was served from a Chinese tea service, accompanied by a perfect selection of dainty cakes. Grace noticed her mother looking at the scones with a hint of envy before biting into one.

She herself felt as though she had swallowed a stone—obviously not due to the quality of the scones, but to being caught in the crossfire of looks exchanged between George and Daniel Stockton. Once, she caught George licking his pale lips, which sent a shudder down her spine. She quickly turned her attention to her teacup, only to be addressed the very next moment by Daniel Stockton.

"You must be missing the season in London, with all the lavish balls taking place there at the moment."

"To be honest, I am missing London," Grace replied coolly. "But I find the beautiful landscape and life at Vannattuppūcci to be more than sufficient compensation."

She worded her reply guilelessly, ensuring it could not cause offence to anyone. Indeed, no one took offence, but it led Daniel Stockton to ask, "Why don't you allow George to show you around the plantation after tea? As future master of this corner of the world, he would no doubt be delighted to escort you."

"But of course," his son replied, blushing deep red. "If you would like that?"

What else could Grace do but accept? Especially since her mother and father were giving her looks that warned her to be polite. When she accepted, as was expected of her, they nodded and smiled to one another.

To cap it all, Victoria grinned broadly at her sister in an unobserved moment.

Grace hardly listened to the chatter over the tea table; her attention was caught by a bright-pink frangipani tree that bloomed in the middle of the English garden. The frangipanis at Vannattuppūcci were also very beautiful, but there was something special about this tree. *Maybe I should persuade George to stop by it later.* Or better still, play hide-and-seek—while she sat in the grass behind the tree, keeping absolutely silent, he could search until he was blue in the face.

As far as she was concerned, the afternoon tea could have gone on for hours, but the dreaded moment of the guided tour arrived all too soon. Daniel invited Henry to his study, where he had something he wanted to show him, while Victoria withdrew with Clara to the latter's room. The ladies decided to enjoy the peace and quiet in the shady drawing room—and George offered Grace his arm.

At that moment Grace was filled with envy of her younger sister. She would have far preferred listening to Clara's boring accounts of her ailments than forcing herself to make conversation with a man who had little of interest to say to her.

George led her out into the garden, having flatly refused to venture out into the tea plantation or the adjacent pickers' village because one didn't want to squander the afternoon under the gaze of those primitive people, and at her request they made for the magnificent frangipani. What at first glance had seemed like a single tree was in fact a number of intertwined trunks. Was this the work of nature or due to the hand of a skilled gardener? Either way, the result was extremely impressive and beautiful.

"A little further along you'll find a bodhi tree," George said, long accustomed to seeing the frangipani and immune to its special qualities. "The natives believe it's akin to the one under which Buddha received enlightenment, and they've established a truly absurd cult around it. It's only through a strict ban that we've managed to stop them constantly leaving flowers under it."

Grace was reminded of the painting of the gods in their entrance hall. Since the maids had seen her leaving the fruit there, and Victoria's subsequent recovery, the number of flowers laid beneath it had begun to increase again. She fervently hoped her father would not let Stockton persuade him to forbid the workers and pickers from leaving their offerings.

As they were standing beneath the spreading branches of the tree, Grace noticed a number of parrots.

"Oh, look!" she cried. "Aren't these birds beautiful?"

George glanced at them briefly and said, "Not long ago I bagged a green parrot, and I managed to stuff it without compromising any of its natural appearance."

Grace's eyes widened in shock, which the young Stockton must have mistaken for admiration, as he added, "You must know that taxidermy is a great passion of mine. I also preserve insects, butterflies and moths. I can show you my collection if you like . . ."

Grace thought of the trophies in Father's room at Tremayne House. Animals he had not shot himself, but had kept in memory of the past. As a child, the animals' black glass eyes had regularly sent shudders down her spine.

"No, thank you," she said quickly. "I prefer to observe animals in their natural surroundings."

If she had hoped that would divert George from his favourite subject, she was mistaken. With a passion she had not expected from this pale young man, he began to talk about the taxidermy process, increasing the queasy feeling in Grace's stomach. When he came to a description of how he had used a preserved parrot's wing to make a piece of jewellery to give his mother for a Christmas gift, it was finally too much for Grace.

"Please excuse me, I'm not feeling well," she said, perhaps a little more sharply than necessary.

"I'll accompany you back to the house," George offered, but Grace shook her head.

"No, there's no need. I don't want to take you away from observing your next . . . specimens."

She turned and began to walk away. At first she restrained her steps with as much dignity as she could muster, but as soon as she thought she had put enough space between herself and Stockton's son, she started to run as though pursued by the ghosts of George's trophies.

Back indoors she tried to calm herself a little. If her objections to George Stockton had previously been rather trivial, she now had something she could really detest him for.

As she rounded the corner and was heading for the magnificent glass door to the drawing room, she heard the voices of her mother and Mrs. Stockton. The tones of their voices caused Grace to stop and listen.

"My dear, our son is really quite besotted with your daughter," Alice gushed. "Since your ball he can't get her out of his head."

"Even though he only saw her briefly," Claudia said with a sigh. "I really don't know what was the matter with her that evening; it was so out of character."

"It's the climate here. Young people are easily affected by it. Even though I've been here twenty years, I've never really grown accustomed to it myself. But you can be sure that our George and your Grace will make a wonderful couple if you will consider their union."

Grace held her breath.

"My dear Mrs. Stockton, we've already considered it. Now all that remains to be seen is how well the young people get on together."

Grace had to press her hand to her mouth to prevent a cry of horror from escaping. Did her mother in all earnestness want to pair her off with that pallid boy? She who had married such an imposing figure as her father?

Her head started spinning so much that she had to lean against the door frame. But she had no time for a fainting fit as she heard Stockton's voice approaching behind her, giving her father yet more good advice about the plantation.

Grace immediately realised which was the lesser of two evils. She straightened herself up and walked into the drawing room.

"Ah, Grace, there you are!" her mother said sweetly. "We were just talking about you."

A modest reply would have been the polite response, but Grace couldn't force out the words. She bottled up the only reply she could make to what she had heard, her lips forming a crooked smile.

A little later Stockton and Henry returned to the drawing room. Stockton's eyebrows shot up in surprise as he saw Grace sitting by her mother—alone.

"Where have you left my son?" he asked, his voice jovial but his eyes boring into her. "You weren't playing hide-and-seek and left the poor lad outside looking for you?"

"No, of course not," Grace replied as politely as she could, modestly lowering her gaze so he couldn't see the horror that the images conjured by George still aroused in her imagination. "I think he wanted to stay out in the garden for a while."

"Ah, then he must be keeping an eye out for some creature or other," Stockton replied almost disparagingly. He clearly wasn't over the moon himself about his son's hobby. "George's passion for collecting knows no bounds, but I'm sure that, one day, a pretty woman will be able to bring his mind around to other things."

He looked at her again before turning to Henry. "Would you object to me showing the young lady our observation tower?" he said. "Maybe if the garden wasn't to her delight, she may enjoy the wonderful view of the mountains—and your property."

"But of course there's no objection!" Henry replied, shooting Grace a look of warning.

The thought of having to go anywhere alone with Stockton made Grace deeply uneasy, but she forced a smile. "Will you come with us, Father?"

Henry declined. "No, I think I'd like to listen to the women's chatter for a while."

Not even Father wants to spend too long with him, Grace thought angrily as she rose with a pounding heart and ice-cold fingers, and took Stockton's proffered hand.

Stockton looked at her with a smile, then led her from the drawing room. As they descended the front steps in silence, Grace wondered where this viewing platform was, and whether it was far. She harboured a slight hope that George or Clara, together with Victoria, would appear and ask to come with them, but they remained absent, as though Stockton had locked them all in some secret chamber.

Stockton dropped her hand as they reached the drive. "Follow me. It isn't far." Stockton's friendly tone merely increased Grace's mistrust. But she pacified herself with the thought that her parents were close by, and although he had looked at her strangely before, he had never made a move to touch her.

A series of steps made from thick timber boards, with steps smooth enough for her to negotiate freely once she had hitched her skirt up a little, led up the mountainside past the terraced tea fields. For a moment, the view and the rustling of the tea plants made Grace forget that she was still in the company of Stockton.

But then he moved so close to her that she could almost feel the warmth of his body, smell his cologne.

"We're nearly there," he said unnecessarily, since Grace could already see the platform. It was set out on an outcrop of rock with a metal railing to protect observers from falling. The small telescope glinted in the sunshine.

Grace had to admit that the view from up here was wonderful. In the distance they could see Adam's Peak.

"The telescope enables you to look closely at the mountain peaks," Stockton said behind her. She felt as though his breath were stroking her shoulder. "I hope you're not prone to vertigo."

"I don't think so," Grace replied, caught between curiosity and anxiety.

"You're plucky. I like that."

With a gentle hand at her back, he steered her forward.

As Grace bent to the telescope, her hips brushed against his body. She looked to the side in alarm, as she hadn't realised how close to her he had moved.

"You can adjust the focus of the lens here."

Before Grace could pull back, he had reached his arms around her. His hand brushed against her hair as if by accident, his arm touched her back. Effectively embracing her, he turned the adjustment screw, then withdrew his hand, but not without briefly touching her waist.

Grace shuddered. What drove him to touch her like that?

The next moment she felt a little silly. *Maybe I'm overreacting,* she told herself as she tried to concentrate on the view. She succeeded in doing so for a while, marvelling at the craggy heights of Adam's Peak and then, lowering the telescope a little, gaining a wonderful view of their own tea fields and the Vannattuppūcci mansion. It looked like a jewel in folds of green velvet.

But then she heard an agitated gasp from Stockton. At first she thought there must be something wrong with him, but as she looked up, she found herself looking into eyes that were dark and gleaming oddly as they watched her. Although she had very little experience with men, she knew instinctively that this was a gleam of lust, of desire. The sensations were making him tremble. His tongue flicked over his lips.

"Grace," he whispered almost inaudibly, a strange smile playing on his lips.

This and his dilated pupils made her shrink back, but the telescope and metal railing prevented her from going far. Stockton took a step towards her and raised his hand to touch her hair.

"Please can we go?" Grace whispered fearfully, her mouth dry. "I'm feeling dizzy. Please!"

Stockton stopped mid-stride. After a brief pause, he managed to draw the lust back into the black depths of his eyes.

"As you wish, Miss Tremayne," he said somewhat stiffly, before offering her his hand. This time Grace did not take it, but descended the steps alone.

The whole of the way down, it took all of Grace's self-control not to run. Stockton made no further attempt to get close to her, maintaining a respectable distance, but she was deeply afraid of what might be going on behind his eyes—almost more afraid than of the subject that Mrs. Stockton and her mother had been discussing.

Back in the drawing room, she found that George, Clara, and Victoria had returned.

"Well, how was the view?" her father asked cheerfully, without noticing that something was amiss with his daughter.

"Beautiful," Grace said flatly. She noticed Mrs. Stockton look quizzically at her husband. The desire in Daniel's eyes had gone, but it seemed as though it had left behind some trace that Alice could see clearly. For the rest of the afternoon Grace could not bring herself to look Mrs. Stockton in the eye, even though she had not been the one who had reached out her hand to the woman's husband or sought accidental physical contact.

Fortunately, the purgatory was over an hour later and they made their way back to Vannattuppūcci. The whole time, Grace had been simmering inside so much that she was unable to speak. Her unease following her walk with Stockton was mixed with her anger at the machinations towards an engagement between her and George.

But no one noticed, since Victoria chattered away cheerfully about all the ailments Clara Stockton had been regaling her with. "It was hard, but I said nothing about my malaria," she added when she noticed her father's dark look.

When the carriage finally came to a halt, Grace felt unbridled anger deep inside. To hear Mrs. Stockton speak, it was as though the engagement with her son was already a fait accompli. How could her mother think of handing her over to the first eligible man that came her way— simply because their plantations were adjacent to one another and the Stocktons were clearly richer than they were?

What would she say if she knew that Stockton clearly had a fancy for her, too? *She'd probably think I was imagining it.* Grace couldn't help feeling disappointed by the thought.

In her room, she tore the hat from her head in a rage and threw it into a corner by the window. She put her hand up to her hair and released the locks. Victoria, following a few moments later, quickly closed the door behind her.

"What's the matter? Have you got an insect in your hair?"

Grace didn't reply, but tore off her dress. She whirled around, her eyes shining like those of a madwoman. Victoria shrank back in alarm. "Should we be thinking of committing you to an asylum?"

"You should be considering Mrs. Stockton for that!" Grace snarled. "She thinks her George and I would make a wonderful couple! And Mother saw fit to agree! As though there were no other suitable young men in the area."

She couldn't bring herself to tell Victoria how Stockton had almost forced himself on her at the viewing platform.

"I doubt you'd want to marry any of them, either," Victoria replied sharply, removing her own hat with more considered movements.

"Of course I'd consider marrying one of them. As long as he doesn't look like George Stockton! How can Mother even think of marrying me off to that insipid boy? Do you know what his favourite hobby is? Stuffing dead animals! When we were out walking he gave me a blow-by-blow account of how he draws out the innards with a hook. I tell you, he's not right in the head!"

Victoria's eyes sparkled with dark delight. Given her own curiosity, she would probably have liked to watch the taxidermy in action. "Maybe you should tell Mother about it."

"She sounded so thrilled with Mrs. Stockton's suggestion that she probably wouldn't listen to me. And we've only been here two months!"

"Even if we'd stayed in London you'd probably have had admirers by now."

"But not ones who slaughter animals and stuff them with wood wool."

"You know Mother believes a girl should marry as soon as possible," Victoria continued unperturbed. "She was only eighteen when she met Papa."

Grace almost burst out that this was their father, who had no blood-thirsty hobbies and was glad that his lack of an aristocratic title meant he wasn't compelled to go fox hunting, but she was only too aware that her feelings for him had changed somewhat since he had punished her for her intervention at the whipping. She loved him, yes, but it was as though a dark veil had been drawn over her love since they had been here. She didn't know if it was he who had changed, or her.

"I know that I'll have to marry one day, and indeed, if I'd been told six months ago that I'd become the wife of a rich landowner, I'd have been beside myself with joy. But now . . ." She hesitated. If she were back in England would she really have accepted that her parents would practically choose her husband for her?

In England I'd have had a whole ball season to inspect the available men. I might even have fallen in love with one of them—without his father slavering over me like a hungry wolf.

Love! That was the real reason. As a girl she had always dreamed of it, and as she grew up, everyone had tried to persuade her that her duty to her family was more important. But the germ of longing was not something to be so easily repressed by duty and obedience.

"I don't love George Stockton, and I probably never will. Doesn't one always know whether one likes another person within just a few moments of meeting them?"

"It's also the case that many women get used to their husbands and love can grow from that."

"Be that as it may. But look at you, immersing yourself in your romantic novels and reading Jane Austen—you'd hardly be satisfied with learning to live with someone, would you? Wouldn't you prefer to wait for your Mr. Darcy?"

As she spoke, Grace realised that she had found hers.

"I'm more partial to Colonel Brandon," Victoria retorted with gusto.

"All right, Colonel Brandon, then," Grace said. "The point is that George Stockton is neither of them. He may be the heir to a magnificent plantation, but I'm sure there are plenty of those around here. What on earth is possessing my parents, wanting to marry me off to that boor? There are plenty of worthier plantation owners' sons in the area."

"But if you married George you could stay nearby. You know Father expects you to take over the running of the plantation."

"Maybe I should take over Tremayne House," Grace pointed out. "If I'm honest I'd far rather be there right now!"

That was not quite true, since there was definitely one thing that could keep her in this place. But at that moment she would have travelled to the ends of the earth to avoid a marriage to George Stockton.

"What do you want with that old pile?" Victoria asked in amazement. "You have to admit that the climate's so much better here and this house is less gloomy."

"True, but just imagine yourself in my position!"

As tears sprang to her eyes, Victoria came and sat by her, laying her arm gently on her shoulder.

"Maybe they'll reconsider. Anyway I don't want you to leave here. Perhaps young Stockton won't be willing, either. Or perhaps he'll fall from his horse when he's riding around the plantation with his father. No one knows what fate has in store for us."

Of course a woman had to fulfil her duty and marry. But why George Stockton? As Grace wondered what had become of the obedient daughter who had dreamed of nothing but her debut and a wedding, she realised that no one else could claim a place in her heart. That had already been taken. Taken by a man whom she didn't even know was free.

14

Vannattuppūcci Tea Company, 2008

The next morning, breakfast was again waiting for Diana and Jonathan, but instead of Mr. Manderley, there was only a small card on which he apologised for his absence, saying he had business in Colombo and would not be back until the following day.

"We'll miss him," Diana said with a smile, as she pushed the card into her trouser pocket on the way to the archive room. "What if we have any questions?"

"The whole building's full of nice people who are dying for a distraction from their real work." Jonathan grinned, then handed her a CD case. "I looked up a few facts about kalarippayatu for you, including a video that will give you a good impression of a fight. Maybe you can use this for your collection."

"Where did you get the CD from?" Diana asked in surprise.

"Oh, you know, the ladies in the admin department. You give them a charming smile, modestly tell them what you'd like and, hey presto, you've opened all kinds of doors. This material is well worth looking at."

Diana took the case. "How's your project going, anyway?" she asked. "I can't help feeling bad that I'm keeping you from your work."

"I hardly think that what I'm doing here could be considered keeping me from my work. As I told you yesterday, I can use some of what we find here for my book. Actually, I'm the one who should be grateful to you and Michael for showing me a completely different point of view. We historians often tend to approach the subject far too cautiously. In this place"—he spread his arms—"you can experience aspects of the conflict before your eyes. What more could I ask for?"

Several hours passed, and the only new thing Diana brought to light was an old prescription for quinine, issued by one Dr. Desmond. The other loose papers, some of which she had hoped might be personal letters, turned out to be delivery notes and business correspondence. Even so, she found that some of them were in the handwriting of her ancestor, Henry Tremayne. Even though she was no expert in graphology, Diana could see that the plantation owner was a strong-willed man.

She was reminded of Emily's funeral service. The event—the "scandal," as Victoria herself referred to it in her letter—must have been serious enough for it still to be reaching the present as a faint echo. No one could make out the words any longer, but everyone could still hear that something had been called.

"Oh my God!" Jonathan suddenly exclaimed.

Diana whirled around in surprise. "What's up?"

"I think I've found something here that you most certainly need."

He handed her a tattered little notebook, its pages wavy with damp. It bore no title, and on the first few pages there was nothing but Tamil characters.

"What's this?" she asked, pointing at the blurred letters. "You know I can't read Tamil."

"The characters are meaningless. It looks like they could be practice notes. But after them I think you'll find a real treasure."

Diana leafed through and saw what Jonathan meant.

"I can't believe it," she murmured breathlessly. Her pulse quickened as though she was at the starting line of a sprint.

After the characters came a series of notes in writing so tiny that it would take a magnifying glass to read them. The lines were cramped up close, as though the author had tried to use every bit of free space in the notebook. Anyone taking a cursory glance would have thought this meaningless scribbling, but Diana held the writing close up to her eyes as though she had suddenly become short-sighted, and recognised the tiny shapes as proper words.

"The writer must have used a really fine nib," she said as she put the notebook down. "I think I'll have to ask Mr. Manderley for a magnifying glass."

"Anyone who used such tiny writing must have been trying to hide something," Jonathan said as though he were an expert in deciphering hidden codes. "This could be where Grace's or Victoria's secrets are lurking."

"If this notebook really did belong to one of the sisters, she can't have thought it important enough to take back to England. Perhaps we shouldn't get our hopes up; it might be meaningless."

"You'll only know that if you read it, won't you?"

Diana nodded and thoughtfully ran a finger over the paper, which felt like fine-grained sandpaper.

"You know what? I'm going to ask the ladies in the admin office for a magnifying glass. After all, the one in the red patterned sari gave me the CD."

Why did that comment cause her a small pang of jealousy?

Diana knew the answer, but suppressed it, since at that moment she wanted to concentrate on the notebook.

"I'll be right back!"

Jonathan got up and left the archive. Diana gazed after him for a moment, then picked up the notebook again and held it close up to her eyes. She noticed a faint scent of cinnamon, like the one that had clung to the objects in the chest. As she tried to decipher the tiny letters, her eyes began to water, and suddenly the tears seemed to transform her pupils into magnifying glasses so she could read the first sentences.

I don't know where to begin. My thoughts are in such confusion, and I have no one to confide in. Without a single friend here, all I can do is confide in this notebook and burn it as soon as I've filled it. Maybe I'll succeed in setting everything down in the right order . . .

Before she could continue, Jonathan had returned with a magnifying glass and a small basket of fruit.

"The admin ladies gave me this when I declined their invitation to lunch."

Diana raised her eyebrows. "Is it past lunchtime?" A glance at her watch confirmed it.

"It certainly is. But as a researcher I know how absorbing the past can be. Read on and let me know when you find something groundbreaking. In the meantime, I'll see if I can find any more gems like this one."

Diana gave him a grateful smile and picked up the magnifying glass. Before turning her attention to the notebook, she took a banana. As she peeled it and slowly ate it, she wondered who had written this message of despair.

Once she had finished eating, she took out the envelope she had found beneath Daphne's coffin. The ink was of the same colour as the writing in the notebook. No wonder—both items had been written here. But had the notebook belonged to Victoria or Grace?

Comparing the two documents directly, she saw that the handwriting of Victoria's letter was more childlike, playful, while that in the notebook was flatter and more angular, as if in their haste the author had given no consideration to fine lettering. But there were similarities in the two hands, as though they had been taught by the same teacher.

Had this really been written by Grace? Had she poured out her soul on to these pages?

Her heart racing, Diana took the magnifying glass and began to read.

The wording was typical Victorian chasteness, yet the inner turmoil that had led her to set it all down was clear. As Diana read on, it became clear that the author was, indeed, Grace.

At one point, Diana caught her breath and looked up.

"You know what?" she said as she snapped the notebook shut.

"What?" Jonathan looked up in surprise from his pile of papers.

"We're going to the Stockton plantation!"

"Now?"

"Why not?"

"Well, what's behind this? Something you've found in that little book?"

"And some!" Diana replied. "My ancestor says here that the whole disaster, as she calls it, began with a visit to the Stocktons'. If I've found such a concrete indication, I'd like to follow it up as quickly as possible."

Jonathan raised his hands in resignation. "OK, you're the boss! Let's see how far it is from here."

He got up and went to the map of the region that hung on the wall by the door. It was quite old, as evidenced by the yellowing paper, but the roads and tracks would not have changed.

"If you're up for an energetic walk, we should make it in about three hours," he concluded, after studying the roads that led further north.

"I'm ready for anything. I have to see the Stockton plantation—and the documents they've got stored there."

Jonathan nodded with a smile, then picked up his bag.

◆ ◆ ◆

Although it was obvious that the plantation was run-down, the mansion still looked magnificent, lording it over the surrounding decay. The paint was peeling from the walls, and some of the windows had been roughly boarded up, but as she stood with Jonathan in front of the imposing gates, Diana could imagine what life had looked like here a hundred and twenty years ago.

"Excuse me," Jonathan called out.

Diana tore her gaze away from the house and only then noticed the man in work clothes who was hurrying across the courtyard.

"What you want?" the man asked in poor English. Jonathan switched to Tamil. Diana did not understand what he said, but she assumed he was explaining their presence and asking him to allow them to look around.

The man said something in reply, then vanished.

"What now?" Diana asked.

"He's gone to fetch the key. He says the estate manager isn't here, but if we promise to leave everything as we find it, we can have a look inside." Jonathan smiled at her, then continued, "The house is really impressive. I'm surprised this plantation has got so run-down, as the growing conditions are the same as those at Vannattuppūcci."

"It must be down to the owner." Diana reached out to touch a delicate tendril of ivy, a plant that looked completely out of place here—almost as though the Stocktons had never intended to fit in in this country. "The things Grace Tremayne wrote about him are anything but flattering."

"So he was a real bastard?"

"A womaniser, by the sound of it. I'm interested to know what became of him. Maybe that will bring us a bit closer to Grace."

Before Jonathan could ask anything else, the worker reappeared, keys jingling. The gate's hinges screeched as it opened, giving Diana goosebumps.

"Let's go," Jonathan said, his enthusiasm in stark contrast to the indifference of the man who let them in.

In the middle of the lawn stood a *For Sale* sign in three languages. "What could anyone do with a building like this?" she whispered to Jonathan.

"A spa hotel, perhaps? Or a museum? The times of the English nobility owning second homes in a place like this are long gone."

"But the tea plants are still here," Diana said. "It's possible that tea cultivation could be revived here again one day."

"Yes, maybe. I'd say Mr. Manderley would be a good candidate—the fields neighbour Vannattuppūcci after all. But I'm sure even he wouldn't want to be responsible for maintaining two substantial houses."

A pity, Diana thought, despite what she had read in the diary.

Looking at the house close up, Diana saw a crack running up the wall, as though there had been an earthquake here. Large patches of paint beneath two of the ground-floor windows were peeling away. The old front door had been replaced by a modern one, which had the effect of a shrill discord slicing through the harmony of an orchestra. *In Germany, alarm bells in the historic building protection offices would have sounded a long time ago,* Diana thought with a pang.

But as soon as they left the hideous door behind, she was immediately immersed in the shadows of past times. Despite the lack of furniture, and the dark patches it had left behind on the walls, Diana could vividly imagine how magnificent the house must once have been. She looked in awe at the marble staircase that led to the upper floor. A stately, dark-haired man in a frock coat stared down at her from a heavy gilded frame. As if drawn to the life-sized portrait by a spell, Diana climbed the stairs towards it.

There was no inscription, but from the style of the man's dress, the landscape, the tea fields behind him, and the distinctive lines of the mansion he was standing in front of, she assumed this must be Daniel Stockton. She also had a vague recollection of the photo from the Hill Club, although her attention had mainly been on Henry Tremayne.

At first glance, this did not look like a man who would feel the need to chase after a young woman. His angular features looked serious, his neatly trimmed beard and well-groomed, lightly greying hair indicating a certain vanity. It was impossible to tell whether the painter had been a little flattering with his body, or he simply did not have the belly that many men gained at his age. In any case, Daniel Stockton was a fine figure of a man. Only the black, impenetrable depths of his eyes suggested the repressed desires of the man described in Grace's notebook.

As she turned, she noticed that Jonathan had been watching her the whole time.

"That's the man from the club photo, isn't it?" He hadn't forgotten.

"I assume so. Who, if not the owner of this plantation, would have had a life-sized portrait of himself hung here?"

"Maybe we'll find something to help us with the relationship of the Stocktons to the Tremaynes. The estate worker's only given us an hour; we should make a start on exploring the rooms."

Diana nodded, and as she came back down the stairs she really felt as though Stockton's dead eyes were boring into her back.

Many of the rooms were completely empty, the furniture long gone, but bare cables hanging from the walls suggested that offices must once have been housed here.

Having found nothing on the ground floor—even the room Diana took to have been the drawing room was bare—they went upstairs past Stockton's portrait.

Some doors were locked up here. Peering through the keyholes, they saw rooms that had probably not even been used when the plantation was still going well.

"Look! We might find something interesting in here."

Behind the door Jonathan had pushed open was a room that still contained some furniture. Diana supposed it was Daniel Stockton's study. The high bookshelves had been relieved of the most valuable volumes, with only a few tattered books lying here and there. The furniture that remained had either been secured or was simply too heavy for thieves. Papers were piled on the wide windowsills—a mess of documents from different periods, yellowed newspapers and faded cardboard folders.

As her gaze swept the room, Diana discovered a pile of brochures with a photo of the mansion in better days on the front cover. Faded by the sun, they lay untidily on top of an old, chipped chest of drawers.

Diana picked up one of the brochures and opened it. A shiver of anticipation ran down her spine as she read it and discovered that someone had actually gone to the trouble of writing up the history of the plantation in two languages, English and Tamil.

Alongside a series of general facts, she found a family photo of the Stocktons, which confirmed her guess at the identity of the man in the portrait.

Daniel Stockton brought the plantation to the heights of prosperity until, at the age of seventy, illness forced him to hand over the reins to his son. He died two years later, following his wife, who had died suddenly twenty years earlier.

Diana glanced at the brief biography. Alice Stockton had died in 1888 at the age of forty-three. There was no mention of whether Stockton had married again.

"I wonder if Stockton had anything to do with his wife's death," she murmured softly.

"What makes you think that, Holmes?" Jonathan said.

"In Grace's notebook I've only seen one date so far, and that was the fourth of October, 1887. It could be possible that Stockton wanted to court Grace himself. If the incident at the viewing platform I read about is anything to go by, he could have had his eye on her for some time."

"But to kill his wife for her?"

"Stranger things have happened," Diana said. "Grace clearly had an aversion to his son, which he seemed to share if she wasn't mistaken. Why shouldn't he have longed for a beautiful young wife?"

"He could have got a divorce."

"Which would have meant a scandal."

She was reminded of the reference to a scandal in Victoria's letter. Had it been anything to do with Stockton? Had he proposed to Grace? Had he done something that would justify sending Grace back to England?

A cold shiver tickled her skin as she imagined that Stockton might not have balked at taking Grace by force . . .

She was immediately overcome by an urge to continue reading the account to gain a deeper insight. But the little book lay back in the Vannattuppūcci archive.

"Maybe Henry didn't send Grace away because she had fallen out with him, but to protect her from Stockton." Jonathan spoke her thoughts out loud.

"But if that were the case, why would he have disinherited her?"

Diana fell silent and looked out of the window. Was the platform where Stockton had harassed Grace still out there somewhere?

A look at her watch told her that they only had another quarter of an hour before the estate worker would come and ask them to leave.

"Let's go and look for the viewing platform," she said, following a sudden impulse.

"Don't you want to see the rest of the house?"

"Yes, but we don't have much time. Maybe we can come back again another time." She pushed the small brochure into her bag. The family photo would be enough to help her in her deliberations. "For now, I want to try see the place where he was alone with Grace."

The directions in the notebook were only very vague, Grace having concentrated on describing her feelings towards Stockton, so Jonathan went to ask the estate worker, who was lurking behind a nearby hedge, smoking. Caught, he quickly threw down the cigarette.

The man's wild gestures were a little bewildering for someone who didn't understand the language, but Jonathan got it.

"This way."

The section of the garden they passed through now was even more of a wilderness than the undergrowth around the martial arts school at Vannattuppūcci. Nature had been left to its own devices here for a long time. The steps Grace had climbed with Stockton were almost completely overgrown, with only a narrow beaten path remaining.

But when they managed to peer through the thick greenery, there were still glimpses of the tea fields.

Halfway up they came across a barrier. The sign that swung from a rusty chain was written in both Tamil and Sinhalese script.

"'No entry,'" Jonathan translated. "It seems there's a risk of falling."

Diana was set to ignore it, but Jonathan grasped her arm as she made to proceed.

"It would be better if you don't go. Your family secret will never be solved if you fall to your death. There's probably nothing left up there anyway."

Diana felt a brief impulse to resist, but then she remembered that Grace had written of a precipitous rocky outcrop.

She gave in and stayed where she was.

"I'd have liked to have seen it so much," she murmured, like a disappointed child.

"Who knows, maybe the place is haunted by Stockton's ghost," Jonathan replied with a comforting smile. "If he sees you, he could get all kinds of crazy ideas, and I didn't bring my Ghostbusters equipment."

That brought a smile to Diana's face, and all at once the time she had wasted on this walk seemed trivial.

As they returned to the house, Jonathan slipped the estate worker, by now waiting impatiently, a few notes and apologised that they had substantially overrun the hour he had granted them. Then he took his leave and turned back to Diana.

"He says we can return any time we like," he told her once they had left the mansion's ivy-clad fence behind.

"No wonder, with you slipping him money like that."

"I know how to make friends in circumstances like these."

Diana studied him for a moment. "Have I actually thanked you for everything you've done so far?"

"I don't think there's any need," Jonathan replied. "Especially since we haven't found the missing piece of the puzzle yet."

Diana smiled to herself. If Philipp were half as thoughtful as this, she might consider trying again with him. But the more time she spent with Jonathan, the more clearly she felt that there would be no going back for her after her return to Germany.

And what then? a small voice asked. *Will you ever find another man you like?*

I already have, she answered herself silently. *I've known it for a while.*

Back at Vannattuppūcci, she felt shattered—but at the same time inspired. The secret seemed to be within her grasp.

After a quick evening meal with Jonathan, they went back to the basement.

"You'll tell me if you find something groundbreaking, won't you?" he asked, making himself comfortable in his chair and closing his eyes for a few moments.

"Of course I will," she said as she picked up the magnifying glass and continued her reading.

15

Vannattuppŭcci, 1887

In the night, two days after their visit to the Stocktons', Grace decided to go and see Vikrama. In this situation she needed the advice of a friend, not a sister who wasn't old enough to understand, and not the advice of a friend who was so far away that her answer would not arrive until after the engagement had been arranged.

After reassuring herself that Victoria was sleeping deeply, she threw on her blue velvet dressing gown over her nightdress and opened the window as silently as possible.

The modesty instilled by her upbringing caused her to hesitate a moment—it wasn't seemly for a young lady to be running around in her night attire—but then she hitched up her nightdress and dressing gown and climbed out of the window.

She had never before been outside on the plantation alone at night. She had never even ventured out into the park at Tremayne House without someone to accompany her for fear that the old ghosts of the house would be out and about at night, so she was amazed that in this place, where the darkness was no friendlier, she felt no fear at all. Who was she going to encounter here?

Having reached the edge of the garden, it occurred to her that she had no idea where to begin looking for Vikrama. She supposed his house must be in the village with the others', but she wasn't sure. Maybe he even had a room in the administration building. It was strange that she'd never thought about it.

She finally decided to make for the village and, if necessary, ask for him there, if her instinct did not guide her to him. She followed the path through the jungle for a while, depending on her memory since she could see practically nothing.

She heard voices from somewhere. Someone was still awake in the village. Or was it Vikrama's friends setting off for their martial arts practice?

When a white-clad figure appeared in front of her, she ran up and cried out, *"Vikrama teedureen!"* which she hoped meant, "Where can I find Vikrama?"

The figure whirled around. "Miss Tremayne, what are you doing here?"

With a start, she realised that this was Vikrama, clearly on the way to his practice session.

"I . . . I was looking for you," she said in a small voice, abstractedly tugging down the sleeve of her nightdress through the sleeve of her dressing gown in her embarrassment. "I . . . I wanted to talk to you."

Vikrama inclined his head to one side, then his body relaxed. He set the white-wrapped package he was carrying down on the ground.

"Is it about the lessons? Your father is keeping me so busy at the moment that I hardly have time to draw breath."

Grace shook her head. "No, it's not about the lessons. I . . ."

She hesitated. Was it really such a good thing to tell him about it? He would probably also say that it was a good thing for a woman to marry. A few young girls in his village were preparing for marriage; Grace had picked up that much on one of her visits.

"What is it?" Vikrama asked. He looked at her in a way that made her feel as though he wanted to put his arms around her—a gesture she would have welcomed.

"All the indications are that my mother wants to marry me off. To George Stockton."

At first Grace could not make out Vikrama's expression, but she noticed him tense up.

"Oh. Then . . ." He said no more, as though the thought he had been about to give voice to had been stolen by the night breeze.

"It's just that I don't want to marry him. I don't love him."

A crease appeared between Vikrama's eyes which, although very slight, made his face look several years older.

"Marriage isn't always about love," he said, his voice betraying a hint of sadness. He moved a little apart from her as though a wedge had been driven between them, then looked at her seriously. "In my village, too, girls are given to men who are chosen for them by their families. Here, girls can only marry within their caste."

"Have you . . . have you got a wife?"

Vikrama shook his head. "No, I'm a half-caste, so I don't belong to any of the castes. I'm welcome in everyone's home, but no one would give their daughter to me. It's set down that Hindus can only marry within their caste. At best I'll find a woman from among the Burghers— people who are part-European, part-native—who don't belong to any caste."

Grace looked at him. Every line on his face seemed so familiar to her that she could have drawn him with her eyes closed. An unexpected warmth spread through her as she looked at him. She was relieved to hear his words. He was free, free to love her. As she loved him.

The prophecy that she would bring bad luck on her family passed briefly through her mind, but she dismissed it as fast as it had come.

Why should she be led by an old man's prattle? In any case, it would probably be more of a misfortune if she were to bend to their wishes and marry a man whom she could never in her wildest dreams bring herself to feel anything for.

He was suddenly next to her, very close, his face just a hair's breadth from hers, his hands on her back. He looked at her briefly, searching for any sign of resistance in her expression, and when he found none, he kissed her. His lips were dry at first, but as they opened, Grace felt the moist warmth inside. She could only yield to him, allow his tongue to slip into her mouth and entwine around hers. Her whole body suddenly felt as though it were on fire, her pulse thundering like a storm in her ears.

As he drew back, she felt as though a cold breeze were settling over her face. She immediately longed to be close to him again.

"I . . ." she began, but fell silent as he took her hand.

"We should find somewhere where we can talk," he said softly.

Grace nodded, then allowed him to lead her into the darkness. As they walked, a thousand thoughts shot into her head, which seemed as loud as if she had spoken them.

When they entered a small wooden house, Grace's heart leapt to her throat. What would happen now? Would they merely talk through the night? Or would they do more?

Whatever it was, she wanted it with all her heart. She longed to stroke his skin and to feel his lips on hers again. She wanted to feel his warmth like before, when he had held her in his arms.

"I . . ." she began again, but the words dried up in her mouth as she looked at him. Their lips found each other again, this time more gently, and their hands wandered over each other's body, as though they were exploring something fragile.

When they drew apart again, he pulled the door shut behind him. The fact that they were now truly alone excited her and almost made her forget any interest she might have had in seeing what was inside the little dwelling. He didn't approach her immediately, but walked around her to lay the white bundle on the table, which more or less forced her to examine her surroundings. The moonlight only showed her vague outlines, but they were transformed into objects when Vikrama lit the lamps that were standing on the windowsill.

The hut was very simply furnished. Against the wall was an old, neatly made bed. A chest of drawers near the door looked like it had been a cast-off from the mansion at some stage. A small Oriental-looking cupboard stood by the door, and instead of chairs there were cushions scattered on the floor. Red paint was peeling from the walls. The floorboards creaked softly beneath his feet as he crossed the room.

Could I live in a hut like this? Grace wondered.

Yes, she could. With the right man by her side she could live anywhere. She knew that now. She didn't need a country house in England, nor a debut before the queen. Just the right man.

"It's nowhere near as elegant as your house," Vikrama said, a little ashamed. His voice sounded strange in the awkward silence. "But it's my home, and I built it with my own two hands."

"It's the loveliest house I could imagine," Grace said, not knowing where she should look. Vikrama's face looked even more handsome in the warm light, like the face of a prince in one of her old fairy-tale books.

"Have a seat," Vikrama said, indicating one of the cushions. The prospect of sitting by him made Grace blush and caused her to remain standing.

"No, I think I'm fine as I am. I . . ." Her stomach suddenly lurched. All at once she was aware of the danger she was putting herself in—at least, that which her mother and Miss Giles had always called danger. "I have to go," she whispered. She knew no more about the relations between a man and a woman than a few whispered hints picked up from overheard servants' conversations, but it was enough to worry her.

"The door's not locked," Vikrama said, as though he sensed her doubts. "I won't do anything to you. You know that."

Everything in her was crying out for him to do something to her. Something she would never forget, something that would drag her out of the circle her parents inevitably wanted to draw her into.

She didn't want to be George Stockton's wife, she wanted to be the wife of this man, this foreigner, who had caught her attention from the very first day.

And so she did not open the door—no, nor did she take a step towards it, but stayed where she was, reeling, gazing with longing at this man.

Vikrama came over, but stopped two hands' breadths from her. As before, she could smell the scent of his skin, feel his warmth.

As he drew her into his arms, she did nothing to stop him. Her body seemed to melt into his as she returned his kiss passionately and now, emboldened, began to caress his chest and shoulders.

He stopped suddenly and drew back. As Grace leaned towards him, he gently held her away.

"We shouldn't be doing this!"

"Why not?"

"I don't want to get you into trouble. You must know that you could get pregnant. I don't want to do that to you."

Grace stared at him, shocked. Those words would not have slipped so easily from an Englishman's lips. But he was right. Even though her body yearned for his, even if she wanted to cast all reason to the wind, her head told her that what Vikrama had said was right. If she got pregnant that would certainly mean trouble. But her heart did not care about the consequences.

They finally separated without a further kiss, without further closeness, but with a promise to meet again. As Grace left the hut, she realised that she had gained the clarification she had been wanting: she knew now that Vikrama loved her as much as she loved him. That was enough to silence the spectre of a marriage with George Stockton, for a short while at least.

On the way back to the house she suddenly felt she was being watched. She couldn't say where the feeling came from, but something about her footsteps sounded strange, oddly doubled, as though someone were trying to walk in step with her.

A twig suddenly snapped behind her. Grace jumped with a small cry, but then realised that the noise was above her and she had probably merely disturbed a few monkeys. As she continued, the suggestion of footsteps disappeared and with it the feeling that eyes were boring into her back. *I probably only imagined it,* she told herself as she finally saw the house loom out of the darkness before her.

From then on Grace stole out of the house as often as she could to meet Vikrama. They kissed, walked hand in hand through the forest, breathed the dust-free air, and marvelled at the beauty of the night, at the secrets each revealed to the other that made them see the world differently.

They would sit together on a boulder, and Vikrama would lay his jacket over her shoulders. His warmth and his kisses awoke in her a longing for more, but although desire burned inside her and lit up her eyes, she did not give herself to him. Their kisses were passionate, but he did not touch her body.

Afterwards, she would spend the rest of the night staring at the bedroom ceiling, languishing with an unfamiliar desire which she had no idea how to relieve.

During this time Grace's mood was as happy as it had ever been. Even her sister noticed the change.

"Are you sleeping better now? You're positively radiant!"

"Yes, I'm sleeping excellently," Grace fibbed. She had no intention of telling Victoria about her love, even if she knew full well that her sister was able to keep a secret.

Grace's happiness continued until the day Stockton suddenly announced he was coming for tea. Too late, she realised she should maybe have feigned illness. But as it was, she was forced once again to listen to his flattery and the unspoken threat of marriage to his son that hung in the air.

This time she had no need to find a flimsy excuse to leave because her mother sent her and Victoria out, saying there was something she wanted to discuss with Stockton.

She's probably talking about my engagement to George, Grace thought bitterly. It took a huge effort of will not to let her feelings show.

"Shall we play hide-and-seek in the garden?" Victoria asked. Although Grace was in no mood for games, she agreed.

"I'll begin—you go and hide!" her sister said as she ran to a frangipani tree.

Next time I should make sure I make a better job of hiding from Stockton, Grace thought as she searched for a hiding place. With Victoria counting down behind her, she noticed a pergola that she had only paid the briefest attention to before. Victoria would take ages to find her there. Her anger against Stockton should have cooled by then.

As she entered the leafy tunnel formed by bodhi trees, she could almost feel as though she were back at Tremayne House, where the gardens had featured pergolas of fruit trees. With her sister's voice in her ears, she ran further into the arched pathway. Dappled sunlight fell through the twigs, landing in bright flecks on the sand beneath her feet. Once she had reached the middle of the pergola, all sound suddenly seemed to have vanished. She stopped, tipped back her head, and closed her eyes. Maybe she should come here more often . . .

"Are you enjoying the peace and quiet, Miss Tremayne?"

Stockton suddenly appeared. The devil only knew where he had come from!

Grace gasped in shock and recoiled.

She suddenly regretted her decision to choose this spot. Stockton must have seen her on his way across the courtyard and followed her.

"Mr. Stockton. Didn't you have something to discuss with my mother?"

Stockton smiled, walking towards her with his hands clasped behind his back. "It was only the briefest conversation. I didn't want to leave without saying goodbye to you first."

The gleam in his eyes certainly didn't suggest a farewell. Grace had seen that expression on Vikrama's face.

As though he had read her mind, Stockton suddenly leapt towards her and pressed her roughly against the wall of tree trunks. The lecherous spark in his eyes scared her terribly.

"At last I'm alone with my little princess."

"Let me go!" Grace grabbed his wrists, but was unable to fend him off. His breath brushed her face as he panted, "I've wanted you since the day you and your sister ran under the hooves of my horse. Not a minute has gone by since then that I haven't thought about you. In the nights when I lie beside my wife I dream of possessing you, of taking you as my lover. I came so close on the viewing platform. If you hadn't taken fright, I'd have had my way with you there and then."

"Mr. Stockton!" Grace exclaimed in disgust. "You can't mean that seriously."

"I most certainly am serious! I've been craving you, my sweet Grace, for so many months! I know your father would kill me if I gave in to my desire. That's why it would be so wonderful if you were to marry my son. My misguided, feckless son, who only has eyes for dead animals! God only knows whether he could sire an heir. But I'll take care of that."

"Let me go, Mr. Stockton!" Grace tried desperately to turn away, but was unable to get free of him. "You're talking nonsense!"

He stopped suddenly. His expression could only be called madness. "Nonsense? We'll see about that. A number of rumours have come to my ears, rumours that I'm sure would interest your father. I wonder if he'd consider those nonsense?"

"I don't know what you're talking about!" Grace's eyes sparked with anger, but tinged with fear. Did he really know? Who could have been watching her? Who could have betrayed her?

She suddenly recalled that Petersen had once crossed her path after a rendezvous. It had seemed a mere coincidence, but when she thought about it now . . .

"I'm talking about that half-caste, that Vikrama. A handsome chap, I'll give him that. And he clearly knows the way to handle you to get what he wants!"

Grace felt as though the ground were opening up beneath her feet.

She lacked the strength to fight off the hand that lifted up her skirt, the thighs that fought their way in between her legs.

"That's nothing but malicious rumour!" she said in an effort to defend herself, all the while wondering when their secret trysts could have been discovered. Whoever it was must have had a filthy imagination if they believed she would have given herself to Vikrama like a prostitute.

"I think you should grant me the same favours as you do that savage," Stockton panted, his arousal deafening him to her words. "It will hardly affect you, since he's already penetrated you."

Grace gasped as he felt for her underwear. Fear and disgust stuck in her throat, so that she couldn't even scream. His breath brushed her face, and a moment later his lips were pressed against her mouth and his tongue choked off any cry she might have made. At the same time his finger found its way inside her. As the blood hammered and throbbed in her ears, Grace thought she would faint from horror.

He stopped in amazement and drew his lips away from hers. "He hasn't . . ."

Grace sobbed with revulsion and anger before finding the strength to push him away.

Stockton recovered rapidly from his astonishment, then suddenly smiled. "Well, if that's how it is . . ."

"Grace?"

Her sister's voice rang in her ears like a liberty bell. Stockton paused, his flushed face going a deeper red. Grace whimpered. Was he going to let go of her at last? Or did he have the gall to assault her before Victoria's eyes?

Her sister called again, and he drew back. Instead of letting her go immediately, his fingers bored into her upper arms.

"Not a word of this to your father, you understand?" he hissed. "If you breathe a word to him about this little meeting, I'll tell him about your trysts with the half-caste."

"You're a bastard, Stockton!" Grace's voice dripped with disgust.

"I may be, but one who gets what he wants! In return for my silence, I want you to meet me the night before your wedding. It won't occur to my son that you're not a virgin. And I honestly don't want to rely on George for the future of my plantation. I want to father an heir with you myself. And I promise you that you'll never experience a deeper desire."

As the grip of his hands loosened, Grace shoved him away. Instead of grabbing her again, he brushed his hair from his face with a trembling hand and held her eyes like a wolf fixes on its prey.

"Think about what I've said, Princess. As long as your father says nothing to me, the matter will remain a secret. And if you come to me before your wedding night, everything I know will be forgotten. You have a gentleman's word on it!"

Grace felt like spitting in his face, but at that moment Victoria came round the corner. She looked from Grace to Stockton in amazement.

"Here you are! Why didn't you answer me?"

Grace felt as though she would die of shame as she struggled for composure. "Mr. Stockton and I were talking. I can't have heard you."

"I was about to fetch Mr. Vikrama to help me look for you."

The sound of his name ignited a spark in Stockton's eyes. He pressed his lips together, but his words still rang in Grace's ears. And she knew he would carry out his threat.

"I'm coming, darling," she said to Victoria and walked away without so much as a glance at Stockton.

It took every ounce of self-control she possessed not to reveal what had passed between her and Stockton. Several times she was on the verge of tears, but the knowledge that Victoria was bound to ask her what was the matter soon made her regain control of herself.

On the way back to their room, Victoria was called away by Miss Giles. Grace returned to the room alone and sank down on the bed. What was she to do now? How could she reveal Stockton's intention without losing face herself? She certainly couldn't tell her parents that . . . Stockton would be bound to dismiss it as slander, or as an attempt by her to seduce him.

No, it wouldn't come to that!

For some reason she was unaware of, her gaze fell on the chest of drawers. She immediately rose and hurried over to it.

She opened a drawer and looked at the palm leaf she had hidden there. Stockton's words thundered through her mind. She was fully aware of the consequences of her plan, but she had no other choice. She had to make Stockton lose interest in her, either as a potential wife or daughter-in-law. *Listen to your heart.* The old man's voice echoed through her mind. At that moment her heart was saying one thing and one thing only, completely at odds with her head . . .

That night she didn't creep out of the house. Her knees drawn up to her chest, she sat in front of the window and tried to shake off the sickening feeling of revulsion that had gripped her. She still imagined she could feel Stockton's hands pawing at her. Could Vikrama ever touch her again without summoning up the lustful face of that swine?

A soft scratching caused her to raise her head. Vikrama was standing outside the window, in his ceremonial white clothing.

Grace looked across at Victoria, who was sleeping soundly. She opened the window and Vikrama beamed at her.

"I'd like to take you with me," he whispered. "You've always said you wanted to see me fight."

It was indeed what she had wanted, but now was not the time. She was unable to feel the delight she should at this gesture of trust, of love.

"What's the matter?" Vikrama asked, his face full of concern at her silence. "Don't you want to come? Is it your time of the month?"

The way he spoke so freely about certain subjects made her smile.

"No, everything's fine. I was just feeling a little unwell, but it's passed now you're here." She leaned forward and gave him a kiss. "I'll be with you shortly."

She quickly slipped into her afternoon dress, which was still hanging over the chair, and having reassured herself that Victoria was sound asleep, she climbed outside with Vikrama's help. She stumbled against him, and for an electrifying moment her hand brushed against his naked breast. Shocked at first, then wondering, she stared at him. She knew the skin of his hands and arms, she knew his lips, but she had never expected the skin of his chest to be so soft and velvety against her own. A flame, ignited in her own breast, shot to her loins, causing a throbbing sensation.

Vikrama seemed to sense the feelings raging in her at that moment; he drew her close and kissed her more passionately than ever, before quickly regaining his self-control.

"We have to go," he gasped. "They're waiting for us. And you don't want your sister to see us."

Grace shook her head and allowed him to lead her through the gap in the hedge.

On the way, they talked in whispers about how each couldn't stop thinking about the other, and how that could have fatal consequences if he was distracted and took a wrong step somewhere on the plantation and tumbled down a precipitous slope. "But at least I'd have you on my mind at the moment of my death," he added with a smile.

"It's not something to laugh about," said Grace indignantly, then reached out and ran her fingers through his soft hair. "But I'm happy that you've fallen for me in every other way."

Vikrama laughed briefly and gave her a kiss.

At that moment Stockton's assault was forgotten. In any case, Grace couldn't have brought herself to tell him about it, because she knew he would go straight to him and demand some kind of retribution. She was firmly committed to her plan, which would mean she could finally be with the man she loved.

Once they arrived at the hut, which was dimly lit by flickering torches, the scene took her breath away. Two dozen young men of varying ages were sitting on the veranda looking at a wooden stage on the ground in front of them, where a number of objects had been set out.

"What is this place?" she whispered to Vikrama.

"Our martial arts school."

"You have a martial arts school behind our house?"

Vikrama kissed her. "Yes, we have. And I'm relying on you to keep our secret safe."

"I will. But how do you manage to keep all this from my father? Did my uncle allow you to fight here?"

Vikrama nodded. "He did. Under the condition that we would never attack one of his people using our skills—it's very dangerous for the uninitiated. Because everyone liked your uncle, we swore that we would only use our martial art if our life was in danger."

"And the same applies to my family."

Vikrama nodded almost reverently. "I have to admit that my fingers have been itching to punish Petersen in our way for whipping Naala, but I'm able to keep myself under control. In any case, I'm sure your father wouldn't treat us with the same tolerance as your uncle. That's why we only meet here in the night-time and leave the place looking as though it's been long since abandoned. Anyone who comes across it in the daytime won't see anything more than a rickety, neglected hut."

He led her on, until they were standing in front of the veranda that ran the length of the hut. The men seemed to be as surprised by her appearance as Grace was about the fact that this building was so close to the plantation. Vikrama briefly explained to them, and to the old man who Grace assumed must be their teacher, why she was here.

Grace was sorry she couldn't understand everything Vikrama said, and resolved to ask him to give her a few more lessons when they met.

"The teacher agrees," Vikrama said, turning back to her at last. "I explained to him that you're trustworthy and won't give anything away."

"And did you also tell him—"

Vikrama shook his head. "I told him you were merely a friend—and the woman who rescued Naala."

"And that was enough?"

"For our teacher, yes. Sit down here, on one of the rocks, to watch."

She obeyed and he returned to his teacher. If she was not mistaken, Vikrama seemed to be his right-hand man. Since the old man could no longer fight himself, it was Vikrama who demonstrated the complicated movements to the young men.

At first they fought one another, which was breathtaking enough in itself. But when Vikrama stepped forward to face one of the older pupils, Grace was completely astonished. She would never have believed that it was possible for people's movements to be so fast and lithe. Like cats they sprang together and attacked each other with short practice swords. Occasionally their limbs seemed to melt into one another, making them look like the dancing Shiva from the picture in the hallway.

When the bout was over, Vikrama and his opponent bowed respect-fully to one another, then to the teacher.

This was repeated a few times with different opponents. Whenever Vikrama was not on the fighting platform she watched him as he sat next to the teacher with a solemn, reverential expression. Not a single sound of encouragement passed the lips of the pupils, with only the clacking of the weapons breaking the silence. Grace wondered how she had failed to hear it before.

When the practice had come to an end and the pupils had gone their separate ways into the night, Vikrama accompanied her back to the house. There were rustlings in the undergrowth all around, and a bird cried out high above the mountain slope, which was bathed in soft moonlight.

"Would you marry me?" she asked suddenly, surprising herself with her boldness, which was undoubtedly stoked by her fear of Stockton.

Vikrama froze momentarily. "Marry you? I'm sure your father would be against it."

"He may well be, but wouldn't it be possible to marry without his blessing? Before your gods, perhaps. Especially since they were on my side when Victoria was ill."

The bewilderment in Vikrama's eyes caused Grace's heart to con-tract. Didn't he want her?

"It would bring misfortune," he said eventually. "I'd bring misfor-tune down on your family. I'm only a half-caste. I don't belong either to your world or that of the Tamils."

"But you love me anyway?" Grace looked into his eyes, search-ing for the truth, and found it in the moist gleam that reflected the moonlight.

"I love you," he replied. "More than my own life. More than any-thing or anyone I've ever loved before."

He took her in his arms and drew her aside between the bushes.

Kissing passionately, they lowered themselves to the ground, on to the soft grass. Vikrama ran his hand over her body, down to her thigh, and Grace was not surprised to find that his touch brought her pleasure. She allowed his hand to slide beneath her skirt and stroke the sensitive insides of her legs. He didn't dare move any further. As though hit by an ice-cold wave, he withdrew, shaking his head.

"No," he whispered, although he knew it was already far too late.

"Please come to me," she implored, reaching her hands out to him. "I have no idea what will happen next, but at this moment I want you."

"It will hurt," he warned breathlessly, still wrestling to keep control.

"I know," Grace said. She felt as though she would burst like a glass bowl with boiling water poured into it.

Vikrama seemed to be weighing up whether to give in to his desire. Then he pulled down his trousers and lowered himself on to her.

As he carefully penetrated her, Grace closed her eyes. She believed she could overcome the pain, but it was terrible. As his hips pressed against her thighs, he paused. The burning passion in his eyes was a little dampened by concern.

"I hope I haven't—"

Grace kissed him. Although she was burning, at that moment she couldn't think of anything more wonderful.

They stayed motionless like that for a while, skin on skin, then the pain receded and gave way to a gentle trace of desire, the likes of which she had never felt before. He began to move, and this time she didn't close her eyes. She wanted to see what was going on in his mind, wanted to watch his desire as she was completely overcome by her own.

When he felt she had reached her climax, he withdrew with a sigh. A few moments later something sticky spurted on to her knee. Vikrama sank down on her, moaning softly.

Still floating on a cloud of joy, she realised that her plan had not worked, as even she understood enough about what happened between a man and a woman to know that the man had to release himself inside her. Vikrama clearly had not, out of consideration for her.

For a while they lay side by side in silence, each listening to the other's breathing.

"Tell me, what's your first name?" Grace asked, her head nestling on his breast. Her whole body was still tingling from her outburst of passion. The fact that her plan had not fully worked was of secondary importance.

"My name is Vikrama. I don't have another. It's not our custom to have surnames."

"So what does the *R* stand for?"

"For my mother's name. It should be my father's initial, but my mother kept his name a secret. Since she was called Rani, she gave me her *R*, as is the custom."

"So the only reference to your family is the first initial of one of your parents?"

"Yes, that's the tradition here."

"Isn't it a bit confusing?"

"A little, but most people take care to ensure that their children don't have the same names as others who might have a similar combination."

They fell silent again, and Grace knew she had to get back soon.

"Shall we do this again?" With a gentle smile he stroked her hair and her cheeks.

"Yes," she replied hotly. "I can't imagine ever wanting another man."

They kissed passionately, then he said, "I'll ask Kisah if she can give you some of her herbs."

"Why?" Grace asked.

Vikrama stroked her belly. "Because I want to stay inside you the whole time, without making you pregnant."

Grace blushed and the next moment felt terribly naïve. Of course she could get pregnant if she slept with a man! The fact that Vikrama had withdrawn, that he was now suggesting the herbs to her, only showed that he didn't want her to get into trouble. He couldn't possibly imagine that she actually wanted his seed to fall on fertile ground.

"And you think these herbs will help?"

"None of our women get pregnant if they don't want to. As long as they're not married, they take the herbs and nothing happens. After the wedding, they stop taking them and they can have babies."

As he spoke, he kept stroking her, reawakening her desire.

"I'll hold back until the herbs take effect."

"And how long will that be?"

"A few days. Then there'll be no more risk."

16

Vannattuppūcci Tea Company, 2008

Midnight had come upon them. As Jonathan pored over the commercial books, Diana leaned back, rubbing her eyes. Her head was spinning, and her body was gripped by a strange excitement. Her find was simply wonderful, but it had a terrible power to hold her and never let her go.

No romance novel could have such strength of feeling as Grace's descriptions of her burgeoning passion and the disaster that Daniel Stockton threatened to bring down upon her.

Diana should have been shocked by her ancestor's confession, but enough dark years lay between them that she could see her as nothing other than a young woman who had fallen hopelessly in love and wanted to live that love to the full—an unthinkable wish in those times.

"You ought to go to bed," Jonathan said, looking rather bleary-eyed and reminding Diana how late it was. "The notebook will still be here tomorrow."

"I doubt I'll be able to sleep after what I've read here."

"Is it that bad?"

"No, not bad, but surprising. And certainly scandalous for those times. At least it's made a few things clear for me. But at the same time it's raised plenty of questions."

"How about a little night-time walk?" Jonathan suggested, pointing to the little window through which the façade of the neighbouring building gleamed in the moonlight. "The mild evening air might help you get your thoughts in order."

That was something Diana desperately needed to do, since her temples were throbbing, a sure sign of an overtaxed brain.

The movement sensor was triggered by them leaving the house, and the front steps were suddenly bathed in light. In the purple sky, with the palm trees standing out against it like silhouettes, a silver crescent moon hung against a backdrop of innumerable stars. A soft rustling filled the air.

"Come with me," Diana said, taking Jonathan by the hand. She led him to the pergola in which Stockton had waylaid Grace. How would the whole story have turned out if he had not threatened her?

"My great-great-grandmother had a relationship with the estate manager," Diana said as they entered the dark tunnel.

"With that man Cahill?" Jonathan asked. "I found his name in the documents."

"No, with a man called R. Vikrama. A mixed-race Tamil."

Jonathan's eyes widened. "Now, that is a surprise."

"And I'm gradually beginning to suspect the reason for the quarrel, the reason for the scandal. Henry didn't want to save her from Stockton. She and Vikrama must have fled somehow."

"Maybe someone found the notebook. Otherwise it wouldn't have been tucked away in that accounts book. Maybe someone had the perverse pleasure of reading what it contains."

"But how would that someone have got their hands on it? Grace must have hidden it well. And she also threatened to burn it. If she'd had the opportunity I'm sure she would have done so. The Tremaynes were very thorough when they wanted something hidden . . ."

She suddenly realised their faces were closer together than they ever had been before. The scent of Jonathan's skin and the lingering scent of his aftershave enfolded her, and she found herself wondering how it had been back then, when Grace and Vikrama stood facing one another and kissed for the first time. It was as though she was whisked back in time, into another life. The next thing she felt was warm lips against hers. It felt as if that was where they belonged.

When she opened her eyes, Jonathan was standing in front of her, looking a little surprised.

"What's the matter? Was I such a bad kisser?"

Diana shook her head with a smile. "It was as though I'd gone back in time. As though I were Grace."

Jonathan grinned broadly. "Well I hope you kissed me for myself, not because you believed it was Vikrama there with you."

"Of course I kissed you for yourself," she replied, laying her hands gently on his cheeks. "But you should know by now that I'm quite a complicated person. And I still have a husband, from whom I need to get a divorce."

"You're not already thinking about marrying again, are you?" Jonathan laughed, making Diana blush.

"You're right. We have no idea whether we could live together. But for my part, I can say that I've fallen a little in love with you."

"Only a little?" he asked light-heartedly, taking her hand.

She saw in his eyes the same wish as the one burning inside her. Her conscience reminded her that she was still a married woman and she shouldn't do this merely to pay Philipp back. *I'm not doing it for that reason, but because right at this moment there's nothing I want more.*

◆ ◆ ◆

Sleeping with Jonathan was completely different from anything she had experienced with Philipp. Although her husband had been neither rough nor inconsiderate, and during the happier days of their marriage, she couldn't have imagined a better lover, Jonathan was now showing her otherwise. His kisses, his movements, were so gentle and sensual that when she was in his arms she forgot about Philipp completely and felt as if she were floating. The dismissive thought that it was no wonder because he was from the land of the Kama Sutra, was swept away by a wave of intense sensations that peaked in a breathtaking climax.

Afterwards, she lay in his arms and looked up at the ceiling, where bright flecks of light were dancing.

"I think this moment is perfect," Diana whispered as she snuggled up against his breast.

"Really?" Jonathan said with a smile, as he stroked her hair. "But I haven't shown you everything yet."

"Maybe we should keep something back for the days to come. I don't want you arriving back in Colombo completely exhausted."

"I think I've got enough strength to draw on." He drew her into his arms and kissed her.

After lying in his embrace for a while, Diana suddenly got up and slipped into her bathrobe.

"What's up?"

"I'm just going to fetch something."

"Sustenance from the kitchen?"

"The notebook."

"Surely not," he grumbled. "Have you had enough of me already, wanting to go reading that book?"

"No, but I want to know what happens next. There's no way I could sleep anyway. Don't tell me you don't want to know what happens to Grace and Vikrama."

She leaned over him, gave him a kiss, and left the room.

When she returned with the notebook and magnifying glass, she sat down by Jonathan, leaned against him like a comfy armchair, and read out loud to him in the lamplight.

"From that moment on, nothing has been as it was before. I creep out of the house at night, meet Vikrama, and we lie together. By day I play the dutiful daughter, patiently bearing my mother's enthusiasm for George Stockton, ignoring Miss Giles's advice, and roaming the estate with my little sister.

Fortunately, there have been no more encounters with Daniel Stockton.

I admit that I'm secretly pleased to imagine that he's afraid—afraid that I might have told my father about our little incident. But that pleasure is a double-edged sword, as it is also a constant reminder that Stockton, on his part, has threatened to betray me.

In the evenings, when I sit by the window and wait for Vikrama, I listen to my inner voice. After our first night, Vikrama brought me a pouch containing herbs, but I haven't touched it.

I hate to deceive him like this, but my heart tells me I'm doing the right thing. Isn't that what the palm-leaf prophecy told me to do?

We've been lying together for three weeks, and it's completely possible that I'm pregnant by now. I do find this thought unsettling, as I can imagine what my parents' reaction would be. But on the other hand it gives me a sense of freedom, because that despicable George most certainly wouldn't want me . . ."

Diana was disappointed to find that the notes broke off at that point.

"What do you think? Did she really get pregnant by him?" Jonathan asked, gently stroking her shoulders.

"It's possible," Diana replied. "She didn't take the herbs, in any case." She gazed down at her arm, then twirled a lock of her black hair that had fallen loose over her shoulders. "I imagine that Grace and Victoria were very light-skinned."

"They were English—as white as milk in tea. No wonder my skin's so light."

"I like 'milk in tea'—such a lovely description. If Vikrama really was the father of her child, the one she later gave birth to in Germany, some of his blood would be flowing in my veins."

"The blood of a kalarippayatu fighter." Jonathan kissed her neck. "Looking closely at the colour of your skin, I'd wager that his blood has been passed down to your family."

Diana reached out and stroked his hip. "I wonder what happened."

"With Vikrama?"

"No, I mean the moment they brought it out into the open. When Grace was forced to confess to her father that she was expecting a baby. I wonder if she told him who the father was?"

"Probably not. She loved Vikrama; she wouldn't have risked him getting into difficulty. Her father would have given him a really hard time if he'd known."

"So why didn't Vikrama ever seek her out?" Diana continued, her thoughts drifting to the letter in her bag. The final piece of evidence? "There was a letter I found in the Tremayne family vault. Her sister Victoria wrote to her, saying that he intended to go to her. I assume that 'he' was Vikrama."

"Perhaps he got cold feet. Or their father saw to it that the foreman made serious trouble for him."

"Serious trouble for a kalarippayatu fighter?" Diana raised her eyebrows sceptically and turned to face him. "We still haven't reached the end, I fear. We've revealed part of the secret, but I think there'll be more to come. We still don't know what happened next and how these intimate notes came to be in the accounts book."

"Well, we still have time. As long as my publisher doesn't start putting the pressure on . . ."

"You've been a real lucky find; you know that?" Diana snuggled up to his chest. "I don't know how I'm going to thank Michael."

"I'm sure you'll think of something." Jonathan put his arm around her and kissed the top of her head.

"In the letter, Victoria asked Grace if she'd forgiven her yet," Diana said after staring out of the window for a while, immersed in his embrace. She had a sudden suspicion, but it was too early to put it into words. "I haven't told you yet, but I found another letter. Over there, in the window frame."

She extricated herself from his arms and left the bed to get her bag.

"You did what?" Jonathan raised his eyebrows in surprise.

"I think the letter could have been from Victoria." Diana handed him the envelope, which felt quite weighty.

"And you still haven't read it?"

Diana shook her head. "No. Somehow I get the feeling that it could be the last piece of the jigsaw. I didn't want to open it until we'd reached a point where we could go no further."

"Well, there's nothing more in the notebook. Perhaps now's the time to open it."

Jonathan handed the letter back to her, and Diana thoughtfully traced the words *By Way of Farewell* with her finger.

"Maybe I should save opening it until it's our turn to say farewell to this place."

Jonathan drew her into his arms and kissed her. "It's your choice. But I'm almost sure this letter will bring all the pieces together."

Diana smiled dreamily, and with a tingle of anticipation passing through her breast, she laid the letter on the bedside table and snuggled up to Jonathan's chest.

Although they hadn't slept a wink that night, they were back in the archive bright and early.

"This is strange," Jonathan said. He got up and brought Diana the book he had just been looking through. "This isn't a normal accounts book, but a list of wages. There's an R. Vikrama listed here, and given the values at the time, he earned good money as the estate manager. But he vanishes from the payroll in December 1887."

"Probably because Henry Tremayne found out who had got his daughter pregnant."

"Do you think she would have given that away to them? She could just as easily have blamed Stockton."

An idea suddenly occurred to her. "The notebook must have been discovered. Even if it was found before they knew she was pregnant, her descriptions are clear enough and would give them every good reason to throw Vikrama out."

"That sounds plausible," Jonathan said. "But there's one thing about all this that seems strange to me. Why doesn't she write about getting pregnant? I would have thought that her father first got on the trail of her secret when they noticed she was pregnant. And if Vikrama had been thrown out by her father because of it, what would have kept him from going to find her sooner—in the letter, you mentioned it was still only a possibility. Why didn't he ever arrive?"

"Maybe he never had the opportunity."

Diana dropped the magnifying glass in surprise. Without her noticing, Manderley had come through the door and must have overheard their entire conversation.

"Mr. Manderley, I didn't see you come in . . ."

The managing director, dressed today in a beige suit with a red tie, had his hands in his pockets.

"There's a good reason for the belief of some people here that there's a curse on this place. One brought down on the estate by my ancestor as much as yours."

"What do you mean?" asked Jonathan in astonishment.

"I knew it would come to light one day. A secret can be hidden away or somehow brushed under the carpet of history, but sooner or later someone will come along who finds it and unearths it."

Diana shuddered.

"We ought to talk about this over a nice cup of tea. Come with me."

As the kettle came to the boil, Diana and Jonathan sat down at the table in the common room. It still wasn't completely clear what Manderley was getting at, but as she had him to thank for apparently bringing them a step closer to the solution, Diana decided to be patient.

"I have to apologise to you, but I couldn't resist snatching a quick look at this notebook you've been reading."

"It was tucked into one of the old ledgers," Diana said. "I'm amazed no one's found it before."

"Obviously the right person never searched for it," Manderley replied as he poured water into the teapot and reddish-brown streaks spread like blood into the water. "Preparing Ceylon tea is an art, but you're richly rewarded with the best possible flavour. This one is from the autumn flush."

Once the hot tea had been poured into their cups, Manderley continued. "When I looked at what you had found, I recognised a name that was mentioned. Cahill. He was Mr. Tremayne's lawyer."

He's read what's in the notebook. Diana flushed and, strangely, felt as uncomfortable as though he'd been watching her having sex.

"He was one of my ancestors," Manderley said. "Our family has been associated with the fate of this plantation for many decades. Even though successive generations have tried many times to leave, to start a new life somewhere else, it's always drawn them back in the end."

"It seems we have something in common."

"Yes, I think so. At least as far as Mr. Cahill is concerned."

Manderley stood up, left the room for a moment, and returned a little later with a small book.

"I think you should include this in your research."

"What is it?"

"My ancestor's memoir. He wrote it shortly before he was committed to the Colombo asylum."

"The asylum?"

"It's incredible, isn't it? Serving his master drove him mad."

"Have you read it?"

"No," Manderley replied. "This notebook was a hot topic of conversation for many years in our family. It was referred to as 'The Scandal.' By the time it was found, it was too late to punish anyone. My grandparents locked it away in a safe at our house, and told all the children that it was dangerous to read it. We eventually lost interest, but when you came here to research the Tremayne family history, I was reminded about it."

Diana looked at the worn leather-bound book. A few fingerprints could clearly be seen on it, and a couple of ink blots tinged the edges.

"It's by the same Cahill who worked with your family. I get the impression it might contain some shocking revelations, but it could also shed a good deal of light on the situation. If there's anything I ought to know, please do tell me."

Their eyes met briefly, then Manderley poured the tea.

All morning Diana could do nothing but stare at Cahill's notebook. Jonathan made himself useful by trying to find any references to the lawyer among the documents. The name Cahill appeared in the payroll, and his signature was on the cover sheet of a commercial contract.

"This signature could be important, to compare the handwriting," he said, handing her the page. It only took a brief look to confirm to Diana that it was his.

That evening they went to bed very early. Diana had put the notebook aside and devoted her attention to other documents because she knew she would need peace and quiet—and Jonathan's presence—to read Cahill's account.

Every time Diana looked at it, the thin black book seemed to have an air of malevolence. She didn't want to know what the stains were that had dried on the cover, warping it in places.

As she touched it, ready to open it, the room suddenly seemed eerie, even though Jonathan was by her, calmly stroking her back.

With a knot in her stomach, she ran her hand over the book. Could it hold the last piece of the puzzle? The reason why Vikrama had never been able to travel to find Grace? Why her father had deleted her name from the family Bible? "Do you really think I should read it?"

"Provided you're not afraid of the account of a madman."

"Who knows what he's written here?"

"You'll only find out if you read it." Jonathan put one arm around her waist, the other across her shoulders, then laid his cheek in the crook of her neck. "I'm here, in case it gets too horrible. The thoughts of a madman can sometimes be like a whirlpool, dragging you down with them."

"That just what I'm afraid of," Diana replied. "Do you really think Manderley hasn't read it?"

"Why would he have lied? Some people simply aren't keen on delving into the dark secrets of the past. Especially if it's a secret like I suspect this one is."

With a sigh, Diana looked at the little book, then shrugged and opened it.

17

The Remarkable Story of John Cahill

Vannattuppūcci, 1887

The arrival of the new owner of the Vannattuppūcci estate had put Lucy Cahill in a state of great agitation. As though Queen Victoria were about to appear in person, her eldest daughter, Meg, was scoffing at her younger sisters, hoping her mother would not notice. Lucy did notice, but chose to ignore it. The arrival of a new mistress would open up a whole range of new opportunities for her.

"I've heard that the Tremaynes have two quite delightful daughters. Will you make sure I get to meet them sometime?" she asked her husband. Maybe she would manage to steer Meg into the girls' circle of acquaintances. That would substantially increase her prospects of finding a suitable husband.

"Sometime, I'm sure," Cahill murmured, not raising his eyes from the newspaper, the coffee cup in his hand hovering over the table.

It was not a newspaper article that had gripped him—he was using the newspaper as a cover to give himself chance to think, as he had done so often during the previous weeks. What would he say to Henry Tremayne? The death of his brother must have shaken him badly. Could he perhaps be planning to sell the plantation? Or would he be kind enough to place its management in Cahill's hands?

"Sometime?" Lucy's voice sliced through his thoughts. "Aren't you concerned about our children's future?"

"I didn't know that our children's future depended on the Tremaynes."

"It would certainly make a difference!" his wife insisted. "If you were to set things up right, Meg and Sophia could be moving in the best possible circles."

As the argument had crept up like a monsoon storm and was likely to become a similarly heavy downpour, Cahill deemed it better to put his paper away and set down his coffee cup, the contents of which had long since gone cold.

"Darling," he began, well aware that it was no use pitting himself against his wife. And he wanted to avoid adding to his inner turmoil before going to Colombo to greet the new arrivals. "As soon as I see a possibility, of course I'll make sure that you're introduced to the Tremaynes. But wouldn't it be better if I weigh these people up myself first? If they're friendly and easy to get on with—and I'm including the daughters in that—we can introduce our daughters to them in no time."

Thinning her lips, Lucy nodded. This answer had not satisfied her, but she knew it was no use rushing things. Cahill was not a man to be rushed.

On the way to Colombo, Cahill kept wondering how many of his former employer's secrets he should reveal. Not the whole truth, since he was the only one who knew it. No, sometimes it really was better to let sleeping dogs lie. Tremayne had to concentrate on keeping the plantation going. The dark stains on his brother's clothing had been buried with him; it was surely not necessary to dig them up again.

The man he encountered in the harbourmaster's office was the precise opposite of his brother. Blond, a little plump, with blue eyes and a light shadow of a beard—and yet a gentleman through and through.

"Welcome, Mr. Tremayne. I'm glad that you and your family have reached Ceylon safe and well." The two men shook hands, then went into the office. Cahill felt a little uneasy the whole time. It was a strain to speak about the deceased Richard Tremayne. Over recent weeks, he had all but forgotten the dead man's face. But of course, Henry Tremayne was expecting an explanation of the incident. As he spoke, Cahill relived in his mind's eye the sight of the plantation owner's shattered body being brought back to Vannattuppūcci. How the workers had lined the road to pay their respects to their beloved master.

Cahill, who was of a more delicate disposition than most would suppose, had felt sick from the sight of so much blood. But he had observed how the remains of Mr. Tremayne were prepared as well as possible for his funeral.

Although he was a Christian, Tremayne had made it known that he wished to be cremated according to the Hindu tradition, and his ashes scattered over the sea. This had appeared completely practical to Cahill, saving him as it did the effort of having his body transported back to England, which would have taken many weeks. Instead, he had sent Henry Tremayne a telegram to Tremayne House, and subsequently sent him a letter, in which he explained that his brother's will had specified he would not have a gravestone.

He was unable to answer the question of how far the police investigation had gone, but he knew that no one would care any more about a dead man whose ashes had been scattered at sea. At the end of the conversation, Tremayne invited him to lunch, a gesture he really appreciated since his stomach had been rumbling for a long time and it was a long way back home to his wife's kitchen.

◆　◆　◆

Everything was going swimmingly. The workers finished the essential renovation works, and Cahill was soon able to give his new employer the news that there was nothing more to stand in the way of the family moving into Vannattuppūcci.

Now he saw Mrs. Tremayne and her daughters for the first time. Wonderful daughters, he found—the eldest in particular was adorable. One day, she would be mistress of the plantation, and although he had rejected his wife's suggestion a few days ago, he now heard her voice again in his head. Maybe it would indeed be possible to bring his own daughters into contact with these girls.

The appearance of Vikrama made him forget the idea for a moment. What was the lad doing here? There was nothing for it, however, but to put on a friendly face. After all, the half-caste, as he secretly called him, was ignorant enough to be completely harmless. Cahill deigned to sing his praises in front of his new employer because he knew that would shed a good light on himself.

The lad disappeared again, and after Cahill had shown Henry Tremayne around the house, his duties were over for the day.

On the way home he met a rider coming the other way. It was safe to say that Daniel Stockton was the richest plantation owner in the region. For a long while it had looked as though Richard Tremayne was set to challenge this position, but then the accident had happened and Stockton's crown was safe.

"Good day, Mr. Cahill. What brings you up here?" Stockton reined his horse in. He was clearly on his way to Nuwara Eliya to meet his friends at the Hill Club. Cahill had tried, at his wife's urging, to be accepted as a member, but in vain. The plantation owners and businessmen did not want a lawyer in their midst, especially not one who did not run his own practice, but acted for one of them.

Despite this stigma, Daniel Stockton always acted with due politeness towards Cahill and the others—or so it seemed, at least.

"I've just accompanied the new owner of Vannattuppūcci, Mr. Henry Tremayne, here."

"Richard's brother?" Stockton's eyebrows shot up.

For a moment he seemed to be wondering whether the new owner would be as obstinate as his brother had been. When he was alive, Richard Tremayne had represented strong competition for him. And there had also been some trouble in matters concerning the land.

"Yes, that's right. He's just moved into the house with his wife and two daughters. If I may say so, they're all very beautiful women."

It was well known that Stockton had a weakness for a beautiful woman; he smiled and leaned forward a little in the saddle. "Then I should visit them soon to pay my respects."

"That would be a good idea, sir. At the moment things are a little chaotic at Vannattuppūcci, but I'm sure that the next few days will provide an ideal opportunity to visit. In the meantime, Mr. Vikrama has offered to show his new employer around a little."

The mention of the half-Tamil brought a scowl to Stockton's face. It was his opinion that, in the absence of a master at Vannattuppūcci, this R. Vikrama had been behaving as though he were the owner of the plantation. Stockton would voice this opinion to anyone who cared to listen, keeping silent about the real reason for his animosity: that he was annoyed he was not able to acquire the house and the plantation as he had intended.

Cahill knew of this, however, and could also believe that, while Stockton would not actually attempt to wrest ownership of the estate from Tremayne, he would nevertheless do all he could to gain access to those fields.

"So, he has daughters, you say?" Stockton mused, ignoring the remark about Vikrama. "No sons?"

"Not yet; at least none that I know of. But Mrs. Tremayne is still quite young. It's possible that an heir may be born one day."

Stockton pulled a face. Then he sat back in his saddle and tightened his grip on the reins again.

"Thank you very much for the information, Mr. Cahill. I'll be seeing you."

"Goodbye, Mr. Stockton," Cahill called after him as he spurred his horse to a gallop.

Cahill found out about Stockton's visit the next time he called to see Tremayne in his office. By then, Vikrama had explained to Tremayne all that was required of him, and Cahill justifiably hoped that the new owner would slip effortlessly into his role. At least, this was the impression he gained from his conversations with him, and there was the physical evidence of a plantation that was once again running like a well-oiled machine.

One afternoon, as he was hurrying across the hall, Cahill saw the young Miss Grace talking to Mr. Vikrama. There was nothing wrong with that in itself, but it nevertheless brought Cahill to a standstill. A dark shadow was awoken in his breast, one he had suppressed and forgotten about for a long time. How the girl smiled at him! And how the lad's gaze roved over her face and her body. Two young people were standing there, hot-blooded and full of desires they had hardly tasted yet.

It's nothing, he thought in an attempt to reassure himself. *It's perfectly understandable that a charming girl like Miss Grace wants to get to know the people on the plantation.* Even though she was nothing like her uncle Richard in appearance, she seemed to have a similar character to his: friendly, open, and warm.

And that was a good thing—as the future mistress of Vannattuppūcci, she would need the sympathy of the workers, since they were willing to work far harder for an employer they loved than for one they merely respected.

◆ ◆ ◆

The weeks following the ball not only saw numerous changes, but also cast something of a cloud over the place.

While Tremayne delegated work that Cahill had previously carried out to Vikrama, reassuring him that he would still pay him the same for less work, and on top of it all really valued his legal advice and representation, Cahill's wife complained that the ball had been far from successful from their own point of view. "They didn't even look at my daughters, especially the elder one," she grumbled. "The younger one was friendly towards our Sophie, but there was nothing more to it than that."

"They're a different class from us, darling," Cahill had said in an attempt to pacify her. "In any case, there's so much for them to take in—I'm sure they haven't got the time to devote to every guest that was there. I promise you, our girls will be given a chance yet."

Mrs. Cahill merely sniffed and appeared to be combing her memory for anything disparaging she could bring up about the Tremayne daughters.

In the days that followed, Cahill wondered where Vikrama was going with Grace and the rather pompous governess.

"She wants to learn the natives' language, so she knows what they're saying about us." Tremayne's assertion sounded serious, as though he suspected some lurking evil intention. Did he believe the people here would deceive him? Or did he have a creeping suspicion that the relationship between Vikrama and his daughter might be more than merely that of a teacher and his pupil?

Maybe I should say something to him, Cahill thought, but rejected the idea. *I'm sure there's nothing to it. Miss Grace only wants company of her own age.* And learning the language was important for the future mistress of Vannattuppūcci. Richard Tremayne had also been able to speak it.

◆ ◆ ◆

The following weeks condemned Cahill to almost complete inactivity. Tremayne delegated mindless clerical work to him, and the drafting of documents, which he then sent him to deliver throughout the region.

"You might as well be a postman," Lucy carped in a caustic tone. "That Tamil boy is going to oust you."

"He certainly won't, darling, don't you worry," Cahill said in an attempt to appease her. But the seed of mistrust had been sown. Had Vikrama really usurped his position? Did Tremayne sense something?

No, that wasn't possible. No one knew about that.

One day, as he was returning from Colombo where he had gone to have a few documents notarised for Mr. Tremayne, he was stopped by Daniel Stockton. He looked rather distraught, and Cahill got the impression he had been waiting for him.

He probably saw me coming through his telescope, Cahill thought uneasily. Everyone said that Stockton could survey the whole area with it and watch just about anything that happened.

"Good evening, Mr. Cahill." Stockton blocked the way of the small carriage, preventing it from moving on. *Like a highwayman,* Cahill thought.

"Good evening, Mr. Stockton. What can I do for you?"

"Oh, a good deal, I believe."

He was surprised at that, and his astonishment increased as Stockton let the cat out of the bag.

"One of the men I've lent to Tremayne has reported that Miss Grace meets regularly with that Vikrama."

"She's learning the language from him," Cahill replied, turning hot and cold beneath his formal suit.

"The language, eh? Mr. Petersen says something rather different. He says they meet mostly at night and have been seen kissing. I hardly believe that's how one learns a language."

Cahill was speechless.

"Have you seen anything of the kind?"

"No, sir. I've only seen them in the afternoons."

"Hm. Well it would be a good thing if you could have someone keep an eye on them. After all, I've chosen her as a wife for my son, and we don't want him to be given a cuckoo in the nest."

Cahill felt light-headed. That mustn't happen at any cost! It didn't bear thinking about.

"I'll keep my eyes open, Mr. Stockton." Something suddenly occurred to Cahill. "What about Mr. Tremayne? Should I tell him about our suspicions?"

Stockton shook his head. "No, not at first. We won't want to arouse his anger when he's got the plantation to see to, do we? You should only tell your boss when you have concrete evidence. Until then, only me." The plantation owner took a pouch of money from his pocket. "For you. A little contribution to your expenses."

Before Cahill could thank him, Stockton had turned his horse and ridden away.

From that moment on, Cahill did all he could to spy on Grace Tremayne. *For the sake of the plantation,* he told himself. *And for the good of the young miss. Young things like her are easily led astray.* During the day, he peered in through her window at times and watched her from a distance at others. He was unable to obtain any proof, since he didn't know exactly when they met and what routes the girl took.

When he encountered Stockton he told him that everything was in order and he was not to worry—who could know what Petersen had seen?

"Anyway, it could well be that Petersen wants to bring the girl into disrepute. You must have heard how she stood up against him when he was whipping a tea picker."

"Yes, that story did reach me." Stockton's thoughtful expression indicated that he had not considered this possibility.

"I'm sure it's just a case of your man seeking his revenge. Miss Grace Tremayne is a well-bred young lady who knows what's expected of her. She would never, ever become involved with one of those savages."

It seemed evident that Stockton believed the explanation because he stopped asking Cahill about the situation.

Cahill found out to the contrary a few weeks later. One day, as he was heading for one of his usual meetings, he found the house in quite an uproar. He took one of the maids aside in the hall and asked her what was the matter, especially since Dr. Desmond was there.

"Miss Grace Tremayne has had a fainting fit. You'd better wait in Mr. Tremayne's study."

Miss Grace had a fainting fit? What could that mean? She was a healthy, robust young woman!

When Henry Tremayne entered the study two hours later, he was as white as a sheet. "Oh, Cahill. I'm sorry, I forgot all about you."

"May I ask what has happened, sir?"

Tremayne sank down on his chair with a sigh. His features were stony.

"My daughter . . ."

"I hope she hasn't had a recurrence of her malaria," Cahill said disingenuously—of course he didn't want to reveal that he already knew it was not about Victoria.

"It's not Victoria, but Grace . . ." Tremayne hesitated, weighing his words carefully. "Maybe we should postpone our meeting. I'm too exhausted at the moment."

Cahill was about to say that he hoped nothing serious had befallen Miss Tremayne, but managed to stop himself. He would find out what was the matter.

When he told Lucy about Miss Grace's fainting, she immediately said, "Could it be that her moral standards are not quite what they should be?"

"What do you mean by that?" There it was again, that dreadful feeling of alternating hot and cold.

"As far as I know, young things like her only keel over when they're pregnant. It happened with me, remember? When I was expecting Meg."

In fact, Cahill had taken little notice of Lucy's trials and tribulations during her pregnancies. One day he had simply arrived home and she had given him the good news.

"I'm telling you, if there's a boy who's been courting her, she'll be pregnant by him."

Her words took away Cahill's appetite for his supper.

The next day there were whispers all around the plantation—Miss Grace must be pregnant. And the master was beside himself because she would not tell him by whom.

Cahill paced nervously up and down in his study. He'd known it all along! It must be that Vikrama. Why hadn't he kept better watch over them? Why had he given Stockton, who was clearly concerned for his son, that story about revenge? Petersen might be a swine, but his eyes were sharp and he was obviously still loyal to his benefactor, Stockton.

This was a disaster! If he didn't know so much about Richard, he might not have cared so much about whether Grace had taken up with Vikrama. But the liaison between them was extremely dangerous, and he should have stepped in sooner for the good of Vannattuppūcci. It was too late for that now.

He never found out exactly how Henry Tremayne discovered that Vikrama really was the father. There was some talk of a notebook that her sister Victoria had found. It seemed that in her youthful inquisitiveness she had read about her sister's escapades, which Grace had written down in a kind of diary, and had been caught red-handed by Miss Giles.

Henry Tremayne's reaction was drastic. He sent Petersen and his friends out to search for Vikrama and punish him.

He hadn't intended his daughter to watch, but the girl found out and ran from her room after Tremayne had given his orders.

Cahill would never forget the girl's wailing as they dragged the lad in. He had just arrived at the house for a meeting with Tremayne, but stood rooted to the spot on the steps up to the house as the scene unfolded in front of him.

"Please let him go!" she sobbed, writhing in the arms of the men who were holding her fast.

"The devil we will, miss!" Petersen sneered. "Your father has instructed us to teach him a lesson, and a lesson he'll get! Drag him over to that tree so I can flay the skin from his body!"

"No!" Grace screamed, so shrilly that Cahill wanted to block his ears. "Defend yourself!" she cried out in anguish. "Please defend yourself! Don't let them kill you! Think of our child!"

Her cries incited him to struggle up against the men who were holding him. He glanced over his shoulder and exchanged a look with Grace—a look that suggested that what happened next would drive them apart forever.

Then Vikrama exploded. With movements the like of which Cahill had never seen before, he released himself from the grip of his captors and set about them. Before they knew what was happening, two were bleeding from the nose and a third was stumbling backwards.

Petersen unrolled his whip at lightning speed, but he was only able to bring it down once. He had raised his arm for another strike, when Vikrama beat against him with rapid blows.

"Damn you all—doesn't anyone have a gun?" the foreman yelled, but Vikrama was away, turning once for a last glance at his beloved before plunging into the darkness.

The men who had been holding Grace released her and stormed after him, disappearing into the undergrowth a few seconds later. The girl sank down on the steps. She gazed imploringly into the darkness, probably hoping with all her heart that he would make it.

When Mr. Tremayne finally came out, the defeated men had struggled to their feet. With swollen lips Petersen reported Vikrama's escape. When he added that he had been striking out in all directions like a man possessed, Grace finally spoke, a strange smile on her face. "That wasn't the devil, it was kalarippayatu, idiot."

Cahill took it to be the name of a demon; Henry Tremayne didn't care a jot what it meant. He grabbed Grace and raised her to her feet.

"What are you doing here? I put you under house arrest."

The girl swayed as if she were about to faint, which was not surprising given her condition. But she remained standing and looked at her father with an expression that would have moved a more sensitive being to tears.

"They won't catch him, Father. They won't catch him; his gods will make sure of it!"

Henry glared at her for a moment as though he were about to slap her face, before dragging her back into the house.

Cahill, whom no one had noticed, sank against the banister for support.

What a night! What a commotion! And all because he had remained silent. Because he had done nothing to prevent this disaster from the start!

I should have told Mr. Tremayne his brother's secret. The consequences would have been bad, but maybe not as dreadful and insurmountable as the present situation!

Exhausted, he took his handkerchief from his sleeve and mopped his brow. He could forget about his meeting with Mr. Tremayne. He might as well go, and return the next day.

◆ ◆ ◆

The following evening, Daniel Stockton galloped into the courtyard. The search for Vikrama had by then spread to both plantations, and after hearing what had happened and what had triggered it, he had also offered his help. His people were now also looking for the former estate manager—but without success as yet. In a rage at this on top of everything else, he drew his horse to a halt and ran up the steps. He didn't spare a glance at Cahill, who was waiting in the hall.

"He should have been shot like a dog!" Stockton raved a little later in the Tremaynes' drawing room, acting as though he were Grace's father.

Well, Cahill thought, *I suppose he would have become her father-in-law if Vikrama hadn't got her pregnant.* Once again his dark secret stirred inside him. Mr. Tremayne would have to know sooner or later. But not yet.

Cahill knew it would be better to withdraw and come back later, but then he noticed a figure on the steps. Miss Grace! He withdrew further into the shadows and hid behind an open door.

The young woman didn't see him, she was so sunk in her thoughts.

"There might be a solution," Stockton was saying, having calmed himself a little.

"And what might that be?" Henry asked.

"There are women in the village who know how to rid a woman of her brat."

His words fell like splinters of broken glass.

"You mean she should go to an abortionist?"

"Not go, but you could bring such a person here. In the house, away from the prying eyes of others, she could get things back to the way they were before."

"But that's a sin!" Tremayne snapped.

"What your daughter did with that bastard was a sin!" Stockton hit back angrily. "If you did this you wouldn't lose face with the others! I would still accept her as my son's wife, if she were no longer pregnant."

Cahill bit his lip as Grace walked past him, erect and with her head held high like a queen. She had obviously overheard Stockton's demand. She stopped in the doorway, hesitated a moment, then entered. And before their neighbour could come out with any further threats, she said, calm and self-possessed, "I intend to keep the baby, Mr. Stockton. You will not bring me to sin against life."

Silence followed her words. Cahill would have loved to be able to see the expressions on their faces. They were probably frozen in shock.

"Father, to protect you from scandal here, I have decided to go to England and give birth to my baby there."

Still there was no answer.

"A savage's brat?" Stockton was the first to give vent to his rage. "Miss Tremayne, please see reason! You could be rid of all your worries, just like that."

"Murder, you mean? Why? Because you want to make me the mother of your heir, as you once put it? Or have you reconsidered your position since our encounter?"

"That's—"

"A lie? Is that how you'd describe it, Mr. Stockton?" Grace paused briefly before continuing. "You've read my account, Father! You were hell-bent on finding the wrongdoer, but that's not Vikrama! This man here is heaped with guilt, so read a bit more closely!"

Stockton's heavy breathing filled the room. "Surely you're not going to take this girl seriously."

"Be silent, Mr. Stockton! This is my house. I'm in charge here. And I would advise you to leave, now, before I forget myself!"

"You'll regret this, Tremayne. I'll make sure that the whole of Ceylon knows what your daughter is!"

He stormed out, fuming, his footsteps echoing through the room. In the hall, he muttered something incomprehensible. A door slammed. Everything fell silent again.

"Father?" Grace whispered softly.

"You will travel to England as soon as possible," Tremayne pronounced, his voice shaking. "You will give birth to the baby, and we will find a family who will accept it and look after it."

"No, Father. I . . ."

"Don't argue!" Tremayne thundered. "Now go to your room and don't come out again."

Grace did not reply. She turned slowly and left the room. From his hiding place in the shadows, Cahill saw tears running silently down her cheeks.

In the days that followed, his services were not required. Rain showers cooled the air, signs of the oncoming winter in these latitudes. In a month's time they would be celebrating the birth of the Saviour.

Cahill withdrew into his study, refusing to speak to his wife or his children. What was to become of the plantation now? The Tremaynes had another daughter; she would inherit Vannattuppūcci. But what about the family's reputation? Stockton would never rest until Tremayne was ruined—all the more so if Miss Grace's assertion was proved.

A week later, a carriage pulled up in front of the house. Miss Grace only took a few things with her. Miss Giles travelled with her, probably to ensure that Miss Grace didn't do anything else stupid.

Cahill did not know what her farewell with her family had been like, but apart from Miss Victoria, no one was standing on the steps to wave the two women off. The carriage left the plantation. Cahill had found out that Tremayne's daughter would be sailing back to England on a post ship called *Calypso*.

After his eldest daughter's departure, Henry Tremayne was never the same. He would shut himself away in his study for hours, alternating between disappointment, rage, and despair.

Then Cahill plucked up courage. He was hardly expecting his news to cheer Tremayne up—quite the opposite. But he had decided to tell him what he knew before anything else happened.

"I don't need anything, Mr. Wilkes," Tremayne called out, assuming it was the butler at the door.

"It's me, Cahill," the lawyer whispered. "I have to speak to you."

Silence followed his words.

"Come in!" Tremayne said finally.

As Cahill entered he was shocked to see the state his employer was in.

It wasn't so much his clothes—there had been other times when he had dispensed with wearing a jacket. But beard stubble shadowed his face, his mouth was a thin-lipped line, and his eyes were sunk in dark hollows.

"What do you want, Cahill?" he asked. Even his voice sounded different, as though it had aged in a matter of days.

"I believe I have something that may interest you."

Henry raised his eyebrows. "Really?"

"There's something you ought to know, now that . . ." His employer's angry expression silenced him. Tremayne stood up behind his desk as though he intended to set about him. But he merely straightened his shoulders and beckoned him forward.

As he closed the door behind him, Cahill was struck by an idea. *Don't make it any worse than it is.* But he had crossed the Rubicon and there was no going back. His employer had a right to the truth, so that the traces of the past could be laid to rest once and for all.

"You must understand that I don't have much time, Mr. Cahill," Tremayne began. He indicated a chair in front of the desk. "So get to the point, please."

Cahill could see from the accounts ledger, which lay open but untouched, that Tremayne's time had been taken up by matters other than work.

"There have been certain developments. Things I didn't tell you when you arrived because I didn't consider them important."

Henry's expression darkened, but he continued to listen in attentive silence.

"Following recent events, I'm sure Mr. Vikrama is still on your mind."

Tremayne's snort suggested that he was all too well aware of him. "What about him? Has he done something else, apart from seducing my daughter?"

"I fear so, although it's not exactly his fault, but your brother's."

"Richard? What does he have to do with it?"

Cahill hesitated, acknowledging a kind of perverse excitement. He would finally be rid of the burden he had carried around for so long.

"When your brother came to Vannattuppūcci, he was attracted to a young tea picker. Good Lord, was she beautiful! Golden skin, jet-black hair, and strange green eyes, the kind more often found in Egypt. As he was the master, your brother had his way with her, again and again. The poor woman believed that he would make her his wife—after all, mixed marriages between Dutch settlers and natives had happened before, and their children were quite highly regarded. But your brother was cut from different cloth. After a while he grew tired of her—too late, since she was already pregnant. When she told him, he flew into a rage and drove her from the plantation. She returned to her home village in disgrace. But after a while his conscience began to plague him. He fetched her back shortly before the birth, under the condition that she would not betray him. She gave birth to the child, gave him a name and brought him up. When she died, Mr. Tremayne considered it his duty to take care of the lad. Totally unaware that Richard was his father, Vikrama grew up here and became one of the most important people on the plantation."

"How do you know all this?"

"Your brother told me shortly before his death."

Cahill tensed. The truth was a little different here, too, but who would be concerned? "He planned to establish his son as his legal heir," he continued. "But his premature death meant things never came to that, thank God. And I never deemed it appropriate to tell Vikrama because you're Richard's brother and have a far more legitimate claim than the lad does. Where would we be if these savages ran the plantations themselves?"

Henry stared at him, perplexed. For a moment it seemed as though Cahill's words would run off him like water off a duck's back. But in truth they were penetrating deep into his soul. "That lad is Richard's son," Tremayne murmured, finding it hard to believe that God would allow a trick like that to be played on him.

"I would have told you sooner, but you were too busy—"

Tremayne's howl of rage silenced him on the spot. With a furious swing of his arm, Henry swept the inkpot on to the floor, where it smashed, causing ink to flow freely across the parquet.

"So this means that my daughter has been made pregnant by her cousin?"

"You could say that." Cahill stepped back as though he feared being struck.

Henry stared at his lawyer in bewilderment. Although his mouth was opening and closing, he was unable to make a sound.

Cahill came over alternately hot and cold as he looked into his employer's face. Tremayne's eyes looked like two bottomless pits that threatened to swallow him up.

"You should have told me immediately that my brother had a bastard!"

Cahill could think of no reply, since his employer was right.

"Does he know who he is?" Henry asked, balling his fists in anger.

Cahill shook his head. "No, I don't think so. Otherwise he'd hardly have got involved with your daughter. After all, they're first cousins. Even the savages here aren't as depraved as that."

Henry sank down on the chair behind his desk, the implications of the situation apparently only now sinking in.

His weakness emboldened Cahill a little.

"I honestly never dreamed that he and your daughter . . . After all, Miss Grace was a true lady, and the young Stockton was courting her. There was absolutely no indication that she and he . . ."

But with hindsight there was plenty of indication. The looks that passed between them, Vikrama's slight smile when he saw her, her face at the window . . .

It appeared that Grace's father was thinking along similar lines.

He jumped up suddenly, stormed around the desk, and grabbed Cahill by the collar.

"You should have kept more of an eye on that fellow. No, you should have thrown him out as soon as you found out who he is!"

"But your brother . . ."

"My brother seems to have been an even greater swine than I thought he was! He should never have got entangled with that woman. It's a small consolation that she didn't tell the bastard anything about his father!"

For a brief moment, doubt appeared to flare up in him. What if she had told him something? But he dismissed the thought with a shake of his head; it seemed simply too dreadful to contemplate.

He voiced but a single solution to this problem. "If he ever has the gall to show his face here again, you will see to it that the bastard disappears once and for all!"

"You mean I should . . ." Cahill gasped for breath.

"You will do it!" Henry snarled. An evil grin spread across his lips. "To make up for concealing this information from me for so long! You will remove all trace of this affair from the world. I mean everything. Then I might see fit to overlook the fact that you deceived me and allow you to keep your position on the plantation. Otherwise, you and your family can pack your bags."

Tremayne's dismissal struck him like a bolt of lightning. He couldn't move. Nor could he take his eyes off his employer, who was boiling with the rage of a man who'd had one of his favourite things taken from him.

What would you have done if it had been your Meg? he thought. The answer was immediate: *I'd kill the bastard.*

Cahill brooded for several days and nights about how to track down and ambush Vikrama. The failed attempt to beat him up made the lawyer keen to exercise caution. *The lad is a skilled fighter—you don't stand a chance against him. He wouldn't even need one of his knives to kill you.*

But before he could corner him, he had to find out where he was. Tremayne's and Stockton's men were still searching in vain for him.

Then fate smiled upon him for the first time in many weeks. One night, unable to sleep, he was sitting at his study window, when he caught sight of a figure slipping through the garden. He recognised him straight away from his movements. What was Vikrama doing here? Miss Grace had been gone for a month, and Tremayne had strictly forbidden him from setting foot here ever again. Was he now making a play for the other girl?

Without a moment's hesitation, Cahill pulled on his trousers over his nightshirt and opened his desk drawer. The metal of his revolver gleamed malevolently. A shot would surely be heard for miles, but there was no other way of taking the lad. Even with a knife he would probably be bested by him. After tucking the gun into his waistband, he left the house. How peaceful the plantation seemed! Only the rustling of the bamboo and the murmur of the leaves on the trees lay in the air like faint whispers.

He could still make out Vikrama, who had by now almost reached the house. *The boy's got a nerve,* Cahill thought with grudging respect.

Keeping to the shade of trees and bushes, the lawyer followed him. All the windows of the house were dark, like dead eyes looking out on the driveway and the fountain.

Despite all his apparent courage, Vikrama did not dare enter through the front door. Concealed in the shadows, he made his way around the building and disappeared from Cahill's view.

What was he up to?

Peering around the corner of the building, he saw Vikrama by an open window. A slim girl's hand appeared and took something from him. A long, cloth-wrapped package. He exchanged a few words with her, which Cahill could not make out, then withdrew. The lawyer's hand was on his revolver. *Not yet.* As Vikrama turned, he quickly ducked back into the shadows. Vikrama started to walk in his direction. As the sound of his footsteps approached, Cahill hid behind one of the dense rhododendron shrubs to wait. Would he return to his quarters? Cahill turned and looked towards the house. What were the chances of a shot waking all the inhabitants and plantation workers?

While he was still considering, Vikrama disappeared into the undergrowth. That was not the way to the living quarters. Where could he be going?

Once Cahill was certain that Vikrama could not see him, he stepped out from the rhododendron bush and followed him.

As he plunged into the undergrowth and listened for footsteps, he suddenly realised where the lad was heading. Into the plantation.

He concentrated on making as little noise as possible. Vikrama appeared to suspect nothing. It was as though the tea plantation that had been his home since childhood made him feel safe. Cahill almost laughed bitterly. *He has no idea that death is hot on his heels. Or does he? Does he suspect something?*

A hot flush flashed through his body, and he broke out in a sweat. It was like that time when he had followed his employer up the mountain, convinced he was saving Vannattuppūcci. If Richard had not intended to reveal his identity to his son and hand over the management of the plantation to him—*a semi-savage,* Cahill thought, still disgusted—he could still be alive.

Cahill had considered it his duty not to let the plantation fall into the hands of a Tamil. His words had been of no use at all. After catching up with him on Adam's Peak they had argued, an argument that ended with Richard falling into an abyss.

Cahill had the shattered body within his sight but, convinced that only Richard's death could prevent a stupid mistake, he had made no attempt to rescue the fallen man. He had convinced himself that this was ultimately for the good of the plantation—and its salvation, for who would have wanted to trade with a plantation that was in the hands of a native?

The situation now was similar; once more he would be the saviour by obliterating the proof of Richard Tremayne's infidelity and his lawful heir. He was no longer able to help Grace, but maybe Vannattuppūcci.

Vikrama was now in his sights, but completely unaware he was being followed. Cahill cocked the revolver as quietly as possible.

Shall I tell this half-caste that it's his cousin he's got pregnant? That he's Richard Tremayne's bastard? No, why waste my breath on him.

He breathed deeply and pulled the trigger.

The shot echoed like thunder from the mountainsides. Who might have heard it? For an anxious moment Cahill saw his own head in the noose, but then he remembered he was here on behalf of his employer. That Tremayne would be grateful towards him for doing the dirty work his men had been unable to achieve.

The shot felled Vikrama like a tree. He collapsed with a groan that was scarcely heard above the echoing gunshot.

Cahill stared at him incredulously, almost paralysed with shock. Then he came to his senses with the thought that he would have to get rid of the body. As far away as possible, so that no one would find it. His despair, his fear of punishment, would help him to find a way.

He needed a spade, and he knew where to find one.

His heart racing, he ran back to the house. No one had been awoken by the shot. The windows were all in darkness.

Back in the plantation, the tea field suddenly seemed hostile, the shadows around its edge whispering reproaches into his ear, the wind singing a lament for the life that had been taken here. The neatly uprooted tea bush looked like a watchman who was not intending to do his duty too well.

It was one thing to kill a man, but another thing entirely to dispose of the corpse. Even after he had wrapped the body in a cloth, he was sure he could feel its eyes following him.

Cahill slaved away beneath the imagined gaze of the dead man and thought he could hear his voice whispering. *You took my father, my love, my life. Can you imagine what the penalty is for that?"*

"No penalty," Cahill muttered to himself. "No one will know."

Once the grave was deep enough, he straightened up and peeled away his shirt, which was clinging to his body with sweat. A pleasant coolness brushed over his back.

It's almost done. He grabbed the dead man's legs and dragged him to the edge of the hole. The makeshift shroud came loose. The dead eyes were open, staring at him. For a moment he felt as if, once again, it was Richard Tremayne he saw before him, smashed on a rock. Seized by dread, he gave the young man a kick that rolled him into the grave. As the body fell with a muffled thump, Cahill thought he heard a groan. Was he still alive?

Fear welled up inside him. But he didn't want to risk another shot.

Once he's covered in earth, he'll soon stop groaning. He quickly set to work, feverishly shovelling dirt back into the grave.

It began in the night. The voice of the dead man, his accusations and his threats, returned as he lay down in bed beside his wife. She was asleep, and as he feared her questions he chose not to wake her to ask whether she had heard anything.

As Cahill closed his eyes, he saw Vikrama's face clearly. The surprise as the bullet hit him, the dying light in his eyes. And he saw Richard Tremayne again. Surprised and full of reproach in that moment before he fell into the abyss.

"I had to do it," he whispered to himself. "Don't you understand? I had to do it."

But the voices would not let him go. They whispered things he did not want to hear: secret desires, black stains on his soul, dark memories. They kept him awake all night, until day finally dawned and it was time to inform his employer what had happened. He must have heard the shot in the night, and perhaps he already suspected that this particular problem was over.

Hours later, sitting in his employer's study, the voices were a little quieter, as though they wanted to hear what Tremayne had to say. They subliminally demanded that he also confess to the murder of Tremayne's brother, a murder perpetrated out of the deepest conviction that it would be a bad thing for Richard's son to take the helm one day. The plantation had to remain in English hands. It simply had to, because in Cahill's world order, there was no alternative.

"I assume the matter has been dealt with," Henry said without turning from the window where he was standing. He looked much more peaceful, more in control. As though a burden had been lifted from his shoulders. Now his daughter's lover was gone, he could convince himself that everything was all right. Grace would have her baby in England, hidden from the eyes of the world. Perhaps they could place the baby in the care of a foster mother and deny it was their daughter's. Anything was possible once Grace had arrived in England.

"Yes, it's done." Cahill took a handkerchief from his pocket and wiped the sweat from his brow. "I've buried him in the new tea field. It was easier than I thought."

His uncertain laugh echoed, distorted, in his head.

"And no one saw you?"

"No one, sir. I feared the shot would wake people, but it didn't."

Tremayne nodded with satisfaction. "Good work, Mr. Cahill. My daughter will have arrived in England by now. We'll find a solution, I'm sure, and you can consider yourself reinstated as estate manager."

"Thank you, sir. You're too kind."

Cahill had no inkling that he would not be enjoying for long the position he had just regained. Only two weeks later he lost the battle with the voices in his head. The fact that he had committed his guilty conscience, his dreadful deeds, to paper did not help at all. That was not compensation enough for the dead.

After running out, screaming and naked, into the courtyard, terrifying the tea pickers and his good wife, he was examined thoroughly by Dr. Desmond and committed to the asylum in Colombo. Confined to a straitjacket in a dark cell where scarcely any light fell, Cahill was delivered up, helpless, to the reproaches and curses of his victims. Regular injections of morphine, considered to be a medicine for his condition, strengthened the voices all the more, so that nothing remained to him but to surrender by giving up the ghost.

18

Vannattuppūcci Tea Company, 2008

Diana looked in the mirror rather sleepily. She had spent almost the whole night reading Cahill's account, and although she had managed to snatch a few hours' sleep, she was flabbergasted by the discovery of these crimes that no one was left to atone for.

While reading she had burst into tears at the screaming injustice, but Jonathan had been there, had held her and rocked her in his arms, giving her the strength to continue reading.

She felt it was justice that Cahill's guilty conscience had driven him to madness. She would have wished the same on Henry, but even though he would never have been aware of it, he had been punished in other ways. His family tree, cultivated over centuries, had gradually eroded, his name vanishing with his two daughters, until finally the only remaining heir was from the branch he would have liked to extinguish for good. There clearly was something like karma in the world.

At breakfast they saw Manderley, who looked at them expectantly but was too reserved to ask outright the question that was obviously burning inside him.

"Did you sleep well?"

Diana shook her head with a smile. "No, but that's not a bad thing. I've been revived by your breakfast, and I've found out more about what happened to my great-great-grandmother."

"Ah . . ." The estate manager kneaded his hands. Usually so self-possessed, at that moment he looked to Diana like a boy expecting punishment. "It's strong stuff between those covers?" He didn't ask directly, but she sensed he really wanted to know what his ancestor had done.

"It turns out that Cahill murdered my great-great-grandfather and buried him beneath the tea field, having previously murdered Richard Tremayne, another of my ancestors," she told him. "After that he was haunted by voices that ultimately led to his being committed to the Colombo asylum—the one that was shown in my old guidebook as a tourist attraction."

"People's outlooks were rather different then," Manderley said, nonplussed, but a little relieved. "I thought my ancestor must have committed a murder, otherwise there would have been no need for people to keep quiet about him. Just think, his name's crossed out in our old family Bible. Someone must have read his confession, perhaps even his own wife, but by then it was too late for a prosecution. If I remember correctly, Cahill died two months after he was committed to the asylum. He swallowed his own tongue."

"That's terrible," Diana murmured, trying to imagine what the man's final hours must have been like. Grace was so good-natured that she would hardly have wished such a fate on him. Or would she?

"I'm sorry about your own ancestor," Manderley said awkwardly. "I always knew there was a dark shadow over our family—a reason we can't leave this place."

"There's no need to apologise. It's a long time ago, and your family has nothing to do with the acts of your ancestor. And if there is a shadow, it's gone now, since you've shed light on the events of the past."

Manderley nodded, then turned his attention to the water he was boiling to make tea.

That afternoon, feeling good that she no longer needed any more information to enable her to reconstruct the events of the past, Diana packed her bag then picked up the letter. She wasn't expecting it to reveal any more great surprises, but she took it to Jonathan's room because it meant fitting the last tile in place in the mosaic.

"The time has come," she announced as he looked up from his packing. "We're saying goodbye to Vannattuppūcci, so we can open it now."

Jonathan took her hand and drew her down to sit on the bed.

After taking a deep breath, Diana broke the seal and took out the two sheets of paper.

> *My dear house,*
>
> *Twenty years have passed since our family came to Vannattuppūcci, taking over your rooms and trying to fill them with life. Now I'm leaving this place forever, as a happy wife and mother of my little Daphne, who is now twelve years old. Someone has to look after Tremayne House before it falls into complete dilapidation. Since my sister, Grace, was disinherited by our father, I feel compelled to return to England with Noel and Daphne and take up my duties there.*
>
> *But before I go, there is something I need to get off my chest. Something that should never come to light, and that I can only entrust to you. I don't want to take it back to England, so instead I intend to leave it here, the place where I burdened myself with guilt.*

Sometimes I'm pursued by images of those days, as though it all happened yesterday. Every now and then I believe I can hear Grace's voice or see her walking through the park. Then the tears come, such is the pain the memory of our happier days brings.

Everything changed on the day Grace broke down and told the doctor she was pregnant. The identity of the father caused my parents great consternation, since Grace refused to say, merely looking to the ceiling with an empty gaze whenever she was asked.

But the truth will always out.

There was a rumour that Miss Giles passed Grace's secret journal to my father after she found me looking at it. But that's not true. I want to unburden her poor soul by stating that it was I who took the notebook to my father. I didn't mean to harm Grace, but rather wanted to show Papa what had driven her to take that step, what had fuelled her love, a love I had known about for some time.

I hoped he would understand, that he would show leniency, since the cause of his anger was Grace's silence about the father of her child.

But my well-intentioned deed ultimately triggered the misfortune. All hell broke loose, and I have probably lost my sister forever.

She sent no reply to the letter I sent her saying that Vikrama would come to her, just as she refused to answer any of the other letters in which I begged her forgiveness and offered my help. I found out that she's living in a small German town and that she's now married and has a little daughter. But she still doesn't answer my letters.

I wonder if she ever found out that Vikrama wanted to come to her . . .

I'll never be able to give her an answer to that question in any case, since Vikrama, that handsome Tamil, suddenly vanished without trace. I assume he's no longer alive because the search for him was suddenly stopped and peace returned to Nuwara Eliya. One of Stockton's bloodhounds probably ran him to ground and did away with him. However great my optimism, I can't think of a better explanation.

Now the time has come; the carriage is about to leave. I'm entrusting this letter to the place where Grace kept watch for her beloved, and where I've left a little memorial in the form of the symbol of our plantation: a butterfly. The sumptuous curtain that used to adorn our room has largely rotted away, but a part remains. I've made it into a scarf to remind me of my time here.

Farewell, Vannattuppūcci. I'll miss you!

With love,

Victoria Princeton, née Tremayne

Diana finished reading the letter and silence fell. Neither she nor Jonathan could say a word. As they sat side by side on the bed, she listened to the rustling of the trees, which seemed like distant whispering from the past.

"So it was Victoria who betrayed her sister," Jonathan said, finally breaking the spell.

Diana nodded. "You could put it like that. That was the guilt she wanted to lay to rest. The guilt Grace knew nothing about."

Jonathan put his arm around her. "I think that means you have everything. The mystery is solved."

"Not quite," Diana said. "We still have the palm leaf. Although I'm not quite sure that I really want to know what it says. Given all that I've found out about my family history, what meaning would a prophecy have?"

"You could check whether it was true. In case you ever have a similar horoscope prepared for yourself."

Diana snuggled against his arm. "Do I really want to know my future? Know when I'm going to fail and when I'm going to succeed? What surprises would be left to me then?"

"I think these horoscopes are just indications for life," Jonathan replied. "Ways to help people change. Especially if they're warned when they're going to make mistakes."

"But don't you think people fulfil their destinies by overcoming obstacles that others place in their way?"

"That's one argument." He rubbed his cheek against her hair. "You know, I like the fact that we have more in common than we thought at first."

"Our Tamil inheritance."

"That's right. You never know, one of my ancestors may even be one of yours. The Indian Tamils who were brought here by the British were from one region. They might perhaps have been on the same ship."

"Well, I hope we're not related like Grace and Vikrama were." That knowledge still made her feel uncomfortable. Cousins of all degrees in royal houses might marry one another, but Diana nevertheless felt uneasy about it.

"No, I'm sure we're not." Jonathan took her hand and kissed it.

An hour later, Diana and Jonathan left Vannattuppūcci, after thanking Manderley and promising to send him a summary of the events for his records.

The driver had arrived early and was waiting by the gate; he drove them speedily along the green-lined road to the small railway station where they had arrived a little over a week before.

As the overcrowded train rumbled towards Colombo, Diana gazed wistfully out at the mountains of Nuwara Eliya. Now she knew that a small part of her roots was here, she found it difficult simply to leave. *I'll be back,* she promised silently. *Sometime.*

Back in the village of Ambalangoda, this time there was no festival. The huts stood in silence along the beach. There were only a few children, romping in the sand, running with loud shrieks after a small light-brown dog that sought to escape its pursuers with its tongue lolling.

"I wonder if Mr. Vijita is back," Diana said anxiously. She took the package out of her rucksack, and the palms of her hands prickled as she opened it. What else did this palm leaf have to tell her? She wondered whether it predicted Grace's or Vikrama's fate, and whether events had unfolded as had been written a thousand years before.

Jonathan made some brief enquiries in the village and came running back to her.

"We're in luck. He's back. He's not completely recovered, but his son says we can talk to him."

The old man's hut was neat and tidy, but nevertheless radiated poverty to Western eyes. There was a simple bed, a small table with somewhat crooked legs, two chairs that looked in little better shape, and a chest of drawers in which the old man probably kept all his worldly belongings—a few items of clothing and his memories.

He was sitting on the bed as they entered, dressed in a shirt and a traditional sarong, his feet in sandals. He greeted his guests with a toothless smile, studying Diana closely before indicating to them to sit.

As he only spoke Tamil and Sinhalese, it was Jonathan who spoke to him, and then handed him the leaf. The old man looked at it, his brow creased, then spoke a few rapid words.

"What did he say?" Diana whispered. "Can he make anything of it?"

"I think so," Jonathan replied, his voice hushed. "He says your palm leaf hasn't come from a library."

"Hasn't it?" Diana raised her eyebrows. "But . . ."

"He says this horoscope was drawn up for a wedding. It's the custom to compare the horoscopes of the bride and groom before they marry, with the intention of preventing unhappy marriages."

The old man said something else in his staccato voice. Jonathan replied, which led to a discussion between the two of them. *Maybe I should have got him to teach me a few words,* Diana thought. *Like Grace did.*

Jonathan finally explained to her, "He's absolutely certain that it's a wedding horoscope."

"But Grace spoke of a palm leaf that prophesied bad luck for her family."

"Then it must have been one that only existed as a copy. Since palm leaves were regularly used by the Tamils as writing paper, the forecast for R. Vikrama was also written on a palm leaf."

"This is Vikrama's wedding horoscope?"

"Yes, it is. He probably intended to take it with him to England, to marry Grace. If Mr. Vijita is not mistaken, this leaf is no more than one hundred and twenty years old."

Diana's first thought was that Michael had been very surprised at the results of the dating analysis.

"That's a pity," she said, a little crestfallen. "A pity that Vikrama never got to marry her."

"That's true." Jonathan thought for a moment, then smiled. "But on the other hand I'm glad things turned out as they did."

"Why?"

"If Vikrama had married your great-great-grandmother, how would your lives have been? Our paths certainly wouldn't have crossed if you hadn't been researching your family history. And that really would have been a pity."

A day later, after a short stay in Jonathan's flat, the time came for Diana's flight. Nothing could have held Jonathan back from going with her to the airport, to snatch a few more hours with her. They had talked a lot the previous evening about the past and the future.

Diana's head was spinning, but she was happy. The mystery of the Tremaynes had finally been solved. She had fulfilled Emily's wish and could now move on with the knowledge of her unusual origins.

Her heart was breaking as the time approached for them to say goodbye.

"I'll miss you so much. You and Sri Lanka."

"Your homeland, in a way."

"Yes, my homeland—to a small extent, at least."

"We'll see each other again," Jonathan said and kissed her passionately. "You get your life in order and I'll make sure I finish my book. Then we'll see how things lie between us."

They held each other for a moment longer before Diana had to go. She waved at him once again from beyond the barrier, then turned so he wouldn't see her tears.

During the flight, Diana took another look through all the documents she had collected, which Mr. Manderley had kindly photocopied for her. Mr. Green was in for a surprise!

By the time the plane touched down in Berlin, she had come to a decision. She would go to England for a while and not only put the facts of her family history in order, but also find out about specialising in English law. During her time away Eva had proved without doubt that she was capable of running the Berlin office excellently. Now the curtain had been drawn back a way to reveal at least some of the mysteries, it was time for her to begin a new life.

Fortunately, Philipp wasn't in when she got home. She looked thoughtfully up at the façade of the building, a façade that had concealed the demise of her marriage well. But now the end had come. Although some of her heart lay in that house, she didn't want to stay a moment longer than was necessary. Having shed so much light on her family's shadows during the previous fortnight, she didn't want to remain in the shadows herself.

She phoned a fellow student who had specialised in family law and asked for an appointment. He had one available the very next day. Then she phoned Eva and told her she'd be there that afternoon.

As she entered the bedroom to change, she paused. A pair of panties lay on the bed. Nothing special, Diana thought, an ordinary pale-green pair with lace, size S. Since it was unlikely that Philipp had taken to wearing women's underwear, this must be a trophy from one of his conquests.

The sight would have made her blood boil a few weeks ago, but now she merely smiled, her resolve strengthened, and set about clearing her wardrobe, packing the clothes she wanted to keep into a suitcase. Everything else found its way into a large black bag, which she intended to leave at a charity shop on her way to the hotel.

After stowing the suitcase and bag of clothes in her Mini, she went up to her study. Philipp had placed a few letters on her desk. Some bills, publicity leaflets, and a postcard advertising holidays in India. Diana threw the junk mail in the waste paper bin without a second glance.

Relieved that she had never been a hoarder, she began to fill two large boxes with books, papers, and writing utensils. She also dealt with the bills, as she didn't want to give Philipp any grounds to complain that she wasn't paying her share.

Finally, she sat down at the desk and composed a letter to Philipp, explaining that she felt it was time they went their separate ways. For both of them. She told him nothing of her family history, but gave the secrets she had just uncovered as her reason for wanting a new start. After wishing him luck and happiness in his future life, she signed it and tucked the letter into an envelope, which she placed in his study.

As she was carrying the first box downstairs, the phone rang.

She was inclined to ignore it, but its insistent ringing eventually led her to pick up. Mr. Green's voice reassured her that she had done the right thing.

"I hope you've arrived safely in Germany, Miss Diana."

"Thank you very much, Mr. Green. Things are going very well. I've got so much to tell you when we meet again—and you've got a thing or two to explain to me."

Although she couldn't see him, she could tell he was smiling.

"My aunt had you in on this, didn't she? You made sure all the clues were placed where I was bound to discover them."

"How did you find me out?"

"During my stay at the Hill Club Hotel you emailed me a picture that none of my family knew about. The location of Grace's grave was always a great mystery. Emily must have passed it on to someone—or my grandmother had it in her bag when she arrived. My mother knew nothing of the graveyard where Grace was laid to rest, so it seems that Emily kept the information close to her chest. That means she must have passed it on to you."

Silence. She was sure he was still smiling.

"I must say that placing the letter under the sarcophagus was a stroke of genius. But that was when I began to suspect you. No one would leave a letter like that lying in a vault."

"Congratulations, Miss Diana! You'd be a credit to Sherlock Holmes."

Diana smiled as she remembered that was what Jonathan had called her. What was he doing at that moment? Was he thinking of her, missing her?

"But I didn't call simply to ask after your health. A gentleman has arrived here asking to talk to you. I told him you're not here, but he insisted I called you because he has something important to say to you."

Diana had a suspicion that made her go weak at the knees.

"Thank you, Mr. Green. Please can you put him on?"

When she heard Jonathan's voice, she turned hot and cold. What was he doing in England? Wasn't he supposed to be finishing his book?

"I must say this is a magnificent house. After a bit of renovation it would make a lovely home, I'd say. What do you think?"

Diana was unable to catch her breath for a moment. "Actually, I'm intending to come to England for a few days. The office is running fine without me, and I've no desire for any further arguments with Philipp. He can have this house and I'll have Tremayne House."

"So the divorce is definite?"

"As far as I'm concerned. I'm going to give the papers to my solicitor today." She didn't tell him about the knickers on the bed. "Then I'm going to talk to my partner in the practice. I don't know whether I'll sell my share or remain as a sleeping partner. But whatever happens I intend to apply to study in the UK."

"You're making a new start."

Diana looked thoughtfully at the fine white thread around her wrist that she'd been given as a good-luck charm at the Tamil wedding. It had survived all her activities and numerous showers, and still lay intact against her skin. "While I was in Sri Lanka I felt as though I were not only on the trail of my history, but also looking for myself. And I think I've found myself now. New beginnings can be quite exciting, can't they?"

"Would your new beginning stretch to you taking on a lodger in Tremayne House?"

Her heart was pounding so loudly that she feared she was getting tinnitus.

"What did you say?"

"Let's just say I've got plans to spend a while in England. I can just as easily finish my book here—and at the same time I can submit it to British publishers. Would it be possible to stay with you for a while?"

Diana had to summon all her self-control not to shriek like an excited teenager. She pinched the back of her hand to steady herself before replying, "I think we have a room free. I'll tell Mr. Green that he should get it ready."

Three days later, Jonathan picked her up at Heathrow Airport. Diana had sorted out the most important things and could now look forward to her new future.

"I've missed you so much," she whispered into his ear after they had kissed passionately.

"But we were only apart for a few days," he replied, a mischievous gleam in his eye.

"An eternity!" Diana said as she took his arm.

Later, as they were sitting in the kitchen being treated to Mr. Green's tea and cakes, they spread out the results of their research on the long table that was notched with the cuts of centuries of kitchen knives. "Sit down, Mr. Green," Diana said after watching the butler bustling around for a while. Of course he would never admit that he was burning to hear all about it. "Since you've played a not insubstantial part in the story, you ought to hear what we've discovered."

Once Mr. Green had obeyed, Diana and Jonathan took turns to tell him what they had found out, the horrifying and surprising alike. Mr. Green listened, his expression impassive as though he had known it all for a long while, but when they came to the madman Cahill's diary, a thoughtful frown creased his brow.

"I wonder how much Mrs. Woodhouse knew of that? She knew that her mother had lived on the plantation until she was twelve. When

Mrs. Woodhouse confided the secret to me, she spoke of a secret surrounding her great-aunt Grace, events that took place in Ceylon."

Mr. Green took a sip from his teacup. "I wonder if Mistress Daphne deliberately took most of what she knew to the grave with her, since I find it hard to believe that Mistress Victoria would have told her nothing about Grace and her illegitimate child."

"Not everyone reveals all they know, not even on their deathbed," Jonathan said thoughtfully. "Sometimes they simply don't want certain things to come to light, especially if they could be harmful for the family or the person themselves."

"It wasn't incumbent on Emily to find out the whole truth, since she wasn't the last of the Tremayne line," Diana replied. "But even if she had, I'm sure she would have coped with it. Emily was very strong."

"She was."

An inner ray of sunshine falling on a shred of memory of Emily brought a smile to Diana's face.

"But I think we still have some unfinished business." Mr. Green rose and left the kitchen.

Diana gave Jonathan an enquiring look.

"Could he have kept a few clues from you?"

"I wouldn't put it past him. He was very good at drip-feeding his information."

Mr. Green returned with a brown envelope and said, "The photo I emailed to you was just one of three. When I didn't receive a reply from you, I assumed you were preoccupied with other things."

"Or we could have been kidnapped."

"I'm sure something like that would have made the news, so I didn't worry. You've given me plenty of evidence in the past that you're quite capable of looking after yourself."

With a smile, he opened the envelope and took out two black-and-white photos. The first showed a gravestone, the other the painting of Victoria and Grace as children.

Diana looked enquiringly at the butler. "Do you know what these mean?"

Mr. Green shook his head. "No, how would I? Your aunt told me nothing about the background, but simply gave me the clues and instructed me to mete them out gradually. But if I may make an observation, since the grave obviously isn't in Britain, you should begin with the painting."

"You mean I should take it down?" Diana shot a questioning look at Jonathan, who feigned innocence.

"Why not? I think the piece of wall beneath it could do with seeing some daylight."

Her heart thumping, she left the kitchen, followed by Jonathan and Mr. Green. As she stood in front of the painting, which had so skilfully captured that intimate moment between two sisters and their mother, her hands were shaking so much that at first she couldn't bring herself to touch it. What would she find here? Some more drawings? She hesitated. What else was left to be revealed?

"Don't worry, Diana. It's only the truth, waiting for you to discover it," her aunt seemed to be whispering in her ear. Then it was as though someone else's hands were helping her to move her own. The hands of Grace, Victoria, and Emily. She carefully slipped her fingers beneath the heavy frame, then removed the picture.

The first thing she saw was an old newspaper article, so age-worn from the time spent in its hiding place that it drifted to the floor like a feather.

Jonathan picked it up and read, "*Calypso* in distress—German freighter comes to the aid of an English mail ship."

"*Calypso?*" Diana said. The name rang a bell with her. Wasn't that the ship Cahill had referred to in his account? She'd have to check.

As she and Jonathan turned the painting around, she saw in the old stretcher beneath the canvas a white sheet of paper, which on closer inspection turned out to be a sheet of drawing card of the kind used for pastels and etchings.

With her pulse beating throughout her body, she turned the card over and her hand flew to her mouth.

"This is the angel's face!"

The lifelike drawing was signed with the same butterfly she had found on the window frame in Vannattuppūcci, which was mentioned in Victoria's confession. There were also the initials V. T.

"Victoria must have drawn this, but how . . ."

It suddenly dawned on her. The angel was not the model for the drawing, but rather, the drawing was the model for the angel!

"Could it be . . . could it be that this man is Vikrama?"

She looked around at Jonathan, who was examining the drawing closely.

"It's very possible—this man clearly has Indian features."

"But he has a beard here, and the angel . . ."

"I've never seen a bearded angel," Mr. Green said. "But it's extremely probable that Mrs. Woodhouse could have used artistic licence to shave him."

"So it would mean that Vikrama is watching over Beatrice?"

"It's a lovely thought, isn't it?"

"Yes, beautiful."

"And a lovely way of making amends for the fact that Beatrice was denied eternal rest with her ancestors, because Daphne took her grandfather's side and saw Grace as he did: an outcast."

EPILOGUE

Poland, 2009

It had taken a while for them to locate the cemetery where the grave was supposed to be. The first photo sent by Mr. Green, the final clue, had not been a great help, since the war and six further decades had changed the face of the landscape. The little village cemetery had almost faded into oblivion. The village itself had been more or less destroyed during the war, in the fighting between the Germans and the Poles, and had subsequently been abandoned. Fortunately, the graves had not been touched, either out of superstition or in the knowledge that the dead had no further claims to make.

Diana took in the entrance gates, their metalwork long since vanished, leaving only rusty hinges behind as evidence. The massive stone pillars rose from the ground like a giant's fingers.

As there was no one left to care for the hedge, it had grown rampant, enclosing everything like the legend of the Sleeping Beauty.

The gravestone leaned crookedly, and there was a small hollow of sunken earth over the grave. After so many years, the wood of the coffin must have rotted away.

Diana stood on the overgrown pathway and reached backwards. Jonathan's hand found hers and held it tight—warm and strong.

Mr. Green's second photo had shown the grave itself, but was too unclear to make out any details. Only one feature could be discerned—a kind of medallion set into the middle of the gravestone.

Despite its age, it gleamed mysteriously through the ivy as though beckoning to her to find it at last.

After clearing away the tendrils of ivy, Diana stood with her head to one side and read:

HERE LIE IN PEACE

SEA CAPTAIN FRIEDRICH SÖDERMANN

1 JULY 1860–4 MAY 1918

V. GRACE SÖDERMANN NÉE TREMAYNE

25 DECEMBER 1868–19 DECEMBER 1931

"*V?*" Diana wondered.

"*V,*" Jonathan repeated in amazement. "It can't be."

"What?"

"In Sri Lanka it's the custom to use the first letter of your father's name in front of your own. As soon as a woman marries, she loses her father's initial and takes the initial of her husband as a sign of the bond."

A storm of emotion seemed to rush through Diana's veins. Her heart raced and her mouth was dry as Jonathan's words raged through her mind.

"She was married to Vikrama?"

"If the gravestone is to be believed, yes," Jonathan replied. "At the very least, she must have felt a strong bond with him and have known about the custom."

Diana sank back on her heels. She stared into space for several long moments.

Grace had been married to Vikrama, according to Tamil custom.

Had her husband known about it? If so, how had he been able to live with taking second place? How could he have borne the idea that

Grace was only waiting for Vikrama to find his way to her one day? Diana supposed that Grace must have told Helena the whole story, and she ensured that her mother's name was recorded here with the *V*, in death at least, if not in life.

And how must it have been for Victoria when she found out that Vikrama had disappeared? Was that why she had hidden the mementos, such as the travel guide, the blue gemstone, the photo, and the wedding horoscope in the secret compartment?

Diana reached out to touch the medallion on the gravestone, which turned out to be a locket. Time had left its mark, and she noticed it was slightly loose.

"Have you got a knife with you?" she asked Jonathan, without really knowing what she wanted with it. She didn't want to take the locket away, unless it was obvious Grace would have wanted one of her descendants to have it.

"Here you are," Jonathan said, handing her a small penknife. The blade made it easy to ease the locket from the stone. Why hadn't anyone done so before? Had the war spread a cloak of forgetfulness over this place?

No sooner did she have the locket in her hand than she saw a rolled-up piece of paper in the hollow it had left behind. Her hand trembling, she took it and unrolled it. Foreign characters! The same characters as those on the palm leaf, which she had handed over to Michael, telling him of her error.

There was also a small note, key points written out in a delicate hand. Diana recognised Grace's handwriting.

"This must be a copy of the palm leaf," she said as she jumped to her feet. "The one she wrote about in her notebook!"

"Perhaps it's simply her own wedding horoscope," Jonathan suggested, but Diana's enthusiasm was unstoppable.

"No, I'm sure this is a transcription of the palm leaf, otherwise she would have had the original."

Diana tried in vain to order her thoughts, which whirled like a hurricane through her mind. Her eyes fell on the weathered locket.

"Perhaps there's a picture of them both in here." Diana felt like someone who had lost her mind, but Jonathan accepted her mania with a smile. As he opened the locket with the penknife, they found themselves looking at the face of a beautiful Indian woman, who looked remarkably similar to the portrait of Vikrama.

"This must be his mother."

"Richard's lover," Diana replied. Her head was spinning. With the locket that probably depicted Vikrama's mother, and the probable copy of the palm leaf Grace had referred to in her journal, she now had the final pieces of the puzzle. All she needed to reconstruct the story.

Diana decided to take her two finds away with her, to keep them for later generations, if there were any. She hoped there would be. Her divorce from Philipp was progressing, she was completely happy with Jonathan, and everything else would take its course, with or without a prophecy.

Indian Ocean, 1887

On the high seas, Grace hardly knew any more whether she felt so bad because of her pregnancy or the seasickness that was affecting many. Winter was not a good time for travelling. There were frequent storms, but once they had passed through the Suez Canal the climate would improve and there was not far to go from there to the shores of England.

Grace didn't care. She didn't care if she froze or boiled, if she lived or died. Every now and then she overcame her deep longing for the darkness. Then her thoughts of her child would break like a ray of sunshine through the clouds, and she knew she wanted to live. Live for her child, live for the hope of seeing her beloved again sometime.

In those moments she would take out the scrap of paper she had been given by the old man at the palm-leaf library.

"Listen to your heart," he had said. Could she have warded off this misfortune if she'd obeyed? Her pregnancy had unleashed the worst misfortune her parents could ever have imagined. But she had experienced this great love . . .

"I think another storm is rising," Miss Giles said nervously. Their time at sea had turned her into a bundle of nerves. She spent most of her time brooding in a corner of the cabin and only spoke to her ward when absolutely necessary—not because she was angry with her, but because of a guilty conscience, Grace was sure.

At first Grace had thought it served her right to be separated from Mr. Norris. After all, she was the one who had exposed Vikrama as the father of her child, through snooping around in Victoria's things and then showing the book with the secret notes to their father. As they boarded the ship she felt like throwing the governess over the railings.

But their time at sea had given her plenty of time to think. Grace could sympathise only too well with what Miss Giles must be feeling. The hope that Mr. Norris would summon her back because she was needed to look after Miss Victoria was the only thing that kept her going. It was a slight hope, since she was more likely to be needed to look after the baby. A baby that would trigger a scandal. A baby that might be taken away from its mother, to keep up appearances.

So Grace tried to suppress her anger, and when she sensed Miss Giles was mourning the absence of the teacher, she comforted her by saying she was sure he would come to find her one day and marry her. Just as she hoped to return to Ceylon. However, this hope weakened, and her fears for her lover grew, with every mile they sailed. If Vikrama had managed to hold on to his life, he would have stayed away from Vannattuppūcci. She prayed fervently that his bold heart would not lead him to do anything stupid that he would regret forever. And she hoped that fate would find a way of bringing them back together.

As the storm broke over the ship, Grace briefly doubted the power of the palm leaf. Maybe it had been wrong when it promised her forty-three more years of life. How could the Brahmans know the misfortunes that could befall people? The storm, which proved to be worse than any they had yet encountered, brought the ship to the brink of sinking. Panic broke out. Everything was in turmoil. As the passengers came out on deck, a huge wave broke over them. Grace heard a scream, and Miss Giles suddenly disappeared. Before she could find out where she had gone, hands drew her aside and she found herself in a lifeboat.

A blanket was laid around her shoulders, and she was engulfed in a babble of agitated voices. Icy, wet gusts stung her cheeks, but she didn't feel them. Her thoughts were on the piece of paper, and she knew now that everything would happen as it said.

"Is everything all right, madam?" the young German officer asked in excellent English as he lifted her from the lifeboat. Her teeth chattering, Grace nodded and allowed herself to be led to the cabin they had allocated her. She didn't notice the man's expression of wonder as he looked at her face, her hair. Yes, at that moment she would have laughed at anyone who claimed that the officer with the blond hair and blue eyes would one day be her husband.

But that changed during the voyage. The young officer took care of her, made sure she was comfortable and personally brought her extra portions of food because he believed that the little life inside her should be well provided for. Once they were back on dry land and Grace was installed in a small guest house in Hamburg—wild horses couldn't have dragged her to Tremayne House—he visited her regularly, bringing her gifts and taking her out for walks.

Some people wondered at Grace's condition, while others believed it was her husband whose arm she linked with hers. Friedrich would playfully threaten with his fists any of his friends who commented that he hadn't lost any time, but Grace could see his eyes shining with pride when anyone took him to be the father of the baby.

Maybe it was his care, or maybe simply the realisation that she needed someone she could rely on until her prince arrived, that made Grace open her heart a little. At first it was sympathy she felt, but it grew into affection for the man whom she married, when she was seven months pregnant, in a little church in East Prussia, his homeland.

It gave her a grim satisfaction to stand before the altar and say yes to the officer, making him the happiest man in the world. She was carrying her sister's letter dated 15 February 1888 close to her heart. One of the servants at Tremayne House had forwarded it to her.

I've forgiven you, Victoria, she thought as she left the church, cheered and admired by the wedding guests. *And it's good to know that I have someone to look out for my descendants.*

That child was born in 1888, the year that went down in German history as the Three Kaiser Year. Grace called her daughter, who resembled her father so closely, Helena. At first she was tempted to give the girl her father's first initial before her name, in accordance with the Tamil custom, but she didn't want people to ask questions.

It was enough for her that Helena looked at her with Vikrama's eyes.

About the Author

Photo © Hans Scherhaufer

Bestselling author Corina Bomann was born in Parchim, Germany. She originally trained as a dental nurse, but her love of stories compelled her to follow her passion for writing. Bomann now lives with her family in a small village in the German region of Mecklenburg-Vorpommern and is the author of a number of successful young-adult and historical novels.

About the Translator

Photo © 2016 Sandra Dalton

Alison Layland is a novelist and translator from German, French, and Welsh into English. A member of the Institute of Translation and Interpreting and the Society of Authors, she has won a number of prizes for her fiction writing and translation. Her debut novel, the literary thriller *Someone Else's Conflict*, was published in 2014 by Honno Press. She has also translated a number of novels, including Corina Bomann's *The Moonlit Garden* and *Storm Rose*. She lives and works in the beautiful and inspiring countryside of Wales, United Kingdom.

Made in the USA
San Bernardino, CA
14 May 2020